Je[illegible]

We h[illegible]ed many [illegible]s in this book over the years. It expresses many of my spiritual ideas and questions.

Many thanks for the ideas you have given me. You will be aware that they have been incorporated into the writing.

Most of all thanks for your support & friendship.

Doug Taylor

Jan. 17, 2014.

Also by Doug Taylor

Lilies of the Covenant
The trials and joys of five generations of the Taylor family in eighteenth-century England, nineteenth-century Newfoundland, and twentieth-century Toronto.

Citadel on the Hill
A history of a church community in Toronto in the first decade of the twentieth century, chronicling the trials and successes of the congregation as it progresses into the modern era.

The Pathway of Duty
An immigrant family from England arrives in Canada in the early years of the twentieth century and struggles to survive in the harsh conditions of Toronto's Earlscourt District. The sinking of the *Empress of Ireland* in 1914, in the icy waters of the St. Lawrence River, dramatically changes their lives forever.

There Never Was a Better Time
Two young brothers immigrate to Canada. This is a humorous and intimate glimpse into their family life in bustling Toronto during the 1920s, as well as the adventures of their brothers, parents, and rascal of a grandfather.

Arse over Teakettle—Toronto Trilogy, Book One
An intriguing tale of growing up in Toronto during the days of the Second World War and the postwar years. Tom Hudson and his mischievous friend "Shorty" find adventure in their seemingly quiet neighbourhood as they yearn to learn about the secrets of the older boys.

The Reluctant Virgin—Toronto Trilogy, Book Two
In 1950s Toronto, a killer brutally murders a young woman in the seclusion of the Humber Valley. Her death threatens the seemingly secure world of Tom Hudson when he discovers that the victim was to be one of his teachers. The police are unaware that they are confronting a serial killer.

When the Trumpet Sounds

Doug Taylor

iUniverse LLC
Bloomington

WHEN THE TRUMPET SOUNDS

Certain characters in this work are historical figures, and certain events portrayed did take place. However, this is a work of fiction. All of the other characters, names, and events as well as all places, incidents, organizations, and dialogue in this novel are either the products of the author's imagination or are used fictitiously.

iUniverse books may be ordered through booksellers or by contacting:

iUniverse
1663 Liberty Drive
Bloomington, IN 47403
www.iuniverse.com
1-800-Authors (1-800-288-4677)

ISBN: 978-1-4917-0870-5 (sc)
ISBN: 978-1-4917-0872-9 (hc)
ISBN: 978-1-4917-0871-2 (e)

Library of Congress Control Number: 2013917055

Printed in the United States of America.

iUniverse rev. date: 10/22/2013

This book is dedicated to the memory of Hilda Whealy (née Aldridge) and her brother, Bernard (Bernie) Aldridge, who generously provided much of the background material for this narrative.

Although this tale is imaginary, it is based on real events. Because it closely parallels the occurrences herein and the lives of people who lived them, I hope that those familiar with the true story will not be upset with the liberties taken. Although it is a work of fiction, great effort has been taken to respect the historical facts and the dignity of the characters upon which this tale is based. All characters are fictional or have been employed in a fictional manner.

Contents

Prologue

Though not quite a teenager, Billy Mercer was tall for his age. In the village, he was well known for his mischievous ways, which often ended in fists flying. As a result, he had acquired considerable fighting abilities. However, on this gloriously sun-filled afternoon, accompanied by his younger brother, Zack, he was seeking a little peace and quiet.

Although it was only the end of March, the weather was unseasonably warm. Taking advantage of the early spring that had arrived this year, 1905, in England's Dorset County, the two boys had escaped the confines of the town. Half an hour prior, they had been climbing a precipitous incline.

They were unaware of what awaited them at its summit.

Billy parted company with his brother a short distance from the top of the hill. Zack told his brother, "I want to examine a bird's nest I spied in a tree among the copse of scrawny oaks over there."

"Okay," Billy replied, "I'll see you up at the top."

Billy continued upward. When he looked back, Zack was clambering up the tree, the lower branches granting access to the nest. Not interested in his brother's quest, Billy continued his trek up the incline, assured that his younger brother was in no apparent danger, as he could climb like a monkey.

When Billy had completed the arduous climb, he sucked in the clear air in short, laboured breaths. Sweat trickled down his forehead; he wiped the perspiration from his brow with his rolled-up shirtsleeve. Resting on a narrow ledge, sheltered from the glaring sun, Billy gazed out across the valley below. In the distance he could see the village, more than a mile away. Directly below him, a narrow stream coursed its way among the quiet pasturelands and thickets of trees. The only sound disturbing the hilltop retreat was the birds as they noisily squabbled over nesting material. Glancing up into the cloudless sky, he watched a lone hawk floating silently on an updraft.

Then he heard Zack's scream.

Springing to his feet, Billy hastily retraced his steps down the slope. Approaching near to where the scream had emanated, he heard boisterous laughter. He hid behind a thicket of alder bushes to assess the situation.

He heard Zack shouting angrily, "Back off. Let me be! My brother will knock the stuffing out of you."

"Your brother must be a real terror," one of the boys mocked. "We're trembling with fright. If we find him, we'll shove *him* in the barrel."

More laughter ensued. The reference to a barrel confirmed to Billy that mischief was pending. He remained hidden, peering cautiously through the branches of the alders.

On the ground beside the boys was a flour barrel, too old to be of any use, since cracks of light filtered between its warped wooden slats. It had likely been tossed aside by a flour or grain merchant in town, deposited at the rear of the owner's shop. Billy knew that it required considerable effort to roll it up the steep slope. He was also aware that no one would have thought it strange to see the boys with the barrel, as it was never too early for lads to retrieve discarded wood for the bonfires of Guy Fawkes Night.

Billy heard one of the boys scream excitedly, "Let's cram the snivelling little brat inside the barrel and roll him down the hill."

Another boy agreed. "That's a great idea. The hill's really steep. The barrel will shoot downward like a cannonball from hell." They giggled at the prospect.

The tallest boy added, "The long ride to the valley floor will bounce the hell out of the mongrel brat."

Another boy chimed in, "He'll likely break an arm or split open his head. Who cares? He'll live."

"Perhaps he won't!"

Their hilarity increased.

Not satisfied that Zack was sufficiently terrified, one of the boys suggested, "Twist his arm and make him yell."

Another shouted, "Yank on the brat's ear."

He grinned smugly as Zack screamed. Each time he cried out, their howls of delight increased.

*

During the delay the lads had unknowingly provided, Billy sized up his adversaries. There were six of them. Two were his own size, and two were shorter than he was, even though he was certain that they were older. Another boy, not as tall as Billy, possessed a pasty complexion and skinny build. He had heard the other boys refer to him as Runty.

Billy quickly surmised that the sixth boy was the leader. In his mid-teens, he was broad shouldered, well-muscled, and several inches taller than Billy. Billy knew he must eliminate this boy from action.

An opportunity appeared when the older teenager foolishly leaned over the barrel to demonstrate to Zack where they were going to shove him. His voice was somewhat muffled, but Billy could hear the words even after the boy shoved his head farther inside.

The lad taunted Zack as he mocked, "Can you hear me out there, little crybaby? Within a few moments, you'll be inside this barrel to begin your ride to hell." He chuckled at the supposed cleverness of his remark while the other boys laughed menacingly.

Finally, one of Zack's tormentors shouted, "Come on! Lift the crybaby's legs and shove him in! We'll send the sniveller on his way."

*

Before the tall boy had time to emerge from inside the barrel, Billy sprang into action and lunged from the bushes. Given the advantage of surprise, and because he was approaching the other bullies from behind, he easily pushed them all aside. He then grabbed and lifted the legs of the boy who was leaning into the barrel, forcefully driving him headlong inside it. The boy's long legs now dangled from the barrel's open end.

Without any pause, Billy pulled the barrel over onto its side and, with a forceful kick of his boot, sent it on a zigzag course down the incline. The other three boys, stunned and immobile, stared in shock as the wobbling barrel descended.

Recovering, the boys turned angrily on Billy.

One of them yelled, "Quick, guys. Punch the daylights out of him."

Billy quickly struck again.

Driving his right fist into the stomach of the boy closest to him, he then swirled around and rammed his other fist into the midsection of another. The two collapsed on the ground. Billy did not strike the sickly looking member of the group, thinking him defenseless and too weak. The boy took off like a scared rabbit, his legs a blur of motion as he fled from the fighting devil that had appeared from nowhere. The two other boys who remained on their feet, though leaderless, felt they still had the advantage of numbers.

Without pausing, Billy struck out once more. Faced with his flying fists, the pair—after a few moments—wisely retreated down the path their leader had so ignominiously taken in the barrel. The two boys on the ground sprung to their feet and likewise retreated.

Billy placed his arm on Zack's shoulder as they watched their adversaries crashing down the path where the barrel had wobbled and rolled just minutes before. With the departure of the boys, the craggy summit returned to its former tranquility.

The hawk had disappeared farther up the valley, and the birds were silent.

Billy thought, *As long as I live, no one will ever hurt my brother.*

*

The following day, the bullies had no difficulty discovering where Billy lived. Fighting Billy Mercer, as some of the townsfolk referred to him, and his brother, Zack, were well known in the town.

Scouting the area near Billy's home, the boys discovered that behind his house was a laneway and that he and his brother invariably returned from their outings into town via the laneway. Two days later, they awaited Billy, confident they could thrash him easily, as this time he could not surprise them or divide their forces like he had done on the hilltop.

*

The sun was stretching into the western sky when Billy and Zack arrived at the head of the laneway. Unaware of what awaited them, they ambled along the dusty pathway. Two fat trout were swinging from Zack's shoulder, evidence that the brothers' efforts at the stream had been rewarding. Entering the lane, they saw the bullies up ahead. The high garden walls enclosed the laneway on both sides, and two of the bullies had quickly closed off the end of the lane where they had entered. They were trapped.

Billy's ability to think fast did not desert him.

He told Zack, "Quick. Step up into my cupped hands and I'll boost you up o'er the wall."

"I won't leave you. You can't take on six of them."

"Don't argue. Quick. Step up."

Reluctantly, Zack obeyed. When he was within reach of the top of the wall, he grabbed the limb of the gnarled apple tree that hung out over.

Billy now positioned his back against the east wall, preventing anyone from striking him from behind. Slowly, the bullies encircled him. The tallest boy grinned maliciously, his fists clenched tightly.

"Not so smart now, are you?" he taunted. "I'm going to bang your head so hard against that wall that it'll knock the wax from your ears."

"You can try," Billy replied. "But before I go down, I'll get in a few good punches. They'll rattle the earwax in that thick head of yours. Your brains, if you have any, will be smashed into porridge."

The leader of the gang knew Billy was right, and since he did not want to be the first to receive the brunt of Billy's fists, he stepped back, urging one of the other boys to start the assault.

"Beg for mercy, you snivelling coward," a boy jeered.

Another boy added, "Falling on your knees should come naturally for you, beggar boy. We hear your family's all filthy beggars."

Billy remained calm. He had no intentions of being baited into giving up his one small advantage. Before they overcame him, he would indeed thump a few heads.

The bullies were too busy to notice that a garden gate had swung open and a fierce-looking elderly woman clutching a broom had stepped into the laneway.

Suddenly, the woman screamed, "You ignorant louses are in me laneway. I'll show you who needs to beg for mercy."

Having uttered her battle cry, the woman took her broom and struck two of the boys across the back. She employed her weapon with the skill of a Robin Hood swinging an oak staff. Her first sweep struck them viciously. Her second strike smacked the other two with such force that they collapsed onto the dirt laneway. Before the boys had a chance to recover, the woman swatted them again. Next, she pummelled the handle of the broom on their heads.

One of the boys, trying to protect his head with his arms, yelled, "Hit the old windbag back."

The tall lad screamed, "Are you crazy? There'll be hell to pay with the town constable. Besides, we can't get near her. She's wielding that damn broom like a sword."

"Call me a windbag, will ye?" she screamed, and again pounded the broom handle mightily on their heads.

"The old bag's a six-armed monster," one of them yelled as he nursed the lump on his head.

Billy grinned. The boys were right. The woman was a holy terror. Taking advantage of the distraction she was causing, Billy struck out. He dispatched two of the boys with powerful blows. They backed off, and it was only a few moments before they decided to flee.

Billy grinned in satisfaction as he watched them retreat down the laneway.

Meanwhile, another of the neighbours, drawn by the commotion, opened his garden gate. Surveying the scene, he muttered angrily, "So this's the cause of the infernal racket that's disturbed me afternoon sleep."

It was the elderly Walter Patchett, eccentric and crotchety. His annoyance soon turned to delight when he watched the boys racing down the lane and the elderly woman defiantly clutching her broom.

Unable to restrain himself, old Walter shouted to the woman, "Pity that you can't have another swing at them, old girl. If the British army had you on their side in the last war, it would've lasted no more than a few minutes."

The defeated lads, now humiliated, decided to retaliate verbally from a safe distance.

"Stick that broom of yours up your arse, you old witch," the tallest boy shouted.

It was Walter who yelled back gleefully, "You young fool, there's no room up her arse for a broom."

Then, chuckling and smacking his toothless gums, he turned to the elderly woman.

"The lad should have told you to shove the broom down your throat. Your mouth, old woman, could swallow half the town."

"Careful what you say, you silly fool," the woman warned as she gripped her broom and stepped toward him.

Walter wisely retreated, chuckling merrily, delighted with his clever retort. Again, he noisily smacked his toothless gums with satisfaction.

After Mr. Patchett had hustled back to the security of his back garden, slamming the gate loudly behind him, Billy was the only one remaining to receive the brunt of the woman's wrath. Before he had a chance to thank her for rescuing him, she turned her anger on him.

"Your friends are worse than crim'nals," she screamed. "You shouldn't be hangin' around with those lazy louts. They'll all end up in jail, alongside yourself." Then, nodding up at Zack, who was perched in the apple tree inside the garden wall, she added, "You'd think you'd set a better example for your young brother."

Billy watched as the woman, like a broody hen with feathers ruffled, retreated to her garden, clucking more verbal abuse as she departed.

Billy told Zack, "We'll be in deep trouble when Father and Mother hear about this."

The elderly woman was the ferocious Mrs. Rowntree, who shared the same dwelling with their family.

Chapter One

Billy and Zack resided in a humble two-storey house on South Street in the village of Comstock in Dorset County, southern Britain, near the English Channel. Ancient hills and sloping pastureland surrounded the town. Two narrow streams, which the villagers hyperbolically referred to as rivers, divided Comstock into three sectors.

Some of the townsfolk enjoyed hearing about Billy's antics, but others expressed the opinion that Billy was too quick with his fists and far too reckless to survive boyhood. One of those who frequently expressed this opinion was Mrs. Emily Rowntree, Billy's battle mate from the laneway.

She often remarked, "That Billy Mercer is an incorrigible scalawag."

Each morning, like clockwork, the cranky Mrs. Rowntree swept the narrow sidewalk in front of her home, the bristles of her well-worn straw broom clicking furiously across the paving stones. Whenever a neighbour-woman strolled along the street, her tongue clicked as energetically as her broom. Like a spider ensnaring a fly, she trapped her victims in her web of gossip. She rarely acknowledged the presence of menfolk. Her dearly departed husband, Harry Rowntree, had never shown any interest in her tittle-tattle. Because he had been the only man with whom she had had any experience, she assumed they were all unworthy of her attention, similar to old Walter Patchett. She considered him a waste of space, a bag of wrinkled skin stretched over hot air.

Despite her boundless knowledge of the "doings" of the town and her lengthy sermons on the morals of those she considered unredeemable sinners, she reserved her most heated dissertations for the sins of Billy

Mercer. Invariably, she concluded her stern disapproval of his antics with a shake of her head, declaring, "Whatever would our gracious King Edward, crowned only three years ago, say if he saw that boy's shocking behaviour? The lad's a disgrace to all England. If I'd birthed a child like him, I'd never have had the courage to sire another—never mind four more."

Billy was twelve years old, the firstborn of the five Mercer children. At five-foot-five, he was tall for his age and possessed a slim, wiry build. When strolling along South Street, he stood out from the other boys—and not just because of his height. His fair skin, which each year bronzed easily under the summer sun, his deep blue eyes, and his handsome features attracted as many favourable comments as his mischievous habits brought condemnation.

Mrs. Rowntree's vilifications did not cow Billy. Whenever he heard her expound on his lack of saintly virtues, he screwed up his face at her or stuck out his tongue. If she were out of earshot, he'd call her, "Mrs. Crabtree," and chant a poem of his own creation: "Crabtree, Crabtree, mean old hag; dump her in a river in a burlap bag."

On one occasion, she overheard him. His poetic offerings did not exactly place him in the ranks of William Wordsworth, she was sure. Angrily, she informed his parents. His father reprimanded him, even though he chastised him more out of a sense of duty than conviction, since he knew that Mrs. Rowntree often baited Billy. The elderly woman was pleased when she learned that Billy's father had disciplined him; she eyed him smugly the next time she met him.

Billy's mother was Melina Mercer, whom his father called Emmy. She was aware that her oldest son was a handful and worried about him. She had always hoped that he would set an example for his younger siblings, but anyone who met the Mercer family soon realized that Billy possessed many shortcomings. They were also aware that despite these attributes, his mother loved him dearly.

On one occasion Mrs. Rowntree told Emmy, "Billy's disrespectful, cheeky, and too quick with what the dog licks its rear end."

"Perhaps he's a tad too exuberant," Emmy replied, ignoring the woman's crude remark, "but he's a good boy at heart. He'll make us all proud one day."

Mrs. Rowntree huffed indignantly. "Yes, as proud as anyone can be of a lad who's bound to be a crim'nal." Then, as she entered the door of her house, she muttered under her breath, "When that boy learns to behave, pigs will fly."

*

Emmy had always been aware that Billy was more physically active and vocal than his siblings. One evening Emmy told Phil, "Even when Billy was a toddler, he never seemed to stand still or keep quiet. His curiosity knew no bounds. Even then, he was always investigating something with great energy, often disturbing some adult or other."

"Aye," Phil replied. "By the time he was three, he rarely accepted anything without asking why. He's as curious about ideas as he is about his physical surroundings."

"His height is now closer to a man's than that of a boy. Since he's usually at home while you're at work—whenever he's not in school, that is—he goes with me when I shop on the High Street."

Emmy now decided to inform her Phil of a happening that had occurred late that afternoon.

"While I was shopping today, some boys were hanging around Bailey's Butcher Shop." She attempted to sound casual so as not to alarm her husband. "You know how bold young lads can be."

"Can we afford meat again this week?" Phil said, interrupting her.

"Shush, that's not the point of my story."

"Well, get on with it, woman," he replied, a hint of a smile creeping across his face. He loved Emmy dearly but took delight in gently teasing her.

"When I came out of Bailey's, three scruffy lads were hanging around outside. I'm certain that they live on the far side of town—ruffians," she added disparagingly. "They were looking for trouble. Spying me, they called me a rude name and tried to snatch a parcel from my wicker basket. I fought them off. I had a fresh fish in my basket from the fishmonger's cart. I struck one of the lads across the face with it. It was wet and slimy, but it did not stop him. He was being encouraged by the other two."

"My goodness, Emmy, this is serious."

Phil's amusement now turned to concern.

"Let me finish. Billy appeared from the bench across the roadway where he was sitting, and though it was one against three, he flew at them, his fists flying. The boys retreated. I think they'll avoid us next time and seek easier prey."

She did not mention that after the boys fled, Billy had placed his arm around her and whispered softly, "Everything is all right, Mama." Billy often told her those words whenever he sensed that she was upset. Sometimes she wondered which was the child and which the parent.

Emmy had no way of knowing that the three boys who had confronted her outside the butcher shop were the same bullies that had trapped Billy and Zack in the laneway after they had tussled on the hilltop, where they had intended to roll Zack down the incline inside a barrel. The minute they saw Billy appear, they retreated. They had no desire for another thrashing. Cowards they were, but nature had not endowed them with total stupidity.

"Emmy, this is indeed serious," Phil said. "Did you report it to Constable Jim?"

"No point. The bullies were long gone."

"Next time, wait until after I return home from work, and I'll go to the market with you."

"I can't wait *that late* to do the shopping. I'll take Billy with me."

Emmy did not intend to relinquish her independence or cower before bullies. It was not her way.

"Besides, Billy should be in school," Phil continued. "Since the government passed the Balfour Act three years ago, you know that he must stay at his learning for at least another year. After that, he can go to the shops with you, as well as earn a few shillings labouring in the farmers' fields outside of town. I know he hates attending school, but attend he must. I'll not have it any other way. The boy needs his book learning. Besides, he's much too young to be brawling."

"I don't disagree, but school was over for the day when this occurred. I must shop for food, and it's proper that Billy accompany me," Emmy insisted. "I know that Billy doesn't like school. I also know that he is more rebellious than our other four youngins. But he's bright and loves learnin' about anything that catches his interest. Besides, I seem to recall that you were not keen on school, either. I also remember that as a boy you were often in trouble, just like Billy. You were also too quick with your fists. Like father, like son."

Phil sighed and made no effort to dispute her remark. "Be that as it may, he needs to take his schoolin' more seriously. I suspect that sometimes he fails to attend. We may be in trouble with Constable Jim if he's caught being truant."

"True, but I think you'd best convince Billy of this."

"Aye, that's the rub," he replied as he stroked his chin. "I've never been able to reason with the lad. He questions everything and has too many ideas of his own. At times, I cannot understand the way he reasons. But I'll try once more."

Phil's brow wrinkled with concern as he thought about the task ahead.

Then he said, "I fear that, in some respects, Billy's ways are quite similar to my own when I was a boy. I don't know whether to feel proud or fearful."

Emmy gazed at her husband. "Even with little education, he'll grow up to be a fine man. I told you about the events today and how even against unfair odds he defended me. Besides, you outgrew the sins of your youth, and he will, too."

Phil glanced up at her, nodded, and replied, "Aye, if he lives that long. Bess is only seven and is becoming more like Billy. Each day she grows more inquisitive, and her mischievous ways become more evident. We might soon have two rebellious-minded children on our hands."

The conversation having ended, the couple sat in silence and gazed at the fireplace, where the flames were rapidly burning toward their final embers. A crackling sound emanated from the hearth as a small chunk of wood collapsed to the bottom of the grate.

As the fire's heat diminished, dampness crept across the room. Phil and Emmy retreated up the narrow staircase to bed, the decision about whether or not Billy should accompany her shopping remaining unresolved.

As Emmy pulled back the quilts on the bed, she thought about Phil's words. She often pondered Billy's future. Yes, troubling times were ahead for the boy. Many days she had no idea where he was or what he was doing. During the last few months, he had been disappearing for an hour or so each evening. Where was he? When she confronted him about his whereabouts, he simply shrugged his shoulders and replied, "Around." This worried Emmy. A town like Comstock presented too many possibilities for mischief for a boy of Billy's age.

*

The following week, Emmy was in Bailey's Butcher Shop again. She enjoyed shopping there since its proprietor was friendly, always offering a pleasant smile. His considerable girth and florid face were a result of his fondness for his wife's pork pies, which he also sold in his shop. His wife's other baked goods were eagerly sought at the bake sales at St. Mary's Anglican Church and at the stall she set up on the High Street each Saturday morning for the farmers' market. Mr. Bailey was a contented man, well fed, and kind in deed and thought. He rarely spoke ill of anyone.

Mr. and Mrs. Bailey had one child, an eight-year-old lad named Franklin, whom they called Frankie. He was an overly active boy and, like Billy, was invariably in trouble for some misdeed or other. Though intelligent, he had no interest in learning from books. The world of nature was his teacher. Not an insect, animal, or plant in Comstock or the surrounding countryside escaped his interest. He was readily able to recite in prodigious detail their life cycles, growth patterns, and habits.

It was late in the day when Emmy arrived at Bailey's Butcher Shop, and as usual, Billy retreated to a wooden bench across the street from the shop to wait for his mother. Frankie spied him sitting on the bench, crossed the street, and joined him. Despite the age difference, Billy always enjoyed chatting with Frankie and listening to his tales about badgers and groundhogs. A natural affinity had developed between the two boys. They flinched as they noticed Miss Snell, the local teacher, entering the butcher's shop.

Billy said to Frankie, "I skipped school twice last week and didn't go today. If my mother learns about it, she'll tell my father."

"I saw that you were away today. I hate going to school. Listening to old Miss Snell is worse than a swarm of bees. She has a face like a skunk. Yesterday, after her lesson about butterflies, instead of repeating back what she said, I asked her something. She yelled at me and told me I was not to ask questions."

Having vented his anger, Frankie screwed up his face in disgust and spit on the sidewalk in front of the bench.

"I think she needs a husband like my father. He'd sweeten her up. My father knows how to make my mother laugh."

"I don't think any man would want to live with Miss Snell. Sometimes I call her 'Smelly Snelly.'"

They both giggled quietly. Then Frankie added, "I saw a badger yesterday that looked like Miss Snell. It was a large male. Perhaps he would make a good mate for her."

The quiet chuckling now turned to outright laughter.

Regaining his composure, Billy continued. "My father says that Miss Snell is almost eighty. He told me that the trustees would have retired someone else years ago if they could've found someone willing to work for the miserable wages they pay her."

"I know what you mean. She looks older than God's dog. She's going bald, and the hair she has left is as white as the snow in the Goddards' meadow in winter. I think her face is wrinkled like a badger's arse."

More laughter ensued. They both knew that they would have their mouths washed out with lye soap if anyone heard them say the word *arse.*

Then Billy added, "She struts up the street like a sergeant major. She can whack a willow rod fiercely across the arse of anyone who displeases her."

Frankie was glad to hear Billy use the swear word, as he was older and it justified his own use of the bad word.

"Want to know what's worse than seeing Miss Snell?"

"What?"

"Seeing two Miss Snells."

They again giggled, but their amusement subsided as they watched the odious woman go inside the butcher shop. Billy feared that his day of reckoning was soon to arrive.

*

Emmy was retrieving her boiling fowl from Mr. Bailey when Miss Snell entered the shop. As she spied Emmy, the old teacher's eyes narrowed, and a look of superiority gripped her prune-like face. Without any greeting or introductory remark, Miss Snell launched into her tirade.

"Your Billy missed two days of school last week. He was also absent today. That lad of yours is a good-for-nothing."

Emmy resented the teacher's assessment of her son. She knew that Billy should be in her classroom, not off in the neighbouring farms earning a few pence for manual labour. She wondered if the elderly teacher had seen Billy sitting on the bench across the roadway.

"I'll speak to my husband. We'll make certain that he attends." Emmy tried to remain pleasant and not get defensive.

"While you're at it, try to make certain that he learns to keep his mouth closed when he is in my school. His impertinency is most annoying. Last week, he questioned the moral of an Aesop tale, the one about the grasshopper and the ant."

Emmy was familiar with the ancient Greek morality tale. It told of a grasshopper that idled away the summer months, eating, dancing, and singing, while an ant worked diligently to store food for the winter. When the freezing weather arrived, the ant was prepared. The grasshopper asked the ant for food but was rebuked by the ant for being lazy and not working hard. The winter frost killed the grasshopper. The tale extolled the virtues of hard work.

"What did my son say about the story?"

"He asked if there might be a second lesson to the tale. He said that the ant's treatment of the grasshopper was not Christian. He dared to suggest that during the summer, the ant should have tried to help the grasshopper see the error of its ways. However, when the winter came, the ant should have shared its food with the grasshopper."

"Billy said that?"

"Yes! Have you ever heard such stupidity and nonsense?"

"Actually, I have. It's in the parable of the Good Samaritan."

"Mrs. Mercer, I know that parable well. They are not the same at all."

"Perhaps not, but the parable teaches us that it's our Christian duty to help everyone in need, not just those with whom we agree. I think my son was trying to say that the ant, similar to the Good Samaritan, should have been more generous with the grasshopper."

"Nonsense. It appears that you are as empty-headed as your son."

Emmy was shocked but not lost for words.

"Miss Snell, if you opened your mind as wide as your mouth, you might understand what Billy was trying to tell you."

Emmy placed the boiling hen in her wicker basket and hastily departed the shop. Noticing that no one was around, she muttered to herself, "I know I shouldn't be so outspoken, but the woman provoked me. Never mind 'like father, like son'; perhaps it's 'like mother, like son.'"

Emmy now having left the store, the old school teacher puffed her cheeks indignantly and clicked her tongue in disgust as she recalled their conversation. "I can see where that young imp Billy Mercer inherited his villainous ways," she told Mr. Bailey.

The butcher smiled half-heartedly but said nothing. Though he rarely took a dislike to anyone, he was not fond of the officious Miss Snell. On many an occasion he had told his wife, "Miss Snell gives me a pain in my lower extremities."

When speaking to his fellow merchants, he employed a less polite version of the phrase. They found much mirth in Mr. Bailey's assessment of the school teacher, as it was not usual for him to voice such an opinion. However, they invariably nodded in agreement.

As Miss Snell continued her rant, she noticed that Mr. Bailey had said nothing. She inquired, "Don't you think I'm right? The ant in the story was entirely wrong."

Finally, Mr. Bailey broke his silence.

"Perhaps the grasshopper in the Aesop fable read Matthew, chapter six, verse twenty-five: 'Take no thought for your life, what ye shall eat, or what ye shall drink; nor yet for your body, what ye shall put on. Is not the life more than meat and the body more than raiment?' The grasshopper simply took the message from Matthew's gospel to heart."

"Nonsense. May I remind you that Reverend Wilmot at St. Mary's would not take kindly to your literal interpretation of that biblical verse?"

"Perhaps not. But remember, the Reverend never stops thinking about what he's going to eat and drink."

"Don't be disrespectful of the good reverend. He hears the voice of God."

"True, but the only time he listens to the voice is when it's calling him to the dinner table."

"You men have no sense of what is proper. I find your remarks quite offensive. I think I'll go to another butcher shop next time."

Having delivered her final remark, the mighty Miss Snell stormed out of the shop.

Mr. Bailey quietly said, "Amen."

*

Later that evening, Emmy sat beside the fire with Phil. The house was quiet, the children in bed. She told Phil about her encounter with Miss Snell. After she had finished relating the details, he laughed and said, "Good for you, Emmy, my girl."

However, Emmy remained indignant. "I had a teacher similar to Miss Snell when I was a girl. I haven't forgotten her cruel remarks. It's no wonder that Billy dislikes attending her classroom."

"Aye, I understand, but Billy needs an education."

"Yes, and he'll get one, but perhaps not from that old windbag Miss Snell."

*

Billy's troubles never seemed to subside. The following evening, Mrs. Rowntree berated him for nothing other than being in her presence. He simply smiled, remembering how she had wielded her broom like a warrior in battle when she confronted the teenage bullies in the laneway. Ever since the incident, he had harboured a degree of respect for her. However, it was out of the question that he stop teasing her.

One evening as Phil and Emmy sat by the fire, as was their usual custom, Emmy thought of Mrs. Rowntree's oft-repeated warning, *Billy's bound for hell.* She reconsidered the matter for the umpteenth time in her life and thought, *My Billy is bound to be one hell of a man.* Then she blushed for thinking in such intemperate language. Phil noticed her cheeks redden.

"What secret desires are you entertaining?"

"I'm feeling a little warm tonight. I'll pull my armchair farther away from the fireplace."

"I think the heat's from your thoughts, not the fire."

"Oh, shush, you silly goat. Can't a woman have a few private reflections?"

"Not those that cause her to blush."

"If I told you my thoughts, it might cause you to blush."

"Better keep them to yourself, then. I have no desire to suffer the heat from the sin of corruption."

They both smiled.

Emmy glanced away from the fire and gazed lovingly at Phil. They had been married fourteen years, and she thought he remained as handsome as when they had first met. When he was a teenager, at five-foot-eleven, he had been the tallest among his friends. His smile was the most inviting of all the boys'. Though he was now older, his head of blond hair remained full, even as it had changed from yellow to light brown. His blue eyes, however, remained as sparkling and attractive as ever. Despite the fact that he worked in a factory where smoke, soot, and dust hung heavily in the air, his face was unlined.

Billy was the spitting image of his father in appearance and manners.

*

In 1901, the Mercer family had relocated from the town of Dorchester to the village of Comstock in Dorset County. That same year King Edward VII had ascended the throne, following the death of Queen Victoria, whom the British people called Mother of the Empire. Comstock was only a mile from the turbulent waters of the English Channel. The move had been difficult for Emmy, but like many of the poor across the land, she had learned to cope and not complain.

Born in Dorchester, Emmy, when a girl, was the shortest in stature of the four children in the Thompson family—shorter, even, than her two younger sisters. Her brother, Bill, only a year older, was much taller. However, despite their differences in age and height, she and Bill were constant companions. He never seemed to mind his younger sister tagging along when he went exploring the streets of the town or the surrounding woods.

Emmy's father, William Thompson Sr., had called her "adorable." Her mother thought her quite pretty, but it was rare for anyone to say that she was beautiful. Her thick brunette hair surrounded a face with plain features. Her deep brown eyes and pert little nose were her only redeeming physical characteristics. On the other hand, the girls thought that Bill was very attractive; his outgoing personality attracted much attention. It helped that he was muscular, was good at sports, and possessed a natural ability to sing and play any instrument that interested him.

However, despite Emmy's short stature and lack of eye-catching features, she did draw the attention of the most attractive boy in the community, young Philip Mercer, whom people called Phil. He saw in Emmy something that he had not seen in the other girls—determination and pluck. She was the most interesting girl he had ever met. It was not long before his fascination with her turned to adoration. The reason for his deepening sentiment was something that had occurred on the High Street, which confirmed to him that she was the *best* girl in Dorchester.

It happened one afternoon. A group of children had gathered, and when an old man ambled up the street begging food, several of the boys threw rocks at him and shouted nasty names. Emmy pushed the boys away and fiercely defended the elderly hunchbacked man.

"Leave the man be," she shouted. "He's hungry and needs a bite to eat."

One of the lads told her, "The man's a criminal."

"His only crime is being too poor to get any food," she responded.

One of the bigger boys added, "The old buzzard stinks. His crime is making the streets stinky." The boy pinched his nose with his fingers to emphasize his point.

"He needs a crust or two of bread. Get out of my way. I'll take him to our kitchen door." She then pushed her way through the group of children, the beggar following behind her.

They dared not challenge her, as they knew that her older brother, Bill, was observing the scene and it was clear that he approved of his sister's actions. They feared his fists. When Emmy and the old man arrived at the back door of the Thompson house, she fetched some day-old bread for him from the family's kitchen.

Her compassion touched Phil deeply. From that moment onward, he spent as much time with her as he was able. Within a few weeks, he realized that he loved her. Fortunately for him, Emmy soon reciprocated his love. The two became an inseparable couple.

As an adult, Emmy remained short, a mere five-foot-three. Shy by nature and prone to recede into the background of a group, Emmy—if someone offended her sense of right and wrong or picked on her—was more than capable of defending herself. Phil had once told her, "Your backbone is of cast iron. I'm glad that you love me, because I fear you would be an awesome enemy."

*

When the Mercers arrived in Comstock, the town that confronted them was humble compared to Dorchester, which they had left behind. In Comstock, houses were far less grand, the townsfolk having constructed them compactly. Only an occasional narrow street or laneway separated the rows of peak-roofed dwellings. Most of the homes were more than a century old, moss growing between their ancient stones.

The Mercer family rented a modest dwelling on South Street where the poorest of the town lived. At the north end of South Street was the High Street, where the wealthier residents of Comstock resided. The Mercer house was semi-detached and similar to the other houses on the street. Its single doorway was flush against the sidewalk that paralleled the roadway. Right inside the doorway was a small vestibule with two doors, one granting entrance to the north side of the building, where Mrs. Rowntree lived, and the other opening into the Mercer home. The vestibule permitted a degree of privacy, as when the outside door opened, people passing on the sidewalk were unable to gaze directly into the interior rooms of the dwellings.

The downstairs of the Mercer home contained a small parlour with a brick fireplace; on its mantel was an old clock, a wedding gift from Emmy's parents. The Mercers had positioned two well-worn stuffed chairs in front of the fire, the larger and most frayed of the two being where Emmy usually sat. She spent many hours there sewing and knitting. The cozy kitchen included a cast-iron stove, a rough wooden table, six straight-back chairs with wicker bottoms, and a tall stool for Zack.

The rear door of the kitchen opened onto a small garden surrounded by a six-foot brick wall. An ancient apple tree leaned against the wall on the west side. It was this tree Zack had climbed to observe "the battle of the broom." The tree offered welcome shade on a hot summer day. In winter, its gnarled branches crackled noisily in the wind. Beyond the wall was a dusty laneway, and on the far side of it was another wall. On the other side of that wall were vegetable gardens and, beyond them, a meadow of wild grass. Bordering this was a gurgling trout stream. It was a tranquil environment, a glorious playground for the Mercer children.

In the days when Phil and Emmy first arrived in Comstock, it was a thriving town. Each Saturday morning its farmers' market had been teeming with the produce of the farmlands that hemmed the town on three sides. On market days, long before the sun crept above the surrounding hills, well-laden carts creaked along the cobblestone streets. On these occasions the High Street was crowded with people who bargained and bartered for their weekly household needs while indignantly scolding dealers about their high prices and short measures.

In the late afternoon, the Bull and Ox Inn on the High Street, as well as the Oak Leaf Ale House on South Street, served many a tankard of ale to thirsty townsfolk and farmers alike. It was a life of hardship and toil for most of Comstock's citizenry, but it was not without its rewards. A successful day at the market was a source of contentment both for farmers and housewives.

In the years following the celebration of King Edward's coronation, the optimism generated by that regal event slowly faded. Harsh times gripped the land. Crops were no longer as bountiful, causing prices for commodities to rise. Even the humble ha'penny became scarce, as people were forced to become more frugal. The decrease in demand eventually affected the town's two main industries—the Buckingham Tannery and the Church Manufacturing Company, purveyor of fine china. Phil worked at the latter as a skilled silver engraver. He laboured long hours, but at least he had employment. For this he was grateful.

Church Manufacturing Company was well known for its unique china patterns, but its real claim to fame were the porcelain chocolate sets, which, before the downturn in the economy, had been highly sought-after items by those with the funds to pay. Most of them were not sold locally, but rather were offered by the finer shops throughout England. A typical set consisted of an impressive ornate box container, six cups with saucers, six sterling silver spoons, and sterling silver holders for the cups. Phil created the designs for the silver items. Though the company highly respected the quality of his work, his remuneration did not reflect that appreciation.

*

At this point Billy was twelve years of age, the firstborn of the Mercer children. Eleven-year-old Mary was second oldest. Next was Ruth, who was ten. They were both quiet, hardworking girls who dutifully assisted their mother in the kitchen. Mary and Ruth had blonde hair like their father.

Elizabeth (Bess) was seven. She was not tall for her age like Billy, but her lack of stature and tender years did not detract from her desire to compete with her male siblings. Bess's hair was brunette like her mother's, and she possessed her mother's dark complexion, but her features were striking like her father's. Her eyes were a deep blue, similar to her brother's, but they shone more radiantly than his because of her dark complexion.

The adults of South Street thought she was cute. A bit of a tomboy, she longed to accompany her brothers on their adventures, but they would not allow it. As a result, when Bess was not playing with the local girls her age, she hung around the kitchen and was usually more annoying than helpful.

Zachariah (Zack), the youngest Mercer child, was six. Similar to Billy, he resembled his father, some commenting that he was a "midget" version of Billy. For his age, he was not as tall as Billy had been, but he possessed a slim, wiry build similar to that of his older brother. However, unlike Billy, he was quiet and less adventurous, even though he enjoyed sharing in his brother's mischievous antics. His older sisters teasingly referred to Zack as the runt of the litter. A runt he may have been, but because of his attractive appearance, he garnered almost as much attention as Billy. At times, he was also as big a tease as his sister Bess.

*

In 1894, the Anglican priest in the ancient stone church of St. George's in Dorchester had baptized Billy as William Paul Peter Mercer. Emmy had chosen his names. William, his first name, was in honour of her older brother, Bill. The previous evening, she and Phil had been discussing him.

"I think that your brother Bill is becoming one of the town drunks," Phil had said. "He's constantly hanging around the Oak Leaf Ale House."

"I admit that I've seen him there, too, but I believe that within my brother is a dormant seed of goodness that one day will sprout and grow."

"My goodness, that's quite poetic," Phil teased.

"Shush, you silly goat," she replied, ignoring his comment. "I remember the days when my brother and I were children, and how we enjoyed each other's company. I miss seeing him."

Phil's tone softened. "I respect how you feel, Emmy. After all, he's your brother. But I fear he's a bad influence on the children."

"I think that's a rather harsh judgment. You realize that Bill is aware of your disapproval. That's why he rarely comes near the house."

"Perhaps that's for the best."

"I'm not sure about that. Although he spends much time in the Oak Leaf Ale House, have you ever seen him tipsy?"

"No, I admit that I haven't. But that's beside the point. He hangs around the alehouse too much. Whatever does he see in that rowdy crowd?"

Phil's remark caused Emmy's temper to rise. She replied sternly, "One time when I met him on the street, I inquired why he spent so much time at the alehouse. He said that the conversations in the alehouse were more interesting than in most places, and that included within St. Mary's Church."

"I doubt that!"

Emmy was not finished. "He also said that there was more Christian charity within the alehouse."

This comment stopped Phil in his tracks. He remained silent for a few moments before he replied. Slowly, a small smile crept across his face and he said, "Well, thinking of Reverend Wilmot, I suppose your brother might be right. Wilmot is not very charitable in his sermons. I sometimes think he might be as bad an influence on the children as the drunks in the tavern."

Taking Emmy by the hand, he caressed her fingers, smiled, and gazed into her flashing eyes. She was unable to resist returning the smile. Slowly, she calmed down, realizing that Phil was respecting her viewpoint even if he did not totally agree.

She asked, "Do you remember why I named our firstborn after my brother?"

"Yes. You told me it was because of your 'abiding' love for him, as you put it."

"Do you remember why I chose Billy's other names?"

"Yes. You chose the name Paul in honour of the apostle Paul, who in his writings stressed faith and obedience. You hoped that Billy would acquire those attributes. You chose the name Peter because you thought that St. Peter was the most humble and human of the disciples, exhibiting qualities that you wanted Billy to demonstrate as he grew older."

Emmy smiled, pleased that Phil had remembered what she had told him those many years ago. Then she said, "I think we both know that Billy is more of a Peter than a Paul. He's not boastful and is clearly all too human, but obedience isn't his best quality."

"Yes, I know. It's as if he and trouble are constant companions. He doesn't seem to seek its companionship; it just follows him wherever he goes."

"Then, when you give your love to Billy, regardless of his shortcomings, try to extend the same love to his namesake—my dear brother, Bill."

"I don't know if I can, Emmy dearest, but I'll try."

*

One evening in mid-April, Billy climbed the narrow stairway leading from the kitchen to the second floor of the house where the family's three small bedrooms were located. By the time he reached halfway up the stairs, the chill descending from the upstairs rooms replaced the warmth from the fireplace. His parents occupied the front bedroom with the large bay window that overlooked the small homes and humble shops on the street below. Billy's was the back room on the left-hand side of the stairs. He shared it with Zack, who was already in bed, but not asleep, when he arrived in the room.

Young Zack adored Billy and often regretted that he did not have the ability to fight against seemingly impossible odds like his older brother. He prayed mightily that someday he too might fight like the biblical Daniel in the lions' den. Actually, he considered Billy braver than the prophet Daniel and had once made the mistake of informing the Reverend Wilmot of his conclusion. Zack still remembered the cuff on the ear he received from the stern minister of God.

Outside the bedroom window, as it was early April, strong winds blew northward from the cold channel waters, creating whistling noises in the hollow chimney. Below, in the back garden, the daffodils and tulips had long since dropped their blooms. Despite the warm weather earlier in the season, the days now were damp and cold. Zack snuggled deeper under the quilts as Billy shed his clothes and climbed into bed.

The light of the moon shining through the small-paned window on the south side of the room cast shadows across the quilts, the old wooden headboards visible in the dim light. Both beds contained straw-filled mattresses supported on the frames by thick hemp ropes that were manufactured from the crop of local fields. The only goose-down mattress was in their parents' room. It was a wedding present from Phil's parents, who had both passed away the year Zack was born. The beds in the boys' room had been in the Mercer family for many generations—no one knew how long—and the hemp ropes needed replacing.

Whenever Billy climbed beneath the thick quilts into the cold bed, despite his relatively light weight, the ropes groaned as they stretched in response to the extra burden. Gazing around the room, Billy was not ready to enter into the world of slumber. His eyes scanned the walls, once white but now dulled with the soot of the passing years. A single faded picture, a watercolour of Comstock Harbour in summer, painted many years ago by his uncle Bill, hung forlornly on the otherwise barren wall. He liked Uncle Bill, even though his father had told him not to see him since he drank too much fermented barley water. No one in the family except Zack was aware that Billy frequently saw and spent time with their uncle.

Rather than hanging their clothes on the pegs to the left of the door, Billy and Zack had tossed them onto the straight-back chair against the rear wall. Their mother frequently reminded them not to do this, but they continued anyway, as it was faster and easier for them. On the far side of the room, moonlight reflected from the white crockery of the "thunder mug," the pot available for their necessary nighttime functions. It was a humble bedroom, but it was Billy and Zack's private domain wherein they shared and discussed their thoughts.

The silence was broken when Zack inquired, "What's a 'billy-prod-stick'?"

"Never you mind," Billy replied, a mixture of amusement and irritation in his voice.

"I heard those boys in the laneway say those words. And today I heard Shirley Ann say them. Your face turned red when she said them. I know they're naughty."

Billy remained silent. He had recently developed an interest in girls, and he "sort of" liked Shirley Ann. However, he knew that Zack was intent on teasing him, so he ignored him.

"I know what a billystick is. Constable Jim carries one. But what's a billy-prod-stick?"

"Be quiet!"

"I'll ask Shirley Ann. She'll tell me because she likes you and I'm your brother. If she doesn't tell me, I'll refuse to tell her where you are the next time she wants to find you."

"How do you know she likes me?"

"Because she tells the other girls that you are 'heavenly divine,' and she grins in a strange way and flutters her eyelashes when she says it."

In the darkness of the room, Billy could hear Zack imitating a kissing noise with his lips on the palm of his hand. Billy was unable to resist smiling.

Zack continued in a syrupy singsong voice, "I think Shirley Ann is your girlfriend. At least she thinks she is."

Actually, there were several girls in Comstock who were desirous of being Billy's girlfriend. When he strolled up South Street, hands thrust deep in his pockets, cap perched on a jaunty angle, many a young girl admired him. Despite his mischievous ways, his appearance was that of an angel on two legs—the most attractive boy the young girls of the town had ever seen. They found his height and slender build pleasing and they thought his bearing almost manly, even though he was not yet a teenager.

"Come on, Billy. Tell me! What's a billy-prod-stick?"

Billy remembered the boys in the laneway. They had confronted him and Zack behind the house. There were three of them in their late teens. They mocked him by saying that his "billy-prod-stick" was too small to help a girl into heaven. He knew what they meant, and he knew that they wanted to fight. Being older than he was, they thought him an easy victim.

Telling Zack to run for it, Billy delivered a few hard punches when they attacked him, and then he quickly slipped over the garden wall to the safety of the back garden of the Mercer home. He knew when it was wise to retreat, as the boys were all older than he was and could have inflicted serious harm. He smiled with satisfaction as he remembered his swift escape and the frustrated yells of the disappointed pugilists.

Zack stubbornly refused to be quiet and go to sleep. "What's a billy-prod-stick?" he asked again. "Tell me!"

"I'll make you a deal, Zack. If you go to sleep, I'll tell you tomorrow."

"Promise?"

"Promise."

Billy knew that the following day he would have to invent a plausible story to satisfy Zack. There was no way he could answer his brother's question with any degree of honesty. His mother would kill him.

The next morning, Billy told Zack that a billy-prod-stick was the same thing as the billystick that Constable Jim carried, but *larger.*

Billy grinned mischievously to himself as he pictured Constable Jim's confusion if Zack told him he knew about a billy-prod-stick.

*

On the final Saturday of April, the warm winds of spring finally swept across the land. The villagers of Comstock had suffered from a deficit of nature during the dreary winter months, but as the gardens and meadows unfolded under the warmth of the sun, they were finally able to reach out and touch the greenery. The townsfolk shed the heavy clothes that had protected them from the winter winds, allowing the soft breezes to caress their pale skin.

Because there was a gloriously blue sky, Billy and several other boys of the village eagerly gathered at East Bay, Comstock's harbour area, which possessed a narrow beach. Donning their swimming costumes, they gingerly entered the chilly waters. Stretching out on the hot sand after their immersion in the numbing waters of the English Channel, they were compensated for the icy waves' tortures by the sand's warmth.

Later, returning home on the pathway that wound its way northward from the beach to the southern edge of the town, Billy strolled past the fields, green and lush from the late spring rains. Sheep grazed quietly. Noisy coal-black crows fought among themselves in a leafy copse bordering the pastures. Arriving at the bottom of South Street, outside the Oak Leaf Ale House, Billy sat on a rickety wooden bench that only remained upright because of the brick wall supporting it.

It was past the hour of five. Many of the men were departing the tavern to return home for tea. Billy sat and waited for his uncle Bill to come out. His uncle was popular with the alehouse crowd, as he was a talented piano player, even though he had never received a music lesson in his life. The men referred to the battered upright piano in the ale room as Betsy Banger, and indeed Billy's uncle could "bang" Betsy's stained keyboard and produce rollicking folksongs and sentimental ballads to which the men sang along with great gusto. Sometimes, he played a favourite hymn or two. The soothing effect of the ale added to the men's emotional response to the songs. As Billy sat outside and waited, he could hear his uncle playing the piano within, along with the loud, intoxicated chorus. Occasionally, the sounds of clinking tankards reached his ears.

*

Unbeknownst to his parents, Billy knew how to play the old piano. Many months earlier, in the late afternoon, before the alehouse became busy with men returning from work, he heard the piano inside the tavern and entered to listen. He discovered that his uncle Bill was the musician. Billy had always liked his uncle, the few occasions he had seen him. He found him easy to talk to and enjoyed his funny stories.

Bill Thompson was gregarious by nature. People in the alehouse said that he had the "gift of the gab." It was true that Bill was rarely at a loss for words. His quick wit helped him avoid many a difficult situation with the rowdy men who frequented the tavern. A few women also visited the alehouse regularly, although their presence was not considered respectable by the housewives of the town. The "tavern girls" ignored the snide remarks they overheard on the High Street and coped with the rough treatment they were subjected to by the male patrons of the tavern. They were highly attracted to Bill, as he was unquestionably the most handsome and interesting man of the lot. His humorous tales and stories, which he told during pauses in his piano playing, were very popular.

The first time Billy had entered the alehouse, his uncle was surprised to see him, but instead of questioning why he had dared come inside, he invited him to sit on the bench beside him. After a few moments of light banter with his nephew, he began explaining the C-scale and demonstrated that when its notes were arranged in a varied sequence they could create a melody. Next, he played other scales and showed how they also produced melodies, but with a slightly different sound.

The next time Billy appeared, his uncle played various notes together. He asked Billy, "Do you hear how certain notes complement each other?"

"Yes," Billy replied. "I like the sound they create."

"That sound is called harmony. Want to try it?"

Bill listened and watched as his nephew's fingers moved across the keys. He was amazed how they moved assuredly to produce the harmonized notes.

"It seems that you and the keyboard know each other."

Billy smiled and continued manipulating the keys.

In the days ahead, during the afternoon hours when the alehouse was empty, Billy slipped inside and continued to receive lessons from his uncle.

One day Uncle Bill told him, "You play well with one hand; try using the other."

Billy nodded. "I'll try."

To the amazement of his uncle, Billy successfully employed the other hand. He made mistakes, but it was obvious that he was capable of accomplishing the task.

"That was good," Uncle Bill said, "for a first try. We will continue working on it together in the days ahead. You have a natural talent, my boy."

Next, Billy learned to play the notes from a song sheet, quickly understanding the relationship between the notes on the page and their position on the keyboard. His uncle Bill realized that before he was able to explain the next stage in understanding the music, Billy's mind leaped ahead to the next level. It was as if a source within him automatically told him what to do. Even more amazing, he never forgot what he learned. If he played a melody once, he recalled it with ease, no matter how much time had elapsed. However, the thing that astonished his uncle Bill the most was that Billy could "feel" the music, instinctively gracing it with embellishments that were uniquely his own. It fascinated his uncle.

Billy never told anyone, except Zack, that he was able to play the piano. He knew that if his parents discovered that he could play, they would instantly know where he had learned, since—apart from the one in the alehouse—there was no other piano available to him. The only other instruments were in the wealthy homes on the High Street. Billy's parents had forbidden him to go near the alehouse, never mind enter it. As a result, he remained silent about his newly acquired skill.

*

On the Saturday afternoon after Billy returned from the harbour, after waiting ten minutes, his uncle exited the alehouse. Being in a generous mood, he dropped a penny into Billy's hand as he deposited himself on the bench beside him. For a second or two, Billy thought the bench might collapse.

Uncle Bill wore a battered hat that looked as if it had survived the Boer War, or perhaps even the Franco-Prussian War of the 1870s. His drooping, untrimmed moustache and four-day beard growth added to his unkempt appearance yet failed to hide his handsome features. Billy could care less. He loved Uncle Bill and enjoyed talking to him. Billy often confided in him the ideas he shared with no other adult. His uncle was insightful; his opinions, highly intelligent. Billy knew that his uncle's humorous stories held hidden meanings and often contained a lesson worth considering. Invariably, Uncle Bill, rather than passing judgment on his ideas, prodded him to question matters further. Billy enjoyed these sessions, especially since he and his uncle shared a common bond: their love of music.

As uncle and nephew sat on the bench talking, several more men, boisterous and reeking of ale, departed the alehouse. At that moment, a mangy male cocker spaniel wandered along the street and deposited itself on the sidewalk beside the bench where Billy and his uncle sat. It was an abandoned animal, much in need of a bath and decent grooming. Billy had often seen it begging for scraps around the local alehouses and the nearby butcher shops. One of its ears was badly mangled, the result of a fight many years before.

Billy ignored the dog.

For some reason, though, the animal suddenly wrapped its front legs around Billy's left leg and pumped as if he had found a bitch in heat. Thoroughly embarrassed, Billy shook his leg violently to dislodge the dog from its passionate perch, but to no avail. The spaniel held on and continued his rhythmic motions of amorous delight. Several men came out of the tavern and observed the scene with great amusement. Their chuckles soon grew into unrestrained laughter. Billy's face reddened proportionately to their growing enjoyment. Having fair skin at a time such as this was a severe disadvantage.

Finally, one of the drunken men gave Billy a knowing wink as he declared, "Don't worry, me boy. The mutt is just having a sample in case it intends to ask you to marry it."

The men howled with delight and continued laughing as they departed homeward.

Billy's uncle Bill chuckled as he stood to leave.

"Don't feel bad, Billy boy," he said. "It won't be the last time that a lad like you will suffer the indignity of an indecent proposal."

*

On Sunday, April 29, as the church bells tolled in the crisp morning air, the Mercer family trekked southward on South Street to St. Mary's Anglican Church. The winds from the channel were gentle, the sun was ascending into a crystal blue sky, and a few cotton clouds dusted the western horizon, remaining distant enough so as not to mar the scene.

Emmy was aware that Phil was not happy about attending the service. She told him, "It's obvious that you aren't too pleased about going to church this morning."

"It's not the service I dislike. I've attended the Anglican church since I was a boy. I've always enjoyed it. It's the Reverend Wilmot that I dislike."

"I understand how you feel. I'm not too fond of him, either. But he's our priest and we owe it to the children to show him respect."

"The good reverend is as wide as he's tall. Old Walter Patchett repeatedly tells everyone that the Reverend is five-foot-five, no matter which direction you look at him. Walter also enjoys telling people, 'Reverend Wilmot's bushy eyebrows, long nose, pointed ears, and beady eyes make him look like a fox, one that has devoured too many hens from a local henhouse.' Personally, I think that when Wilmot preaches, he's more like a bull."

"I know what you mean. He bellows like old Mr. Halliday's bull."

"That's the truth. He accepts no disagreements about his interpretation of the Holy Book. According to him, if you agree with him, God guarantees you a pew in heaven. If you disagree, the fires of hell are already singeing your toes. I think my toes are already burning."

"Shush, you silly goat. I'm aware he leaves much to be desired, but we should try to be respectful."

"I find it increasingly difficult. I think he's one of those Christians who keeps his Bible on an upper shelf, well beyond his reach. He only takes it down when he requires proof for a preconceived idea that he has no intention of exploring in the first place. He believes that this qualifies him as a preacher of 'conviction.'"

"Shush! The children might hear you."

"I'm not saying anything that Billy doesn't already know."

"I suspect you're right. I think Zack knows, too. But still …"

"Well, you must admit that the Reverend is a ridiculous sight. When he's on parochial visits, he stomps up South Street in his heavy black boots as if he's trying to stamp out the evil in the town. I also notice that he reserves his most frequent visitations for parishioners with well-provisioned larders. It's as if he believes that those with pantries containing lots of food and bottles of spirits are in greater need of his spiritual guidance than others are. His huge belly is testimony to this deeply held religious conviction."

"My, but you're wound up this morning."

"Well, you must admit that when his mouth is not bellowing boring sermons and lectures, he gobbles as much free food as he can. Each year, his stomach grows larger. Thankfully, his excesses of the flesh don't include promiscuity, or else the town's orphanage would bulge at the seams like his frock coat does."

Emmy tried not to smile as Phil continued his tirade.

"The Reverend and Billy are not exactly on good terms. Old Wilmot resents Billy's asking him questions during Bible classes. The Reverend fears that Billy's inquisitive nature might lead him to think about the Bible in ways of which he might disapprove. Wilmot thinks that it's better to quash Billy's impertinence, rather than have him thinking for himself, which he thinks leads to sin."

"I know, I know. But Billy is to blame, as well. The Reverend has not forgiven him for placing a large puff-mushroom under the cushion of his pulpit chair at last autumn's Harvest Festival Service."

Phil grinned. "I remember it well. When the Reverend sat down on it, the force of his fat rear-end crushed the puff mushroom. The rude sound echoed throughout the nave. Everyone mistook it for flatulence. No one dared laugh aloud, but as I recall, everyone's amusement remained throughout the entire hour-and-a-half-long sermon. It didn't help that the closing hymn was 'Heavenly Gales Are Blowing.'"

Emmy could no longer hide her grin.

However, despite knowing that Phil was right, she again stressed, "I'm not disagreeing with you. I'm simply saying that we must show respect for the Reverend. We need to set a good example for the children, especially Billy. Lord knows he needs no encouragement to be disrespectful."

*

Passing by the weathered stone wall of the churchyard, Phil and Emmy entered the narthex through the south door beneath the old square-shaped tower. The site had been a place of worship since the time of the Normans, although the present-day church had been erected in the fifteenth century. When seated in the nave, the couple felt the cold and damp of the ancient structure. They gazed toward the lectern, awaiting the arrival of the Reverend Samuel Thackeray Wilmot.

Phil and Emmy watched as the Reverend made his grand entrance. His beefy hand firmly gripped the wood railing as he heaved his bulk up the narrow stairs that led to the pulpit. At the appropriate time in the service, he launched into his sermon with all the energy of an Israelite attacking the walls of Jericho. His jowls shook as he emphasized the main text of his sermon, "The wicked flee from the wrath of God."

Phil whispered to Emmy, "I've never seen a 'wicked flea.' Have you?"

"Shush," she replied. "Try to set a good example for the children. Besides, how would I know if a flea has been wicked?"

Emmy's remark encouraged Phil to offer another frivolous comment. "Wilmot believes fleas are wicked because they're too small to eat."

Emmy was unable to resist smiling as Phil nudged her gently with his elbow to reinforce his silly remark. In response to Phil's inane musings, Emmy pretended to cough, placing her hand across her mouth to hide her grin. However, several of the busybody women of the congregation noticed her amusement. A knowing look passed among them. They were certain that the cause of her smile was something naughty.

Ignoring his wife's predicament, Phil made matters worse when he whispered, "The Reverend must end the sermon soon. It's past his feeding time."

Emmy tried her best to ignore him, but she had the worst desire to laugh aloud. She bit her tongue, the pain allowing her to contain her amusement. The service ended with Robert Lowry's hymn "Shall We Gather at the River?"

In a voice that Emmy could hear above the robust singing, Phil said, "I bet the Reverend wants us to gather at the river to enjoy a picnic lunch, where he'll devour everything, including the wicker picnic baskets."

At the end of the hymn, the congregation fervently chanted amen with enthusiasm, grateful that the morning's devotions were over for another Sunday.

*

Following the service, Zack asked his mother, "Why doesn't Reverend Wilmot ever preach any 'pudding' sermons?"

"What are 'pudding' sermons?" she inquired.

"Sermons that make me feel all warm inside, as if I'd just eaten a piece of plum pudding. Billy sometimes tells me 'pudding' sermons."

"What do you mean?"

Zack gazed up at his mother as he explained. "Last night, Billy told me the story of the Prodigal Son, the way he would tell it. Billy says he's not sure that it's fair that Reverend Wilmot condemns the brother who stayed at home. He says that before the father killed the fatted calf, he should've asked the son working in the fields to come and greet his long-lost brother. He should've explained that the calf was to show that he loved both his sons. Billy says that a smart father wouldn't ignore a son who stayed at home to help him. For the father to say, 'All I have's yours,' Billy says doesn't sound as if he meant it, when the way he acted didn't show it. Billy says that the lesson of the story is that we should treat everyone good, even those who fail us. Billy says that even if I failed you and Father, you'd still love me as much as if I didn't fail. Billy made me feel warm inside, as if I'd eaten pudding."

Then Zack stressed emphatically, "*That's* a pudding sermon."

Emmy looked at Zack and said, "I understand what Billy was trying to tell you. His ideas often show another way to think about the stories."

Then, turning to Phil, being careful that Zack would not hear her, Emmy said, "Whenever I hear Billy's interpretations of biblical stories, I'm not certain whether to reprimand him or encourage him."

*

The following week there was another incident that brought attention to the biblical story of the Prodigal Son. It occurred in a roundabout way. Reverend Wilmot chose to read from a text other than the Bible for his Sunday morning sermon. To illustrate the point he wanted to make, he used the story about God's denying Moses entry into the Promised Land because of his disobedience.

At the conclusion of the sermon, he shook with rage as he thundered, "As a result of Moses' wilful act of disobedience, God denied him entrance to the Promised Land. Anyone in this parish who acts contrary to God's will is doomed to bottomless perdition, there to dwell in adamantine chains and penal fire." By now, everyone was familiar with the flowery words the good reverend employed to tell about the torments that awaited those who did not follow the path of righteousness. They were not aware that the words were lifted from the poetry of John Milton. However, they knew that as far as the Reverend was concerned, there was only one way to interpret the Bible—his way.

In the afternoon, when Billy and Zack attended the boys' Bible class, they mischievously hid the Bibles to create a fuss and shorten the length of the class. The Reverend was certain that Billy had performed the deed. He grabbed Billy by the ear and marched him into his office. With a certain degree of glee he thundered, "Billy, you have wilfully disobeyed God."

"But I only hid the Bibles," Billy protested meekly.

The Reverend roared in reply, "It's against God's law to hide Bibles."

"I don't remember reading that in the Bible," Billy mumbled quietly. The Reverend was unable to hear the remark, but he didn't care. He was certain that it was disrespectful. Sitting down in his armchair, which creaked under the load of his considerable girth, Reverend Wilmot glared angrily at Billy while noisily drumming his pudgy fingers on his desk. The Reverend's scowl and increasingly reddened face made Billy fear that the preacher was about to thrash him. He was right. The only thing that held him in check was that he knew that the boy's father would never allow him to perform such a deed. Disciplining Billy was one thing, but facing the wrath of Phil Mercer was another.

As the moments passed, Billy's curiosity overcame him.

He quietly asked, "Reverend Wilmot, may I ask a question?"

"For heaven's sake, what is it?" he replied, exasperation evident in his voice.

"If you disappointed a friend or a person in this parish, what should the person do? Should the person forgive you, or should the person hold a grudge against you?"

The Reverend calmed down as he observed the earnest expression on Billy's young face. Against his better judgment, he answered his question.

"If I ever wronged a person, which is highly unlikely, then the person should naturally forgive me. After all, I'm the priest of this parish."

"Then forgiving you would be the right thing for the person to do?"

"Most assuredly."

"Then I don't understand, sir. Wouldn't a loving heavenly father do the same? After all, in the parable of the Prodigal Son, Jesus taught that though the Prodigal Son disobeyed his father, the father forgave him and killed the fatted calf for him. In your sermon about Moses, you said that God told Moses that he would not see the Promised Land, but I hope that God did not mean that Moses would not enter heaven. Moses had served God faithfully. Despite his act of disobedience, wouldn't God welcome him into heaven? And if someone sins against us, shouldn't we forgive him?"

The boy's words stung the Reverend. His arguments made some sense, but somewhere beneath them, the Reverend was certain, there were shoals that would wreck his view of the world. This he was unable to tolerate. He believed that his parishioners should accept his views or be damned to hell. Yet here was a young boy who was questioning his interpretation of the events he had described in the sermon he had preached that very morning. He knew he must squash such independent thinking.

The Reverend paused, puffed his chest to prodigious proportions, and replied testily, "It's not your place to question my sermons. It's up to you to obey your betters. Now, get out of here!"

Billy turned and walked out of the office. He decided that he would not mention the incident to his father, even though he suspected that his father was not fond of Reverend Wilmot. Billy knew that his father would tell him that he should not have hidden the Bibles.

As the Reverend Wilmot watched Billy depart, he was certain the lad was a miscreant beyond redemption. Yet there was something about the boy's words that bothered him. However, he was not certain what it was.

*

The summer of 1905 gradually burnt into the final embers of autumn, the warm months in northern latitudes capriciously fleeting. One morning, the cruel winds of early winter echoed through the narrow streets of Comstock and swept across the empty pasturelands bordering the town. It froze the cow dung; the well-worn boots of the dairymen were now immune to nasty immersions when they crossed the meadows.

As the days grew colder and the prevailing winds gained strength, the few remaining leaves on the ancient oaks fluttered to the ground. In the now empty fields, where the wheat and hemp had been harvested, the remaining stubble quivered in the gales. Then, one morning, a heavy fall of snow buried everything beneath a layer of white. With the advent of icy temperatures in Comstock came anticipation of the merriment that would ensue once the yuletide season arrived.

Late one evening, an unsolicited decoration mysteriously appeared, hung on the door of the vicarage. The next morning, Reverend Wilmot discovered the dry, flat, hollow-centre piece of cow dung the shape and size of a large Christmas wreath. Several sprigs of green holly, with their accompanying red berries, added to its festive appearance.

The prank brought much mirth to the pub-goers. One elderly man in the alehouse declared, "Whoever placed the 'dung on the door' was merely commenting on the quality of the Reverend's sermons."

All the men in the pub laughed, even though none of them had suffered the vicar's sermons at St. Mary's.

Old Walter Patchett declared, "The wreath represents an important event in the Christmas story—a gift from a wise man."

*

The Mercer family was never to forget the yuletide season of 1905. A few days prior to Christmas, a telegram arrived from Grandmother Mercer requesting to visit. Phil wired back, granting his permission. The following week, she arrived from Dorchester on the evening train. She had asked that Phil arrange for her to stay four nights at a modest hostelry on the High Street. Knowing that there was no spare bed in the small house on South Street, she declined her son's kind offer to make room for her within the Mercer home. She said that she would manage just fine at an inn.

Because she had parted ways with Phil and Emmy on harsh terms many years before, she was uncertain of receiving a warm welcome. If her reception seemed cool, at least she would have the option of retreating to the inn. Her fears proved to be unfounded, however. In the darkness of a frigid evening, Phil and Emmy greeted her warmly at the train station and escorted her to the inn for the night. The following morning, since Phil was at work, Emmy accompanied her from the inn to the Mercer house on South Street.

Phil's mother was ramrod straight in stature and exceptionally fashionably dressed. She had gained no weight since Emmy had last seen her. She was trim and full-bosomed and, despite the years that had passed, remained an attractive woman. Emmy noticed that her face was still unlined, and though she was nearly sixty years of age, her chestnut-brown hair showed only a sprinkling of grey. Emmy smiled as she remembered Phil's once saying, "My mother's specialty is 'greying' others."

It was not long before Emmy noticed that, in other ways, her mother-in-law was not the woman she had previously known.

*

In the evening, after Grandmother Mercer had returned to the inn, the children were in bed, and Phil and Emmy sat by the fire, Emmy told Phil, "Today I noticed that your mother seems less demanding and more open to discussion, as opposed to lecturing."

"I agree that she seems different. There's been much to discuss, and I want to make the most of our time together. This evening, after I returned from work, we talked about many things. The subject of our parting years ago, we avoided. But still, by the time I escorted her back to her hotel on the High Street tonight, it was as if old wounds had healed and we were once more united."

"That's a good sign."

"Yes. Sometimes I think about the reasons we parted ways."

"She didn't approve of our marriage."

"Her attitude caused us many problems."

"I remember. It was the reason we relocated here to Comstock."

"I wonder if the reason she's changed is that she's getting older. She's been alone now for many years. My father died when she was a relatively young woman. Several years after his death, Frank [Phil's brother] disagreed with her over some matter or other. He eventually immigrated to Canada. They remain out of touch to this very day."

"It now appears as if your mother wants to make amends."

"Yes, it appears that way."

Phil continued, "Billy has not seen his grandmother since he was six years old. He seems overjoyed. I watched him this evening. He's fascinated by her tales of Christmases past, when Frank and I were children."

"I know what you mean. Her odd sense of humour has captured his heart."

"I think he particularly enjoyed the story she told about your father this evening beside the fire. Did you hear her?"

"No. I was outside chopping wood. What was the story?"

"She told the children about a nosey neighbour who once asked your father how he intended to celebrate his tenth wedding anniversary. Your father told the old gossip, 'I took my wife to Blackpool for our fifth anniversary, and for our tenth, I am going back to pick her up.' Your mother said that the old woman was shocked, but that the children's grandfather just chuckled merrily as he watched her depart in a huff."

"I'm sure that my mother's laughter was as hearty as the children's."

"It was, indeed."

"I watch your mother as she hugs the children. She is definitely not the same woman I knew years ago. I don't know what's happened to change her, but I don't think it's just ageing."

*

Billy had his own thoughts about his grandmother. He suspected that she, too, had had a rebellious spirit in her youth. All adults who spoke differently or had uncommon habits, Billy thought, also had an independent streak. He confirmed his suspicions about his grandmother the following Sunday when he overheard her speaking to Reverend Wilmot at the church door after one of his all-too-long Sunday sermons.

Reverend Wilmot smiled obsequiously at Grandmother Mercer as he said, "Good morning to you, my good woman." It was obvious that he knew who she was and that she was visiting the Mercer family. Grandmother Mercer had heard that no morsel of tittle-tattle ever escaped the Reverend, whose ears were as sensitive to gossip as his stomach was to food.

"How charming you look," he gushed in a syrupy voice. "I am certain that you have never been as fine-looking as you are today." As the Reverend had never seen her before, she knew his words were mere treacle. "I hope that while you're in Comstock," he continued, "I may be permitted to call on you and your family before you return home. We can share a cup of tea and a few treats." He licked his lips in joyous anticipation as he thought about Emmy's rich, flavourful raspberry tarts.

"I trust you enjoyed my sermon," the Reverend continued boastfully while smiling condescendingly.

Grandmother's eyes narrowed slightly as she considered Wilmot's ingratiating manner. She knew verbal nonsense when she heard it and resented the Reverend's being so brazenly patronizing. She would have kept silent and ignored his comments if only he had not asked her about his sermon. For her, it was like igniting a spark near a container of coal oil.

"If I might suggest, Reverend, you might try shortening your sermons a little. If God cannot make clear his message in an hour, then he will make it no clearer a half hour later."

"My dear lady," Wilmot replied, extending his rotund stomach, "do you realize that you're giving advice to a man of the cloth?"

"Yes, and do you realize that you are addressing a lady who has heard preachers' sermons drive away more people from the church than the devil could ever persuade to leave? If you're a man of the cloth and a servant of God, then try listening to his voice more and speaking less. It might be a good idea if you also shortened your lengthy prayers to heaven above and devoted more time to the needs of those living here on earth."

Grandmother Mercer knew that her censorious words had stung the Reverend Wilmot. She tried not to look at his rotund belly. Realizing that several members of his flock were listening, she decided to say no more. As she departed, she saw that the Reverend was smiling half-heartedly as he returned to greet the other parishioners.

She regretted her outburst. In a way, she felt sorry for the Reverend, who was trapped between the desires of his stomach and his desire to admonish others for their sins of the flesh. Besides, she had broken her vow to be less outspoken and to curb her tongue. During the last few years, she felt that she had been mostly successful in this enterprise, but then along came the annoyingly pious Reverend Thackeray Wilmot. However, telling him what she thought had indeed been satisfying. A small smile crept across her face as she entertained the idea that the Reverend's mouth ran longer than a racing horse in heat. The man would try the patience of Job. Using a vulgar and a biblical comparison to describe the annoying reverend did not bother her. She was a woman of many contradictions. However, she was glad that no one could read her mind.

*

On Christmas morning, Grandmother Mercer arrived at the door laden with gifts. Billy received the first book that he had ever owned. Previously, other than the books he had read in school, only the Bible had been accessible to him. Having read it many times cover to cover, Billy found himself puzzled over some of its stories. He pondered these passages, but other than confiding in Uncle Bill and Zack, he had never expressed his opinions aloud. He wanted to discuss his thoughts with his father, but he was not comfortable broaching contentious subjects with him.

Billy saw that the book Grandmother Mercer had chosen for him was a leather-bound copy of Thomas Hardy's novel *Far from the Madding Crowd.* He knew it was an unusual choice for a boy his age, and also that it was an expensive present.

Grandmother Mercer told him, "I think that everyone should read Thomas Hardy's works as, after all, the town where I live, Dorchester, is the centre of Thomas Hardy country. Give it a try," she said as she handed it to him. "The book's advanced vocabulary may cause you some difficulty, but I'm certain you'll successfully understand the story."

She was right. Billy devoured it easily and loved the story. He was particularly fascinated by the character Bathsheba Everdene. The novel reinforced Billy's passion for reading and created a desire in him to find more books. The other children enjoyed their gifts, too, but none of them was to experience the type of impact that the Hardy book had on Billy. It was the beginning of his lifelong love affair with literature.

When Christmastime was over, Grandmother Mercer returned to Dorchester. The entire family was saddened. They regretted the lost years, but there was to be no crying over spilt milk. The yuletide season of 1905 had been special, thanks to Grandmother Mercer, but the days ahead were precious, too—and no one in Comstock was looking forward to them more than Fighting Billy Mercer.

*

Between Christmas and New Year's Day, while sitting in the quiet of the vicarage, Reverend Wilmot pondered his problems with Billy. After much soul-searching, he concluded that the lad was a tool of Satan. Recalling the events of the previous months, he thought about several pernicious deeds that he was certain Billy had performed. He remembered the day when his wife had discretely placed his clerical collars on the clothesline inside the back shed and a thief had stolen them. A few hours later, the townsfolk saw several mongrel dogs running in the High Street wearing white collars around their necks. *No one but Billy would perform such a perfidious deed,* he thought.

It was fortunate that the Reverend was unaware that when one of the canines had peed against the tree outside Armstrong's Bakery, an elderly woman had chuckled loudly and exclaimed, "I do believe the dog is spraying holy water. I'm afraid to see what the animal will deposit as a communion wafer." The story was the talk of the town for several days.

Reverend Wilmot had no proof that Billy had committed any of the deeds that brought ridicule on his head. However, he was certain of his conclusion when he mentioned dogs several times in his sermon the week after the incident. Each time, he noted a tiny smile on Billy's face. It convinced him that the boy was the perpetrator.

The more the Pastor suffered, the longer his sermons became. He saw no reason why he should suffer alone, and suffering in silence was not within his capabilities.

*

Mrs. Rowntree had also been the brunt of several pranks, and similar to Reverend Wilmot, she was certain who was responsible. She could elaborate on Billy's misdeeds without any provocation; she rarely missed an opportunity to do so. Sitting by the fire with her ten-year-old tabby cat on her lap, she told the animal, as she scratched behind its ears, "Young Zack shot a dried pea from his peashooter at me this morning. I was bending over the well drawing a bucket of water. It hit me on me old arse. That boy's following in his brother's footsteps."

Sammy, the tabby cat, purred as he replied, "Meow."

"I knew you'd agree with me, Sammy, me love. I've lived in this house since the day I was married at age twenty-two. After me dear Harry passed away, the years have been 'arsh. For the past five, I've shared with the Mercer family. God knows that Billy and Zack add to me difficulties."

Sammy nudged her hand to be petted.

"I'm now in me eightieth year. At least I've not become a fatty like many of the old gossips in the town. With no husband to help me, me damn chores prevent me from gettin' fat."

She sighed, and Sammy meowed sympathetically.

"I've been a widow now o'er twenty years. Harry and I ne'er had any children."

The cat stirred, hearing the bitterness in Mrs. Rowntree's voice.

"When I first married, me wanted a daughter and a little brother to keep her company, but life dealt me a bad hand." She paused, stroked Sammy's tail, and added, "However, I've thrown a few bad hands to some I've met on South Street." She chuckled for a moment or two. "However, me thinks I've thrown the most 'bad hands' at Billy." She cackled merrily.

Sammy continued purring as she talked on. "Sometimes me thinks Billy's not really a bad lad and that I should ignore his damn pranks. However, I just don't seem to be able. There's something about Billy that almost makes me want to love him, but I can't when I know he's a lad who's bound for hell."

Placing Sammy on the chair on the other side of the hearth, she stood up and walked over to the hallway mirror. Gazing at her image, she sighed in exasperation, as she did not find her reflection pleasing.

"I know the girls in the Mercer household think I'm a witch. Two days past, little Bess asked me if I could fly through the skies on me broom on dark winter nights. I suppose Billy and Zack told her about the 'broom war' in the laneway."

Continuing to gaze into the mirror, she asked Sammy, "Do you think me face is wrinkled?" Hearing no reply from the cat, she confessed, "I admit that me nose is long and crooked. Perhaps I do look like a witch. Two of me front teeth are missing. I hate smiling. Perhaps that's why the Mercer girls think me a witch."

Sammy meowed loudly. He wanted her to sit down again so he could jump up on her lap. However, she thought that his meow had a different message.

"What's that, Sammy dearest? You don't think me looks like a witch? Well, thank you. Tomorrow I'll try to be more cheerful, but life smacks me across the face each time I try. It makes me forget about trying to be pleasant."

She ran her fingers through her frizzy grey hair.

"I've never been able to frighten Billy and Zack. But lately, I've noticed that Bess doesn't fear me, either. That child is too much like Billy. However, there's something about the way Bess looks at me with her piercing blue eyes that worries me. At least Billy and Zack I knows are rogues, but Bess? I simply cannot understand her."

Sammy began circling the chair where they had been sitting. Finally, he ignored his mistress and leaped up on it. Mrs. Rowntree did not notice.

"I wonder if Billy ever feels guilty about playing pranks on me? Lately, he's been speaking kindly, even given me a few smiles. What do you think about that, Sammy?"

Sammy meowed loudly.

"I'm certain that you're right, my pet. I think he's mocking me, too. He's a bad rascal. I don't think we can ever forget he'll end his days in a jail."

Sammy remained silent.

Continuing without the cat's approval, she told him, "Just last summer, I caught Billy dumping two small trout into the well that I share with the Mercers. The well is fifteen below the ground, and the water many feet deeper. Despite me trying to get the damn things out, it was impossible. Now, each time me draws water, I see the bleedin' fish. However, I must admit that our well water's the cleanest in all Comstock. No insect ever lives to spread disease.

"Sammy, do you remember the time I went to the kitchen window looking for you, and I saw Billy stealing a pair of me bloomers? I'd hung them on the clothesline to dry. They were hidden from the street behind the evergreen bushes. Before I could rush next door to tell Mrs. Mercer about it, I heard laughter from the street. Me opened the outer door and peeked out. The mangy spaniel that hangs around the alehouse was running around wearing me red bloomers.

"I told Mr. Mercer about the prank, and he kept Billy in his room for a week after school each day. He was let out only after he done his chores. I thought he'd learn a lesson, but the very next day he was back at his pranks."

She paused and, turning to the cat, added, "However, lately I've noticed that his pranks are not so often and a little gentler. Me wonders if he's begun to realize that I've a hard life and doesn't wish to add to me problems?"

Sammy was now rubbing against her legs. He had leaped down from the chair. Listening to his mistress's troubles had made him hungry.

As Mrs. Rowntree walked to the cupboard to fetch his bowl, she said, "Me dearest Sammy, I don't think Billy'll ever learn his lesson. Me thinks his pranks will continue in the days ahead. He's bound for hell."

Sammy meowed loudly. To him, hell was any place where there was no food.

"I knew you'd agree," Mrs. Rowntree told her feline companion.

*

During January 1906, Billy attended school irregularly, frequently skipping class to labour in the barns of various farmers, earning a few pennies a day. The last week of January, Grandmother Mercer shipped to Comstock, via train, a large trunk of books. Among them were adventure tales for Bess and Zack. However, for Billy and the older girls she had included ten books that Thomas Hardy had penned, as well as numerous editions of the classics and some history, science, philosophy, and geography texts.

The books became Billy's window onto the world. They allowed his mind to soar beyond the hills of his hometown, carrying him to the exotic isles of the South Pacific, across frozen Arctic wastelands, and into Africa's steamy jungles. Greek mythology and philosophy, Roman legends and law, and biblical history raced past his eyes on the printed pages. When he read Plato and Socrates and other ancient works, he was quick to see relationships between them and the Bible. His reading broadened his knowledge of the ideas and teachings they presented. Also, he noticed they shared certain themes. Billy's mind was open to the greatest scholars of the ages, but they did not dim his enthusiasm for the teachings of the Bible. His readings allowed him to conceptualize important ideas, which resulted more in his asking questions than finding answers. Billy was never to be the same again. A man's mind was now trapped inside a boy's body.

Zack, Bess, and the older girls followed Billy into the brave new world of learning, even though they mainly read only the adventure stories. They often sought Billy's help to understand some of the words. Billy was pleased to share the excitement he felt with his siblings. He never failed to encourage them.

During late February 1906, Billy developed a more responsible attitude toward life. He attended school more often and was increasingly respectful of Miss Snell. She was uncertain how to interpret Billy's change of behaviour and continued to berate him. He ignored her fits of bad temper and, on occasion, smiled at her. This infuriated her even more. However, he ignored her outbursts and absorbed the ideas the classroom presented. Billy also displayed more tolerance toward Mrs. Rowntree, ignored her harsh rebukes, and smiled at her more frequently. Like Miss Snell, she was also suspicious of his behaviour.

One morning he overheard Mrs. Rowntree discussing him with a neighbour woman.

"When that Billy Mercer smiles, I remembers something that I once heard. 'The devil can beguile and enchant as he leads us down a path of sin.'"

"Perhaps," the other woman replied, "but despite his villainous ways, there's something about Billy that pulls on the strings of me heart. Try as I might, I'm unable either to sever the strings or to understand them. I suppose that there's something about the boy that's beyond my understanding."

Mrs. Rowntree gazed sternly at the woman but said nothing. However, it made her think!

*

April delivered more than showers of rain; it brought forth "showers of change." Four successive events occurred that were to alter the life of the Mercer family forever. The first happened early in the month, on a warm spring Saturday evening on the High Street, after the shopkeepers had shuttered their windows for the day. The pleasant weather encouraged many residents of Comstock to stroll forth upon the avenues of the town.

It was Saturday, April 7, and Billy and Zack were among those who were walking along South Street. They were homeward bound after a successful trouting expedition to the river on the west side of town. Their fishing poles and bait bucket in hand, and with five plump trout on a line slung over Zack's shoulder, they received more than a few admiring glances, even though their trousers and shirts were soiled from the day's activities.

Zack was now seven years old, a handsome lad, each day growing more like his older brother in mannerisms and appearance. His blond hair was a tad lighter than Billy's, but his eyes were the same cornflower blue. Similar to Billy's, his skin was flawless, except for a small birthmark on the left side of his forehead, which was usually hidden by his hair. It was becoming obvious that within a few years he would attract as much attention from the girls as his brother did. It was also apparent that he would likely never be tall like Billy. When he was fully grown, he would likely be less than average height.

As the brothers strutted down South Street, proud of their catch, they noticed that a crowd had gathered outside the Oak Leaf Ale House. Then they heard music—a brass band. Whenever one appeared, it immediately attracted the attention of those strolling on the streets of the town, especially on a warm evening. In this era, only a limited number of people had ever heard live music, other than in the churches, and thus a musician or the occasional barrel organ on a street corner invariably attracted a crowd. Concert halls existed only in the larger urban centres, and if there had been one in Comstock, the price of a ticket would have been beyond the means of most. Thus, a brass band was worthy of much attention.

Billy noticed that on the street, across from the notorious Oak Leaf Ale House, people had gathered and were listening to the band. However, they carefully maintained a healthy distance from the notorious pub. A few teenage couples, realizing that the townsfolk were preoccupied, unassumingly continued their way southward toward the quiet cemetery of St. Mary's, one of the few places where a young couple could meet and not provoke stern disapproval or idle gossip. The churchyard was sacred ground and was deemed a place where immoral behaviour was unlikely. Many an infant's existence began within the walled cemetery of the ancient St. Mary's Anglican Church in Comstock.

When Billy and Zack arrived at the place on South Street where the crowd had gathered, they saw Uncle Bill among the crowd. He was intently observing the scene. Worming their way through the bystanders, Billy and Zack joined their uncle.

"What's happening?" Billy inquired of Uncle Bill.

"It's a Salvation Army band—from Dorchester."

"Why are they here?"

"They've come to save sinners. Do you wish to be saved?" Uncle Bill offered Billy a mischievous wink as he spoke.

"Saved from what? A runaway horse?" Billy teased in reply.

"No, saved from a sinful woman like the one over there." Uncle Bill nodded his head to indicate a plump elderly woman who at that moment was stepping out of the alehouse, and none too steadily.

Billy looked at her and grinned. He was aware of the hidden meaning in his uncle's remark. He replied, "I think that woman likes you, Uncle Bill. I've seen the way she grins at you whenever I'm in the alehouse." Billy smirked and awaited his uncle's retort.

"My boy, I gave up sinful women last March during Lent. I gave up turnip, too. It's a sin to eat such a bitter vegetable."

Billy smiled at the mention of turnip. "Perhaps you should save the woman for yourself."

"My boy, you're incorrigible."

"Naw, I just can't be changed," he replied, offering another grin. His uncle looked into Billy's eyes and saw that they sparkled with mischief, thoroughly enjoying the verbal duel. He placed his hand on Billy's shoulder and gave it an affectionate squeeze.

"I might not be able to change you, but I have a feeling that when you're older, a few of the girls will have had their hearts melt into butter after meeting you."

Their conversation ended when the band started to play. The sound was soft and as rich on Billy's ears as a bit of chocolate would have been on his tongue. He thought the music far nicer than the sound of the alehouse piano and the ancient pipe organ in St. Mary's, which had been installed through funds raised to celebrate the British victory at Waterloo in 1815.

Uncle Bill gazed down at Billy and inquired, "What do you think of the sound of the band?"

"I really like it. The trumpets are great," he enthused.

"They're not really trumpets. The Salvation Army bands uses cornets instead."

"They look like trumpets to me."

"The two instruments are similar. Cornets are the same shape as trumpets, but they're shorter."

"Whatever you call them, I'd love to learn to play one."

"Perhaps someday you will."

"If wishes were horses, I'd ride home," he replied.

Uncle Bill smiled as he continued listening to the band's music.

"They sound like an angels' band," Billy told his uncle.

"Do you think the angelic trumpets from on high have descended to Comstock's South Street?"

Billy smiled. "Not really, but I've never heard anything like it before."

"I don't think the Oak Leaf Ale House qualifies as a stable like the one in the story of Bethlehem."

"True, but on a Saturday evening, I've heard people say that it smells like one."

They both grinned.

"Listen, Uncle Bill," Billy instructed, "the band is playing a different melody. I don't recognize it."

"It's new to me, too."

"The man just referred to it as the 'Founders' Song.'"

"I don't know what that means."

"I believe it means that the hymn was composed by the founder of The Salvation Army."

They listened as the preacher read aloud the words.

O boundless salvation! Deep ocean of love,
O fullness of mercy, Christ brought from above,
The whole world redeeming, so rich and so free,
Now flowing for all men, come roll over me.

The band performed two more verses of the hymn and the preacher spoke briefly, exhorting sinners to repent. The outdoor prayer service was reaching its climax, and as the drummer laid the big bass drum on its side, the preacher cried aloud, "I invite those who wish to be free of their sins to step forward and kneel beside the drum."

Billy watched as a well-dressed man came forward, a handkerchief wiping tears from his eyes.

A few moments later, Billy noticed that Uncle Bill's eyes were moist. Something had profoundly struck his uncle's heart, but Billy was unable to decipher exactly what it was. The preacher man held his songbook high in the air as he urged, "Join the heavenly throng by kneeling at the drum."

His uncle Bill did not go forward, but a small tear trickled down his cheek. Perhaps his uncle wished to change his life even though he had not gone forward and knelt beside the drum. Billy knew about "life-changing moments," as he had experienced some himself. Was Uncle Bill facing a moment of spiritual truth through the medium of music? Could music accomplish this? If it were possible, then this was another revelation for Billy to ponder.

The poignant moment was broken when the drummer gave a loud bang on the drum and the band commenced playing again. While the musicians performed three more verses of the hymn, Billy hung on every note. The brass instruments fascinated him, particularly the cornets, which, to him, would always be trumpets. He had heard the Reverend Wilmot preach from 1 Corinthians 15:52: "For the trumpet shall sound." To Billy's mind, there was something majestic about a trumpet. It was indeed heavenly, he thought. He edged closer to the musicians to gain a better view. Zack followed him.

Billy told Zack, "I'd love to have a cornet."

Zack responded, "I'd like a trumpet, too."

"They're cornets."

As was the case many other times in his young life, Billy truly wanted something that was impossibly beyond his reach. Though young in years, he had learned that understanding complex ideas presented a similar challenge. He had often stood on the brink of knowledge but had failed to cross over into its depths.

Next, the preacher lowered his hymn book and commenced reading aloud the final verse of the song. He again pleaded, "Sinners, give your hearts to God."

Billy said to Zack, "I'm not sure what that means, but I'm ready to give my lips to God if he will give me a cornet to play."

"Or a trumpet," Zack added.

Following a lengthy prayer, the band packed up their music and assembled in a military formation in the middle of South Street. To the beat of the bass drum, the men set forth and marched up the street to the Masons' Hall, where they would hold the evening's church service. As they marched along, they played a lively tune. Dogs barked and women waved as they passed the small homes flanking the avenue.

With the departure of the band, Uncle Bill wandered away.

"I wonder if Uncle Bill is headed to the Masons' Hall?" Billy said to Zack. Then he asked, "I wonder if God knows how much I want a shiny new cornet?"

*

The second event of that April was less dramatic, but its impact was more immediate. A letter arrived from Canada in the afternoon post on Wednesday, April 18. As Billy passed the envelope to his father, he noticed the small Canadian postage stamp bearing the regal profile of King Edward VII. When his father gazed at the envelope, Billy caught the look of surprise that flitted across his face. Mr. Mercer knew only one person in Canada who would send him a letter—his brother, Frank.

Phil Mercer sat in his chair beside the fire and eagerly tore open the envelope. "Read it aloud," Emmy requested. He began in a voice that was unsteady.

My dear Brother,

Sarah and I send greetings to you and your family. I trust that this letter finds you in good health. I regret that I have not written to you during the past few years, which have too swiftly disappeared. The past is regretfully gone, and the future is before us. I beg your indulgence as I explain.

Here in Toronto, I met a fine girl named Sarah, who immigrated to Canada from Nunhead, near London. We were married five years ago. We have no children.

Before I reveal to you the purpose of this letter, other than to apologize for my hasty departure from your life, I wish to inform you about my life here.

Toronto is a bustling city, thriving and embracing the new century that is now in its sixth year. Employment opportunities in this young city are aplenty, and the wages much better than in England. The shops teem with the bounty of the farms and the produce of the surrounding market gardens, and though prices are not cheap, they are within the reach of those who are careful with their pennies and purchase wisely. There is a mood of optimism in this young land. Our prime minister, Wilfred Laurier, said it best when he declared, "The twentieth century belongs to Canada." Canadians believe it and act accordingly.

I followed in our father's footsteps and became an apprentice in a silver-plating company. I work on King Street, in the heart of the business district of Toronto. I seemed to have inherited Father's skills, as my employer has recognized my efforts and promoted me. I am now a foreman and earn a respectable wage.

Sarah, my devoted wife, has shown great promise as a seamstress and now fashions ladies dresses. Living a frugal lifestyle, we saved sufficient funds to purchase a house on Draper Street, from whence I am able to walk to work. The women on nearby Wellington Street create sufficient demand to keep Sarah occupied in her trade. It is a good life, and my only regret is that I have been unable to share my life with you and your family. We have acquired friends here, but the lack of family leaves a longing in my heart that cannot be fulfilled.

Now I must inform you of the main purpose of my letter. A friend of Sarah's is immigrating to Canada next month. His name is George Meaford. Sarah knew his wife when she was a girl and lived in Nunhead. The joy Sarah has experienced at the news of their impending arrival lifts my heart, but it also reinforces the loneliness and sorrow I feel when I realize that you and your family are so far away.

I have two requests that I beg you to consider. I write to you in the hope that you might consider bringing your family to Canada. A house across the street from me is for rent. I know the owner personally, and he has assured me that he will hold the house for you if you should choose to immigrate. As you are all British subjects, there would be no problems with immigration.

I realize that it is a major decision, and also that my request is sudden. However, do not allow the suddenness of the request, or the difficulties that such a major decision would entail, deter you from considering the matter. Think about your children. Opportunities here will be far greater for them than in Comstock. As well, we would be together again as a family. It is my sincere wish that you deliberate on my suggestion.

The other request that I wish to broach relates to my departure from England, which I did under duress. The problems between Mother and me were never resolved. I know how she holds firmly to her ideas, and though it is said that faith can move mountains, it might require an even greater force to sway Mother from her opinions.

Dear brother, would you approach her on my behalf? I feel that you might be better able to move a mountain than I (smile). I know your relations with her have also been distant, but I believe she would accept an appeal from you better than from me. If you are successful, or even if you detect a glimmer of hope, please inform me. I will take the matter in hand and write to her. If she is adamant that she does not wish to have any contact with me, then I will learn to live with the disappointment. However, I sincerely hope that you are successful.

I send my kindest regards to Emmy and the children. I have never met any of them. I learned about your marriage and the successful births of your children through a neighbour of yours who immigrated to Toronto last year. Because Sarah and I have not been blessed with children, my desire is great to have family members close to us. This feeling has increased as the years have passed.

Please write to me when you have made a decision. I will abide by your wishes, but I truly hope that when Christmas of 1906 arrives, we will all be together. Gathering around the yuletide tree with the voices of children echoing in our parlour, and the love of family around us, would be the greatest gift that God could ever bestow. May God bless you and your family.

Sincerely and affectionately, your devoted brother,

Frank Mercer

*

The third event was also sudden. It occurred on the Saturday evening of April 21. Emmy was gazing through the second-floor bay window that overlooked the cobblestone street. It had been raining since early morning, sheets of rain slashing across South Street, water gurgling noisily as it drowned the gutters and overflowed the street in the low-lying sections. When a loud clap of thunder struck, she jumped and gasped aloud. It was like a cannon exploding in the heavens.

As it was nearing the time for Phil to return from work, she parted the curtains and glanced out the window. In the background, she could hear the kettle boiling on the stovetop. Peering amid the gloom of the evening, amid the raindrops dribbling down the glass, she saw Phil. Judging from the slope of his shoulders and his plodding step, she was certain what had occurred.

Entering the house, Phil placed his sodden overcoat on the peg on the kitchen wall beside the back door and deposited his weary body in his chair beside the fire.

"You need a cup of hot tea," Emmy said soothingly. Tenderly, she placed her hand on his shoulder as she passed the mug to him.

"Thanks, love."

"Are you all right?"

"I don't really know. The last few months, it's as if I've suddenly grown old."

Emmy said nothing, patiently waiting for him to speak.

"The news is bad, Melina." He never referred to her as Melina unless he wished to express something serious. There was no need for him to say anything further. Emmy's heart sank into her boots. She had been right. She reached out and placed her arms around him.

"They laid me off work today. There aren't enough work orders for the company to keep me on."

"You've been in fear of this for many weeks, my dearest."

"Aye, losing the job and being unable to support the family is eating away at me."

"Drink your tea. You'll feel better."

Phil sighed, slowly exhaling the air from his lungs.

"We'll get by," she said. "Our savings are meagre, but they will keep the wolves from the door for a few weeks. I can take in laundry and do more sewing for the neighbours."

His pride wounded, Phil was close to tears as he took Emmy's hand and looked into her eyes. "Yes, my love. We'll survive. But I feel like a failure. I've worked so hard to build a future for us. Now it seems that the days ahead will be bleak. What am I to do?"

"Have you thought about your brother's idea that we immigrate to Toronto?"

"Yes, but we don't have the funds for the passage."

"Write to your mother. She might assist us."

"We have just recently reunited with her. How can I ask for help when it means departing from her life forever?"

"I understand. But I think she might help. Canada might be the answer to our prayers. Write to her and explain everything. Any money she loans us, we'll repay."

*

The fourth and final event that was to shape the lives of the Mercer family occurred five days later, on Thursday, April 26. In the early morning hours the skies finally cleared, the moisture-laden clouds having escaped beyond the eastern horizon. Sunshine washed over the hills surrounding the town, splashing over the rain-soaked streets and soggy herb gardens. An unseasonably warm day was ahead.

Temperatures were rarely high in Comstock because of its proximity to the English Channel, so people considered seventy-five degrees a heat wave. Phil was standing on the narrow walkway in front of his house when Mrs. Rowntree arrived with her broom to perform her daily ritual.

"Mornin'," she said briskly.

"Good mornin'," Phil replied, not anxious to engage in conversation with the sour woman.

"Even the floods of Noah can't wash the dirt from this street. Just the other day I said to Mrs. Moulton …"

Her tongue stopped clicking as she watched a lad arriving with an envelope from the telegraph office. He handed it to Phil. Dying to know its contents, she looked directly at him and said, "Well, open it, my good man. What news does it deliver? I hope it's nothing bad."

Phil did not reply. He opened the front door and entered the vestibule. Mrs. Rowntree attempted to follow him, but he gently closed the door. Inside, he went into the kitchen, where the morning's fire had died away but where the hearth still emanated a hint of warmth. As the day was heating up fast, he decided to sit in a kitchen chair near the rear window, since it looked out over the cool greenery of the garden.

With shaking hands, he opened the envelope and unfolded the paper. The wire said:

> Will provide the money if you take me to Canada
> with you—Stop—Love—Stop—Mother

A tear trickled down Phil's cheek. Not only had God answered his prayers, but he had also reunited him with his brother. As well, their mother would be nestled once more within the family circle. A smile flitted across his face as he thought of Frank's joy once he heard the news.

*

In the days ahead, the Mercer family was engaged in a whirlwind of events. As their moving preparations neared an end, Emmy told Phil, "Though our few possessions were rich with memories, they brought only a few shillings when we sold them."

"Aye, prices are cheap for second-hand goods, as so many others are departing from England."

"We've given away many things to friends. No one would buy them."

"Billy is broken-hearted at losing the books your mother sent, but there's no other choice. However, *Far from the Madding Crowd* he's determined to keep and has slipped it in his suitcase among his clothes."

"It was his first real book. The 'first' of any experience is always so precious."

*

Monday, May 21, arrived—departure day. Early in the morning, they gathered their suitcases in the parlour. "Within the hour, the hired cart will be here to transport us to the train station," Emmy told Phil.

"I've mixed feelings about leaving our home on South Street."

"I know what you mean. It was drafty in winter, and when the winds blew north from the channel, the windows rattled and the flames in the fireplace flickered."

"I won't miss the rattling windows and chilly drafts."

"Neither will I. However, the fireplace was where we gathered every Christmas morning. It was where the children listened to you tell stories, and it was where we sat in the evenings to share our thoughts about the day."

"I don't know if the journey ahead is paved with adventure or mishap, but the village of Comstock has filled my heart with precious memories."

Then, gazing out the window, Emmy said, "The horse and cart have arrived to carry our belongings to the station."

*

Sitting at the back of the cart, Billy, looking back for a final glimpse of the house, saw Mrs. Rowntree standing in the doorway, observing their departure. She gazed at him, giving him a look that he was unable to interpret. He told Zack, "I wonder if Mrs. Rowntree's wondering who she'll hit with her broom now that we're leaving for Canada."

Zack grinned.

Billy looked back at her once more. He smiled and waved her a fond farewell. He was unaware that after he and his family disappeared from sight, Mrs. Rowntree slipped out the door and hurried along the cobblestone street in pursuit of the cart.

Chapter Two

When the Mercer family arrived at Comstock's British Rail station, located at the south end of town, a railway worker hauled their steamer trunk and bulky suitcases into the baggage car. The Mercers clambered aboard, and a porter assisted them in placing their smaller suitcases in the overhead rack. They had reserved seats, and since the train would not depart for ten minutes, they descended from the coach onto the platform to bid goodbye to those who had gathered. Although it was a workday, a few close friends and family members had come to offer them a final farewell. Emmy's maiden Aunt Matilda, whom she loved dearly, several of her female cousins, and Phil's great-aunt Susanne were there.

Emmy was suddenly aware that someone was standing close to her, on her left. Her mouth dropped open with surprise as she gazed into the smiling face of her brother, Bill. Attired in a neatly pressed suit, he had shaved, trimmed his moustache, and combed his hair. He looked like a new man. Emmy threw her arms around him and held him close.

After breaking from her embrace, he said, "My dearest Em, I couldn't let you depart without seeing you."

Tears came to Emmy's eyes. Bill was the only one who ever called her Em.

"Bill, it's good that you came. You look so fine and handsome."

"Em, I have finally turned my life around."

"I always knew that you would do well."

"I came here today because I feared I might never see you again. Canada is on another planet. However, my future appears brighter, but I face it without you, Phil, and the children. I can never express the depths of my regret for having lost so many years when I could have been with you and your family."

Emmy stroked his face gently. "We'll miss you." She paused and added, "Other than me, Billy will miss you the most."

Billy had never even hinted that he had spent time with his uncle. As well, his mother knew nothing of the piano lessons, but she had suspected that the two had met and talked, as Billy frequently employed some of her brother's favourite expressions. Emmy had shared her suspicions with Phil, who had nodded his head but offered no comment. He, too, had noticed the mature vocabulary that Billy increasingly used when expressing ideas and had suspected the source was Emmy's brother. However, neither he nor Emmy was aware of the depth of the relationship between Billy and his uncle.

"Billy is a rare lad, Em. Another of my regrets is that I will not be there when he makes something of himself. I don't know what it is that Billy possesses, but it's a rare quality."

"He has your name, Bill."

Bill smiled wistfully. "Aye! That he does. But unlike me, he's destined for great things. You mark my words."

Bill had uttered aloud the thoughts that Emmy had always held dear in her heart. He hugged Emmy for several minutes, kissed her on the cheek, and then went over and hugged the children.

He gazed back at Emmy, smiled, and then took Billy aside.

Placing his hand gently on Billy's shoulder, he said, "My lad, you've seen me many times at the alehouse, and we've shared many an hour with our music, but I've never shared your life. I know I gave you a ha'penny or two along the way, but I never gave you the time that you deserved. I will regret it to the day I die. Try to remember me with kindness, even though I failed you. When you step aboard that train, a new world will open for you. I regret that I will not be at your side to share it. Never forget that music can enter a man's soul when nothing else can ever gain entry. God has given you a gift; use it wisely."

Billy gazed up at his uncle, unable to express the love he felt for this man whom his father had forbidden him to see. He was also unable to tell his uncle how much the love of music that he had implanted in his soul meant to him. Billy also believed that music was a gift from God, a precious gift. A tear crept into his eye. He reached out and threw his arms around the uncle whom he loved so dearly. A silent understanding passed between them, though no further words were spoken.

Uncle Bill held Billy close and hugged him, not wanting to let go of his nephew. When they finally stood apart, Uncle Bill looked at Billy tenderly, knowing that he might never see him again. Billy saw that his uncle's eyes were misty. Uncle Bill turned to depart, fearful that he might burst into tears. However, before he was able to escape, he saw that his brother-in-law was blocking his way.

Phil placed an arm around Billy to prevent him from walking away, and he gazed intently at Bill. The two men faced each other. They had not seen eye-to-eye throughout the years, and there was an uneasy silence. Then Phil smiled and offered his brother-in-law his hand. Bill grasped Phil's hand firmly and returned the smile.

Billy listened as his father said, "Bill, I apologize for the way I've treated you during the past few years. You hung around the alehouse so much that I feared you might be a bad influence on the children, especially Billy. I was wrong. I know that you have had long talks with Billy, and I sense that you encouraged him to think for himself. Emmy has told me about some of Billy's ideas. I've thought about them. I'm not certain his interpretations of the Bible stories are proper." Then Phil paused, smiled slightly, and continued. "However, I can see the justice in them, as well as the depth of thought. I see your influence. Billy is a better boy for having been in your presence."

Bill was overcome with emotion. "Thanks, Phil," he finally replied. "Your words mean a lot to me. The music of the band playing outside the alehouse drove a stake through my heart. I knew that I was wasting my life. I am indeed like the Prodigal Son in the Bible story, but I'm trying to return. It's too late to kill the fatted calf for me, but try to remember me kindly."

"If I had time, I'd not only kill the fatted calf, I'd also slaughter half the herd." Phil grinned as he looked at Bill. They shook hands again, and then Phil embraced his brother-in-law. For Billy, this was the beginning of his looking at his father in a different light. He loved his father dearly, but he had felt that he did not understand divergent viewpoints. He now knew that this was not true, and in the future he might be able to confide in him the way he had previously confided in Uncle Bill.

Following the reconciliation, Billy went over to talk with Shirley Ann, the girl on whom he had been "sort of" sweet. They chatted for a few minutes, but Billy was too enthusiastic about the horizons that beckoned to dwell on the past. When they parted, he returned to where his parents were standing.

Billy was unaware that there was another reconciliation pending. Mrs. Rowntree suddenly appeared amid the well-wishers. Because several of her front teeth were missing, she rarely smiled. However, on this occasion, her lopsided grin encompassed her entire face. She solemnly shook hands with his parents, and then she gazed at Billy, the boy she had many times described as "bound for hell."

"Well," she said to Billy, her smile continuing as she spoke, "you may yet end up in hell. But me thinks you'll lead the devil a merry chase. Me wishes you a safe trip to Canada, me boy."

Next, the strangest thing happened. She embraced Billy, the hug almost squeezing the life out of him. Then, brushing the hair from her face in embarrassment, she gazed down at Zack.

"You look after your older brother, me lad. You know he'll find trouble, even in the sanctity of a church."

Then she cackled loudly as she told Billy, "I'll remember the mischief you played on the Reverend Wilmot until the day I die. I've never cottoned to the old buzzard." She did not mention the numerous tricks he had played on her.

Finally, Mrs. Rowntree gave a wistful smile, displaying the gaps in her front teeth, and then escaped among the crowd. Billy watched her depart, grinning while he scratched his head. He had suspected that Mrs. Rowntree was a kindred spirit. He'd been right. He was learning one of life's greatest lessons: Do not always believe appearances—even milk can masquerade as cream.

In Mrs. Rowntree's case, rich cream had masqueraded as skim milk.

*

The farewells now over, Billy boarded the train. Leaning out the window, he waved to friends standing on the platform. Then, with a sudden jolt, the train commenced its forward motion, the coach windows slowly moving past the pillars supporting the vaulted iron roof of the station.

The train puffed its way eastward, parallel to English Channel coast and toward Dorchester, where they had prearranged to meet his grandmother at the station. From Dorchester, they would journey to Liverpool—a distance of 189 miles as the crow flies, but much farther by way of the snaking rail lines.

When the train arrived at Dorchester Station, Billy and Zack gazed out the window.

"The place is crammed with people," Zack told Billy in amazement.

"Yes. A few minutes ago, a train arrived from Weymouth."

Zack yelled as he pointed, "Look! There's Grandmother Mercer. She's standing beside her two big steamer trunks. She's brought half of her household. She has a pile of suitcases, too."

"She's on the platform where the northbound train will arrive within the hour. We're on the opposite track, so we'll have to haul our luggage up over the bridge that crosses the tracks and then descend to the other side."

*

When they arrived on the platform where Grandmother Mercer was standing, she smiled, greeting them with strong hugs.

Mrs. Dorothea Mercer had always been a robust woman. When she was a child, she had been beautiful and strong-willed, but also demanding. Even now, many men referred to her as handsome. However, her crustiness had mellowed, although she remained a powerful personality. In recent years, her close friends had begun referring to her as Dot rather than Dorothea, a familiarity she would never have allowed when she was younger.

She had been the driving force behind the ACW (Anglican Church Women) in the parish of St. George's in Dorchester. She had supervised the preparation of every sandwich, cup of tea, and fancy cake that the women served at church functions. Her Harvest Festival Dinners had been the talk of the town. Other churches envied them but were never able to duplicate them.

However, during the last few years, other talk about Dot had circulated among the pews. She had held her head high, but she was aware of the gossip. Her close friends in St. George's Parish lamented her departure, while some were pleased to see her go. The latter group was regretful to learn that with her departure to Canada, they must step forward to serve the needs of the parish. They were to discover that work always looks easy when you are not the one having to do it.

*

The railway attendants placed the luggage of the Mercers in the baggage car of the train that would transport them north to Liverpool. A tumult of noise and confusion reigned, the confined walls of the station magnifying the babble of excited voices. The hiss of escaping steam from two mammoth locomotives preparing to leave rose to the heights above the tracks and then descended earthward again. The Mercers, laden with luggage, plodded toward the coach.

By early evening, the train reached the outskirts of the port city, decreasing its momentum as it approached Liverpool Central Station. After a brief stop, the train continued to the port area, jerking to a standstill at dockside. A busy harbour scene confronted the Mercers.

Billy told his father, "The wharf area's a hive of buzzing activity."

Phil smiled at his son's description. "Yes. We've arrived late, and many of the workers are taking a break, but others are still loading cargo onto the ship."

"Look at the number of stray dogs. They're barking like crazy, begging for scraps from the workers who are taking their teatime."

"Actually, I was looking at the size and number of cranes, sheds, and machinery," his father replied.

Billy grew poetic as he replied, "Everything plays a role on this stage. Compared to Comstock's port of East Bay, this is a theatre so large that it seems to be a stage encompassing the entire universe."

Phil again smiled at Billy's thoughtful description, but he was unable to resist pontificating a little on his own. "The port of Liverpool's one of the greatest of all the European harbours, for centuries associated with trade and passengers on the Atlantic. It's of sufficient depth that vessels are independent of the levels of the tides. The residential area of Liverpool is situated on the east side of the entrance to the immense Mersey River estuary, about three miles from the sea. At this point here, where we're standing, the river is about three-quarters of a mile in width, although the inside basin widens to about three miles. The port area is the largest in Britain."

Billy glanced at his father. "It's quite a port. And this is just the beginning of our adventure."

"Yes, we've a lot to see in the days ahead."

*

The ship that was to be their home for the next six or seven days was the steamer *Southwark,* a vessel of the Dominion Line, chartered by The Salvation Army's Immigration Department. Its well-worn decks instantly betrayed that the ship was not one of the luxurious floating palaces of the sea. The humble vessel carried immigrants to Canada, and on the return voyage its steerage section was loaded with cattle. Discounting the few first-class cabins, The Salvation Army had booked the remainder of the ship's passenger space. The hiring of ships and the assisting of immigrants was a service they performed for Salvationists and the public alike. Many a corps (congregation) in the British Isles was being decimated because so many of their soldiers (members) had departed for lands across the sea.

The *Southwark*'s hull of steel displayed signs of rusting, but it was smooth to the waterline. Thick pilings along the side of the wharf protected the hull from the damaging effects of its rubbing against the pier. The ship's massive size, however, allowed it to sneer at the petty manoeuvres of the swirling tidewater surrounding it.

Grandmother Mercer had paid for two second-class cabins. The girls were to share a cabin with their grandmother, and the boys were to bunk with their parents. The fares included meals in the dining room.

Even before the end of the nineteenth century, third class, sometimes referred to as tourist class, had become more common. By the first decade of the twentieth century, these cabins were gradually replacing the steerage sections on ships. These had been located at the bottom of the holds, at the stern of the vessels, where the cables to steer were located. Steerage was a noisy, stuffy, and uncomfortable section in which to make an Atlantic crossing, but the *Southwark* still maintained steerage class since the ship required the space for cattle on the eastbound voyages from Canada to Britain.

For the westbound trips, the crew scrubbed the steerage section as best as they were able, reconfigured the space, and inserted partitions in the areas that had contained stalls. However, the pungent odour of the cattle never entirely disappeared. The Mercers overheard a man say, "Steerage accommodations remain only fit for cattle."

*

Emmy was grateful to be in a second-class cabin, rather than steerage. After surveying the small space that was to become her home for the following days, she began unpacking their few possessions, taking out only those belongings needed for the day.

"Cabin space is certainly limited," she told Phil.

"Yes. But it's amazing how everything is designed to conserve space."

"Our personal items of clothing and warm sweaters, I'll place in the small drawers built into the walls of the room. I'll arrange our toiletries on the tiny shelf above the bed."

"I was told that the 'head' is down the hallway toward the stern. We share the facility with all the other passengers on this deck level."

Ten minutes later, Emmy said, "Let's go up to watch the ship sail out of the harbour."

Ascending the stairs at the ship's stern, they arrived on the open deck. Phil noticed that they were on the starboard side facing the city and the busy dock area.

*

Leaning on the railing, Billy and Zack observed the final preparations for departure. A crew member had told them that it took six days to load from wheelbarrows the coal needed for the long voyage. Cargo and food supplies had been brought aboard in the final two or three days before sailing. The vast quantities of mutton and chicken were now in the cold-storage section of the ship.

Zack whispered to Billy, "It's a good thing that Reverend Wilmot won't be onboard. The food supply would disappear in a single day."

They both smiled at the shared memory of the ravenous reverend.

"I think the workmen have completed the final tasks," Zack said.

"The workers are called stevedores," Billy told him. "They take the passengers' steamer trunks from the baggage coach of the train."

"The last of the stuff to be placed onboard is being put inside the ship now," Zack said as he pointed to the men pushing the last carts toward the opening in the hull.

"They're hoisting them up by ropes and pulleys suspended from the mastheads. The pulleys are operated manually, although the more modern vessels have small steam engines."

Billy and Zack remained silent as they observed the last of the crew scramble aboard. On the pier, men cast off the thick ropes, called hawsers, which held the *Southwark* in position at dockside. The ropes hit the water with a loud splash. A blast from the *Southwark*'s whistle startled the Mercers; the hollow sound echoed throughout the vast harbour. Then, within less than a minute, the ropes that had dropped into the murky water were hauled aboard. The *Southwark* was at last free from her berth, the gap between the dock and the hull widening.

Several tugs awaited on the port side to assist the ship in its departure.

"What are those small boats going to do?" Zack asked Billy.

"They'll help guide the ship out into the ocean."

"What's the other little boat?"

"That's the pilot tender. Onboard is a man who'll guide our ship down the narrow harbour toward the open sea."

"How do you know all this stuff?"

"From books."

Zack nodded and remained quiet.

They watched as the pilot tender pulled alongside the *Southwark* and its pilot boarded her. Later, after he had guided the vessel down the mighty estuary of the Mersey, the pilot would depart from the *Southwark*. The ship's propellers at the stern commenced turning as the tugs hauled the vessel from the port side.

While the ship eased away from the dock, Billy and Zack continued to observe the scene with fascination. They huddled close together, as the breezes blowing from the salt water were chilly in these early weeks of May, even though the late-day sunshine felt warm against their faces.

The ship set its course due north, between the confines of the land. When the river mouth widened, the *Southwark* turned west. They glimpsed the suburb of Bootle on the starboard side and New Brighton on the port side, each coming into view and receding from sight.

The *Southwark* held thirteen hundred immigrants, only a tiny portion of the great wave of relocating peoples that had begun the previous century and continued relentlessly until the First World War slashed its wounds across the European landscape.

Billy and Zack were but a speck among the masses.

*

Within an hour of her departure from Liverpool, the ship began heaving in the waves. As the minutes passed, the swells grew ominous in size, harmonizing with the brisk winds of early spring. As sunset approached, dark billowing clouds tumbled across the sky, obscuring the sun's setting into the vast depths of endless ocean. Then, when darkness descended over the waters, severe gales blew relentlessly upon the North Atlantic. With each passing moment, the rolling motion of the vessel increased.

Emmy remained below in the cabin, lying on the berth. Each time the ship thrust upward and subsequently plunged downward, it left her stomach somewhere in between. She became nightmarishly seasick. The small bowl beside her bed became her most necessary companion. Phil assisted as much as he was able, but there was very little he could do to ease his wife's debilitating seasickness.

The weather remained turbulent the following day. Emmy was deathly pale, moaning quietly. The essence of her being heaved with the mountainous swells caused by the blustery winds and agitated seas. She stretched out lifeless on the berth, at times holding Phil's hand while he gently applied a cold towel to her forehead. He did his best to assist her. Shortly before mealtimes, he went to the dining parlour and brought back a mug of broth, hoping that she might be able to consume a little.

Sometimes, after meals, he went directly to the galley where a sympathetic kitchen helper gave him a little extra soup. He managed to coax her into sipping sufficient amounts of broth to prevent her from becoming dehydrated.

Emmy was unable to share the children's enthusiasm for the heaving of the ship. The rocking motion made her thoroughly sick. Billy and Zack considered it a game and raced around merrily in the ship's corridors, much to the annoyance of some of the other passengers. The girls also found the trip entertaining, especially Bess. She ran as wildly as her brothers. They met other young passengers, made new friends, and played games.

During the night, the boys heard Emmy's moans, as they shared the cabin with their parents. They were saddened by her plight but were helpless to assist. The next morning, their father assured them that staying out of the cabin during the daytime and allowing her to rest was as much as they could do.

Billy sometimes fetched her broth and repeatedly told Emmy, "Everything is all right, Mama." He had always been her protector and so his words encouraged her, but the sickness would not release her from its grip. Sometimes Zack held her hand, repeating Billy's words, assuring her that everything would be all right.

*

Grandmother Mercer was as indomitable at sea as she was on land. It was as if she had dared the rolling waves to upset her sense of well-being. The first day aboard, within a few hours, she walked the corridors with the equilibrium of a seasoned sailor. She enjoyed her afternoon tea in the lounge as much as if she were in the Dorchester Hotel in London. In the evening, she appeared at the dining room with a robust appetite. All her life she had coped with adversity. Now that she was older, adversity might cause her to alter her course, but it never prevented her from sailing onward.

During the second and third days aboard, the seas remained rough. A freezing wind from the north chilled any passengers who ventured out on the decks. The turbulence of the North Atlantic created uncertainty among many passengers, as they questioned the wisdom of the path they had chosen. Most did not complain aloud, because they feared that such rumblings would create a mood of despair.

*

Unknown to Billy and the other Mercers, there was a man onboard the *Southwark* who was to have a great influence on their lives. George Meaford, a carpenter by trade, was twenty-seven years old and, at this point in his young life, was particularly optimistic about the future. Just a few days before, he had married Evangeline (Vangie) Smith, the love of his life. It was Vangie who knew Phil Mercer's sister-in-law, Sarah, in Toronto.

When George first met Vangie, he had thought her the prettiest and most charming girl he had ever known. She was a year younger than he was, possessing fine features, porcelain-clear skin, hazel eyes, and dark brown hair. A petite five feet in stature, she was reserved by nature, but when she spoke she demonstrated intelligence and insight. These qualities added to the favourable impression others had of her. George had met her at the Nunhead Corps of The Salvation Army, where he attended services.

George was a second-generation member of The Salvation Army, his parents having raised him in a home steeped in its beliefs. Though the Army undertook many charitable endeavours, it was a church that had been founded on Methodist teachings. The church dominated George's family life. At an early age, he learned to play the trombone; when a teenager, he had joined the Nunhead Band. A naturally talented musician, he was promoted two years later to end-chair (principal) trombonist.

For that decade in the twentieth century, George was considered tall at five-foot-eleven. With a slender, well-proportioned build, dark brown hair and moustache, and piercing blue eyes, he commanded the attention of those he met.

For George Meaford and Vangie Smith, the remaining few weeks of single life were full of bustling activity. However, another decision that they made brought forth even more busyness. After much discussion, they decided to immigrate to Canada. They purchased train tickets to travel from London to Liverpool, and they also booked passage on the *Southwark* to sail to Canada. Their new life as a married couple was to begin aboard a ship on the Atlantic, on their way to a new land across the sea.

*

On the third day at sea, Wednesday, May 23, the ship continued heaving mightily in the seemingly endless swells of the North Atlantic. Billy and Zack were racing along the deck corridor above their cabin. Bess trailed behind them. After ten minutes, pausing to catch their breath, they heard the soft sound of music floating above the ever-present throbbing of the ship's engines. Someone inside one of the cabins was playing a brass instrument. Despite being barely audible, Billy thought that it was a trombone. He had heard the instrument when the band had played outside the Oak Leaf Ale House.

Within moments, he discovered the origin of the music and sat down on the wood floor of the hallway to listen. Zack and Bess looked puzzled, but they sat down beside him. The person was quietly playing hymns. Billy recognized several melodies from Reverend Wilmot's insufferable services. Then the musician performed a quiet rendition of the hymn he had heard the Dorchester Band play outside the Oak Leaf Ale House—"O Boundless Salvation." Billy realized that he was likely listening to a Salvation Army bandsman.

To their disappointment, the music stopped. After a few minutes' silence, Billy hesitantly knocked softly on the door. When the door opened, Billy said, "Sir, can I please hear a little more music?" Billy was staring up into the face of George Meaford. His handsome face featured a small, well-trimmed moustache that turned up at the edges when he smiled. The man reminded Billy of his uncle Bill.

"I am sorry," the man replied. "My wife slept poorly last night due to the ship's heaving. I was playing her to sleep. She's now become drowsy and I don't wish to disturb her."

With boyish enthusiasm, Zack chimed in, "Then come down the hallway and play, Mister."

George could not help but smile again as he gazed at the two lads, their faces portraying an eagerness to hear more of his trombone. It was obvious that they were brothers. Then he noticed the young girl beside them, likely their sister. She had a mischievous grin on her face, but her manner indicated that she was as enthusiastic as her brothers to hear more music. Hesitating for a moment, he gazed back at Vangie. She was asleep.

Reaching for his instrument, he also grabbed his *Salvation Army Tune Book* and then quietly closed the door as he stepped out into the hallway. At the end of the corridor was a space where suitcases were placed when passengers disembarked the steamer. There was sufficient room for the three children to sit on the floor, allowing other passengers to pass. George sat on a small crate.

"Sir, will you show me how you position the slide of the trombone to make the different notes?" Billy inquired.

"Certainly, young man."

Next, Billy asked him to play the C-scale, and then the F- and G-scales. In the fifteen minutes that followed, George demonstrated the lip formations and showed how the trombone's slide expanded and contracted to produce the various sounds. He repeated each scale several times as Billy listened to the differences in the sounds.

"Can I try it?" Billy asked.

George smiled as he passed the instrument to the boy.

Billy stood to his feet and, for several minutes, blew through the instrument, adjusting his lips to produce the various sounds. Then, to George's amazement, Billy performed the three scales correctly, deftly moving the trombone's slide into the correct position for each note. He had memorized the positions while George had been performing. With a rudimentary implementation of proper lip formations coupled with the correct slide positions, he produced the notes and placed them within the various scales with reasonable accuracy. It was remarkable. George had taught many lads in the congregation at Nunhead, but none had ever demonstrated a grasp of the instrument on the first try.

Ten minutes later, George was even more amazed when Billy began selecting various notes from a scale to produce a melody. With only two misplaced notes, he played the melody of "O Boundless Salvation." George was not aware that he had heard the melody previously, prior to his playing it in the cabin for Vangie.

"Where on earth did you learn that melody?" George inquired.

"From a band I heard in the village where we lived."

"Would you play it again?" George requested.

"Sure." Billy played it a second time, and this time he made no mistakes.

"Remarkable," George muttered.

Gaining confidence, Billy next played several simple folk songs, and though not without errors, the performance was again remarkable. However, even more extraordinary was that after his first attempt at a melody, he corrected his mistakes and next time performed it correctly with relative ease. The more Billy played, the more fascinated George became. He remembered how long it had taken him to produce a clear note and learn the slide positions. However, this boy instinctively knew how to tighten and relax his embouchure to raise and lower the pitch. The boy was a rarity—a true natural.

George listened as Billy explored the possibilities the trombone presented him with. The sound was rough and the tone left much to be desired, but there was no denying that the playing was exemplary.

Unable to restrain himself any longer, Zack sprang to his feet and pleaded, "Let me try."

Billy glanced at George for permission and then handed his brother the trombone. George was again amazed. A lad Zack's age usually made only rude noises, but this small boy actually produced a few good notes. Having watched his brother, he moved the slide up and down, and each time he stopped blowing, he giggled with amusement.

"If I had a few more lads like you two," George told them, "I could build a good Army band in Canada."

"Let me try, too," Bess pleaded, but George said that he must return to his cabin to check on his wife. Bess's mouth fell in disappointment, her shiny blue eyes betraying her feelings.

Being left out seems to be my lot in life, she thought.

*

The following morning, George and Vangie entered the dining room. George saw Billy and Zack sitting at a table with their father, three girls, and a stern-looking elderly woman. He introduced Vangie and himself to the adults and smiled at the boys.

Phil told him, "Your name is familiar to me. Are you the same George Meaford who knows my wife's friend Sarah Mercer in Toronto?" George confirmed that he was.

Vangie replied, "Why, that's amazing. Sarah has been my friend for many years."

George said, "Even in the middle of the vast Atlantic, it's a small world." Then he added, "May I join you at the table?"

Permission was readily given. During the course of the meal, George explained about the music the boys had played and said, "I hope that I have your permission to continue the lessons."

Phil replied, "Certainly. Learning music will give them something to occupy their time and keep them out of mischief."

"Hopefully their learning music will more than just occupy their time."

"Of course, I did not mean to imply that it was just something to pass the time. It will be beneficial to them."

Bess spoke up, "Can I learn, too?"

"Sorry, young lady. I only have two cornets in my cabin, and I need my trombone to demonstrate the techniques."

Bess resented being left out, but she asked, "Can I at least listen?"

"Certainly."

*

In George Meaford's cabin were two cornets he was delivering to the Queen Street Citadel in Toronto. Salvation Army churches were referred to as citadels, temples, corps, and sometimes barracks. The interiors of their places of worship were called halls. Being an "Army of God," the church employed many military terms.

George was pleased that both boys would receive lessons at the same time. They began the next morning. In the days ahead, George received complaints from a few passengers about the "ungodly racket." He spoke to an understanding crew member who allowed them to enter a small unoccupied space in the cargo hold, where they indulged in their "noise" to their hearts' content.

*

The fourth day on the ship was May 24, the celebration of Queen Victoria's birthday. In the afternoon, passengers gathered in the dining room to sing patriotic songs. In the evening, after a relatively peaceful day's sailing, Emmy discovered that she was able to tolerate the scent of food when Phil brought her a cup of broth. She decided to join her husband and the children, who were already in the dining room sitting with the Meafords. It was then that Emmy met the couple.

As it was her first time in the dining room, she consumed only soup. The following evening she managed two boiled eggs, toast, and two cups of strong tea. On their fifth day aboard, she consumed a small portion of lean chicken and a boiled potato. Because she was eating, her strength was returning, so the adults lingered longer at the table while the children raced away to join other children on the decks or in the corridors.

"Your boys have a natural ear for music," George told Phil as Emmy listened intently. "In Toronto, I would consider it an honour if you contacted me and allowed me to continue their lessons. We have arranged to rent a flat above a shop on Queen Street, near Portland Avenue. You said that you would be residing in a house on Draper Street. I believe that our residences are in the same neighbourhood. The Salvation Army congregation we will be attending is located at Queen and Tecumseth streets. They have a boys' band. If you have no objections, your sons could join the band. I will be the church's junior bandmaster. Please consider it."

"We're Anglicans," Emmy replied, even though the comment had been directed at Phil. "However, The Salvation Army does good work. Our church modelled its Church Army after your organization. My husband and I will discuss the matter and give you a reply."

"That would be fine. God has given your boys a talent. It would be a sin to hide their talents under a bushel, as the Bible says."

*

Later in the evening, although it was cold and windy, the Mercers strolled out onto the deck for a few minutes. Enjoying a little time alone, Emmy said to Phil, "I wonder if the girls will envy the opportunity Mr. Meaford is offering the boys?"

"I'm certain that Bess will feel left out."

"I fear you're right. I heard Bess ask Mr. Meaford, 'Doesn't The Salvation Army have a band for girls?'"

"That sounds like Bess. She believes that she can do anything the boys can do."

"She usually can." Emmy smiled.

Then they saw Grandmother Mercer coming toward them.

Emmy and Phil were surprised that she was out on deck in such cold weather, but they knew better than to say anything. Similar to Bess, she would likely tell them that she could do anything they could do. As they chatted, Phil told his mother about Mr. Meaford's request.

She told them, "I'm not certain that I want my grandchildren joining The Salvation Army. I admit that the Army does good work, but their open-air meetings are rowdy, and I've heard that their services contain wild antics and much theatrical preaching. Some say that they are more show than worship. However, I'll say no more. The decision is yours. I'm trying to learn to hold my tongue, even though keeping silent has never been one of my virtues."

Phil and Emmy tried to hide their smiles, but she was aware that they were amused.

Strutting away indignantly, she said, "I know how to keep quiet. But if anyone asks my opinion, I'll certainly give it."

*

On Monday, May 28, 1906, the *Southwark* arrived safely in Halifax's harbour. Despite the turbulent weather during the first three days of the voyage, it had been a swift crossing. Halifax was a welcome sight for the sea-weary Mercer and Meaford families.

Standing on deck and watching the approaching shoreline, Phil told Billy, "Halifax is Canada's busiest Atlantic port. It's situated on a peninsula, where the ocean tides surround its rocky shores on three sides. Its outer harbour is almost a mile wide. To enter the inner harbour, ships sail through a narrow passageway into the Bedford Basin, which takes up several miles of waterfront and has excellent dockage."

When the ship reached the calm inner waters of the port, Grandmother Mercer joined them on deck. She said, "It's such a relief to reach land."

"I think we all feel that way, especially Emmy," Phil said.

She replied, "However, despite the roughness of the crossing, I feel that I've coped rather well. The only thing separating us from our new home is the trip by rail to Toronto."

*

Grandmother Mercer was the last of the family to step onto the gangway to disembark. As she waited for the family's luggage, an elderly woman began conversing with her. The woman was British, returning to Canada after visiting relatives in the Old Country. The expression on her face indicated that she was clearly not looking forward to the final portion of her journey.

"The railway cars you see over there," she said contemptuously as she nodded her head toward the wharf, "are uncomfortable and crude. They refer to them as colonist cars."

"Why are they called that?" Grandmother Mercer inquired.

"It's because the cars transport mainly colonists from Britain. Sometimes I feel that the railways don't consider colonists to be real people. The cars are no better than those used for cattle."

"I suppose we're in for a difficult trip."

"You have no idea. The trip to Toronto will be noisy, dirty, and crowded. The coaches have meagre amenities, and the hard seats contain only a thin covering of well-worn leather." The woman added, "The soot from the engine is thicker than molasses in January."

After Grandmother Mercer climbed aboard the train, it soon departed. She told Emmy, "The air in the car is certainly stuffy."

Emmy nodded in agreement. "The smoke from the engine pours over the train coaches and seeps inside the cars. Soot floats in the air. The windows look as if they haven't been cleaned for months."

"The soot creeps in every tiny space and settles on the seats and our clothes. I fear that clouds of it will billow in through the window if I raise it to catch a little outside air. The never-ending noise of the wheels on the rails adds to the discomfort. My head is splitting."

"At times, it's difficult to chat without shouting."

The click-clacking journey continued hour after hour. As darkness fell, the porters rearranged the benches to create beds. Grandmother muttered, “The beds are hard and have no mattresses or blankets.” Then she gazed disparagingly at the upper bunks above the seats and close to the ceiling. “The upper bunks certainly look uncomfortable. Thank goodness I don’t have to climb up into one.” Then she nodded her head toward the back of the car and said, “At the rear of our coach, there’s a small coal stove to allow passengers to cook any food they carry. It’s a pity we brought nothing to cook.”

“Yes. There was no time in Halifax to purchase anything.”

Grandmother continued, “I saw the facilities. Everything drains onto the tracks below. There’s also a sink for washing, and it, too, drains through a pipe directly onto the tracks. The railway company reserves the Pullman cars for the well-to-do, which is certainly not us.”

Emmy replied, “I guess we must endure the discomforts in silence.”

Grandmother got the message and said nothing more. Then she gazed over at her grandchildren. They were relishing every moment of the adventure. She had many other thoughts about the dreadful coaches, but heeding Emmy’s advice, she kept them to herself.

*

The Mercers and Meafords arrived in Toronto’s Union Station on the evening of Wednesday, May 30. On the platform, attendants deposited the Meaford family’s steamer trunk (with few personal belongings inside) as well as the two trunks belonging to Grandmother Mercer. One of the smaller suitcases contained Phil’s silver engraving tools. Billy’s uncle Frank and his wife, Sarah, stood waiting for them on the platform at the station.

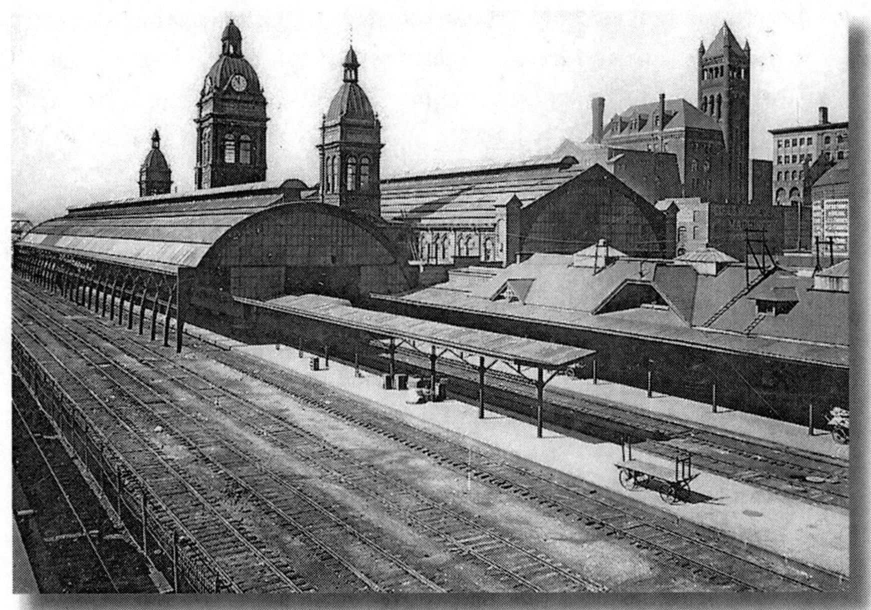

The tracks at the rear of Toronto's old Union Station, built in 1884. The single tower that stands alone on the right-hand side of the photo faces Front Street. The station was demolished following the opening of the new Union Station in 1927. This station remains in use today. *City of Toronto Archives, Fonds 1244, Item 5040*

Billy noticed that Uncle Frank was uncertain how to greet his mother, but she quickly removed his misgivings when she warmly embraced him. Billy felt that she was demonstrating that the past belonged in the past. It was a tender moment, a reunion Billy observed closely, as he had never met his uncle Frank. He was surprised by how much he resembled his father. He knew that his grandmother and Uncle Frank had not been in touch for many years, but he was unaware of the reason.

Without any introduction, the woman in the broad-brimmed hat with the peacock feathers, who was their aunt Sarah, embraced Billy and his siblings with strong hugs. Billy instantly liked her. Uncle Frank shook hands with Billy rather formally, but there was nothing formal about his smile. Within the few moments they stood on the platform, amid the hissing steam and the commotion of porters shouting for people requiring their assistance, old family ties were renewed and new ones forged.

Arrival area of Toronto's old Union Station. *City of Toronto Archives, Fonds 1244, Item 9999*

One man in the group was unknown to Billy. His uncle Frank introduced him. "This is Captain Bramwell Sendry. He's the Corps Officer, as they refer to priests in The Salvation Army, at Toronto's Queen Street Citadel congregation."

The Captain shook hands with Phil and Emmy, and then Frank introduced him to George Meaford. When George and the Captain shook hands, Billy thought that the chemistry between the two men had created instant rapport. He did not know that their letters had crossed the Atlantic over the past year. They were about the same age, shared a love of Army music, and both had connections to the Nunhead Corps in England.

Billy whispered to Zack, "The Captain seems nice, but rather aloof. His smile hasn't much warmth."

Zack said nothing, only edged closer to his older brother.

Billy listened as the Captain explained to Mr. Meaford, "I've arranged transportation for you and your wife to take you to the one-bedroom flat you'll be renting. It's on Queen Street, above Mitchell's Hardware Store."

Then Uncle Frank turned to Phil and Emmy. "I've hired a cart to deliver your luggage to our house on Draper Street. However, you'll ride in the coach with Vangie and me."

It was not long before they arrived at Draper Street, where Uncle Frank's home was located. The steamer trunks were placed inside the door of the house the Mercers were going to rent, but they were to sleep in Frank and Sarah's home for their first evening in Toronto. Frank had told them that he did not want them to begin their new life in Canada in an empty house.

Billy gazed up at Frank and Sarah Mercer's bay-and-gable house on the west side of Draper Street. As he entered the home, he looked around. The rooms were spacious, but they were also warm, cozy, and well furnished.

Aunt Sarah asked if anyone wished to have tea.

They all readily accepted. An hour later, they headed for their bedrooms, too tired to say anything other than, "Good night."

*

After everyone was in bed and the house was quiet, Emmy gazed through the bay window into the darkened street. Her eyes lingered on a small cottage-style semidetached house on the opposite side of the road. She knew it was to be theirs. With its mansard roof overhead and a bay window on the ground floor, it looked like a home from a dream. Sleep came uneasily that night for Emmy even though she was thoroughly exhausted.

Frank and Sarah Mercer's bay-and-gable home on Draper Street.

On Thursday morning, the sound of clattering milk bottles and the clip-clop of a horse's hooves on Draper Street awakened Emmy. The twittering of the birds reminded her of Comstock. Phil stretched and yawned noisily as he watched Emmy rise from the bed and stroll over to the window. She peered out into the street, her eyes drawn toward the small house across the roadway that was to become their home. Phil quietly crept up behind her, wrapping his arms around her. For a few moments they held each other, enjoying the warmth from their bodies in the chilly room, taking pleasure in the love they shared.

"We're finally here. Can you believe it?" Phil whispered as he kissed the lobe of her ear.

"Sometimes I need to pinch myself to assure myself that it's real. The house we're to rent is far nicer than I ever expected."

"Yes, we're fortunate. Toronto will give us opportunities far beyond anything that Comstock had to offer."

"I hope the neighbours here are friendly."

"Well, anyone would be better than that old Mrs. Rowntree."

"Oh, hush," Emmy gently chided. "Remember, she came to the station to see us off. She even gave Billy a big hug."

"I remember. I thought Bess was going to pee her pants laughing."

"You men are so disrespectful. Bess was highly amused, but I have no knowledge of the condition of her bladder."

"Never mind how Bess reacted," Phil continued. "I almost peed my pants when I saw Rowntree on the platform."

Emmy chuckled. "At least I now no longer must endure her telling me, 'Billy is bound for hell.'"

"She obviously doesn't believe that any longer," Phil said. "She hugged our handsome Billy so hard that I thought she was going to ask him to marry her."

Emmy smiled as she broke the embrace and turned to look into Phil's eyes. "That's what Mrs. Rowntree needs—a good man."

"That's likely true, as long as it isn't Billy or me."

"Well, I don't need a good man. I already have one."

Emmy and Phil kissed tenderly, unaware that the milkman down on the street was observing them. They never knew that as he grabbed the reins of the horse to continue his deliveries, he said, "Come on, Gertrude, me old love. This neighbourhood is becoming a little too wild for the likes of us."

*

Draper Street, where the Mercer family was to reside, was short, only one block in length. Wellington Street West was located at its north end; Front Street was to the south. It was one block west of Spadina Avenue. This was a workingman's community, unlike Wellington Street at the north end.

Following a hasty breakfast, Phil and Frank moved the suitcases across to the Mercers' new house. As they entered, the steamer trunks blocked the hallway. Climbing over them, the men began a thorough examination of the interior. Then everyone began unpacking.

Emmy said, "The only furniture we have are the three mattresses that Frank purchased. They're on the floor in the bedrooms."

Phil told her, "When we have sufficient funds, I'll buy lumber to make headboards and bedframes. Frank offered us a loan, but I refused. Although he's a foreman and his wages are better than most, he has little spare cash after he pays his monthly mortgage. My mother's savings have dwindled after paying our passage aboard the ship, train fares, and travelling expenses, but she insists that she still has sufficient funds to assist us with our daily needs."

"Thank the Lord for your mother's generosity," Emmy told him.

The small house on Draper Street that Phil and Emmy rented.

In the evening, when Grandmother's largest steamer trunk was empty, it became the family's humble table. They were all surprised when she retrieved teacups and a teapot from another of her trunks.

She told them, "I wrapped them in a quilt, and they've miraculously survived the journey, although one of the saucers is chipped. They look grand now that I've placed them on the trunk, which Emmy has covered with a linen tablecloth she brought from home. We can use the empty suitcases as seats for the adults, and the children can sit on the floor."

When they gathered for their meal, Emmy said, "I think we should hold hands and offer a brief prayer of thanks for our safe arrival."

At the end of the meal, Emmy told Phil, "Tonight we'll sleep on the mattresses on the floor, but it won't detract from the joy of being in our new home."

*

On the afternoon of Saturday, June 2, George Meaford visited the Mercers. He told them, "I'm amazed at how well you've settled in. It's so quiet here on Draper Street. The flat that Vangie and I are sharing is on busy Queen Street. It has noisy streetcars and much foot traffic. However, we like it. It'll be a good home." Looking around the room and smiling, he added, "I see that you're arranging things rather well. While I'm here, I wish to extend an invitation to dinner on Sunday, and inquire to see if you'd like to attend the Army church service with Vangie and me."

The Mercers accepted, all except Grandmother, who replied, "Thank you for the invitation, but I promised to attend the Anglican service with my Frank and Sarah, at St. John the Evangelist Anglican Church. It's within easy walking distance of the house here on Draper Street."

*

On Sunday, June 3, the Mercers attended their first Salvation Army service. The band was under the baton of an elderly gentleman, and George was playing in the trombone section. He was able to play any valve instrument, but the slide trombone was his preference.

Billy watched every player in the band and hung on to each note, especially those of the cornets, which to him remained as glorious as trumpets.

He told Zack, "Playing a piano is okay, but I'd rather play a cornet." He then added, "You know, I think I want to become a Salvation Army bandsman."

Chapter Three

On Monday morning, Phil walked to the Toronto Silver Plate Company at 420-426 King Street West, where Frank was employed. Frank had arranged an interview for him with the owner of the factory. The company was a prosperous enterprise, and as Phil approached the buildings, he marvelled at their size.

Inside the factory, in the waiting room outside the manager's office, Phil fidgeted with the brim of his cap, clutching it tightly in his hands. When his name was called, a secretary ushered him into the office of Mr. Eugene P. McCallum. Phil shifted from one foot to the other as the manager eyed him. He now knew how Daniel felt in the lions' den.

After a few words of greeting, Mr. McCallum said, "Your brother, Frank, tells me that you are a skilled tradesman, well acquainted with working in silver."

"Yes, sir. Over home, I worked at the Church Manufacturing Company."

"I am familiar with the company. In what capacity were you engaged?"

"I was responsible for the engravings on the silver holders that held the cups for the chocolate sets."

"We don't get much call for such luxury items here in Toronto."

"I understand that, sir, but I am able to engrave on any silver object any design that's required. Most of my designs are my own creation."

Other questions followed. A half hour later, Mr. McCallum said, "You may begin next Monday morning. Be here bright and early at seven a.m."

Phil stepped lightly, almost jauntily, as he exited the factory. Passing the shops on the south side of King Street, he walked west to Portland Avenue, turned south toward Wellington Street, and was soon home.

Though he needed the money, he was pleased that he had a week to himself. Spare time was a luxury that had rarely passed his way, so he was grateful to have a few hours to work around the house and see a little of his adopted city. Having lived the past few years in Comstock, the large town of Dorchester was now a stranger to him. Toronto made Dorchester seem like a miniscule hamlet. As a result, although he found Toronto fascinating, he was challenged to adapt.

That afternoon, Emmy told Phil, "Tomorrow I must take the three youngest and register them in school. Billy is thirteen and remains of school age, but he wants to find a job in one of the grocery stores on Queen Street. I'd prefer he attend school, but we need the money."

"I still think he should be in school."

"I agree. But he's determined, and he's tall enough that they will think he's of an age to work."

*

Following the final meal of the day on Wednesday, in the lingering light of a seemingly never-ending June evening, Billy was excited when his father announced, "I've decided that we should explore more of the city."

Billy chimed in, "Though Toronto's much larger and grander than Comstock, to quote a phrase I heard back in Comstock, 'It's an insignificant outpost of empire.' However, it's an outpost that I want to see more of."

Grandmother Mercer added, "Or, as I like to say, Toronto's an undistinguished pimple on the rump of the Britannic Lion."

Billy laughed but continued, "Maybe the city's unimportant in the eyes of the empire, but I'm glad to be here."

"Well," Grandmother Mercer admitted, "I guess it has its good points. It's thoroughly British. Anyone or anything that isn't like the Old Country, I view suspiciously."

Queen and Spadina, looking north on Spadina Avenue in 1910, the Bank of Hamilton (today, the CIBC) is across the street, on the right-hand side of the photo. On the left-hand side is the Mary Pickford Theatre. It became Bargain Harold's, and today it is the site of a McDonald's. *City of Toronto Archives, File 1231, Item 2046 (1)*

It was not long before they left the house to go tour their new town. Arriving at the intersection of Queen and Spadina, Billy gazed at the impressive Bank of Hamilton on the northeast corner, and then at the Mary Pickford Theatre opposite it on the northwest corner, its ornate turret above the third floor dominating the street. He wondered if someday he might be able to attend one of the moving picture shows. Then he thought about the admission price and sighed with disappointment.

While he was examining the theatre, an unsavoury character was watching him and his family with an amused look on his face. Billy noticed him and felt embarrassed, as he thought that the man likely considered them country bumpkins gazing at the big-city sights.

When Billy looked north up Spadina Avenue, in the distance, in the centre of the avenue, he could see the ornate tower atop an impressive building. He was unaware that it was Knox College. Spadina Avenue impressed him; it was the widest street he had ever seen. Near the intersection at Queen, there was a below-ground men's washroom. He watched as a man wearing a bowler hat descended the stairs to the facility.

The unsavoury man who had been watching Billy and his family assessed the threat that Phil might present to his plan. A sly grin slid across the man's face. He was certain that Billy was as green as grass, as were the others who were with him. He was also confident that they were unaware of his interest in them.

University Avenue looking north from south of College Street to the Provincial Legislative Building, c. 1910, with chestnut trees flanking the roadway. *City of Toronto Archives, Fonds 1568, Item 0310*

Walking east along Queen Street, Billy arrived at University Avenue. When he crossed over, in the distance he saw the turret on the great stone building at the head of the street. It was the province's Legislative Building, visible through the forest of chestnut trees flanking the roadway. In the years ahead, when the city widened the street, these magnificent giants were destroyed. On this warm evening in June, from Queen Street, Billy noticed the late-day sun illuminating the pink Credit Valley sandstone blocks of the structure.

He heard Bess declare, "It looks like a palace."

Zack told her teasingly, "Girls think that all big buildings are palaces and imagine that they are princesses locked up inside them, and that a knight is going to come along and rescue them."

"I don't need any knight to rescue me."

"That's true. You'd likely hit the knight on the head and steal his horse."

Billy smiled as he watched Bess grin at her brother's backhanded compliment, ignoring his assault on her honesty.

Billy was now unaware of the stranger who was observing them, as the man was following a safe distance behind.

Within minutes, Billy and the others arrived at the heart of the downtown area. At the head of Bay Street was the immense City Hall, which had been occupied now for seven years. The building was in a prominent location, its façade looking southward toward the lake, and its great tower dominating Bay Street. Gazing down Bay Street toward the northwest corner at Bay and Richmond, they stood in awe at the ten-storey Temple Building, headquarters of an insurance company, the Independent Order of Foresters.

Looking north up Bay Street from near King Street in 1908, the Toronto City Hall located at the top of the street and the tall Temple Building near it on the left-hand side. *City of Toronto Archives, Fonds 1244, Item 0595*

"My goodness, just look at its height," Billy exclaimed to his father. "Uncle Frank told me it's the tallest building in the entire British Empire. It has heating and air-conditioning systems, marble fountains with taps that spout iced water, mosaic floors, rich wood panelling, and fireproofing."

The Temple Building on the west side of Bay Street, at Richmond, one block south of Queen, in 1907. The structure was built in 1895 and was the city's first real skyscraper. *City of Toronto Archives, Fonds 1244, Item 7036*

As the family continued along Queen Street, the passing streetcars sometimes drowned out their conversation. Billy had read about the streetcars and so he was a font of knowledge about them. While he was busy expounding to Zack, he did not notice that the man following them was edging closer.

Billy told Zack, "Except for the chassis, the bodies of the streetcars are entirely of wood. I've read that in the United States they're building streetcars of steel. Uncle Frank warned me that the various streetcar lines can be confusing."

Earlier in the week, when Uncle Frank had explained the streetcar routes to Billy, it had caused his mind to swirl in amazement. In Comstock he had walked everywhere, as there were only two main streets. He had never realized how difficult it would be to adjust to living in a city of 215,000 people. Frightening! However, upon reflection, he admitted that it was also exciting.

Finally, they all arrived at Yonge and Queen streets, the centre of Toronto's retail trade. Billy gazed at the stores of the T. Eaton Company and the Robert Simpson Company. They were indeed grand, but he felt slightly intimidated. Their windows displayed an array of goods beyond his wildest imaginings.

Yonge Street at Adelaide Street, looking north to Queen Street. The building on the right-hand side of the photo, on the northeast corner of Yonge and Adelaide, is the Lumsden Building, constructed in 1909. It remains at this same location today. *City of Toronto Archives, Fonds 1231, Item 0339*

Yonge Street in 1911, looking north from King Street. *City of Toronto Archives, Series 0372, SS 0100, Item 0239*

Turning to his father, Billy said, "The stores are huge. Simpson's is six storeys high. Back home the shops were small."

"True," his father replied. "But we'll get used to them."

As they continued to look into the windows at Simpson's, the man whose intentions were dubious edged close to the Mercers and pretended to look in the windows as well. Through the reflection in the glass, he was able to determine exactly where Billy's attention was focused. Knowing the boy was distracted, the stranger bumped against him.

Quickly apologizing, he smiled obsequiously, tipped his hat, and began to stroll away. However, Billy sensed something was wrong, felt for his billfold, and realized it was missing. The man did not get far. Billy raced after him and grabbed him from behind by the collar. At the same moment, his father felt his pocket and realized that his billfold was also missing.

The man was taller than Billy and powerfully built. About forty or fifty years of age, he was old enough to have learned to defend himself and young enough to put up a good fight. His clothes were unkempt; when Billy grabbed him, the man's hat fell to the sidewalk. Sweat stains rimmed the hatband, which matched the discolouring on his trousers and jacket.

He was a street-tough.

The man quickly turned, raising his fist to strike Billy. Before he could deliver the blow, Phil grabbed his arm. The man struck Phil instead, but he had quickly turned, the blow glancing off the side of his cheek. It stung but was not injurious. Phil's retaliatory blow was so forceful that it knocked the man off his feet. However, the ruffian's resilience was amazing, and he was on his feet again within seconds.

Billy thrust the next jab.

Though not as forceful as his father's, it struck hard, and the man went down again. However, he was not finished. Standing upright, he held up his fists and danced like a prizefighter. Dodging the man's punches, Phil waited for an opening and hammered him squarely on the nose. The man dropped to the sidewalk, blood gushing down his face.

The man stood, threw their billfolds to the ground, and fled.

*

Zack had watched the encounter closely, etching the man's face indelibly in his mind. It was a handsome face, but it was devoid of any humanity, as if he cared nothing about the pain he inflicted on others. Actually, Zack had noticed the man prior to the fight, as he had thought the man walked rather strangely. Zack was unaware that when the thief was a young man, he had injured his hip in a street fight and ever since walked with a slight limp.

This was not to be the last time that Zack and Billy were to encounter the thief's violent fists.

Zack had viewed the incident with the thief differently than his parents did. "The fight was super," he enthused. "I wish I could've smacked the guy."

Finally, Phil told him to desist and added, "I don't want anyone mentioning the incident to Grandmother Mercer. It might worry her."

*

The sun dipped toward the horizon as they trudged homeward west along Queen Street. The children were tired. Phil offered to carry Bess in his arms, as she was only eight. She would have no part of it. Zack was every bit as exhausted, but he also refused any assistance. He told his father, "Billy will walk home on his own, and so will I."

When they entered the house on Draper Street, the final slivers of twilight were fading. There were none of the usual complaints when Phil told the children to go to bed. Their exhaustion trumped their need to protest. Phil knew that they likely wanted to discuss "the fight" in privacy.

After the children were upstairs, Phil relaxed with Emmy. He watched as his mother put on the kettle to boil for tea, and he listened as Emmy talked about the events of the day. Grandmother Mercer listened, too, as Emmy described the sights in Toronto's central business district. Phil sensed that his mother was aware of Emmy's tension. He wondered if she suspected that something had happened that she was not telling her.

"Imagine," Emmy said, trying to sound enthusiastic, "the ten-storey Temple Building almost touched the sky."

"It is indeed quite a city," Grandmother replied. "At times, I'm not sure what to make of it. It's certainly not like Dorchester. Tomorrow I intend to go to the shops on Queen Street. They're not far away. Will you go with me, Emmy?"

Emmy nodded her agreement.

The evening now over, Phil gently placed his arms around Emmy as they went up the stairs to bed, the love they shared visibly evident.

*

Every neighbourhood in Toronto had a street with a concentration of retail shops where people gathered to engage in animated conversations and exchange news while they shopped. Queen Street was the major shopping district for the homes half a mile north and south of it. When only a few items were required, people visited a corner store.

It was to Queen Street that Emmy and Grandmother Mercer gravitated. Similar to the shops of Comstock, these stores sported colourful canvas awnings over their front windows to cover the merchandise that was displayed on the stalls outside. The awnings also protected customers from the heat of the summer sun and the drizzling rains of autumn. Grandmother Mercer and Emmy noticed that the price of a bottle of Coca-Cola was five cents, a newspaper two cents, and the better cuts of beef an outrageous twenty cents per pound.

As it was their first visit to the shopping district, the two women had arrived early in the morning, just as the shops were opening.

Grandmother told Emmy, "I've always found it fascinating to watch stores coming to life to start a new day. I loved watching it in Dorchester, and it's just as interesting here in Toronto."

"I know what you mean."

When they walked past a ladies' clothing boutique, Grandmother said, "Look at that dress. I'd love to buy it. I'd wear it to church." Sighing, she admitted, "I guess the dress is merely a dream. It's the princely sum of fifteen dollars."

Emmy had seen the dress and had also liked it, but she also knew that to own it was impossible.

Emmy and Grandmother felt self-conscious as they entered the first store—Hutchinson's Butcher Shop. A small bell above the door tinkled as they came in and then walked across the sawdust-strewn floor. The shop owner was busy with a customer, but he glanced up and greeted them.

"Good morning, ladies. It's always nice to see new people coming into the neighbourhood. I'll tend to you in a few moments."

The casual greeting pleased Emmy. As she examined the cuts of meat, she whispered to Grandmother, "The large department stores won't be as friendly as this shop. Their customers come from all parts of the city. They won't recognize anyone."

"True," Grandmother replied, careful to keep her voice low so that the butcher and the woman customer did not hear her. "The butcher is wrapping soup bones and stewing beef for the woman at the counter. She likely has as few pennies as we have. Shopping here on Queen Street is not that different to shopping in England. Back home, I always spent my coins carefully."

"You know, Queen Street reminds me a little of Comstock. It's like a village—a village with honking vehicle traffic and clanging streetcars—but a village nonetheless."

As they talked, Grandmother Mercer was secretly watching Mr. Hutchinson. In a conspiratorial tone she told Emmy, "I think the butcher is almost sixty, but he has a full head of brown hair. There's grey in his sideburns, and his large moustache is full, although it needs trimming. It droops at either end. Although he has extra pounds around his middle, because he's tall he carries it rather well."

Emmy was enjoying Grandmother's assessment of the butcher. "Do you think him handsome?" she asked.

"Not bad, not bad at all."

They both raised their gloved hands in front of their faces to hide their grins.

Having finished serving the previous customer, the butcher now turned to serve Emmy and Grandmother.

"Again, I wish you good morning," he said as he smiled at them. "What can I get you on this fine day?"

Grandmother informed him of their needs and then watched the butcher as he stepped to the end of the counter to fetch a large cut of stewing beef. However, as he chopped the meat into small pieces, she was aware that he was eyeing her surreptitiously. She hoped that he was thinking that she was a good-looking woman. She turned to see if Emmy had noticed the man's roving eye, but her daughter-in-law was busy examining the expensive cuts of meat, even though she knew they were unable to afford them.

A typical butcher counter in early twentieth-century Toronto, with vegetables in crates beside the counter. *City of Toronto Archives, Fonds 1244, Item 0339a*

As they departed the shop, Grandmother said to the butcher, "I thank you kindly for your excellent service. Being a widow, I always appreciate the assistance of a gentleman."

Mr. Hutchinson's smile widened as he replied, "It was indeed a pleasure to meet you. I hope I see more of you in my shop."

Grandmother Mercer returned the smile. She had purposely dropped into the conversation the fact that she was a widow.

Emmy noticed the exchange and the looks that accompanied it. A small grin crept across her face.

Grandmother had noticed her grin and told Emmy defensively, "It's never too early to plant a few seeds in fertile soil." Then she blushed, feeling that she was being too forward. However, despite her embarrassment at being discovered, she continued. "I hope the butcher's not married. The last thing I want is someone thinking I'm being bold with a married man. I don't want to create any gossip like in Dorchester."

"Don't worry. I know something about the butcher that you don't. A neighbour told me that Mr. Hutchinson has been a widower for the past five years."

"My, my. That's interesting. May the good Lord bless the neighbourhood grapevine."

*

When Saturday evening arrived, the Mercers strolled around in Clarence Square on the east side of Spadina Avenue. Mary and Ruth delighted in running around the grassy space and hiding behind the mature trees as they played hide-and-seek with Bess. Billy stayed close to his father as they talked about their impressions of Toronto and reminisced about their life in the Old Country.

After considerable discussion, Phil summarized by telling Billy, "I love our new home here, but I miss my mates in the factory in Comstock."

Billy responded, "I'm enjoying Toronto, too, but sometimes I think about the wide-open meadows surrounding Comstock."

"I suppose you don't miss having Mrs. Rowntree berating you every time you step out onto South Street," his father teased.

"Actually, I do sort of miss her. I never told you, but she once defended me against a group of older boys in the laneway. They would have thrashed the daylights out of me."

"Was that the time when she wielded her broom like a knight crusader attacking a bunch of heathen infidels?"

"You know about that?" Billy's expression registered his surprise.

His father chuckled. "Are you kidding? Zack gave me a blow-by-blow description of the battle. According to him, he was a warrior knight observing the conflict from the top of a castle wall."

"Actually, he watched from the old apple tree in our back garden."

"I guess that does sound closer to the truth. But you have to remember your brother's imagination."

They both smiled.

Phil continued. "I must confess that I never really liked Mrs. Rowntree. She had too sour a disposition for my tastes. Every time I met her, she was complaining about something."

"I know. But deep down, she liked us. Even after she rescued me with her broom, she scolded me. She would never admit that she liked us until that day at the train station."

"I think it was you she liked, not the rest of us."

"Whatever. My point is that she was not really the person we thought she was."

"I think you're probably right. However, I think you were the only one who ever saw the good in her. I know I didn't."

"Perhaps her sour disposition was her way of keeping people away so she could convince herself that it was the reason she was alone."

"I'm not certain I follow your logic. But I'm glad there's no Mrs. Rowntree on Draper Street."

Billy grinned as he confessed, "There are times when I wish I could go back to South Street, just to ruffle her feathers. I admit that knowing that she rather enjoyed the fuss would take some of the fun out of it."

As they departed the park, Phil asked, "Are there other things you miss since we left Comstock?"

"Sure. But our new life here is good. I'm content."

"Son, we didn't really give up that much in the Old Land compared to what we have to gain here. However, remember always to hold your head high. You're an Englishman." Then he added, "But never forget you're now a Canadian, too. In the years ahead, try to give back to this land that has taken us in."

Billy walked along the street with his father, enjoying the close communion that had developed between them.

*

After they returned home, the family prepared to attend church the following morning. Billy's mother laid out their church clothes, including the shirts and shirt collars she had ironed and starched. In the hallway, while Billy and Zack scrubbed the mud from their boots and shined them, Billy listened to his parents in the kitchen. They were unaware that he was eavesdropping.

He heard his mother say, "It has only been a week since we arrived here, but the days are rolling one into another, just like back in Comstock. Despite the hardships of getting settled and the long hours putting the house in order, I feel at home under the roof of this small house. By the way, when will you purchase the wood for the bedframes?"

"When we've the money, my dear."

"Yes, I guess that applies to everything we need." There was a pause, and then Emmy asked, "Are we going to The Salvation Army in the morning?"

"Well, I'm trying to consider what's best for the children. George Meaford says that Billy and Zack have great talent. The boys have their hearts set on leaning to play instruments. I don't feel comfortable allowing George to teach them if we don't attend their services."

"What about the girls?"

"I believe they've a girls' choir. They call them the Sunshine Singers. Can you imagine Bess as a Sunshine Singer?"

"Not really. Her antics usually create more clouds than sunshine. However, I must admit that I enjoy the congregational singing at the Army. It's livelier than the church in Comstock. But I was baptized in the Anglican church. It's my spiritual home. We've lost the town that was our home. Must we now lose our church?"

"Losing Reverend Wilmot isn't such a great tragedy." Billy heard his father chuckle. "I think Billy misses him. He was one of his main sources of amusement."

"You men are so disrespectful. But I notice you're avoiding my question. Where do we go to church tomorrow?"

"Well, I think we should go to The Salvation Army. If the boys are involved with the music there, it'll keep them out of trouble. We must look to the future. I think the Army offers good programs for the children. What do you think?"

"I think you're right."

"Well, I guess we sing the hymns tomorrow to the beat of the big bass drum."

"I suppose your mother will go with Frank and Sarah to St. John the Evangelist."

"I am sure she will."

"I don't know what it would take to get her to change churches."

As Billy climbed the stairs to retire to bed ahead of his parents, he felt pleased with their decision. In the morning, he would be able to hear the cornets.

*

Billy sat in church Sunday morning listening carefully to the Queen Street Citadel Band as they played the opening song, "Come Thou, Almighty King." He had never generated much interest in the music at St. Mary's in Comstock, but the band here was an arousing accompaniment to the hymns. Plus, he enjoyed the robust congregational singing. Some members swayed as they sang, even when the hymns were relatively sedate. Some in the congregation shouted, "Hallelujah," or, "Praise the Lord." One elderly man yelled, "Fire the volley." Billy had no idea what that meant, but he felt as though he should duck because scattershot might come flying through the air. He was not aware that it was another military term the Army used to say, "Fight for the salvation of sinners."

Listening attentively to the band, Billy instinctively sensed how the various instruments blended to create the full sound. He realized that the solo cornets usually carried the melody, but that at times various other instruments played sections of it, as well. The horns, trombones, and euphonium augmented the harmony, with the basses providing the anchor. He listened especially to the cornets, as soon he would have one of his own to play.

The previous Friday, Mr. Meaford had told Billy that if he wished to join the junior band, he should attend the practice on the following Tuesday evening. He had said, "The cornet that you played on the *Southwark* is to be yours, if you want it."

Billy had nodded his head enthusiastically.

On this morning, he thought the sermon was lively but, though not as lengthy as one of the Reverend Wilmot, still too long. He remembered what his grandmother had told Reverend Wilmot, and he smiled to himself.

During the sermon, he had trouble sitting still. His mind was only able to absorb what his rear end was capable of enduring. On this Sunday morning, he stopped listening after half an hour. He felt a wave of blessed relief when the preacher ceased, the prayer service was over, and the band commenced playing the final hymn.

*

A few blocks away, Grandmother Mercer had already departed from the service at St. John the Evangelist and was returning home to the house on Draper Street with Frank and Sarah. Grandmother walked alongside Sarah, and Frank walked behind them, talking to another man from the congregation.

She told Sarah, "I see that church life here in Canada is similar to Dorchester."

"Yes. Almost everyone attends one church or another, and those who don't, the neighbours frown upon."

"Women wear their best outfits," Grandmother Mercer said. She enjoyed talking about fashion styles. "The colour grey is in vogue this year."

A woman passed and greeted the two women with a polite nod of her head, her large bonnet tipping slightly as she shuffled along in her long dress that reached nearly to the ground. She then nodded to Frank.

After the woman had passed by, Grandmother Mercer continued. "The men are still wearing dark brown wool suits, same as last year. The shirts are also the same as previous years—white. The carefully knotted ties have not changed, either. No new styles. I see that most manufacturers still do not sew the shirt collars onto the shirts. The wives or mothers of the men remove them separately for laundering and starching. I've heard that the standard price at a laundry to starch a collar is ten cents."

"That's why I wash and iron Frank's collars at home."

"Young girls are still wearing short, frilly dresses that are miniature versions of their mothers' attire. I wonder if they'll ever make styles that are just for children."

"At least the boys look different than their fathers. They have a cap, knee-length trousers, and long black stockings. This has not changed since I was a girl."

"Every boy yearns for long pants to look more like his father."

"True, but they're grateful for the long stockings on Christmas Eve. They're wondrous for 'stuffing.'"

"In England, proper style dictates most of the daily activities, as well as what people wear. In Toronto, it seems that everyone maintains a similar sense of decorum, adhering to it with a religious-like zeal," Grandmother Mercer told Sarah. Then she spoke conspiratorially as she confided in Sarah. "I've mixed feelings about church life and dress codes. Though I'm beginning to feel at home here, as the customs are familiar to me, I secretly wish I could kick up my heels a little."

Sarah looked at her mother-in-law with amusement as she continued speaking. "I think a large red feather in my bonnet would be simply grand. I'm tired of dark-coloured dresses. I long for one in sky blue or forest green. I've even considered placing an order with a dressmaker."

Sarah giggled as she took Grandmother Mercer's arm. "I've never seen this side of you," she said.

"I have many sides you've never seen. However, a new dress must wait. We need my bit of money for more important things."

"True."

"Besides, I was never able to kick up my heels in Dorchester, either." She uttered a quiet sigh.

At this point, the man to whom Frank was talking had departed, and Frank was close enough to hear his mother's sigh. He asked her, "Are you thinking about your life back home in England?"

"Of course," she replied.

*

During the week that followed, Billy secured employment delivering customers' grocery orders for McMillan's Dry Goods and Grocery Store on Queen Street. He used a wooden pushcart that the store provided.

He liked Mrs. McMillan. During his first few days on the job, he learned that her given name was Elizabeth and that that she was the sole proprietor of the business. Another delivery boy told Billy that her husband had passed away from consumption three years prior. He thought that Mrs. McMillan's dark eyes shone with intelligence, and he quickly learned that she tolerated no nonsense from her employees.

He was stricken when he met Mrs. McMillan's fourteen-year-old daughter. Her name was Jenny, and she was a year older than Billy was. He thought her exceptionally pretty. She had long, dark hair, generous brown eyes, and fine features. Her skin was flawless, her white teeth perfectly aligned, her lips full. When she smiled at Billy, butterflies fluttered in his stomach. This was a new sensation for him. Then he thought about Shirley Ann, the girl in Comstock he had "sort of" liked. She had not created butterflies in his stomach. He was now thirteen, a teenager, and girls were attracting him more and more.

When Jenny gazed in his direction, he shyly dropped his eyes. A bully he knew how to confront, but an attractive girl was another kettle of fish.

He soon learned more about Mrs. McMillan. She was a few years over forty and was a shrewd businesswoman. Courteous and friendly with her customers when the occasion demanded, she rarely shied away from speaking her mind, he noticed. A tall, slender woman, her features were fine and her dark hair was beautiful, similar like her daughter. Because she owned a profitable business, eligible bachelors eyed her greedily. It was also obvious to Billy that when elderly women of the community entered the store, they were highly suspicious of her. Billy figured that this was because of the way their husbands gazed at her.

Jenny soon began conversing with Billy. In one of their conversations, she had inquired about Billy and his family.

"My mother and I attend the Anglican Church of St. John the Evangelist on Stuart Street. Your uncle Frank and aunt Sarah attend there, too. My mother has known them for many years. She recently met your grandmother, Mrs. Dorothea Mercer. She likes her."

One afternoon, while Billy was waiting for an order to deliver, he was stocking cans of fruit on a shelf. Jenny told him, "My mother and I attend church regularly. My mother says that she believes strongly in the teachings of the Anglican faith, but unlike so many of our neighbours, she doesn't believe that any church has a monopoly on divine truth. She says that the beliefs of other denominations and faiths have much good in them, too. She says that as long as they contain the gentle kindness and compassion of Christianity, she could attend those other churches, as well. If an Anglican church is not available, she says we could attend the Presbyterian or Methodist church." She paused before adding, "She says she could even attend The Salvation Army."

On another occasion, Billy heard Mrs. McMillan talking to a customer who said, "I don't approve of The Salvation Army and their noisy services. Their uniforms and strange ways are not good for this neighbourhood."

Mrs. McMillan replied, "I have no problems with The Salvation Army or its teachings. I think that they are a positive influence in the community."

Billy noticed that the customer did not look pleased, but she said nothing more. He thought that Mrs. McMillan had no difficulties expressing her opinion, even if people disagreed with her. Secretly, he hoped that one morning he would see Jenny and her mother at the Army.

Alongside Billy in McMillian's Dry Goods and Grocery Store were two male clerks and two other delivery boys. Billy noticed that Mrs. McMillan was frugal by nature, extending credit abstemiously while insisting on payment on time. She was a demanding employer and possessed a sharp tongue, but Billy thought her scrupulously fair. He also noticed that whenever she spoke to him, her voice and manner seemed to soften.

"Billy," she told him one morning, "take this order to Mrs. Jones on Tecumseth Street. Count the money she gives you carefully and check your change. She'd squeeze a penny until King Edward's nose bled." Mrs. McMillan grinned mischievously as she added this final remark.

"Yes, ma'am. I'll give her the old eagle eye."

"All right, Eagle Eye. On your way." She smiled as she watched Billy depart from the store.

*

Billy worked hard each day. On Tuesday evenings he attended band practice, and during the long evenings of spring he and two friends, whom he had recently met, explored the avenues and laneways of the neighbourhood. Billy still missed the dusty roads, pastures, and farmlands surrounding Comstock, but the laneways of Toronto helped ease his sense of loss.

Roy and Brian were close to Billy's age. Roy was tall and skinny, with a lock of blond hair that fell over his forehead. He was always brushing it back, unaware of his habit. Whenever caught misbehaving, he grinned sheepishly, hoping to avoid punishment. Brian was also a prankster, but his dark eyes were intelligent and thoughtful. When caught in some misdeed or other, he attempted to fib his way out of the situation. Because of good looks and agile tongue, he often succeeded in avoiding punishments that fell on others.

One spring evening, the threesome sallied forth in search of adventure. Zack did not accompany them. Billy's new friends were not as fearless as he was, so he became the leader of the triumvirate by default. Being more mature than they were, Billy should have known better than to be involved in their pranks and mischievous deeds, which always seemed to involve their stomachs. However, despite his intelligence and ability to think deeply, he was a typical teenager at heart.

One evening in the laneway behind Queen Street after the sun had set, Billy suggested to his friends, "Let's slip over a backyard fence into a strawberry patch. We can eat the ripe fruit. I like it when the red juice dribbles down my chin."

They all laughed and then proceeded to a garden that had a strawberry patch. Once they had eaten their fill, Billy said, "Let's throw the unripe berries at each other like we're shooting bullets."

They were busy at war when Roy warned, "A light just came on in the kitchen window of the house. We'd better get out of here."

The boys retreated over the fence like snakes amid the rocks, vanishing from sight.

Another evening it was Roy who said, "Let's raid a cherry tree tonight. There's one in front of that old ladies' house on Front Street. Billy, you're the best climber, so we'll let you go up into the upper branches. You can toss down cherries to us. We'll stand below and hold out our shirts to grab the cherries as you drop them."

"Are you sure you can manage such a difficult role?" Billy said with a degree of mock sarcasm.

Roy grinned and said, "We'll do our best." Billy laughed and off they went toward Front Street. All went well, until they heard a shriek from an upstairs window of the house. It alerted them that it was time to beat a hasty retreat.

It was Billy who planned their next endeavour. He knew of a rhubarb patch in a backyard garden on Draper Street, several houses north of his. "We can boost our rear ends over the back fence and yank up the stalks."

"Sure," Brian chimed in. "We'll wipe the damn mud off the stalks on our trouser legs and then suck out the sour juice. Our faces will be turned inside out with the sourness."

Roy said, "Your face always looks that way—sour."

"Neither of your faces is very sweet," Billy mocked.

Ignoring the remark, Brian replied, "We'll have a contest to see who can suck the most stalks dry. The last one to quit wins the contest."

Later that night, there were no winners as the boys painfully managed their gut aches but were unable to contain the need to rush to the backhouse or chamber pot.

However, their most ingenious and profitable prank was on Mr. Wilson, a greengrocer on the north side of Queen Street, east of Bathurst Street. Again it was Billy who devised the plan.

"Wilson will pay us a penny for each wood fruit basket we take into his store. We can spend the money at the penny-candy store."

"Here's what we do. We climb over Mr. Wilson's back fence and sneak into the shed where he stores the baskets. We remove the baskets and then go into the store and exchange them for cash. Afterward, when Mr. Wilson tosses the baskets back in the shed, he'll have no idea that he just bought baskets he already owned." If a person were charitable, one might say that Billy was encouraging his musketeers to engage in an early-day version of recycling.

After receiving their money, the boys grinned impishly as they slapped each other on the back and strutted eastward along Queen Street toward Martin's penny-candy store, near Vanauley Street.

*

Now into the first week of July, Billy noticed at bedtime that Zack pulled from under his pillow an all-day sucker wrapped in waxed paper.

"Where'd you get the money for that?" Billy inquired.

"Same place as you get the money for your candy," he replied with a knowing grin.

"And where's that?"

"From Mr. Wilson's baskets."

"But that's stealing," Billy replied.

"Well, you did it."

"Who says?"

"Roy's brother, Eddy, who's my friend."

Billy stared at Zack and knew that he had no reply or excuse. His younger brother had simply imitated his own actions. What had seemed to be a smart and daring thing to do no longer appeared clever. He had always known that Zack followed his example, but he had never considered the type of consequences this recent development presented. Being the older brother entailed responsibilities, but when he was the one performing the deed, it had seemed all right. However, he did not want Zack to steal. Actually, he had not considered it stealing until Zack had done it. Then a horrible thought struck him. *What if Mr. Wilson had caught Zack?*

That night, staring at the dancing shadows the moonlight created on the darkened ceiling, Billy knew that his world was again changing. He was no longer a carefree lad roaming the byways and fields of Comstock. He was thirteen, a teenager with a man's responsibilities. His earnings helped the family put food on the table. His parents would be upset if they knew he had almost destroyed someone's strawberry patch and uprooted most of a neighbour's rhubarb.

During the days ahead, Billy saw less of Roy and Brian. He heard that they were frequenting streets to the north of Queen Street, getting into mischief that captured the attention of the constabulary.

As Billy slowly weaned himself off of their company, his cornet became his new companion. Zack listened to him practise and followed his example. Mr. Meaford had given him the other instrument that he had brought over on the *Southwark*. He, too, now attended the junior band practices.

Sometimes they "horsed around," making animal sounds with the instruments. Because of the racket they created, their parents teasingly told them that they should reconsider their decision to attend The Salvation Army. Throughout July and August, Billy and Zack faithfully attended band practices, and much to Billy's relief, Zack did not steal any more baskets from the fruit market.

Billy progressed rapidly with his music. Reading music from a solo cornet tune book, he played the old-time hymns with ease. His grandmother purchased a music book of English folksongs and almost cried as he played her favourites from the days when she was a child.

One day, Billy's grandmother told him, "It's amazing how Zack can 'belt forth' a song with the force of a much older child. I think that *belt forth* is the appropriate description, because although he plays forcefully and places his small fingers correctly on the valves, his youthful style lacks finesse."

Billy smiled as he replied, "He'll improve. He's only seven."

However, Zack's playing attracted the attention of Bess, who was eight. She had always wanted to play an instrument.

"I want to learn, too," she demanded. "It's like a game, and I want to play."

Mary, who was now twelve, chimed in, "I want to learn, too."

Then Ruth, who was ten, added, "I don't want to be left out. Can I join the gang?"

"Please, Billy," the girls chorused, "we want a turn on your instruments."

Though at first unwilling, Billy finally gave in, and Zack slowly nodded his head in agreement. What had begun in a corridor below deck on the *Southwark* had now evolved into a family enterprise.

*

On the evening of Monday, September 3, Phil decided that the family should again explore the city. They had been in Toronto for two months, and Phil's job at the Toronto Silver Plate Company had been going well, earning him a small raise in pay. Summer was ending. He knew that Emmy had worked hard to fill the preserving jars with fruit and vegetables for the winter season. She deserved a break. Besides, it was the final day of the children's summer holiday before four of them returned to school. He decided that they should splurge and take a streetcar ride.

The forested streets of Toronto beckoned. Each summer, on streets such as Queen, Spadina, Avenue Road, and Yonge, open-bench streetcars plied the routes. Phil chose Queen Street for the family's first streetcar excursion.

An open-sided Toronto streetcar in 1906, at the terminus of the College streetcar line in High Park. *City of Toronto Archives, Series 71, Item 9896*

Phil watched intently as the Queen streetcar approached. When it arrived at Spadina Avenue, he and Billy helped Zack and Bess step up on the running board. The conductor hopped along this same running board to collect their fares—two cents for each of the children, and five cents each for the two adults. Phil paid the twenty cents slowly, carefully counting out the five pennies and three nickels.

Earlier in the week, an air mass had drifted up from the Gulf of Mexico. The day had been hot and muggy, such weather the bane of Torontonians in summer. Even at this evening hour, the air remained humid. Phil sat on the bench seat as the streetcar continued eastward, the forward motion creating a much welcome breeze.

Soon, daylight was fading in the western sky, the coloured lights decorating the sides and roof of the streetcar, making it glow brighter and adding to the festive mood that, really, required no enhancement. An open-air car was a sufficient attraction in and of itself.

He noticed that sitting beside Emmy was a stout elderly woman. He had seen her board the streetcar at Yonge Street, wedging herself between Zack and Emmy. The woman's cheeks were plastered with far too much bright red rouge. She wore her rumpled hat on a jaunty angle and a grin on her face that was more of a leer, betraying an absence of sobriety. The woman was loquacious in the extreme and chatted incessantly to Emmy, who did her best to remain polite while trying to ignore the intoxicated woman. Phil was highly amused as he observed them.

When they passed Jarvis Street, Phil heard the woman say to Emmy, "Don't you love these tree-lined streets? You know, Dearie, another favourite streetcar route of mine for an excursion is Sherbourne Street. It has enormous trees and big homes. If you visit it after dark, the trees shade the roadway from the streetlights. It's perfect for catching a few kisses from a willin' gentleman …" She paused, winked, and added, "Or even an unwillin' gent."

She chuckled and gave Emmy a sly grin and a nudge with her elbow.

Phil noticed that Emmy was uncertain how to reply, so he simply smiled politely and said nothing.

Sherbourne Street in 1905. In that decade, it was an avenue with stately homes, flanked by mature shade trees.

The Queen streetcar continued eastward toward the Beaches. For many people in the city, this was cottage country. Though the woman now whispered to Emmy, Phil was able to overhear her. In a conspiratorial tone the woman said, "Beaches are great places to watch the men, though the bathing costumes reveal damn little."

"Please, madam, be careful what you say. I have my children with me."

"Aye, I notice you've a handsome husband with you, too. If you ever grow tired of him, Dearie, you can throw him my way. He's a damn lovely creature."

Emmy was lost for words, and Phil was doing his best not to laugh out loud. He sensed Emmy's relief when the car rumbled noisily through a residential neighbourhood; at least now the children wouldn't be able to hear the woman's coarse language.

The streetcar now reached the end of the line. The elderly woman stepped unsteadily onto the running board and toddled down the street, but not before giving Emmy a wink and saying, "Remember what I said about tossing 'things' my way, Dearie. If you're ever in the Beaches again, ask for Bold Bessy."

"Who was that?" Zack inquired.

"I haven't the faintest idea. But I'm glad she's gone," Emmy told him.

Phil knew that Zack was puzzled by his mother's comment.

"Look," Zack said, as he pointed at the woman and chuckled, "I think she just fell over an ashcan beside that driveway."

Phil gazed down the street and saw that, indeed, the woman had fallen on her rear end. Attempting to salvage her dignity, she struggled to her feet and adjusted her rumpled bonnet. Then she waved at Emmy and laughed heartily as she continued on her way.

"I think she's been to church and partaken of too much sacramental wine," Phil said as he grinned.

"Yes, the 'spirit' does seem to have seized her," Emmy replied.

On the return journey westward, Phil assisted the children in boarding an enclosed streetcar. Several men were standing at the open area at the back, a favourite spot for some passengers in warm weather. Phil found seats for the family inside the streetcar.

Phil explained to Zack, "During the day, the open area at the back is where people place their parcels and where carpenters deposit their toolboxes. Deliverymen put small crates there. After placing the objects on the floor of the porch-like area at the rear of the streetcar, riders who don't wish to remain in the open go inside to find a place to sit."

"I wish we could stand in the open area," Zack said.

"Perhaps next time. It's a warm night and the area's full."

Then he directed Zack's attention to the front of the streetcar. "See the motorman in his private compartment at the front of the streetcar? That's where he handles the controls. Notice the sliding door? He can open and close it to get in and out. The door's now open. See how he bangs the small metal disk on the floor beside his boot? The disk operates the bell. He bangs it with the heel of his boot."

They both listened to the loud clanging of the bell, which sent pedestrians and horse-carts scurrying.

Zack smiled with delight, but then sadness crept into his voice as he lamented, "I wish I could ring the bell."

"Perhaps someday you will."

A Toronto streetcar with open space at the rear where passengers stood. *City of Toronto Archives, Fonds 1244, Item 0496*

The streetcar continued westward toward their home. When the family entered the house on Draper Street, they were tired but happy. Phil told Emmy, "It's not every day that we have the chance to travel to such faraway neighbourhoods. Streetcars are indeed amazing! What a city."

*

The following year, the author Rudyard Kipling visited Toronto and addressed members of the Canadian Club at McKonkey's Banquet Hall on King Street West. His remarks were rather vague and devoid of any real praise for the city; apparently he found the appearance of the downtown area none too positive. It was a pity that he had not been on the open-sided streetcar the night when Phil and the Mercer family journeyed to the eastern terminus of the Queen Street line.

*

By the middle of September, autumn filtered across the ravines and tree-lined avenues of the city. Billy returned home one evening after finishing his final delivery at McMillan's Grocery Store. The shadows of evening were deepening as he passed the home of Mrs. Greenberg, a neighbour on Draper Street. The elderly woman was pulling weeds from her front lawn. She was stout, her size indicative of her expertise in the kitchen. Her grey hair, pulled back tightly into a bun, sat prominently at the back of her head. Her face, creased with innumerable wrinkles, testified to her constant worrying. Despite this, she rarely failed to deliver a smile. Billy felt guilty when he saw her because last June, he and two of his friends had raided her rhubarb patch.

She smiled as she said, "Hello, Billy." Then, shaking her head in frustration, she told him, "I suppose I'll never see the end of these weeds."

"How's your back today?"

"It's killing me. Mr. Greenberg is unable to bend down at all, so I guess I'm fortunate that I'm still able to tend to the gardening."

"Yes, Mrs. Greenberg. Pulling weeds is indeed hard on the back."

"Well, I like to have my lawn neat. I guess the winter winds will soon end its growth, but then I'll have to shovel the snow from my sidewalk. A woman's chores never seem to end."

"My mom says that, too."

"Well, I bet she does. She has five of you to tend to."

"I help her as much as I can," Billy replied defensively.

"Oh, I'm sure you do." After a brief pause she continued, "This morning I baked two rhubarb pies. I don't have much rhubarb this year. Some ruffians pulled up most of it in the spring, and the remainder, they trampled under their feet. However, I salvaged enough for a half dozen quart jars. Come into the house. You can take one of the pies to your mother. I promised her this morning that I'd send it to her."

As Billy stared at the pie, he realized that his hunger was almost as large as his guilt. He knew he must do something to ease his conscience. By the time he entered the back door of his house, he knew what he must do. Placing the pie on the kitchen table, he noticed that Bess was setting the table for dinner. His mom was dumping potatoes into the water boiling in a pot on the stove. Emmy glanced at the pie and smiled.

"May the Lord bless Mrs. Greenberg," she said. "I'm not certain that those are the correct words to say, as she is Jewish and does not believe in the Lord. However, that neighbour lady has more Christianity in her than many Christians. God bless her for sending that pie."

The next morning, Billy arose earlier than usual. Before he left for work, his nimble fingers plucked every weed from Mrs. Greenberg's lawn. By the time he left for the grocery store, the lawn was free of weeds and he had managed to assuage a little of his guilt.

*

When October arrived, Mrs. Greenberg's flowerbeds and backyard garden needed clearing. Summer's warmth had drained from the land and frost had killed the tender plants; only the chrysanthemums and geraniums soldiered onward. Now when Billy returned from work, daylight was gone by the time he reached Draper Street.

One evening, though it was almost dark, Billy saw that Mrs. Greenberg remained outside later than usual, toiling in her front garden. She stopped and leaned on the rake to rest as she watched Billy approach.

"How was your day, Mrs. Greenberg? Bake any pies?" he added with a grin.

"My son used to ask me that," she replied, a pensive look etching across her face.

"I didn't know you had a son."

"Yes, well, I don't see him much. He's a grown man now. He lives north of College Street. He's done quite well for himself."

"I bet he misses your pies. It's a pity that the smell of the pies baking in your oven can't float as far north as College Street. I bet he'd run down here to Draper Street in a flash."

"That's a nice thought, Billy."

"Here's another nice thought. Tomorrow I'll clean up your backyard garden for you."

"That would be wonderful. I'll talk to Mr. Greenberg. We'll see if we can afford a few pennies to pay you."

"No, ma'am. Your pies have already paid for my service," he said. Then he winked and strolled down the street toward his house.

Mrs. Greenberg watched him depart, sighed, and then mounted the stairs to return inside the house. As she closed the door, she became aware how chilly the air outside had become. However, as the warmth inside the hallway enveloped her, she thought of the boy's friendship. Then she thought of her own son. Perhaps he *would* visit her one day. On the following Saturday, when she attended the small house of prayer on the north side of St. Andrew's Street, she would pray for such a blessing.

*

As October ended, nights became increasingly heavy with frost. The winds from the northwest blew unseasonably cold. On Draper Street, the gnarled limbs of the trees were stripped bare of their summer's growth. The residents lit their coal-oil lamps earlier each evening, the glow visible in the houses' windows. Nature was creeping inevitably toward the winter solstice.

The greenery of summer gone, the backyard gardens were now blackened and bare. Tomato plants, which in early September had been bounteous with fruit, were now shrivelled, reclining forlornly against the barren earth. Among the withered stalks lay a few red rotting tomatoes, as well as green ones that were too small to merit a place on a kitchen windowsill. Though useless for the table, in the hands of young boys they became perfect missiles for mischief.

Billy had delivered two extra grocery orders to customers shortly before the store's closing time, and darkness had wrapped around the streets by the time he reached the corner of Wellington Street to walk south on

Draper. Ahead in the dim light he saw three boys, approximately his own age, loitering outside Mrs. Greenberg's house.

Then he heard one of them shout, "Fat Jew lady, fat Jew lady, come outside. We have a present for you."

Mrs. Greenberg's door remained sealed against the night while the cruel chants continued. As Billy approached closer, he saw the parlour curtains in the Greenberg house open slightly. The Greenbergs were aware what was happening, and Billy was certain they feared the impending events. Suddenly, one of the boys fired a rotten tomato at the Greenbergs' door. It hit with a dull thud, splashing its putrid contents over the door, the juice and seeds spilling over the straw welcome mat on the doorstep. Then a hard green tomato hammered the door, and the boys doubled over with laughter.

"Jew lady, Jew lady, come get some tomatoes for your kitchen," the tallest of the boys shouted as he let fly another green tomato.

Billy approached the boys and shouted at them to stop. They ignored him. The tallest lad cursed him and threatened to punch in his face. When they attempted to seize him, Billy's fists struck like a boxer's, his blows hitting them from every direction.

At first, the boys were too shocked to react. The tallest boy was the first to recover; he raised his fist for a retaliatory strike. Billy hit him in the stomach with his right, and then he struck his chin with his left. The boy went down and remained unable to rise from the roadway.

Watching their leader succumb, the other two boys came to his aid. Billy delivered a few forceful blows and quickly danced out of reach. One of them bellowed with rage as he fell to the ground, and the other boy followed him after he received a nose punch that drew blood.

The tallest boy now stood to his feet. Billy grabbed a rotten tomato that had miraculously remained in his enemy's hand and crushed it into his face. The boy went down again, howling with rage. When Billy turned to deal again with the two pugilists on the ground, he saw that they had fled up the street.

The remaining boy, the leader of the triumvirate, deciding that retreat was preferable to another bashing, scrambled to his feet and raced after them.

At the north end of Draper, at the corner on Wellington, the three boys stopped and gazed back at Billy. Not quite believing that they had been beaten by a single opponent, they watched him in stunned silence. The silence did not last. Not wanting to depart the scene without saving face, from a safe distance they bravely chanted, "Jew boy, Jew boy, lover of Jews."

Billy grinned and menacingly walked slowly toward them. They turned and fled. The last Billy saw of them, they were running toward Portland Street, their tails between their legs. Mrs. Greenberg's door cautiously opened a crack as she peered out at her rescuer.

Seeing that it was now safe, she opened the door wider. She said, "Billy, there aren't enough pies in the world to repay you for what you did. I'm sorry that you had to fight for us. Mr. Greenberg has a heart condition. I was afraid for his life."

"You're my friend, Mrs. Greenberg. Friends defend friends."

"Are you hurt?"

"I'm fine."

"You were like David against Goliath."

"Naw, it was more like a rat-catcher against three rats too stupid to know how easy it is for rats to lose their tails."

"I hope the boys don't return."

"Don't worry, Mrs. Greenberg. They won't. But if they do, next time they'll have more than their tails chopped off."

Mrs. Greenberg smiled in appreciation of his feeble attempt at humour, thanked him again, and quietly closed the door. When Billy entered the kitchen of his home, his mother gazed at him. She saw that his cap was dirty and crumpled and his hair dishevelled. Then she laid eyes on the bleeding cut on his hand.

"My goodness! What happened?"

"I took away some cheese from some rats," he replied. He refused to say anything more. His face had not been touched, and his shirt hid the bruises on his ribs.

*

Two days later, Emmy met Mrs. Greenberg on the street. Despite the chilly temperature, they chatted for a few minutes. It was then that Emmy learned the true story of the rats and the rat-catcher.

As she continued homeward, Emmy thought about the day Billy had defended her from the bullies outside the butcher's shop in Comstock. Then she smiled remembering how she had smacked one boy across the face with a wet fish.

She did not approve of her son's fighting, but she also knew that there were times when there was no other way.

*

In the beginning of November, Frank and Sarah invited the Mercers to dinner at their house. As it was only across the road, Emmy placed a shawl over her shoulders and quickly walked over to the house. Despite the darkness, she was able to catch a glimpse of its bay-and-gable peak, which towered above the street unlike her home's humble mansard roof. She helped Sarah serve the food; the highlight was a blade roast Sarah had simmered in a pot for over an hour.

After the meal, Emmy, Sarah, and the four younger children went upstairs to the sewing room at the back of the house. It was where Sarah sat to knit and sew on winter afternoons, as it faced west, allowing a plenteous supply of afternoon sunlight. Zack and Bess made a bit of a fuss because they wanted to join the men, but Emmy insisted that they remain with her.

Frank, Phil, and Billy entered the parlour on the ground floor and sat by the fireplace, the flames crackling merrily, spreading warmth across the room. After they had seated themselves, they stared silently for a few minutes at the mesmerizing flames. Frank said to Billy, "I understand you're doing well at the grocery store. Mrs. McMillan speaks highly of you. She's a demanding employer, so you must be doing a good job."

"I try, sir."

"You've been in Toronto for over five months now. What do you think of your adopted city?"

"It's amazing, sir. Compared to Comstock, it's a world of wonders."

"Have you been down to the harbour area, south of the street named The Esplanade?"

"Yes, sir."

"Do you know that they created the land south of Union Station with landfill? There's talk that they intend to dump more soil into the harbour to extend the city farther into the lake. This means they will need new ferry docks."

"I saw the Island ferryboats last summer—the Primrose, Mayflower, and Blue Bell. I was amazed at the hordes of picnickers I saw going to Centre Island, Ward's Island, and Hanlan's Point."

Toronto Island ferries moored in the harbour, c. 1910. Unlike those of today, these ferries have smokestacks because they were powered by coal-burning engines. *City of Toronto Archives, Fonds 1244, Item 0237a*

Frank smiled amusedly when Billy used the word *hordes* to describe the picnickers crowding the ferryboats in hot weather. Indeed, they were hordes.

Billy continued. "I also saw the *Luella,* the small boat that carries people only to Ward's Island. I was amazed at how fast the passengers boarded the large ferries. They load the upper and lower decks at the same time, using a two-level platform."

Frank inquired, "What else did you notice?"

"In summer, the entire harbour area is beyond anything I ever imagined. I saw boat races as well as people rowing, canoeing, and sailing. Along the water's edge, I saw people playing cricket, golf, and lawn bowling."

"Wait until you see the harbour area when it freezes," Frank informed him. "It's ideal for skating, hockey, and sailing iceboats. The Toronto waterfront is a constant source of pleasure and amusement for everyone, as in this city no one lives far from the lake."

Iceboats on the frozen harbour at the foot of Yonge Street in 1908. *City of Toronto Archives, Fonds 1244, Item 0444c*

"I know what you mean," Phil chimed in. "This past summer, we went to the lakeshore to catch a view of the lake boat *Turbinia.*"

"Yes," Frank replied, "I caught a glimpse of her as she departed through the Western Gap for an excursion to Hamilton. Did you know that the ship is often chartered by The Salvation Army for moonlight excursions?"

The *Turbinia* in Toronto Harbour, c. 1910. *City of Toronto Archives, Fonds 1266, Item 3065*

*

In September, the elderly bandmaster of the Queen Street Citadel Band had retired and the Corps Officer (minister) asked George to take the baton. He accepted, and another bandsman took over the junior band.

Despite the demands of his new role, George continued to instruct Billy and Zack on their cornets. He was unaware that the boys shared everything he taught them with their sisters.

George and Vangie had progressed well since their arrival in Toronto. They regularly read *The War Cry,* the weekly Salvation Army periodical. It informed them about events throughout the city and the greater Canadian Territory. It was in *The War Cry* that George had read that the Army had reorganized the Toronto Staff Band, which was to visit their church. The band consisted mostly of staff employed at the Territorial Headquarters, hence the term *staff band.* However, to supplement the numbers, they also accepted bandsmen from among the various corps bands in the city. The Salvation Army Headquarters was on Albert Street, east of Eaton's Annex Store.

It crossed George's mind that sometime in the future he would like to apply to become a member of the Toronto Staff Band.

*

December 1906 was to be the first Christmastime in Canada for the Mercer family. The yuletide season brought memories of Comstock and their friends back home to the forefront. As they sat around the kitchen table on Draper Street on Christmas Eve, Phil mentioned the fireplace of their home on South Street. He told them, "I dearly miss our relatives and friends in England. Greeting them was always an important part of the holiday season."

There was a chorus of agreement.

However, Phil introduced a bit of reality to the nostalgic mood by reminding them, "We're better off here than we were in England. I have a job, and there's food on the table." Then he glanced at the children and added, "We also have Uncle Frank and Aunt Sarah here. Some folks from the Old Country have no relatives in Canada.

Grandmother Mercer smiled and nodded in agreement.

Phil then read aloud the following article from *The War Cry,* as it expressed some of the sentiments he felt about their first Christmas in their adopted land.

So, this is your first Christmas in Canada? Well, the writer sincerely hopes that it may be a happy time, with not too many memories of "last year," when, with parents and perhaps brothers and sisters, you sat around a fire in the old home and talked over the events of the months that had passed since last you met in a similar way. But it will pay you to live in the present, or as St. Paul said, "Not forgetting these things which are behind, and pressing toward the mark."

Merry Christmas.

Pausing, Phil gazed at the faces of his family as he repeated the final two words of the article. "Merry Christmas!"

Following the evening meal, and as pre-arranged, Frank and Sarah arrived from across the street. Phil warmly greeted them at the door and ushered them into the parlour. The festivities commenced when everyone shared Grandmother's platter of Christmas cake. The adults sipped on tea, which Bess referred to as swamp water.

A few cards had arrived in the mail from overseas. Phil read them aloud and passed them around. Billy gazed for a long time at the card from Mrs. Rowntree. Scribbled in the elderly woman's handwriting were the words, "Fondest greetings from Comstock. Best wishes to everyone for a merry Christmas. Tell Billy not to tease the hell out of the old women in the neighbourhood."

"My, such language that Mrs. Rowntree employs," Sarah said, more out of a sense of duty than any real conviction, as she knew the children were listening.

"Yes," Grandmother Mercer replied. "I met her that Christmas when I stayed with the family in Comstock. That Mrs. Rowntree is a hell of a woman. I'd love to talk with her again."

Before anyone could rebuke Grandmother for her intemperate language, they all burst into laughter. Wishing to change the subject and avoid any questions about Grandmother Mercer's using the word *hell*, Phil instructed, "I think the children should prepare for their Christmas Extravaganza, as I've named it."

The children scrambled out of the room to fetch their brass instruments.

When everyone was ready, Billy announced, "First we'll play an arrangement of 'Hark the Herald Angels Sing.'" Then he explained, "Zack will play the lead on his cornet, as we rehearsed. The girls each have their own parts. I'll play the part scored for the euphonium on my cornet." Turning to his siblings, he added, "And don't fluff it."

*

Uncle Frank watched as Billy glanced at the music sheets to be certain that everything was ready. He thought Bess looked very serious as she lifted her cornet and stared at the music. Sarah was grinning in anticipation.

He whispered to her, "I wonder what kind of noise we'll hear? Ruth's holding her dented tenor horn as if it were a Stradivarius, and Mary is clutching her old trombone as if it's Gabriel's trumpet."

Turning to Phil he asked, "I know Billy and Zack received their instruments from the Army. But where'd you get the instruments for the girls?"

"George Meaford got them as cast-offs from a Knights of Columbus band. The instruments are not too pretty to look at, but they sound none the worse for wear."

Frank stopped talking when he heard Billy say, "Ready?"

He watched as Billy gazed around at his brother and sisters. Then, facing his audience, Billy said, "This may sound a little weird. I had to arrange the parts to suit the instruments we have. Beggars can't be choosers," he added with a shy grin.

From the instant the first notes poured forth, Frank could not believe his ears. The harmony was balanced and tuneful. The old sacred carol had never sounded better, and it was immediately obvious that the children had rehearsed for many hours to produce such a quality performance. When they finished playing, the adults applauded enthusiastically. Grandmother glowed with pride, while Emmy and Phil smiled and encouraged their offspring.

"Play 'Good King Wenceslas' next," Emmy requested. She had heard them rehearsing and knew their repertoire.

A half hour later, after playing all the pieces they knew, the children put their instruments down and basked in the praise of their elders. Cookies were distributed and more swamp water consumed.

"I don't understand," Frank said as he clicked his teaspoon on one of Grandmother's china cups. "I know that Billy and Zack go to junior band practice at the Army and that they receive private lessons from George Meaford, but how did the girls learn to play?"

"Billy teaches them," Phil replied. "George teaches Billy and Zack, and they help the girls."

"It's uncanny," Sarah said. "They all have special talent. How can so much talent be in one family?"

"Perhaps beggars can't be choosers," Grandmother said smugly, "but they can certainly choose to sound great."

"If that is a sample of Army music, perhaps we should attend the Christmas morning service at the Queen Street Corps," Frank declared as he gazed at Sarah, who nodded in approval.

Frank saw his mother's smug look disappear. She muttered under her breath, "Listening to the grandchildren perform on the brass instruments is one thing, but enduring the infernal racket of an Army service is quite another."

*

The next day, not wishing to attend church alone, and because she did not want to dampen the children's enthusiasm for the Christmas celebration, Grandmother Mercer reluctantly accompanied the family to the Queen Street Citadel. When the bandsmen entered the sanctuary to take their position on the platform, she noticed a familiar face among the bass players. It was Mr. Hutchinson, the handsome widower who owned the butcher shop on Queen Street.

She turned to Emmy and said, "I talked to 'Mr. Gerald' just two days ago, when you and I picked up the Christmas turkey. He never mentioned to me that he attends the Army."

"Oh, I thought you knew. I never thought to mention it," Emmy replied.

When the service ended, Grandmother Mercer told Emmy, "I think the band sounded quite good this morning. Perhaps it's because the children have attuned my ears to the sound of brass instruments. Whatever the reason, the Army services don't seem so bad, after all."

Emmy was unable to resist suggesting, "Maybe it's because Mr. Gerald is in the band."

*

The winter months of 1907 flew past. As the days lengthened, warm weather slowly inched its way across the land. When the hot weather descended on the streets of Toronto, the wealthy exited the city to escape the heat, travelling north to the grand lodges or cottages. The Muskoka area was most popular. The Mercer and Meaford families, being of modest means, found that trips to the city's recreation areas were their only options—the Toronto Islands, Humber Bay, Kew Beach, Scarborough Beach on Lake Ontario, and High Park. These destinations were only a streetcar or ferryboat fare away.

The Twenty-Fourth of May holiday fell on a Friday, and some people in the city were thrilled to have a three-day weekend. Those who worked on Saturdays were not so lucky (a six-day workweek was common for many workers). Mrs. McMillan granted Billy the day off, and as Mr. McCallum was to close the Toronto Silver Plate factory for the entire weekend, Phil planned to take his family to Centre Island on Saturday, realizing that it would likely be less crowded than on Friday. Frank and Sarah Mercer decided to accompany their relatives. Grandmother Mercer tagged along, as well.

To save carfare, they all walked to the ferry docks. Along the way, Billy's uncle Frank said to him, "I really enjoy the islands. I can't wait to feel the refreshing breezes from the lake as we cross the harbour. We Torontonians view the Islands as an integral part of our city, yet their quiet atmosphere is a world away from the bustle and grime of the downtown core."

Phil was listening and noticed that his brother referred to himself as a Torontonian. He had to admit that he was beginning to feel the same of himself. Toronto no longer seemed like his adopted city, as it was giving birth to a new life for him and his family.

This was Phil's first journey to the Islands. However, the family had previously been to the harbour area. "The day we visited," he began, "we walked. We went down Bathurst Street. Fortunately, a train was not shuttling back and forth on the multi-track level crossings on Bathurst Street, south of Front. Those tracks are a real nuisance. They funnel all the rail traffic from outside the city into Union Station. As there are ten tracks, the chance of a train's making a crossing is highly probable. Peanut vendors locate themselves near the tracks to sell their goods to customers who wait for the trains to clear from the rail bed. I've been told that people often miss catching a ferry while they are trapped waiting for the tracks to clear."

People crossing train tracks in 1911 to reach the ferry docks.
City of Toronto Archives, Fonds 1244, Item 0259e

"I like watching the trains and the people selling stuff," Zack said.

"If I were your age, I might, too," Frank replied.

A half hour later, they were aboard the *Mayflower,* gliding over a lake smooth as glass and shimmering with sunlight. The swooshing sounds of the waves at the bow of the ferry were hypnotic. As they drew closer to the Islands, the crowd's excitement increased. Finally, the ferry nudged against the pilings beside the dock and eased into its berth. The crowds now surged toward the exit at the south-facing bow of the ferry.

Having visited the Islands before, Frank suggested, "I'd recommend we walk either to the section of Centre Island where there is a sheltered pavilion, or a place where there are plenty of picnic tables. After we secure one, we can wander over to the business district.

Twenty minutes later, they had secured a picnic table. Grandmother Mercer agreed to remain at the table to reserve it and to guard the picnic baskets. No one was better at defending a picnic table from poachers than Grandmother Mercer. The remainder of the group set off to visit the shops and food stands, accessible after they crossed the Lagoon Bridge, which spanned Long Pond. The boathouse of Edward English was located beside the bridge near the northwest corner, and next door to the boathouse was Art Sainsbury's Confectionery Store. Billy and Zack loved the candy store. Boys their ages always did.

Toronto Island ferry: the *Mayflower*. *City of Toronto Archives, Series 71, S0071, Item 5058*

The house on the left is on the south side of Long Pond, with the Edward English boat rental across the lagoon on the north side. *City of Toronto Archives, Fonds 1244, Item 0153*

View of bridge over Long Pond, looking west. May 1913. The boat rental of Edward English, with its turret, is visible behind the bridge. *City of Toronto Archives, Fonds 1548, Item 3187*

"I see that the shops of the Islands are on Manitou Road," Phil said after they crossed the bridge.

"Yes, and over there is the Algonquin Hotel. Farther along the avenue are a hardware store, a drugstore, and a theatre, as well as many food stands and souvenir shops."

"There are lots of different foods for sale," Zack exclaimed, his heart always close to his stomach.

"Oh indeed, yes," Frank replied with a knowing grin. "You'll love the 'chip' stands. In the British tradition, they serve them with vinegar and salt."

"Look," Bess exclaimed as she pointed to a popcorn kiosk, making an exaggerated sniffing noise as she enjoyed the fragrance of the fresh popcorn. Her efforts drew a mild rebuke from her mother. Bess flashed her blue eyes and continued her assessment of the popcorn.

"I bet you can smell the popcorn clear across the lake," Bess enthused.

"Bet you can't," Zack replied.

"Bet you can."

"Quiet, you two," Phil said. Then he added, "I doubt we can afford either the chips or the popcorn."

*

Toronto Island ferry the *Trillium* in 1910. It is the only ferry that has survived into the modern era. *City of Toronto Archives, Series 0071, Item 10962*

*

On June 1, Vangie Meaford took Bess and Zack to Riverdale Park, the site of the city's zoo and roller-skating rink. The entrance to Riverdale Zoo was on Winchester Street, east of Parliament Street. Bess was unable to contain her excitement, as she had always longed to see live lions and tigers.

As they stepped down from the streetcar, Vangie warned Bess and Zack, "Watch your step. Look where you're walking instead of gawking ahead."

"Yes, Mrs. Meaford," they chorused, but they never took their eyes off the gate that led to the zoo.

Inside, they walked the paved path that passed by the animal cages. The odours emanating from the cages mingled with hay and manure assaulted the nostrils, but the children took no notice of it. The only scent they detected was that of the popcorn, which, when combined with the other scents, created an odd fragrance. They were unaware of this oddity as well.

"Look at the monkey," Bess screamed with delight as she pointed to a saucy one that was gripping the bar with one hand. Making loud chattering noises, it reached its other hand out through the narrow bars, hoping for food. When it bared its teeth, Bess mimicked its expression and then giggled with delight.

Zack had never seen zebras before and chuckled as he exclaimed, "They look like donkeys in pyjamas." Then he laughed harder, proud of his joke.

"That's silly," Bess told him.

"I know. That's why it's a joke."

Visitors in front of the monkey enclosure at Toronto's Riverdale Zoo. *City of Toronto Archives, Fonds 1231, Item 0567*

Inside the snake house, Bess would not admit that she was frightened, but Mrs. Meaford detected her fear and put her arm around her shoulders. Zack gazed at Bess and teased, "Girls are such 'fraidy cats."

"Cats are braver than dogs," she replied and stuck out her tongue. Zack and Bess laughed at each other and continued walking.

When they visited the building with the lions and tigers, Zack stood close to Mrs. Meaford, hoping that Bess would not notice—but she did.

"Who's a 'fraidy cat now?" Bess cried in derision as she again stuck out her tongue at her brother. Zack said nothing.

They spent the remainder of the afternoon wandering around the park, viewing the animals in their cages. Shortly before it was time to depart, they stood on top of the hill and gazed at the parkland below, where the Don River lazily wound its way toward the lake. The sun was now leaning toward the west, its fading light casting long shadows across the hillside and down into the valley that stretched before them.

Bess stifled a yawn, but she would rather have died than admit she was tired. On the homeward journey on the streetcar, she fell asleep. Mrs. Meaford placed her arm around her to keep her upright in the seat. Zack sat in a window seat, breeze blowing through his blond hair, feeling that life did not get any better than this.

*

On the final Saturday in June, Uncle Frank and Aunt Sarah decided to take the Mercer girls and Zack on a journey far beyond the city to the town of Weston. It was near the Humber Valley, another popular summer retreat for Torontonians, though many considered it too distant to visit often.

Frank and Sarah, along with the children, travelled to the Junction area of the city at Keele Street and Weston Road. There, they climbed on a Weston Road trolley car that would take them northward through the town of Mount Dennis and eventually to the village of Weston, well beyond the city limits.

As they journeyed along, Uncle Frank explained to the children about the Weston Road trolley car. "It's an unusual streetcar," he began. "It cannot turn around when it reaches the end of the line because there is only a single set of streetcar tracks."

"I don't understand," Zack said. "If the streetcar doesn't turn around, how will we be able get back to the city?"

"The car is double-ended—there's a set of controls at either end of the trolley. To make the return trip, the motorman steps outside the streetcar and pulls down the pole attached to the overhead wires. Did you see the pole when we got on the streetcar?"

"Of course," he replied defensively, feeling that his uncle was talking down to him.

"Well, he places that pole flat against the roof of the trolley, raises the pole at the other end of the car, and attaches it to the overhead wire. Then he climbs up into the streetcar again. Do you see the long handle that the man uses to operate the controls?"

This time, Zack merely nodded. He disliked it when adults underestimated his ability to understand things. Billy never did this with him, which was another reason he enjoyed being with his older brother.

Uncle Frank continued. "He removes the long handle from the controls at the front of the streetcar and takes it to the other end, where there is another set of controls. Then he is ready to go in the opposite direction along the same set of tracks that we are on now."

"Does he clang the bell when he starts off again?"

"Sure does!"

"I wish he'd let me clang that bell. I think that when I grow up, I'd like to be a man who runs a trolley."

"I think you'd be a great trolley man," Aunt Sarah chimed in.

This is not a Weston Road streetcar, as it is from the 1920s. However, it has poles at either end to allow it to travel in opposite directions. *City of Toronto Archives, Fonds 1231, File 1231, Item 0220*

Turning to his wife, Frank said quietly, "I knew the children would love the Weston Road streetcar. I must admit that I enjoy it as well. I never tire of hearing the motorman clanging the bell."

"Yes, dear. The desire to ring a streetcar bell never leaves a man."

Frank smiled at her remark and gazed fondly at his nieces and nephew. He thought, *If they're lucky, the simple pleasures of childhood will never leave their hearts. It's when they do that a person becomes old.*

The streetcar finally arrived at its terminus near Lawrence Avenue, on the edge of the town of Weston. They walked westward on Lawrence Avenue, descending into the valley where Lawrence Avenue crossed over the Humber River.

Frank and Sarah sat on a bench beside the stream, under an enormous shade elm. Mary and Ruth wandered around the area, stopping to watch a group of boys playing baseball. Zack and Bess removed their shoes and socks and joyously waded into the river, splashing as they chased a school of fish that darted away from their toes. The gurgling noises of the stream as it gushed over the flat rocks and around the large round stones failed to drown out the laughter of the "fearless twosome."

They bravely lifted rocks in search of a monster crayfish and rushed around with a cloth net to snare a colossal minnow, which in their eyes was equivalent to the whale in the tale about Jonah. Many things of childhood seem gigantic.

Sadly, their time beside the river came to an end. The thrill of again riding the Weston Road trolley ameliorated their sadness about departing the valley. Clambering aboard, the children rushed to secure window seats. From their highly prized positions, they gazed in awe at the tram operator, who was preparing for the southward journey on Weston Road.

"Wish I could ring that bell," Zack lamented.

The trolley man gazed around the car before departing, and though he had not heard Zack's plea, he saw the look on the boy's face and guessed what it meant. He motioned for him to step to the front of the trolley. Uncle Frank nodded in approval, and Zack bolted toward the front of the car.

Frank thought that no boy in the world had a greater thrill than Zack felt on this day. As the tram noisily descended the steep hill south of Lambton Avenue, he rang the bell as if he intended all the angels in heaven and a few of the souls in hell, as well, to notice his bell-ringing skills.

In the valley where Black Creek flowed, the streetcar crossed a bridge over the narrow stream and climbed the incline on the other side. At the top of the hill, it stopped at Rogers Road. When the trolley again proceeded southward, people on the street glanced up to see what was causing the streetcar's bell to ring so often. They smiled as they realized it was a small boy enjoying himself. It was as if he had trapped happiness in a glass jar and, for a few precious moments, held it in his little hand.

Horses struggling to climb the hill as they plod southward on Weston Road toward Rogers Road. In the valley behind them flows Black Creek. The single track for the streetcar that "did not turn around" is visible in the background. The hill in the background is where they built the Kodak plant in the years ahead. It has since been demolished. *City of Toronto Archives, Fonds 1244, Item 1191a*

The lake steamer *Cayuga* at a pier in Toronto Harbour. *City of Toronto Archives, Fonds 1244, Item 0259*

*

On the evening of Saturday, July 6, Frank and Sarah, along with George and Vangie, joined a large group of "soldiers," as they referred to members of The Salvation Army, on a voyage on the steamer *Cayuga*. The ship's trial voyage across the lake had been on June 5 of this year. It had sailed from Toronto to Lewiston, New York, making the trip in an amazing one hour and fifty-five minutes. The following account appeared in *The War Cry.*

> **Excursion by Moonlight**
> **A Pleasant Trip, Enlivened by Music and Song**
>
> The city corps of Toronto united last evening for a cruise on the lake. The SS *Cayuga* was chartered for the occasion, and the whole affair was under the direction of Brigadier Taylor. At 8:30 p.m. sharp, she steamed out from the wharf with a crowd of about six hundred people onboard, mostly Salvationists and their friends. The lake was rather choppy, and a cool breeze was blowing, but everyone enjoyed the three hours' cruise around, and the time passed pleasantly in listening to the music, chatting with friends, or admiring the scenic effects produced by a thick cloudbank, a full bright moon, and the rippling waters.
>
> As the boat neared the wharf at Toronto, the band struck up "The Maple Leaf Forever" and then concluded by playing "God Save the King."

The excursions became part of the "good old days" for the Mercers and Meafords. Most of us can recall events in our lives that will forever stand out as golden moments in our past. Because an Army band was present on this voyage, Frank Mercer and George Meaford particularly enjoyed the evening.

Their wives appreciated the music, too, but they relished more the opportunity to be away from home for a few hours, free of the many hands-on domestic chores that were part and parcel of living in an age without electrical appliances.

*

The summer months flew by, and soon ships such as the *Cayuga* commenced transporting Niagara's harvest across the lake to the shops, street vendors, and fruit stands of Toronto. The stores along Queen Street were infused with the fragrance of peaches and Concord grapes, the odour of early McIntosh apples adding to the symphony of smells. McMillan's Grocery Store, where Billy worked, did a roaring business as shoppers carted away the bounty of the fields and orchards surrounding the city. Still, customers clicked their tongues and complained vociferously about the high prices.

One day, after returning from delivering a grocery order, Billy saw Mrs. Greenberg enter the store. He smiled at her as she stepped to the counter with a large basket of early McIntosh apples, which she wished to purchase. Mrs. McMillan greeted her warmly. The women talked a few moments, and then Mrs. Greenberg requested the other items from her list. Another woman was observing the transaction, and Billy could see that she was growing impatient.

After Mrs. Greenberg departed, the woman whispered to Mrs. McMillan in a conspiratorial manner, "That big Jew woman certainly takes her time."

"Mrs. Greenberg is a valued customer. She can take all the time she wishes," Mrs. McMillan replied, her voice decidedly frosty.

"I believe in Christian charity, but waiting for a Jew is beyond the pale."

"Let me tell you something. Mrs. Greenberg never purchases more than she is able to pay for at the end of the month, and she always settles her account on time. Last Christmas, she gave me a pudding and a mincemeat pie to show her appreciation for the service she received at my store. A Jew or not, she understands the meaning of Christmas more than most of my Christian customers. And another thing: Mrs. Greenberg never speaks poorly of anyone."

The woman replied in a huff, "Perhaps I had best take my business elsewhere."

"That's an excellent idea. And before you leave, kindly pay the tab that you have owing for the past month's purchases."

Billy heard the entire exchange and smiled to himself. It left an indelible impression of him. In the days ahead, he remembered Mrs. McMillan's words.

*

Billy's ability on the cornet grew by leaps and bounds. More than ever, George Meaford knew that he was tutoring one of the rarest of students—one with an innate gift—who was better than more mature musicians.

One evening in the apartment above the store on Queen Street, after a music lesson had ended, Billy and George Meaford sat for a few moments to chat about the events of the past week. George sensed that something was troubling Billy and inquired if there was anything he wished to discuss. Billy was hesitant, but he finally decided to confide in his mentor.

"Mr. Meaford, this week in the grocery store I overheard several women saying cruel things about Jews. How can Christians justify this type of thinking? Jesus was a Jew."

George paused as he gazed at Billy, finally replying, "It's difficult to explain, but many Christians believe that the Jews were responsible for crucifying Christ."

"That's nonsense. The Jews were present in the crowds when they put Jesus to death, but the Romans crucified him. The Jews had no power to enact such a judgment. Judea was under Roman rule. The Romans allowed him to be put death to appease a small group of powerful Jewish elders, but the final decision was Rome's governor's, Pontius Pilate. Besides, according to the Scriptures, it was Jesus' destiny to be crucified, so no man or group was responsible. Christ was born to die."

"I see that you have been reading your history books as well as your Bible."

"My grandmother gave me books when we lived in England, and she still buys me books in the second-hand shops on Queen Street."

Billy's mature thinking had always surprised George. He found it difficult to believe that the boy was only fourteen years old. Billy had obviously given the matter considerable thought and was seeking an honest and forthright discussion. For the next few minutes, George did his best to explain the position of many Christians on the subject, while pointing out that he thought that prejudice against Jews was wrong.

"So you think that Jews are treated unfairly, too?" Billy finally said.

"Yes."

"Such blatant prejudice goes against everything Christ taught," Billy asserted. "Mrs. Greenberg, our neighbour, helps the poor on our street, shares pies and cakes with people, and always has a kind word for everyone. I'm certain that she knows that I was one of the boys who destroyed her rhubarb patch last year, yet she forgave me. Seems to me that she obeys Jesus' teachings, but she's not Christian."

"I see your point."

"What's more important?" Billy asked as he gazed at George earnestly. "To call yourself a Christian but ignore Jesus' teaching? Or be a non-Christian but actually do as he taught?"

George knew that Billy had hit upon one of the great problems of the church—hypocrisy.

"I think that actions speak louder than words," George replied. "Saying you believe in something is hypocritical if your actions do not reflect those beliefs."

What George did not know was that the opinion he gave Billy on this mild September evening about actions being more important than words would come back to haunt him.

"Other things bother me," Billy continued.

"What things?"

"Can I tell you what I really think?" Billy asked cautiously.

George nodded his head.

"Having read the Old and New Testaments many times, it seems to me that there is a distinct difference between God as revealed in the Old Testament and as revealed in the New."

"What do you mean?"

"The God of the Old Testament seems more like the Greek gods that I've read about in books. He is vengeful and jealous, demands that people worship him unquestioningly, and cruelly punishes those who disobey him. He is to be greatly feared, similar to Zeus or Poseidon. I realize that God's love shines through on some occasions in the Old Testament Scriptures. God showed he loved David, and he also loved the people of Israel. But in the Old Testament stories, God destroyed Israel's enemies without mercy. In Genesis, he punished a sinful world by creating the

Great Flood, showing love only for Noah and his family. Would not a God of love have compassion for the sinners and lead them to see the error of their ways? Was drowning them the only option? These stories seem to indicate that some people are beyond God's love."

Before George could consider an answer, Billy continued. "However, in the New Testament, Jesus taught and demonstrated that no one was beyond the love of God. The two versions are contradictory."

George knew that this was a profound thinking for a lad Billy's age, but he was also aware that many people would consider Billy's words blasphemous. However, George remembered that when he was a teenager, he had asked his parents questions that had shocked them. He knew that Billy was struggling to understand the great God mystery at a level beyond his years. He could not condemn Billy for his honest search for understanding.

Billy continued. "Let me give another example. When the chariots of the Egyptians followed the Israelites into the Red Sea, which God had parted, God closed the waters of the Red Sea after the Israelites were safely on the other side. Correct?"

"Yes, that's what the Bible tells us."

"That's what Poseidon would have done, but not a heavenly Father. Didn't God love the Egyptians, too? Were they beyond God's love?"

"The Bible says that they were the enemies of Israel and that their pharaoh had disobeyed the warnings of God as revealed through Moses."

"True. But it was Pharaoh's heart that was hardened against God's commands, not the hearts of his soldiers. They had no choice but to follow Pharaoh's orders. Unlike Pharaoh, they had not heard the words of Moses. Many of the Egyptian warriors had wives and children. A God of love would not have closed the waters on them. He would have forced them back to the safety of the shore. Love should be extended not only to friends, but also to enemies. That's what Jesus taught."

George said nothing, observing Billy closely.

"Another thing," Billy added. "God killed the firstborn children of the Egyptians in the households where people had not placed blood over their doors. Why would a God of love commit such an act? The babies were innocent and deserved his protection."

Although Billy now remained silent for a few moments, George sensed that he was not finished. He was right.

Billy kept speaking. "However, I think that the story tells us that God is all-powerful and can accomplish things that are beyond belief. Perhaps the story is a way of teaching that message. After all, the drowning of obedient warriors and the killing of innocent babies doesn't seem right. It sounds more like a Greek morality tale."

George said nothing again. He was aware that Billy had read the writings of Plato, Socrates, and many other ancient scholars, as well as Greek and Roman legends. How was he to answer him? He had not read those books and now felt inadequate to the task.

The hour was late, and the boy's thoughts required considerable discussion. No simplistic answers would suffice. In the past, George had also struggled with contradictory ideas of faith. He still did. Though he knew that any venture into the unknown could end in failure, he felt that it was important to explore the boundaries of faith, as sometimes it led to new understandings. Whether or not he agreed with Billy was not the issue. George was aware that if he lost the ability to understand an honest quest to comprehend the ways of God, then he was in danger of losing the ability to examine his own faith. Billy was seeking answers to the timeless and universal mystery that humankind has sought to understand since its earliest days—the mysteries of life and God. The two concepts were inseparable.

However, before George was able to tell Billy that it was time to end their discussion, Billy continued. "The story of Abraham and Isaac bothers me, too. God instructed Abraham to take his son Isaac up into the Mountain of the Lord and sacrifice him. In the final moment before the kill, an angel stayed his hand. However, the Bible says that God knows all our thoughts, so he already knew that Abraham would obey if God truly demanded his son's life. To demand such an act of an elderly father was extremely cruel, not the type of demand a God of love would make. But a god like Zeus would make such a demand."

"Do you think that this is another story that teaches us something?" George inquired.

"Well, I would hope that if such an event actually happened, it was not commanded by God. However, it's an excellent parable to teach us about placing our trust in God."

George again remained silent and gazed thoughtfully at Billy. He was uncertain who the teacher was and who was the student. Billy, however, was uncertain how to interpret the silence. Did Mr. Meaford disapprove of his ideas, or did it simply mean that the evening had ended? Billy placed his cornet in its case and prepared to leave. He glanced at George for a moment or two but said nothing more. He felt that perhaps he had already said too much.

More and more, George realized that Billy's exceptional talent was not only in music. How was he to answer the boy's questions?

*

After Billy had departed, his footsteps no longer audible in the stairwell, George sat in his favourite chair and gazed out over Queen Street. A slight breeze was rustling the white curtains beside the open window. The hour was growing late and the street was quieting down. A westbound streetcar trundled past with only a single passenger inside it. A young couple, arm in arm, strolled along the south side of the street, oblivious to anything other than their blossoming love.

George enjoyed this hour of the evening when they day's activities had ended and the harsh light of the sun had mellowed. Night was descending softly over the street, the lamplights twinkling in the darkness. He thought of the words of the hymn by Lowrie Hofford:

> Abide with me; 'tis eventide!
> The day is past and gone:
> The shadows of evening fall;
> the night is coming on!

George pondered Billy's words. The boy's thoughts sorely challenged him. George read his Bible regularly and prayed that he might understand the contradictions contained within the Scriptures. He had also struggled with the Bible's metaphorical language, realizing that he should not interpret it literally. If he selected certain verses to justify a moral position, his conclusion at first might appear to be correct. However, in failing to include other verses, he learned that the conclusion soon became false. Unless a person considered a moral truth by examining the Bible in its entirety and taking into account the spirit of the verses, he or she might be wrong and thereby become a false prophet.

Similar to Billy, George was also aware of the differences in the view of God as revealed in the Old and New Testaments. He, too, had problems reconciling the two versions. It was as if Christ had wiped away the fear-and-damnation path to the divine and replaced it with a path of obedience to God through love. He had long ago concluded that he must consider contentious moral issues carefully and fully, and then filter them through the love and compassion that Christ taught, as opposed to accepting the preconceived interpretations of others.

In past centuries, some of the actions of the church had been cruel and sinful—the Inquisition and the Crusades, for example. Many churches had also supported slavery and had preached that it was God's divine will. George had to admit that there were verses in the Bible that supported this view. He also knew that churches had used the Bible to justify prejudice against Jews. In the modern era, humankind had no excuse for accepting these pernicious doctrines. He considered persecuting those whose views differed a sinful deed. Denying the role of women in the church was also not right. He felt that Jesus would never have approved of such actions. George was pleased that The Salvation Army viewed women as equal to men and had always allowed them to preach from the pulpit.

George knew that he was treading upon quicksand. Then he had another thought, one even more out of step with the teachings of the churches. Had the biblical writers purposefully created the contradictions within the Scripture? Was it possible that the writers of the Old and New Testaments had intended to challenge people to think, as opposed to creating a source of definitive answers to pertinent issues of faith? Was this the *true* evidence of the divine hand within the sacred texts?

Over the years, George had met many people who preferred to accept matters of faith without examining them. He knew that it made their lives easier, as thinking, questioning, and contemplating were troubling. However, doing these things had led George to a more meaningful understanding of God. He was unable to accept that God simply laid down laws that people must unquestionably obey because of the fear of judgment and condemnation. "Fire and brimstone" theology had no relevance for him.

God was love.

George knew that if he and Vangie had a child and laid down the law to the child, demanding obedience through fear, then they would eventually lose the child. But if they guided the child through love, the love would remain in the child's heart forever—even unto eternity. George felt that this was also true of his heavenly Father.

When George listened to his inner voice, he remembered these words in the book of Galatians 5:22—"The fruit of the spirit is love, joy, peace, long-suffering, kindness, gentleness, goodness, and faith." When he heard his inner voice express these sentiments, he believed it to be the voice of God. It was during these moments that his faith came alive and he caught a glimpse of the divine. Thoughts that harboured envy, hate, condemnation, judgment, and pettiness were of his lower nature; these were not the voice of God.

Prejudice against Jews was wrong. Even Billy knew this. Then he thought of the attitude held by many that the Chinese were capable of operating only restaurants and laundries, and that black people were intended to be household servants. Then he thought about the terrible prejudices that Protestants and Catholics harboured toward each other. Surely, a God of love would never approve of such narrow-minded behaviour.

Prior to talking with Billy, George had never heard anyone question whether or not God loved the ancient Egyptians, both soldiers and infants. The idea was new to George. He admitted that it deserved consideration.

However, dare he share his thoughts and doubts with Billy?

Having struggled for years to understand the mysteries of God, George still struggled. Sometimes he gained insight, and at other times, he was baffled. He knew that he would never truly comprehend a God who was able to create a universe. It was far beyond the capabilities of the human mind. However, he felt that it was important that he seek truth and understanding and then live his life according to these truths. This was what Billy was trying to do, as well.

As George sauntered down the hallway to the bedroom, he felt inadequate to satisfactorily answer Billy's questions, but he was convinced that he should not discourage him from seeking spiritual understanding.

He also knew that his bond with Billy was unique and that it extended far beyond the love of music they shared.

*

The days grew shorter. October was ending. The nights became increasingly chilly. Trees on Draper Street shed their leaves. Lights in the house windows glowed earlier. One evening, Grandmother Mercer and Emmy were busy in the kitchen preparing dinner when Billy returned home from work. They glanced up as he walked in the door. Grandmother gazed at Billy and saw that he was carrying an apple pie. His face was flushed with excitement as he placed the pie on the table, unwrapped his wool scarf from around his neck, and unbuttoned his coat. He tossed both articles of clothing on a kitchen chair, but they fell haphazardly to the floor. Before his mother had a chance to tell him to go hang them on the peg on the back porch, Billy blurted out, "Guess what?" Before his grandmother or mother replied, he added, "Mrs. McMillan gave me a raise in pay."

"You're a hard worker," his grandmother replied. "We're proud of you."

"That's not the best news. I won't be delivering groceries anymore. I'm to work behind the counter, serving the customers. Mrs. McMillan gave me an arithmetic test, which was ridiculously easy, and said I would be able to manage the money just fine."

"That's great news."

"There's more news. I asked Mrs. McMillan if Mary could have my old job and deliver grocery orders. I told her that Mary is thirteen and can work after school and all day Saturday. She told me that she had never hired a girl to deliver groceries."

"What did Mrs. McMillan finally decide?" Grandmother Mercer inquired.

"She thought about it for a few moments and then said she supposed a woman can do any job that a man can do. She said that if Mary wants the job, it's hers."

"Good for Mrs. McMillan," Grandmother said.

"I stopped at Mrs. Greenberg's on my way down the street and told her the great news. She gave me the pie to celebrate my promotion, and she called me 'her Billy.'"

"Your promotion's wonderful," his mother said.

"So's the pie," his grandmother added.

Billy thought, *Working in the store, I'll see more of Jenny.*

*

A small notation in *The War Cry* of November 28 mentioned the needs of the Toronto Staff Band. George Meaford read the article carefully. It stated that a great improvement had been noticeable in the playing of the band and that a set of new trombones would make a decidedly greater improvement to the instrumentation.

Being an accomplished trombone player, plus the bandmaster of the Queen Street Corps, George decided to apply for admission to the band. Besides, a new trombone would be wonderful.

However, it still bothered George that he had found no satisfactory way to answer Billy's spiritual questions.

*

Christmas of 1907 produced many happy memories. The Mercer children performed their Christmas Extravaganza again to everyone's delight, including George and Vangie Meaford, whom they had invited to the event. When George heard the girls perform on their instruments, he was amazed at their progress, especially Bess's.

He said, "I wish the girls could join the junior band at the corps. Unfortunately, they only allow boys to participate."

A short time after, Frank spoke privately to George Meaford.

"I am grateful that you have been tutoring Billy. As his uncle, I would like to help him too. Is it all right with you if I pay so that Billy can also receive cornet lessons from a professional teacher? I've paid off my mortgage on the house here on Draper Street, and have a few more funds at my disposal."

George was offended at first, but after considering he replied, "Certainly.

We should do what's right for Billy. He has great talent. However, I hope that he'll continue to receive lessons from me."

"Certainly, George. I never meant it to be any other way."

*

At the conclusion of New Year's, the cruel hand of winter 1908 gripped the land. Though the residents of the city grumbled about the bitter Arctic winds, in due order the miracle of spring finally arrived.

The final week of May, a member of the band of the Queen Street Citadel was to marry a woman who attended the Lippincott Citadel Corps. It was to be the "Hallelujah" wedding of Bandsman Samuel Easton to Sister Lily Langworthe. Frank was to be the best man, and the officer who was to perform the ceremony had been the Divisional Commander in Nunhead when George Meaford and Samuel Easton had been boys. Samuel had heard Billy play and requested that he perform a cornet solo at the event. Mrs. McMillan agreed to allow Billy the time off from work.

Before the ceremony, the Lippincott Band performed several selections outside the Lippincott Street Hall and then proceeded to take their places inside, on the platform in the sanctuary. Billy opened the ceremony with his solo, along with band accompaniment. Next, the bride appeared, and the band played "The Wedding March," after which George left his seat in the band and went to the altar to "stand" for the groom as the officer solemnly read the vows.

At the conclusion of the wedding ceremony, the couple knelt at the mercy seat to consecrate their marriage. Every Salvation Army church contained a mercy seat. It was placed at the front of the sanctuary, near the pulpit. Usually it was a bench-like structure, but in some instances it was simply a few chairs. It was where sinners knelt to confess their sins. In the book of Exodus, Chapter 25, God gave instructions to the Israelites for constructing the Ark of the Covenant. He commanded them, "Make a mercy seat of pure gold. … I will commune with thee from the mercy seat."

In services, when the preacher gave an altar call, those who wished to confess their sins and be saved came forward and knelt at the mercy seat. The act of confession held deep spiritual significance for Salvationists.

When the newly married couple prayed at the mercy seat, they were expressing their faith in a typical Salvation Army manner.

At the reception following the wedding, many guests passed favourable comments about Billy's solo. It was the first time that members of the Lippincott Corps had heard him play, and they were amazed at the professionalism evident in a boy so young.

*

Over the summer, Billy grew several inches in height; many people expressed surprise when they learned his age. In addition, they noticed that his demeanour and speech were exceptionally mature. Some members of the congregation at Queen Street Citadel questioned why he was not playing in the Queen Street Senior Band. He certainly looked and acted like an adult. Not wishing to create an awkward situation, George simply told them that despite appearances, Billy was too young.

However, George had approached the Corps Officer several times about Billy's entering the senior band. It created tension between the two men. George admired and respected Bramwell Sendry. He enjoyed his company and considered him a good friend. He feared that a disagreement over Billy might mar their relationship.

Captain Sendry, though only in his mid-thirties, acted and thought like a much older man. His flaming red hair caused him to stand out in a crowd. Bramwell was aware that the younger members of the corps referred to him as Captain Red. The adults smiled when they heard the children use the nickname, as they considered it a term of endearment. However, Captain Sendry was highly sensitive about any situation that might bring ridicule upon him. He was a stickler for details and continually insisted that everything at the corps be conducted according to the *Orders and Regulations of The Salvation Army*." This sometimes created conflict when he dealt with the young, who were perpetually seeking ways to push the boundaries of "proper" behaviour.

Captain Sendry respected George Meaford. He had rarely encountered a man who better demonstrated Christian faith in his daily life. Though Bramwell was the Corps Officer, at times he felt that George was better suited to the task. This bothered him and created conflict within him, as it gave him a feeling that he was inadequate to meet the demands of his calling. His worst fear was that he might act defensively if George presented ideas that were counter to his own.

George also felt conflicted. He felt unable to delay the decision of whether or not to allow Billy into the senior band. He realized that Billy had never been to the mercy seat, so he was aware that he must handle the situation with great care.

*

One evening after Billy's lesson at George's flat above Mitchell's Hardware Store, George broached the topic. "Billy, would you like to play in the senior band?" The expression on the boy's face gave him his answer, so he continued.

"Your ability is not in question, but there's a problem," George said.

"Is it because I have not knelt at the mercy seat?"

George nodded his head. "Captain Sendry believes that only those who have been 'saved' can join the band."

"Saved from what? A runaway horse?" Billy said with a slight grin, thinking of what he had said to his uncle Bill in front of the Oak Leaf Ale House.

George smiled, as he knew that Billy was verbally toying with him.

"You know what I mean. You have never been to the mercy seat."

"I know, Mr. Meaford," Billy replied, now becoming serious. "I've given the matter considerable thought."

"And what have you concluded?"

"For me to go to the mercy seat would simply be a public demonstration of what I already believe."

"Is this wrong?"

"No. I think it's the right thing to do if a person believes that it helps him spiritually."

"And what do you believe?"

"I think that my kneeling at the mercy seat is not as important as trying to live my life according to what the mercy seat represents."

"What do you think it represents?"

"The Beatitudes sum it up. But also, I should seek daily to understand

God and attempt to discover what he wishes me to do with my life. For some, kneeling at the mercy seat might be a moment when God is revealed to them. However, for me, I see the path to understanding God as a continuing journey of contemplation, not a moment of instant revelation, such as kneeling at the mercy seat."

Billy paused and then added, "I know that I should also try to turn the other cheek when someone picks a fight with me, although I admit I have a tough time doing it. My fists are usually faster than my tongue."

George smiled, appreciating Billy's honesty. However, he considered the lad's tongue every bit as fast as his fists, perhaps even faster, and his way of explaining his beliefs very mature. Warily, as he was mindful of Billy's intellect, he attempted to explain the concept of the mercy seat according to the Army's teachings.

"In the Army, if a person kneels at the mercy seat, we say that the person has given his or her heart to Jesus," George said.

"I understand this, Mr. Meaford, but these words are a metaphorical way of expressing what I have already done."

George hesitated, uncertain how to better explain the mercy seat.

Before he was able to gather his thoughts, Billy continued. "There's something else that bothers me about going to the mercy seat."

"What's that?"

"It seems wrong for me to go to the mercy seat simply because others consider it the right thing to do. From what I've read in the Bible, Jesus had little time for those who quoted the sacred laws and performed rituals in the temple without regard for their meaning. For me, kneeling at the mercy seat would simply be a ritual."

George now remained silent, gazing at Billy, sensing that he was not finished speaking.

"When I was a boy in Comstock," Billy went on, "the school teacher told me that I had no right to express my personal ideas. The Reverend Wilmot said that I had no business questioning the meaning of the stories in the Bible. Only he had the right to do that, he told me. However, in my quiet moments, I try to understand all the ideas that I have heard, read, and been taught. I also know that I must not force my ideas on others or expect others to try to find their way to God in the same way I have. Everyone must find their own way. The important thing is that they seek an understanding of God that respects others and reflects the love that Jesus taught.

"However, there's a problem. If I express these ideas aloud, it leads to angry discourse and sometimes hostility. However, when I express my faith through music, people listen. At first, they may simply respond to the beauty of the melody, but later, as they learn the message of the music, they often think about the ideas contained within it. I believe that if I am able to hear the voice of God through sacred music, then perhaps others can, too."

Billy's words struck a chord in George. George listened carefully as the man within the boy continued.

"I think that God will judge me by what I do, not by the rituals I perform in the church. Actually, even going to church can become a mere ritual if a person does not practise the teachings he or she hears. It's how I live my life that's important. As you told me, Mr. Meaford, actions are more important than words."

George's words had come back to haunt him. However, he was forced to admit that he did indeed believe that actions spoke louder than words.

Silence descended into the room.

Billy observed his mentor closely, fearing that he had revealed too much of his inner thinking. He had never truly shared his ideas with anyone, but Mr. Meaford was not *just* anyone, in Billy's eyes. He had never intended to tell Mr. Meaford how he felt. He admitted that this "Army stuff" was new to him, and perhaps he did not fully understand it. George Meaford was a man he admired, and Billy wanted to be like him.

Watching Mr. Meaford closely, Billy feared he would censor him for being so outspoken or tell him that his ideas were nonsense. He was aware that words were not as important as actions, but when they were expressed aloud, words did indeed have power.

Realizing that Billy was staring at him, and observing the serious expression on the boy's face, George smiled to reassure him. Placing his hand on Billy's shoulder, he squeezed it gently and said, "I appreciate your honesty. Let me discuss your ideas with Captain Sendry."

"I don't think the Captain will approve of my ideas."

"Perhaps, but don't worry. I'll do my best to make him understand how you feel."

Changing the subject, George said, "You played the music well tonight. It was a difficult composition, but you mastered it."

"Do I get to join the senior band?"

"Like I said, let me talk to Captain Sendry."

*

After Billy departed, George thought about Billy's words. The idea of expressing faith through example and through music was akin to his own notions. George had learned to listen to his inner voice, and his inner voice told him that Billy was on the true path toward understanding. Slowly, he realized that Billy had already found the answers to some of his own questions. The lad might question whether or not the stories in the Bible actually occurred, but it was clear that he understood and accepted the lessons that they taught. Besides, George knew it was true that some Christians obeyed Christ's teaching with their lips, not their hearts. These people could quote Bible verses at length, but they failed to understand the lessons contained within them.

George knew that Billy would never be dearer to his heart than he was on this warm evening in August.

*

Dorothea Mercer had observed Billy's musical progress and now approved of his playing his cornet in the junior band at the corps. Like Billy, she considered the cornet to be a trumpet. Though she remained an Anglican at heart, she reluctantly admitted that she enjoyed the Army services, despite their boisterous style. Besides, it was pleasant to chat with the handsome Mr. Gerald Hutchinson after the services. She enjoyed his company and was aware that he liked conversing with her, too.

August was drawing to a close. Though it remained summer on the calendar, the Labour Day weekend was approaching, and everyone in Toronto knew that the delights of the season of hot weather were ending. Early on the Thursday morning prior to Labour Day, there was a slight chill in the morning air as Bess and Grandmother Mercer strolled toward Queen Street. Grandmother needed to shop for a few articles the family needed. Emmy was at the home on Draper Street baking bread, the younger girls having departed the house earlier with their friends. Billy and Phil were at work, and Zack was moping around the house being a nuisance.

As Grandmother entered Mr. Hutchinson's butcher shop, her shopping basket already filled with fresh fruits and vegetables, she glanced up and smiled at the butcher. He glanced disapprovingly at Bess, who was kicking the sawdust on the floor with her shoe as she gawked at the display of meat in the counter. She wriggled her nose with disgust as she gazed at the headless chickens and geese hanging from the large iron rod behind Mr. Hutchinson's counter. The butcher had wrapped waxed paper around the bloody ends of the necks, a few drops of blood dripping to the floor. Bess wandered outside the shop to pet a dog that was reclining on the sidewalk beside the curb.

"Good morning, Mrs. Dorothea. What can I get for you today?"

"Good morning, Mr. Gerald." When they were alone, they used each other's given names, but they still maintained a degree of formality by adding the appropriate titles. However, they fooled no one. Their friends were aware that they were attracted to each other. There was no cruel gossip, as they were both unattached, mature adults. But there was gossip nonetheless.

When Bess and her grandmother departed the shop for the homeward journey, Dorothea was smiling, as she had accepted an invitation to accompany Gerald for a stroll along Queen Street on the following Sunday afternoon.

On one occasion, Gerald Hutchinson explained to Grandmother Mercer, "I immigrated to Canada from a small village in Yorkshire in 1890, and through hard work I've prospered. My dear wife, Martha, laboured alongside me to build the business. It is because of her labours that Hutchinson's Butcher Shop is now successful."

Grandmother Mercer replied, "You have many loyal customers."

"Thankfully, that's true. With the income from the shop, my wife and I purchased a fine home, a short distance north of Queen Street on Palmerston Boulevard. Martha loved the house and worked hard to make it a home. Consumption infected her lungs, and after three painful years, she succumbed to the disease."

"I'm sorry to hear about your wife."

Gerald paused, smiled slightly, and gazed at Dorothea.

In an effort to cheer him, she said, "I'm certain that a few widows are eyeing you."

"Perhaps, but the eye that interests me the most is yours."

*

When Sunday afternoon arrived—on the Labour Day weekend, September 6—Gerald appeared at the door of the Mercer home on Draper Street. He had shined his shoes carefully. His suit was pressed, and his shirt collar was freshly laundered. There was no evidence that he was a widower, that there was no woman in his house. When Zack opened the door, Mr. Hutchinson looked as well groomed and anxious as a teenager on his first date with a new girl.

Zack blurted out in a loud voice, "Grandmother, your boyfriend's here." Mr. Hutchinson blushed like a schoolboy.

Escaping the giggles and surreptitious glances of the children, Dorothea and Gerald departed the house, walking north toward Queen Street. The stores were closed for the Sabbath, but as it was a pleasantly warm afternoon, many strollers were taking advantage of the sunny weather to window-shop and greet neighbours.

The women who frequented Gerald Hutchinson's butcher shop were aware of his sense of humour. He often told corny jokes to his customers, and though he remembered the jokes expertly, he often forgot how many times he inflicted the same one on the same person.

His favourite story went like this: "Did you hear about the butcher who backed into the meat grinder? He got a little 'behind' in his orders."

On this sun-filled September afternoon, Gerald inflicted several more of his jokes on Grandmother Mercer.

"Do you know how they get the water into a watermelon? They plant them in the spring."

Next he asked her, "Did you hear about the cross-eyed teacher? She was unable to control her pupils."

Dorothea Mercer laughed politely at the butcher's corny jokes as the two strolled together along Queen Street. Gerald spoke to many people who passed, and Dorothea nodded to them regally, her large-brimmed hat tipping imperiously each time she acknowledged a greeting. When they reached the southern boundary of the grounds of Trinity College on Queen Street, they entered through the impressive gates that had been erected in 1903, five years earlier. The large pillars and wrought-iron railings created a grand entranceway to the college.

Entrance gates of Trinity College on Queen Street at the north end of Strachan Avenue. The Tower of Trinity College is evident at the head of the pathway. Today, the gates lead into Trinity Bellwoods Park. *City of Toronto Archives, Fonds 1548, Item 20559*

Gazing north up Strachan Avenue toward Queen Street and the gates of Trinity College, c. 1910. Sadly, the city demolished the historic building in 1956. Today, Trinity College grounds survive as Trinity Bellwoods Park. Fortunately, the great gate that Dorothea and Gerald passed through in September 1908 still exists on Queen Street. Note the empty fields and the

plank sidewalks. Today, Strachan Avenue is no longer in direct line with the gates. It was moved slightly to the west of them. *City of Toronto Archives, Series 072, SS 052, Item 0170*

They wandered amid the mature trees and spacious grounds where Garrison Creek quietly gurgled as it meandered southward through a small valley before eventually crossing Queen Street on its way toward the lake. They admired the impressive Gothic Revival college building with its ornate brickwork, turrets, and pinnacles.

The afternoon sun was angling toward the west as they departed from the Trinity College campus. Dorothea told Gerald, "It's a pity that the afternoon has passed so quickly."

"True! Good times always fly by."

"I was hoping that we had time to see the new public library they're building further west of here, near Lisgar Street."

"Oh, come on! We'll make time. It's only a few more blocks."

Walking a little faster, they arrived at Lisgar and Queen streets.

Dorothea told Gerald, "Even though the new library is under construction, I can see that it's going to be a handsome building. I like its compact classical design and impressive doorway, which is already in place. I read that Andrew Carnegie, the American iron magnate, donated the twenty-five thousand dollars to construct it."

Library on Queen Street near Lisgar Street, which opened in 1909. The building remains on Queen Street today, but it is no longer a functioning library. *Toronto Public Library Collection, T 30609*

Dorothea continued, "When it opens next year, I want to bring my grandson Billy here and get him a library card. He reads every book I buy for him, but this library will expand his world of reading even more. He's bright, understands what he reads, and thinks about the information. Sometimes I don't understand his ideas. But I approve of his questioning everything. I've seen many bright minds wasted by accepting everything at face value. It's those who question things that make new discoveries."

"Aye, Billy is indeed bright. He's an excellent cornet player. He plays well enough to be in the senior band."

"Then why isn't he?"

"I don't know."

Dorothea glanced at Gerald with a raised eyebrow. He did not catch the ironic nature of his statement, what with her having had just told him about those who fail to question things.

"Perhaps you'd better find out," she said.

*

George Meaford knew it was imperative that he speak to Captain Sendry about Billy. George was fond of the Captain, and even though the man was prickly at times, he never doubted his devotion to his ministry. To ignore Bram's opinions was not an option. George knew that somehow he must reach out and attempt to kindle understanding in his heart.

Following an unusually long Sunday evening prayer meeting, the hour was late. The Captain had finished putting away the hymn books and was entering his office at the rear of the building when George approached him.

"Captain, may I have a word with you?"

"Certainly, George," he replied wearily. It had been a long day. "What's on your mind?" They walked into the Captain's office together.

"I'd like to discuss Billy Mercer."

"What's the lad done now?" he replied with a forced grin.

George smiled. It was true that Billy was often at the bottom of some mischief or other, and he gave the Captain a knowing smile as he pulled out a chair and sat down. Captain Sendry seated himself behind his desk, waiting for George to speak.

"I know Bill is only fourteen, but he's tall for his age and plays the cornet like a mature bandsman. I think it's time that we considered allowing him into the senior band."

It was obvious that the request had not really taken the Captain by surprise, as they had discussed the matter previously. He paused, stroked his chin, and gazed intently at George. For an awkward moment or two, the men sat in silence. The Captain continued to rub his chin as he considered his answer.

Finally, he said, "I've not changed my mind. I think he's too young. The demands of Army banding are heavy, and I think a lad his age isn't ready. He should be sixteen to play in the senior band. Besides, I don't think he plays all that well."

"Captain, you're a good man with a good heart and a fine brain, but you've a tin ear," George replied with a teasing grin. "The boy is the finest player, for his age, in the entire city."

The Captain returned George's smile and then added, "Aye, he's good, I suppose, *for his age.* Give him a few years to mature."

"Captain, I'm suggesting that his musical ability and maturity are already at a level that qualifies him for the senior band."

"Well, I bow to your opinion about the boy's musical abilities," he replied. "You're the bandmaster. But there's a problem. The boy's never knelt at the mercy seat. I'm not certain that he is even saved. He shouldn't be playing in the junior band, ne'er mind the senior."

"Be that as it may, Captain, the lad lives his life as a Christian. Going forward to the mercy seat isn't the only way to be saved. I do not feel comfortable standing in judgment of him because he's never been to the mercy seat."

"I understand how you feel, but Army regulations state that he must be saved. That means kneeling at the mercy seat."

"I believe you're interpreting the regulation a little too narrowly. Kneeling at the mercy seat is an act of penitence, that's true, but it's better not to kneel and believe than to kneel and not believe."

"I appreciate your opinion, George. But the ideal we seek is that he kneel and also believe. It's not an either–or situation."

Again, the two men sat in silence. Other than the quiet ticking of the clock on the bookshelf, there were no other ambient sounds. The church's sanctuary was empty, and at this hour on a Sunday night the street outside was quiet. The squeaking of the Captain's chair when he leaned to place his elbows on the desk finally broke the silence.

"George, I respect your viewpoint. There's some truth to your argument, but I cannot ignore regulations. Billy must wait until he is older. However, if he goes to the mercy seat, I might reconsider."

"I respect your viewpoint, too, Bram, but if we make Billy wait, I fear we'll lose him."

Again there was an awkward silence.

"Let me suggest a compromise," the Captain said. "Do you think that Billy would be content with performing solos with the senior band, including open-air services and special concerts?"

"But he'd remain in the junior band. Right?"

"Yes."

"Well, it's a thought."

"Remember, he's only fourteen."

"True, but it's only delaying the inevitable. Billy is unlikely to go to the mercy seat. At some point, if you deny him entry to the senior band, I feel it's only fair to tell him why."

"I suppose. But remember that he has plenty of time to change his mind. Meanwhile, I'll think the matter over, and we'll talk again tomorrow night."

"That's a good idea. Sleep on it, Bram. When we meet again, I wish to make a confession to you."

Bram's eyes narrowed as he wondered what George was referring to. Then the Captain added his final comment. "I repeat. Billy's only fourteen."

"Yes, fourteen—going on forty."

*

The following evening, the two men met again in the Captain's office at the Citadel. George sensed that Bram was tense, as his jaw was jutting out, his eyebrows were furrowed deeply, and a determined look had seized his face.

"I suppose you haven't changed your mind, Bram," George began.

"I've given the matter serious thought and prayed about it. I cannot permit Billy to enter the senior band unless he kneels at the mercy seat."

George gazed down at the officer's desk. Bram had arranged everything immaculately, everything in its place, neat and orderly. George lowered his eyes and drummed his fingers on the desktop. Then, after a brief pause, he looked up at Bram. "Well, Bram, I wish you to consider carefully what I'm about to tell you. You may wish to find a new bandmaster."

"What on earth do you mean?"

"Similar to Billy, I've never knelt at the mercy seat."

"Never?"

"I was raised in a Salvation Army home. I absorbed my faith from my parents. As I matured, I considered spiritual matters carefully. Finding my way to God was no easy task. There was no eureka moment for me, such as kneeling at the mercy seat. Perhaps there were a few mini-eureka moments, but no truly defining moment. God spoke to me within my home, through the words of my parents and through my reading. God also spoke to me through music. For me, the path toward an understanding of the mystery of God was a sustained and thought-provoking journey."

Bramwell gazed intently at George as he spoke. "My search to understand God still continues, and I believe it's a journey that'll never end. At times, I doubted the existence of God. However, just because I'm unable to prove empirically that God exists, I never felt that I could simply dismiss his existence. That would be akin to a scientist's dismissing a problem he cannot solve by simply saying that the problem doesn't exist. It's intellectually lazy."

There was an awkward pause before George spoke again. "Fortunately for me, I continued to explore the God mystery. Slowly, my faith was strengthened by an inner voice, the revelations I received during my prayer sessions and from my constant questioning, not by arbitrary-seeming edicts delivered by others. Slowly, the revelations guided my life. I know I'll never prove the existence of God through intellectualization and that at some point I must accept certain things on faith. But blind faith, never questioning one's beliefs, is inexcusable. Through the years, many well-accepted beliefs have been proven to be clearly wrong. They were often based on interpreting the Bible too narrowly. I feel that I've slowly learned how my Creator wishes me to live. As long as I possess breath, I'll continue to explore the God mystery."

"I find your thoughts somewhat confusing and contradictory."

"I understand. Pondering the mystery of life is indeed frustrating. However, the mystery of life is the mystery of creation, and the mystery of creation is the mystery of God."

"That sounds like very convoluted reasoning."

"Perhaps. The search for the divine is not easy. I admit that it's easier to accept the edicts and rules of others, but God has given us an intellect for a reason. We must use it!"

"As a clergyman, I have always tried to obey the Bible's teachings and follow the rules of The Salvation Army."

"That's excellent Bram, as far as it goes. But I am now going to ask you to consider a problem that concerns me personally. It cannot be solved by biblical quotes and examining the *Orders and Regulations* of the Army."

The expression on Bram's face registered his puzzlement and concern.

"Bram, because I've never knelt at the mercy seat, do you consider me 'saved'?"

Bram hesitated, unsure how to respond, so George decided to explain further.

"If a person feels the need to kneel at the mercy seat, then it's the right thing for that person to do. However, I believe that the act of kneeling isn't as important as the meaning behind the ritual. I think that the same is true for Holy Communion in other churches. If a person feels that Communion helps in his or her spiritual life, then it's proper. However, to participate in the Communion simply as a ritual is of dubious value. The same is true of the mercy seat."

Bram remained silent and gazed intently at George. The ideas his friend presented were contrary to everything he believed. Yet how could he doubt George's faith? He was the most sincere and dedicated Christian he had ever met. The ensuing silence between the two men hung in the air.

George's voice was soft as he again spoke. "Do you wish me to relinquish my leadership of the band?"

Without hesitation, Bram replied, "No, of course not. You're a fine Christian."

"Then we have arrived at an impasse. I can remain bandmaster without having knelt at the mercy seat, but Billy cannot play in the senior band without kneeling."

"I realize it seems contradictory, but that is how it must be."

"Will you explain this to Billy?"

"No, George, not at this time."

*

The next week, there was another incident involving the *Orders and Regulations* of The Salvation Army. Captain Sendry caught two members of the junior band smoking cigarettes in the laneway behind the citadel. He immediately expelled them from the junior band. When George heard about the incident, he visited Captain Sendry at the Officer's Quarters (the rectory), and they sat down over tea to chat about the situation.

"Captain, I wonder if perhaps we've been a little too harsh with the two boys caught smoking."

"The Army rules are clear. Boys who play in the band must refrain from smoking. They promised to do so when they signed their junior band commissions. Need I get my copy of the regulations to show you?"

"There's no need. I'm aware of the rules."

"Then the matter's closed."

"Perhaps it's closed in a manner that neither one of us wishes."

"What do you mean?"

"If those two lads are not permitted to play in the band, they'll stop attending Sunday school and, of course, the band practices. We'll lose them. Would it not be better to devise a suitable punishment, practise what Christ taught, and forgive them? Boys their age often try to smoke a cigarette. They're curious and try to imitate the older boys. It's not as if they committed a sin. They simple failed to obey a regulation."

"Disobeying a regulation is a sin."

"I don't remember Christ saying that."

"Don't play with words, George. You know that what the boys did was wrong. It's a sin. I've told them that in Sunday school many times."

"Surely you don't think they smoked the cigarettes in defiance of you?"

"Well, remember the number of times I've preached against the sin of smoking."

"I've also heard you pray, 'Forgive us our trespasses as we forgive those who trespass against us.'"

Captain Sendry was troubled. He was unaccustomed to having his words questioned, especially by someone he respected as highly as George Meaford.

"I am not questioning your faith, Bram, and I know you have the best interests of the lads at heart."

But Captain Sendry's heart was hardened. "I'm sorry, George. I must act as my conscience tells me. I cannot have smokers in the junior band. It's a bad example for the other lads."

George departed from Captain Sendry's house that night heavy of heart. Unfortunately, he was correct. The two boys never again darkened the doors of the Queen Street Citadel. They were lost to the Army forever.

*

Captain Sendry remained troubled over his refusal to allow Billy to enter the senior band. The words of George Meaford had upset his view of spiritual matters, and as he took his ministry seriously, he wanted to be certain that he had made the correct decision. One evening he saw Billy departing after junior band practice and summoned him into his office.

"Billy," the Captain began, "I've given much thought to Bandmaster Meaford's proposal that you be allowed to enter the senior band. It pains me to refuse his request, but I feel that you are not sufficiently mature to handle the responsibilities of such a position."

"I want to play in the senior band, but if you believe that it is not right for me, then I respect your decision."

The Captain gazed at Billy's youthful countenance and his heart bled for the boy, but deep in his heart he remained unsure of the boy's spiritual maturity. However, the Captain didn't wish to appear obstinate. *If only Billy would go to the mercy seat,* he thought.

Finally, in exasperation, he exclaimed, "Why won't you kneel at the mercy seat?"

Billy gazed directly into the eyes of his pastor, his voice soft as he replied, "I understand why you wish me to kneel. But the rituals of faith are only important if they possess meaning for the person performing them."

"I understand your intent, Billy, but God communes with us at the mercy seat."

"True, but God can commune with me in almost every aspect of my life. I hear him talking to me when I make decisions, when I interact with others, and when I seek him in quiet moments of reflection."

Captain Sendry was disappointed, but he remained convinced that Billy should kneel at the mercy seat. Upon further reflection, he wondered if the lad's ideas were a result of his conversations with George Meaford. It was unlikely that a boy Billy's age would have arrived at such conclusions on his own. However, sensing that Billy was unlikely to change his mind, he smiled gently at him and wished him a good night.

After Billy had departed, the Captain sat in his chair behind his desk and pondered the conversation. He felt that he had arrived at the right decision about Billy's entering the senior band, but in his heart he remained troubled.

*

With the departure of September, autumn transformed the greenery of summer into the golden hues. The blue smoke of curbside fires drifted lazily in the air on warm afternoons, the pleasant odour permeating the autumn haze. The small bonfires provided an excuse for neighbours to gather and chat about their children or the state of local affairs.

Almost every home throughout Toronto possessed a small garden that supplied the needs of the kitchen table. In the fall of the year, they burnt the dead twigs and leaves from these gardens in backyard fires. Children gathered around to watch the flames lick hungrily upward, devouring the dry leaves with a pleasing crackling noise. They ignited similar fires in the chill of evening to roast marshmallows or cook wieners on a stick. The end of summer was certainly not without its rewards and pleasures.

In the days ahead, the sunshine became weaker, and soon the dark season sullenly draped itself across the city. As warmth faded, pewter skies appeared. Heavy clouds billowed expansively and more frequently as the winds of winter gained strength.

*

Christmas of 1908, as in previous years, was a humble affair for the Mercer family. It was their third festive season in Canada, and the occasion became another treasured event in their lives. They participated in the richness of the corps activities—a Christmas supper, several musical festivals, and sacred carol services.

Then, in what appeared to be a fleeting moment, New Year's Eve and the watch-night service arrived and disappeared.

The year 1909 descended onto the vast dominion.

Chapter Four

On the first day of the New Year, a story about Mrs. Greenberg circulated among the residents of Draper Street. As previously mentioned, she was a stout woman. On New Year's Eve, a cup of tea in her hand, she sat down on her favourite armchair beside the stove. Unaware that her cat was sleeping on its cushion, she crushed it to death. When the neighbours heard about the incident, one of them teasingly said that she had devoured the cat's nine lives in a single "sitting."

Though Mrs. Greenberg was horrified, the neighbours remained amused. In the days ahead, when retelling the story, they added unkind but humorous details. They told the postman that the accident had flattened the cat so successfully that Mrs. Greenberg had placed a postage stamp on it and slipped it into a mailbox to send it overseas.

"The cat had been a foreign species," they said, "and she wanted to return it to its homeland for burial." By the end of the week, they finally buried the story as well.

*

In the second week of January, overnight, the temperatures dropped drastically, and the first major snowfall of the year silently blanketed the city. The Mercer family awakened at morning's first light to peer through their frosted kitchen window at the bleak boreal landscape. The storm had buried their back garden, the tops of the fence posts, and the roof of the toolshed, which were all adorned with snowy hats. To the north, a mantle of white decorated the storefronts along Queen Street. To the west, the storm dusted the gates of Trinity College, draping winter magic across the mature trees within the spacious grounds.

Gates of Trinity College on Queen Street in winter, the tower of Trinity College capped in white. *City of Toronto Archives, Fonds 1244, Item 1516*

*

Although it was Phil's third winter in his adopted homeland, the extreme cold of the Canadian landscape continued to surprise him. He had experienced snow in Comstock, but the amounts had been small compared to Canada's, where bone-chilling temperatures gripped the land.

Early each morning, before the children rose from their beds, his first task of the day was lighting the fire in the stove in the kitchen. Next, he shovelled the walkway. He chatted with neighbours who were similarly clearing pathways from their doors to the sidewalk. The scraping noises of the wooden shovels against the frozen earth and stone walkways filled the frigid air.

When Phil returned inside the house, Emmy had breakfast waiting for him. He ate and then departed for work. The Toronto Silver Plate Company had been his place of employment now for the past two and a half years. The training and skills he had acquired in Comstock allowed him to earn a modest income. However, he was concerned. There were rumours that the company would soon be laying off workers if customers' orders did not increase in the months ahead. As Phil was one of the newer employees, he feared he might lose his job.

Despite the harshness of the climate, activities within the snug Army Hall on Queen Street continued throughout the winter. Phil and Emmy attended services each week, along with Grandmother Mercer. Billy and Zack went to the junior band practices each week, as well. Mary, Ruth, and Bess practised their instruments at home whenever time permitted.

*

During the winter months, George Meaford continued to improve the skills of the Queen Street bandsmen. He told Vangie, "Being bandmaster, I miss playing in the band, but sometimes playing trombone solos in the musical concerts helps compensate."

"It's good that you play sometimes," Vangie replied. "Billy takes such delight in listening to you. He dreams of one day performing as well as you do."

George grinned, "He already does. During the past few months, Billy has performed some excellent solos in the musical services, but he's less aware of his musical accomplishments than he is of his failures. No matter how well he plays, he yearns to be better."

"Yes, that's Billy, all right."

Changing the subject, George said, "With the arrival of spring, the home-construction trade is swinging into high gear in the city. Because so many immigrants are arriving daily, there's a constant need for new housing. Because of this, builders are increasingly expanding into the area above the Davenport Road hill."

"Yes, I've heard you say this before."

Gazing north on Bathurst Street toward Davenport Road in 1913. The single streetcar track is visible on the left-hand side of the street, even though it is partially covered in mud. The tracks end at Davenport, and there is only a mud road and plank sidewalk ascending the hill toward St. Clair. *City of Toronto Archives, Fonds 1244, Item 7366*

St. Clair Avenue, looking west from near Yonge Street, c. 1909. The photo illustrates the rural qualities of the landscape above the Davenport Road hill, even near Yonge Street. *City of Toronto Archives, Series 0372, Item 0022*

"The isolation of the area above the hill around Dufferin Street makes the price of land up there cheap. People refer to the area as Muddy Earlscourt, because the soil is heavy clay and drainage is poor."

"A neighbour told me that in Earlscourt, in rainy weather in the spring or fall, there're endless pools of muddy water. Although the area is mostly empty fields, orchards, and farmland, as you say, the number of houses is increasing."

"Yes, and I'm finding more and more work up there. Despite no sewers, water lines, or electricity, the district is a magnet for those who live in the crowded downtown. Another attraction is that the city has not yet imposed building codes. St. Clair Avenue, its main street, is unpaved, although a few shops have appeared near Dufferin Street, as well as at Oakwood Avenue."

"It's a long way to journey up there. The closest streetcar line is from below the hill at Dovercourt Road and Van Horne Avenue. To reach Earlscourt, people walk from there."

"True."

"At the Queen Street Corps, there's a rumour circulating that the Army will be opening an outpost in the area."

"I always find the term *outpost* rather amusing. I know it's the Army term for a new church, but it sounds as if it's in the Wild West."

"Well, in a way, Earlscourt is the Wild West," Vangie said with a grin.

"Actually, it's to the north of the city. Perhaps we should refer to it as the Wild North."

Vangie smiled at George's remark. He paused before he continued, as he feared that his forthcoming proposal might alarm her.

"Because the Army is likely to establish an outpost in Earlscourt, and because travelling to work up there is extremely difficult from our flat here on Queen Street, I think that we should considering relocating."

Vangie's stomach dropped to her shoes. She had feared this might happen. However, even though she was prepared, the prospect of moving up to the "wild, wild north" above the hill still surprised her.

The reality of the situation had not truly dawned on her before.

*

George talked to Frank Mercer the following week. Because of the pending decision about moving up to the Earlscourt area, George inquired of Frank, "How in heaven's name did such a height of land, which everyone calls the Davenport Road hill, ever get plunked into such a flat area as the one the city occupies?"

"Well, don't forget it's about two miles north of the city's waterfront."

"Yes, I know. But it looms over Toronto like a monstrous obstacle, preventing any northward expansion."

"It has an interesting geological history."

"Really?"

"At one time, it was the shoreline of the ancient Lake Iroquois. During the last Ice Age, about thirteen thousand years ago, the waters of this lake covered the present-day downtown area of the city. Eventually, the waters receded, forming the Great Lakes of today."

"When the first settlers arrived here, they huddled around the shoreline. But as the settlement grew, they must have encountered problems when they came in contact with the hill."

"Yes, they did. In the seventeen-nineties, when Governor Simcoe ordered his troops to construct Yonge Street as a military supply line, they came up against the enormous height of the land."

"The hill must have presented quite a challenge."

"Yes. The slope of the ancient shoreline parallels Davenport Road. It sweeps across the city from east to west. Even today, the hill remains a formidable barrier to the city extending northward, and it will until they construct more public transportation lines on the major north–south streets. Until that is accomplished, living above the hill means isolation and difficulty."

"When did they construct the first streetcar line?"

"In 1890, electrified streetcars commenced rumbling up Yonge Street. They extended the line in the years ahead as far as Summerhill, and eventually up over the hill beyond it. This was the first public transportation that travelled up the incline. They soon developed a community around the intersection at Yonge and St. Clair. One of the early homesteaders named it Deer Park, as many deer inhabited the surrounding forests."

"I know that area. I worked on a house there last year."

"As you know, there's a streetcar line on Avenue Road that extends up over the hill. But I fear it'll be many years before another streetcar line goes that far north. There's still no line on Bathurst Street that climbs the hill."

"You've done a lot of reading."

"Yes, I consider myself a Torontonian and want to learn about the city."

"The hill's magnificent, I suppose, but when I must climb it to get to a building site, all I see is a steep incline that I must overcome."

"I know what you mean."

George paused to think over the information Frank had provided.

Finally, he said, "I doubt that I'll live long enough to see any public transportation mount the hill at Dufferin Street. But Vangie and I must decide if we'll move into the area anyway."

*

During the summer of 1909, George told Vangie, "Employment opportunities above the Davenport Road hill are increasing. I think we need to think again about moving up to the Earlscourt District."

"It's a difficult decision. There's much to consider."

"Yes, I'm aware. There's the problem of establishing a home in such a remote location. Also, the Queen Street Citadel Band needs me, and giving up the role of bandmaster is not easy, as I've enjoyed the many hours I've spent with the men. I dread breaking the news to the Mercers, especially Billy. As well, it's necessary to discuss our decision with Captain Sendry. Though I've sometimes disagreed with him, I consider him a close friend." Waiting a few moments, he turned to Vangie and asked, "What do you think about relocating?"

"Do we really have a choice?"

"Not really."

*

Captain Sendry was stunned when George informed him that he and Vangie were relocating to the wilderness above the Davenport Road hill. Losing George, as well as his wife, Vangie, who was the Home League Secretary (leader of the women's group at the church), was a harsh blow.

The Captain shook George's hand and said, "I wish God's blessing on you and Vangie, as well as on your new endeavour."

When George informed Phil and Emmy about their decision, the Mercers were saddened that they would be living so far away. Billy was especially concerned, as he was losing his music teacher.

However, fate was soon to intervene.

*

A week later, Mr. McCallum called Phil into his office and regretfully explained that the company was no longer able to employ him. However, he said he would give him an excellent reference.

As Phil was leaving the office, Mr. McCallum followed him out the door. Placing a hand on his shoulder, he said, "Phil, you've been an excellent worker. I wish I could continue to employ you here at my factory. However, I know of a job that might suit you."

"Yes, sir?"

"I know it might be difficult, but would you consider a position to the north of the city, above the Davenport Road hill?"

"What type of position?"

"A friend of mine, Mr. Harold Peevy, has opened a small jewellery shop on St. Clair Avenue. He's a good man. He owned a shop on Queen Street, but last year he decided to move to that godforsaken patch of earth they call Earlscourt."

Mr. McCallum stopped speaking. It suddenly dawned on him that talking disparagingly of the Earlscourt District was not exactly wise if he wished George to consider moving to the area.

"St. Clair Avenue? A jewellery store? Away up there?" Phil replied, ignoring McCallum's last remark.

"Oh, I know it's a long way north of here and that the streets aren't even paved. But the area is expanding rapidly, and Mr. Peevy believes there're opportunities for those who can seize them. He needs an engraver for watches, silver trays, cups, and the sort. However, until the area prospers a little more, he'll sell costume jewellery, pocket watches, and inexpensive household items. The engraving skills that he'll eventually need are right up your alley. He's prepared to hire a man immediately, even though there won't be much engraving at first. You'd mainly be a sales clerk. The pay won't be much, but I know that you're a frugal man. Think about it."

"I'll speak with my wife."

"Take your time to consider it. You have five children. You will have to find a new home to rent if you move."

"I'm aware of that."

"Let me know your decision. If you decide to accept, I'll contact my friend by sending notification in the post. Good luck, Mr. Mercer."

Mr. McCallum closed the door behind himself after he entered his office. He shook his head in disbelief as he sat down again at his desk. "I'd never move to such a backwoods area," he muttered.

*

When Phil broke the news to Emmy, she was dismayed, but she realized that they had little choice. Jobs were as scarce as hens' teeth, as Grandmother Mercer liked to say. The following day, the decision was sealed, and they commenced their search for a rental property in the Earlscourt District.

*

The Earlscourt District of Toronto had received its name from the estate of Major Foster, whose lands encompassed a large tract near St. Clair and Dufferin. He likely named it after the famous Earlscourt District in London, England. The main thoroughfare of the Toronto district was St. Clair Avenue. In reality, it was a muddy road with narrow sidewalks made of planks of lumber. Dufferin Street's sidewalks were similar. There was barely enough space on the street to accommodate a baby carriage, since there were only a few inches to spare on either side of the wheels. If people encountered anyone with a carriage, they had no other choice but to step down from the wooden walkway into the deep mud to allow the carriage to pass.

In spring, when conditions were particularly bad, the mud sometimes trapped an individual in the muck until several neighbours arrived and grabbed the person's arms to pull him or her to freedom. Much teasing and mirth often accompanied the rescue, though it rarely came from the individual held in the grip of the mud.

*

The first week of May in 1909, the Mercer and Meaford families located houses to rent on Boon Avenue, a street one block west of Dufferin. The houses were a short distance north of St. Clair Avenue.

Several weeks prior to relocating, Grandmother Mercer told Emmy, "I've decided to move in with Frank and Sarah. I feel that I'm not able to cope with the pioneer condition confronting you in Earlscourt. You've been at my side since the day we met in the train station in Dorchester. I'll dearly miss you, and I fear what will confront you in your new home above the great hill."

"I understand," Emmy replied.

She, too, dreaded the move. While seeking the rental property, she had viewed with dismay the roadways, sodden fields, and muddy streets of Earlscourt. The spring rains had recently departed, but the oceans of mud remained.

The muddy streets of the Earlscourt District in 1908, with the wooden-plank sidewalks. *City of Toronto Archives, Fonds 1244, Item 0030*

*

The day the Mercers left behind their small house on Draper Street, Emmy had a sense of foreboding. Phil was too busy packing the cart they had hired to worry about what lay ahead. The girls and Zack thought they were embarking on a great adventure. Billy wondered if he would ever see Jenny McMillan again.

Emmy saw Grandmother Mercer watching them as the horse pulled the cart northward up Draper Street toward Wellington Street, the animal's hooves clomping noisily on the stones of the roadway.

"What have I done?" she said under her breath.

*

On the Saturday afternoon of May 15, late in the day, the Mercers arrived at their new home on Boon Avenue. By the time the last of the sun's rays dipped below the horizon, their possessions were inside the house, scattered about the rooms. Makeshift beds accommodated them the first night. Everyone was too grateful for the quilts to think about the crude conditions of the small rental property.

Early the next morning, shortly after daybreak, Emmy rose from bed and walked into the kitchen to begin the morning's chores, staring in dismay at the small room. Phil entered a few minutes later.

"It'll take considerable work to make this place livable," Emmy lamented.

"Aye, I fear you're right. The exterior walls have only a tarpaper covering."

"I can feel the cool breezes creeping in around the door and window frames."

"I'm afraid the builder did a poor job sealing them."

"I can feel the cold drafts on my cheeks."

Phil placed his arms around Emmy to comfort her.

Looking up, Emmy continued. "In several places, the light is shining through the small holes in the roof. The chilly air is creeping up between the cracks in the floorboards. It'd be even colder if it weren't the spring of the year. I knew the house was in rough shape when we agreed to rent it, but now, in the morning light, I see that its shortcomings are much worse."

Phil held Emmy closer and kissed her tenderly on the cheek. As he stroked back the lock of hair that had fallen over her forehead, he smiled and said, "We'll be all right."

"You're right," she said, returning his smile. "Nothing has ever defeated us before, and this shack of a house is not going to do it now."

"That's the spirit, Emmy girl. Laugh and the world laughs with you."

"Yes, and up here in Earlscourt, if I cry, I'll indeed cry alone. Besides, I can't cry. I might discourage the children."

"At least we have a well, even if it's one that we share with the other houses on the street. I understand that six or seven men from this area dug it last year. It's a good thing that I visited the well last night before we went to bed, so as to fetch water for the morning's tea."

"Where, exactly, is the well?" Emmy asked.

"It's at the south end of the street, near St. Clair Avenue. I fear that during the days ahead, it'll require considerable effort to haul the many pails needed for cooking, cleaning, and bathing. However, we'll all take turns. We'll manage."

*

Following a frugal breakfast, Emmy asked Billy, "Will you accompany me to the well to fetch the day's supply of water?" Billy grabbed a pail and smiled at his mother. As they departed to trudge south on Boon Avenue, pails in hand, they looked back and saw Zack standing in the doorway.

"Wait for me," he shouted. "I can help. Besides, I want to be with Billy."

While they were pumping water, a neighbour and his two teenage sons arrived. Emmy smiled at the man, but he did not respond. Because he was ramrod straight in his bearing, she thought that perhaps he was ex-military. Judging by his appearance and the ages of the boys, she guessed that he was nearly fifty years old. His was a sour countenance. Lines etched deeply into his face, combined with his long nose and beady little eyes, gave him the appearance of a weasel. Drooped across his upper lip was an oversized black moustache resembling those of the villains she had seen on the covers of children's books in the library. As he gazed at her, he continually curled one of the ends of the moustache between his fingers.

Then, to Emmy's surprise, he declared pompously, "I am Pastor Sneadmore Treadwell, a lay preacher." Then, in a cursory manner, he introduced the two boys with him. "Jeremiah here is fourteen, and the other boy is a year older. They're obedient and God-fearing, though the older one is less God-fearing than he should be. I have a daughter, as well."

The fifteen-year-old smiled weakly at Emmy and said, "My name is Ezekiel."

Emmy noticed that Treadwell had introduced the younger boy first but had not mentioned the name of his eldest. She thought this indicated that he was not fond of him. She considered it odd but thought nothing more about it.

Eventually, Emmy was to learn that Mr. Treadwell favoured Jeremiah over his older brother, as he considered Ezekiel too independent in his thoughts and deeds. Also, Ezekiel resembled Treadwell's wife, and people often passed remarks about the boy's good looks. This annoyed the Pastor, who considered attractiveness a spurious gift of the devil. If this were true, then Mr. Treadwell was homely enough to qualify for sainthood.

After he completed his introductions, Emmy continued assessing Pastor Treadwell. He was six feet in height with well-muscled arms. He held his chin high as if he were looking down at the world around him and, Emmy thought, at her in particular.

"I live my life in accordance with God's laws and pray for God to forgive those who engage in the sins of the flesh," he informed Emmy. "Those who fail to obey God's laws will burn in hell, as he is a vengeful God. He smote the Egyptians and will put the sword to all who live in sin. Do ye live in sin?"

Emmy was shocked by the man's directness and so ignored his question. She was also surprised to hear him employ the biblical word *ye.* She continued drawing water from the well and avoided eye contact with her neighbour. However, she could not help but wonder if the man had forgiven God for giving him a face that resembled the contents of a bait bucket. Then she felt guilty for thinking such an unkind thought.

Turning away from her odious neighbour, she glanced at his two sons.

The sons of Mr. Treadwell were dressed tidily, their well-worn trousers clean and ironed. Their hair was neatly combed but plastered down with too much oil. Emmy thought it strange that the boys were so immaculate, considering their ages and that life in the Earlscourt District was so rough-and-tumble. As she observed them, she felt that the younger boy, Jeremiah, was sneering at her. Also, he seemed to eye Billy and Zack in a challenging manner, as if itching for a fight. The older boy, however, flashed a friendly smile.

Mr. Treadwell expanded his chest as he again commenced expounding. "I have lived in the Earlscourt District for almost five years. I was one of the first men to venture above the Davenport Road hill. I am a respected leader in this community. I live my life in accordance with the teachings of the apostle Paul, and I obey God's laws. Obedience and fear lead to heaven. My wife follows in my footsteps."

Treadwell stared at Emmy as if she were a sinner who would never be able to attain his level of righteousness. Despite his unattractive features, Treadwell gave no indication that he was anything other than pleased with himself. Then she noticed that even though he was merely getting water from the well, his clothes, like his sons', were of much higher quality than those most people would wear to perform such a menial task. His trousers had been freshly ironed. The cuffs of his well-starched shirt were spotless, and despite his obvious efforts to disguise the fact, it was clear that they had been turned several times to extend their wear.

"I have given my wife three children," he boasted.

Emmy noticed that he seemed to imply that his wife had little to do with the births. She pitied any woman married to such an overbearing man.

"I insist that my children be intelligent and trustworthy," he continued. "I was born in a prosperous section of London, in a dwelling far superior to most folks'. My youngest child, only a year old at the time, and despite my considerable abilities at prayer, died on the ship that transported me to Canada."

Emmy thought that his voice contained a degree of scorn, as if the child had died to spite him.

Treadwell continued. "It is fortunate that I possess great strength and superior character, or else I would never have coped with the dire conditions in this primitive part of the city. In winter, during the coldest days, it pains me that my wife can rarely wash the floors," Mr. Treadwell dramatically lamented. "The soapy water freezes before she can mop it up. I've often told her to work faster."

His words added to Emmy's pity for the man's wife. They also inspired fear of what the winter ahead would deliver into her own house. It also dawned on her that Treadwell's wife might be able to mop up the water faster if her husband helped her.

Then, as it became Mr. Treadwell's turn to fill his buckets, he added, "Around here, people tend to overheat their stoves and cause fires. Pity that they cannot endure the cold the way I do. When a house fire breaks out, men fetch buckets of water from this well. We rely heavily on our neighbours. Anyway, a good fire might remind them of the flames of hell that await them if they don't repent their wicked ways."

Emmy grimaced at his unkind words. She was used to relying on the kindness of her neighbours, but the primitive conditions of the neighbourhood were another matter. *What have I gotten myself into?* she thought.

*

On the way home, Zack told Emmy, "I don't like that man. He's prune-faced."

Emmy gazed at her son, hiding her amusement. She did not like Mr. Treadwell, either. She hoped the other neighbours were friendlier.

Arriving home, Emmy poked a few pieces of wood into the stove to boil the kettle. The stove was the sole source of heat in the modest abode. It was in the small kitchen, and it burnt wood or coal. Emmy knew that there was always the danger that it might overheat and cause a fire, which would spread quickly because of the enclosed nature of the dwelling and the materials used in its construction.

For the remainder of the day, Emmy, Phil, and the children laboured without ceasing. By the time darkness closed over the land, they had arranged their few possessions within the rooms. The crackling fire inside the old stove cheered them. Following a simple meal, Emmy slipped over to the Meafords' and shared her thoughts with Vangie, who was similarly dismayed.

*

The next morning, Zack and Bess were with Emmy as she walked over to Dufferin Street, where she turned southward toward a shop that was on the brow of the Davenport hill. Gazing down at the city below, she saw the abundance of cleared land immediately to the south of Davenport Road.

She said to Zack and Bess, "In the distance you can see the skyline of the city, huddled near the lake, and if you look closely, you can see the tall towers of the City Hall and St. James Cathedral. It's difficult to see their spires because of the haze from the coal fires in the homes. To the east, at Bathurst Street, there're homes at the base of the hill, but here at Dufferin Street, there're very few."

There was a pause before she made her final comment. "Civilization is slowing creeping northward. I wonder if it'll ever reach Earlscourt?"

Looking south down the hill on Bathurst Street toward Davenport Road. The homes had already crept to the base of the Davenport Road hill, unlike farther west at Dufferin Street. On the southwest corner of Davenport and Bathurst (upper right-hand corner of the photo) is a small sliver of the huge tract of land owned by the McNamara brothers for their market gardening. There is a single streetcar track on Bathurst Street, but it terminates at Davenport Road. *City of Toronto Archives, Fonds 1244, Item 0700*

*

Emmy's next task was to enroll Zack and Bess in the Earlscourt Public School, located at Ascot Avenue and Dufferin Street. Ruth, who was now fourteen, and Mary, at fifteen years of age, were too old to attend school and hoped to find work as domestics. Billy was also to seek employment.

Emmy had told Phil, "St. Clair Avenue resembles a bombed street with mud-filled craters. On the south side, between Dufferin Street and Oakwood Avenue, are a farm and an orchard. Whenever I shop in the area, I gaze at the empty fields bordering the street on the north side. The spring rains have created ponds, and there are wild ducks on them. The ducks remind me of those on the river in Comstock. However, Earlscourt doesn't have markets and fine buildings, such as those in Comstock."

*

Billy was now sixteen and needed to find employment. He decided to begin his search at the nearest grocery store. Walking along the wooden sidewalk on St. Clair, he arrived at a shop where the sign above the door stated, "Thomas McCarthy—Greengrocer and Dry Goods." The sign was awkwardly angled, as several nails had loosened on its left-hand side. The small windows on the front of the shop facing the street were dirty, and the curtains looked as if they had not been washed in many months. It was certainly not like the well-kept shop of Mrs. McMillan.

When Billy entered the store, he noticed that Mr. McCarthy's store was smaller than the one where he had worked on Queen Street. Its floor had not been swept for days. A few black pellets littering the floor looked suspiciously like rat droppings. Jars and tins, which Mr. McCarthy had removed from the wooden boxes but not yet shelved, lay strewn across the counter. It appeared as if the place had not been cleaned since the days of Noah and his ark.

Stepping up to the counter, Billy gazed at Mr. McCarthy, who was busy serving a customer. Many stains decorated the storekeeper's apron. When Mr. McCarthy stepped out from behind the counter to scoop several pounds of flour from a barrel beside the door, Billy noticed that the shopkeeper's trousers were in no better shape than his apron, and his shirt appeared as if it needed a thorough soaking in a laundry tub.

Examining Mr. McCarthy's face, he noted that despite the unshaven cheeks and unkempt moustache, the man's features were handsome and his face was relatively unlined. However, his dull, unfocused eyes made it appear that he had given up on life.

When the customer departed the shop, Mr. McCarthy perched wearily on a tall stool behind the counter and peered at Billy. His disinterest was evident. He did not ask what he wanted, which Billy thought strange. Finally, after a few awkward moments, Billy introduced himself and informed the man that he was seeking employment.

"Well, now," Mr. McCarthy drawled indifferently. Then he took a deep breath as if exasperated, and inquired, "Do you have any experience?" Billy knew that his interview was not beginning well, but he summoned the courage to explain about his experiences at Mrs. McMillan's shop.

When he completed his prepared speech, Mr. McCarthy said, "You worked behind the counter, did you?" His untrimmed, bushy eyebrows shifted upward, and his eyes narrowed as he peered at Billy who, despite the man's unresponsive attitude, sensed a spark of interest.

"Yes, sir. Mrs. McMillan gave me this letter of reference."

Billy retrieved the creased page from his pocket and unfolded it. After positioning it on the counter, he smoothed it out with his hand. Scattered grains of rice on the untidy counter caused small bumps to appear in the paper.

Mr. McCarthy gazed at the letter, making no effort to pick it up. To fill in the gap, Billy told him, "Honestly, sir, I'm a hard worker, good at arithmetic, and honest."

"Are you, now?"

"Yes, sir." Billy smiled and, for some strange reason, added mischievously, "I'm so honest that I even told the minister back home in Comstock that his sermons were too long and greatly boring." Billy wasn't certain why he had uttered such a disrespectful statement.

"Comstock, you say? Do you mean that old rascal, the self-righteous Reverend Thackeray Wilmot?" Mr. McCarthy responded. For the first time since Billy had entered the store, he saw a flicker of life in the shopkeeper's eyes.

"Yes, sir. That's the man. I know I shouldn't have been so outspoken."

"Don't you worry, my boy. That sanctimonious old devil married my wife and me. That was more than twenty-five years ago, long before you were born. It was likely one of the few good deeds he ever did. Mind you, he ate more than his share at the marriage meal. My! My! You told old Wilmot that his sermons were boring. Now, that was not really nice and not really honest, either. His sermons were far worse than boring. They were so unbearable that they often ruined my entire Sunday. He caused more indigestion for his parishioners than a stew with skunk meat."

He paused and then added, chuckling as he spoke, "The Reverend never met a widow whose food he didn't fall in love with. The good Lord gave him a mouth that was useless for sermons, but it was as wide as a great valley for devouring food. Dear old Gobble-guts Wilmot. My! My! What a small world." Then he broke into laughter and slapped his knee, his uncontrolled mirth almost causing him to fall from his perch on the stool. Retrieving a soiled handkerchief from his back pocket, Mr. McCarthy wiped his eyes and blew noisily into the stained cloth. "Old Wilmot," he exclaimed again. "My! My!"

Billy was not certain what to think.

Regaining his composure, the shopkeeper said, "Me lad, I'll tell you what I'll do. My brother is tending to the store on Monday next while I deal with a penny-pinching banker downtown. I'll drop in to see this Mrs. McMillan of yours and inquire about you in person. I'd also like to be assured that she runs a tidy shop. Other than my poor dear wife, I've never met a woman who had a proper head for business. You come back here next week, and I'll tell you if you have a job."

Turning to depart the shop, Billy smiled as he thought of Mr. McCarthy worrying about Mrs. McMillan having a "tidy shop" when his own looked as if it had been hit by a tornado. The bell above the door tinkled as Billy opened it, but above the sound he could hear Mr. McCarthy's laughter as the man said aloud to himself, "Old Gobble-guts Wilmot. I don't believe it."

*

Thomas McCarthy kept his appointment with his banker and, with the previous year's shop proceeds, paid off the small mortgage on his property.

Then he travelled on the streetcar to Queen Street West and inspected the shop of Mrs. McMillan. The sight of the tidy shelves, immaculate floors, and well-arranged counter impressed him mightily, but the most impressive sight of all was the handsome widow McMillan. She reminded him of his wife. A tear came to his eye as he thought about the days when his wife had been at his side. He returned home from the downtown shop determined to see more of Mrs. McMillan.

The following week, Mr. McCarthy instituted great changes to his grocery store in the Earlscourt District and, even more surprising, to his personal appearance. When Billy arrived at the shop on Tuesday, he noticed that Mr. McCarthy had shaved. His hair was combed, and he was sporting a clean collar on his shirt. His apron remained soiled, but it was cleaner than the one he had worn the previous week.

Billy received not only the job but also the task of transforming Mr. McCarthy's shop even further. The grocer told him that he wanted his shop to resemble Mrs. McMillan's. By the end of the week, everyone in the Earlscourt District noticed the change, as well as the improved appearance of the widower McCarthy. Many of the women remarked how handsome the shopkeeper looked. They also commented favourably on the good-looking young man who now worked in the shop.

"Mercy me, I think I even saw Mr. McCarthy smile," one woman remarked.

However, no one knew that Thomas McCarthy had formed a plan to woo the widow McMillan.

*

Mr. McCarthy was almost fifty years of age. He had been a widower for the past seven years. His wife's death had taken a great toll on him. His dark brown eyes were sad because he performed his daily chores without any enthusiasm or apparent interest. The shop was a place to earn a living, nothing more. His store was the only one in the immediate area, and because he had no competitors, he maintained a profitable business. When his wife had been alive, the store had attracted customers from a much greater distance. But Mr. McCarthy no longer cared.

The women of the area felt sorry for him. For some, his handsome looks and manly bearing outweighed his poor personal hygiene. The widows of the community considered him a man who could be easily redeemed by the "proper" woman, certain that if given a chance, they were capable of accomplishing the challenging task. Not everyone felt this way, however. The self-righteous Mr. Treadwell viewed him as a slovenly sinner who was beyond redemption.

*

The summer months of 1909 passed rapidly. Every Sunday morning, the Mercers and the Meafords trekked down over the Davenport Road hill and walked to Dovercourt Road and Van Horne Street (Dupont Street), where they boarded the streetcar to travel downtown. Visiting their former neighbourhood and attending the services at the Queen Street Corps was a welcome relief from the primitive conditions the families endured during the weekdays. Listening to the band, in which George Meaford continued to play his trombone, increased Billy's desire to play in the senior band, but Captain Sendry remained adamant that he must first kneel at the mercy seat. Unable to attend junior band practices now that he lived in the Earlscourt District, he was also unable to play in the junior band.

It was an odd thing, some of the people said, that they were not employing the talents of the young player. They were unaware of the reason.

Zack remained discontented, too, as he was now unable to attend junior band practices. At ten years of age, he was too young to play in the senior band. Besides, following his brother's example, he had not been to the mercy seat, either. Both boys' lives were in tune with God, but the ritual of the mercy seat was a necessity, as far as Captain Sendry was concerned. To compensate, Zack concentrated more on his cornet. He carried his mouthpiece in his pocket and practised on it as he wandered throughout the neighbourhood.

Billy continually improved his performance on the cornet. He no longer received lessons from the professional teacher his uncle Frank had hired, but he continued under the tutelage of George Meaford.

*

The third Sunday in August was blisteringly hot. Waves of heat rippled from the sidewalks and roadways, and humidity hung over the gardens and back fences, warping a few of the planks. After the morning service, George's and Phil's family met for lunch at the home of Frank and Sarah Mercer on Draper Street. Following the meal, the woman and the Mercer girls entered the kitchen to begin washing the dishes, while the men retired to the parlour, their stomachs well contented.

George mused aloud to Phil, "Billy can almost make the cornet talk. I think he's a better player than I'll ever be. He's now sixteen. When he turns eighteen, I'll encourage him to audition for a position with the Toronto Staff Band. He'll be a real asset to the cornet section. I truly believe that no player in all of Toronto will be his equal. In my opinion, Zack will follow right behind him. He, too, is amazing."

Phil listened with silent pride. He remembered the many times Emmy had told him, back in the days when they lived in Comstock, that Billy would "make us proud one day." It appeared that she had been correct.

"Do you think it will be a problem that he has never knelt at the mercy seat?" Phil inquired.

"It may, especially if Captain Sendry's consulted in the matter. However, I can vouch for the fact that Billy is as fine a Christian as I have ever met. He'll make an excellent bandsman."

"Are you biased about his spiritual qualifications because of his abilities?"

"I've thought about that and carefully considered it. However, after discussing the matter many times with Billy, I realized that I needn't worry." He did not mention Billy's troubling way of questioning the Bible.

"I believe that he's saved," Phil responded, "but I wanted to be certain that you believed it, too."

George changed the subject by saying, "I suppose you are both aware that your mother is frequently seen in the company of Mr. Hutchinson, the bass player in the Queen Street Citadel Band."

"Mr. Hutchinson the butcher?" Frank inquired.

"Yes, the very man."

"Do you disapprove?"

"No, of course not. I've learned my lesson."

Phil thought about the remark that his brother, Frank, had made, and wondered what he meant by, “I’ve learned my lesson.” Was this the reason for his estrangement from their mother? The disagreement had led his brother to immigrate to Canada.

*

Meanwhile, when Phil and Frank discussed other matters of mutual interest, Billy and Zack had departed from the house and crossed the street to visit Mrs. Greenberg. They knocked politely on her door. It was several minutes before they noticed her pulling aside the parlour curtain and cautiously gazing out. When she saw Billy and Zack, her face lit up. Then they heard her heavy footsteps in the hallway, followed by metallic sounds as she unfastened each of the three locks that secured the door.

“My goodness. It’s my Billy and his delightful young brother.”

She invited them in with a wave of her hand and led them down the hallway to the kitchen at the rear of the house.

Plunking her considerable bulk in a well-worn rocker, which groaned under her weight, she beamed at them as she motioned for them to pull out a kitchen chair. Mr. Greenberg observed the young visitors from his seat beside the fireplace, which, because the day was hot, remained unlit. He gave the boys a weak smile and then shivered as if a chill had suddenly passed through him. Despite the heat, he pulled the shawl draped over his shoulders tightly around his neck.

“Would you boys like a slice of peach pie?” Mrs. Greenberg asked as she shifted her weight, leaning toward the icebox to open its door.

“We just finished our lunch at our aunt and uncle’s house.”

“Is that a yes or a no?”

“It’s a yes,” Zack interjected quickly, afraid of missing the opportunity to enjoy a slice of what he was sure was the best peach pie in all Toronto.

With great effort, Mrs. Greenberg extricated herself from the confines of her chair and reached inside the icebox to retrieve the pie, which was at the rear, on the bottom shelf. Cutting two generous slices, she deposited them on small plates that made them appear larger than they really were. Before she was able to reach the cutlery drawer for forks, Zack was munching on the delicious treat, holding it indelicately in his hand. Passing

Zack a fork, she smiled as she watched him wolfing down the pie, ignoring the fork.

"Our son, Herman, used to gobble pie like that," she said, her amusement obvious. Turning to Billy, she continued, "Billy, you once told me that if the baking smells from my kitchen could float on the breeze as far north as College Street, then our son might come down to visit us."

"Yes, I remember telling you that."

"Well, I guess the smells *did* travel all the way up to his street. Last month, he came to visit us. He was with a lady friend. I think he might want to marry her. It was wonderful to see him and to meet the girl who might soon become part of our family."

"I am very happy for you, Mrs. Greenberg."

"Thank you, Billy. Our son's now twenty-five years old. I think of you as my second son. You've always been so kind to me."

"What about me?" Zack asked, his words muffled as he chewed a large mouthful of pie.

"Of course. Of course. I'd never forget you, Zack. You're my third son."

She gazed fondly at Zack, his blond hair and cornflower blue eyes creating an angelic appearance that she found irresistible. She wanted to hug the lad but knew that he would squirm in discomfort. Feasting her eyes on him, she noticed that he was enjoying the pie with such pleasure that if he were a kitten, he would have purred.

Then, from across the room, Mr. Greenberg's voice shattered the idyllic moment. "Yes, Herman came to visit us," he muttered grumpily. "He doesn't even use the name we gave him. He now calls himself Harry Green."

"I am not comfortable about that, either," Mrs. Greenberg replied. "However, I was so pleased to see him that I didn't discuss the matter and run the risk of an argument."

"I think he doesn't want people to know he's Jewish," Mr. Greenberg said. Then he fell silent. Mrs. Greenberg knew that her husband was likely correct. Being Jewish closed many doors in the business community. Although she felt that her son's denial of his faith was wrong, she understood the reasons. Life was harsh for those of humble means, but it was worse if you were Jewish.

"Your peach pie is great," Billy said, attempting to change the subject. He understood the plight of the Jews in Toronto and wished he were able to help Mrs. Greenberg in some small way.

"The peaches arrived across the lake on the *Cayuga* just yesterday. I also bought several baskets of Concord grapes to make jelly. I hope you will visit me again later in the season. I'll give you a few jars to take to your mother. I'm certain that your sisters will enjoy the jelly, as well."

"Yes, ma'am," Billy responded. "All my family loves your baking and preserves."

Zack nodded his head enthusiastically. Having devoured the piece of pie, he wiped the crumbs from his mouth with his hand.

Mrs. Greenberg sat down again, basking in the praise from the lads. She glanced again at Zack, who was now licking the pastry crumbs from his plate. Without saying a word, she cut another piece of pie for him. She wished her son was more like these boys, but she understood that life for Herman was more difficult than for others. When he sought employment, the job usually required that he work on Saturdays. This he was unable to do, if he adhered to the tenets of the Jewish faith. She also knew his girlfriend was likely responsible for her son's recent visit. The girl had made it clear that she would only marry a man who would raise her children within the Jewish faith.

As Billy and Zack returned across the street, Mrs. Greenberg observed them from her veranda. The loneliness in her heart had diminished slightly. The boys had cheered her, and she felt certain that her son would pay another visit before too long.

*

As August ended, the sun peeked above the horizon later each morning. The days became shorter, but the final week of the month remained as hot as the weeks preceding it. Zack had pushed the word *autumn* from his mind. He had been thoroughly enjoying the freedom that summer presented, any thoughts of returning to the confines of the classroom remaining too far ahead in the future to be of any concern, despite its being only a few days away.

On Tuesday, August 31, he sprang from his bed and gazed out of the window of the house on Boon Avenue. The previous evening, when the blood-red sun had dropped below the horizon, his father had told him that it was the sun's way of promising another hot day.

It seemed to be true. The early morning breeze wafting gently through Zack's bedroom window already contained a hint of the heat that by midafternoon would surely blister the city. Zack whistled a merry tune as he entered the kitchen for breakfast, knowing that after he hauled four pails of water from the well, the remainder of the day was his own.

Last evening, before going to bed, he and Bess had decided they would visit Wilford's orchard to pick apples from the branches at the top of the trees, which the hired pickers could not reach from their ladders. Bess had agreed to help Zack haul water from the well, enabling them to depart earlier for the orchard.

Bess was a year older and an inch taller than Zack. On this morning, she had tucked her long brunette hair inside the boy's cap she wore every day. Bess had always been a bit of a tomboy. She was aware of Billy's ability to defend himself and saw no reason not to do the same. If any of the neighbourhood boys teased her, she tolerated it for a while, but if it became cruel and persistent, she was not afraid to use her fists.

Zack had once told Bess, "When you fight, you're as dangerous as a cobra."

She accepted the compliment by saying nothing. He never told her that he had been inspired to make the remark after seeing a picture of the snake in a book at the library. The caption under it had said, "Beautiful but deadly." In the case of Bess, though it was an exaggeration, it was partially accurate. She certainly knew how to defend herself against any unwarranted teasing from the boys, but because Zack was her brother, he was unaware that Bess drew the boys' attention because they considered her attractive.

After they had placed the final two buckets of water on the counter beside the dry sink in the kitchen, Zack said to Bess, "Let's get to Wilford's orchard before the other kids climb the trees and get all the apples. We've got on our old overalls, so if Mother finds out we've been climbing, she won't say too much."

Assessing Zack's clothing, Bess added, "Those overalls of yours are older than God's dog. You have more patches on them than the thousand-year-old quilt on my bed."

"My overalls are great for climbing or exploring Garrison Creek, especially where the trees are thick, where it crosses St. Clair Avenue."

"Ya, sure, and my old cap is a princess's crown."

Zack grinned but said nothing more. They sauntered in silence southward on Boon Avenue toward St. Clair. Mr. Treadwell saw them as they passed, but he took little notice. He knew Zack but did not recognize the girl who was with him. However, it crossed his mind that the two filthy creatures belonged together. "Dirt begets dirt," he muttered to himself.

Twenty minutes later, Zack and Bess were climbing among the upper branches of the tallest apple tree in Wilford's orchard. The workers had already stripped off most of the fruit, but on the uppermost branches there remained a few large red apples. From their perch near the clouds, they had a clear view of the plank sidewalk along the south side of St. Clair Avenue, as well as the rooftops of the few shops and houses that dotted the street. They watched a cart and wagon rumbling westward, likely going to the Heyden House Hotel on the northwest corner of St. Clair and Old Weston Road. The horse's hooves created clouds of dust as its iron shoes disturbed the dry soil of the roadway. From his vantage point, Zack was able to see Mr. McCarthy's shop where Billy worked, and farther along the street, Mr. Peevy's Jewellery Store, where his father laboured six days a week.

Zack had met Mr. Peevy many times. On Saturdays, when he was not attending school, his mother sometimes asked him to deliver a pint preserving jar of cool well water to Phil, and occasionally, a few freshly baked cookies. His dad shared the cookies with Mr. Peevy, who was a small man with a thin moustache that constantly twitched. Zack thought that he resembled a mouse. The man's hands, small and delicate, were ideally suited to repairing watches, but they added to his rodent-like qualities. The fringe of hair around his head was white. He had once told Zack that he was a thinker and that he had thought so much that his brain had worn out his hair. Zack had grinned at the corny joke, appreciating that the smile Mr. Peevy gave him demonstrated that he liked him.

Then, from his perch in the trees, Zack spied Mr. Peevy. He was outside his shop, smoking his pipe and peering around. "I think Mr. Peevy is looking for a piece of cheese," he told Bess.

"Is his moustache twitching?"

They both chuckled. Bess knew that Zack thought the jeweller resembled a mouse. Ignoring the world beyond the tree, Zack concentrated on picking an apple that was slightly beyond his reach. Bess had already retrieved a large red specimen from an upper branch, and she was noisily crunching on its crisp flesh, juice dribbling down her chin. She grimaced as she chewed the pulp, enjoying the sweet, tart flavour.

It was not long before Zack reached the apple he was seeking, finished consuming it, and was stuffing the core into his shirt pocket. He told Bess, "I'll dispose of it after we've left the orchard. An apple core left on the ground, old eagle-eyed Mr. Wilford is certain to see. It will make him work the pickers harder, so there'll be no fruit left on the trees."

Zack began his climb to the ground below. Halfway down, he noticed a broken limb and adjusted his course to avoid its sharp end. However, as he turned to grab the next branch to facilitate his descent, he misjudged the distance. The branch caught his overalls and tore them. He heard the ripping sound and winced.

Bess giggled when she saw the huge tear in the seat of his pants, the rip exposing Zack's underwear.

On the ground, Zack gingerly explored the gash with his fingers. Bess finally controlled her laughter and offered her assistance. As he turned around to allow her to see the damage, she chirped, "Your underwear's showing."

"Never mind my underwear. How large is the rip?"

"Well, it's of a size that you could drive a horse and cart through."

"It's that big?"

"Actually, it's not a tear in the cloth at all. The branch caught one of the patches that Mother sewed on your overalls and tore it down on three sides."

"Oh, goodness. If I walk home in these trousers, everyone will see my underwear. If I hold the patch closed, they'll know the reason. Besides, even though the overalls are only my play clothes, Mother will be upset."

"She'll understand."

"Yes, but she'll also tease me about showing my underwear to the world."

"I have an idea," Bess said. "You wait here. I'll run home, get a needle and thread from Mother's sewing basket, and repair the tear so that no one will ever know."

"Are you sure you can sew that well?"

"I can do plenty of things that I never tell you about. Wait by the bushes, over beside the plank sidewalk, until I return. I won't be long."

Twenty minutes later Bess returned, entering the orchard from the west side.

"Take your trousers off so I can repair them," she instructed.

"I can't take my trousers off. Someone might see me."

"You must remove them. I have to stitch the tear from the inside. Otherwise, it will be obvious someone has repaired them. Off with your trousers."

"I can't."

"Then I can't sew them. It's your choice."

Reluctantly, Zack removed his trousers. Thoroughly embarrassed, he covered his crotch with his hands, even though nothing was exposed since he was wearing underwear.

As Bess turned his overalls inside out and commenced sewing, with obvious amusement she gazed at the hapless Zack. "What are you afraid I'll see?"

"Nothin'," he snapped.

"Well, you're right. It's nothin'. Mary and Ruth changed your diapers. They told me that you ain't got nothin' much."

Zack was mortified but managed to reply, "You braggin' or complainin' because they told you about me?" he asked.

"If I ever saw you without your underwear, I'd be complainin'."

"Then you'll never have anything to complain about."

Zack's face was now beet red. Despite his embarrassment, he dropped his hands to his sides as if daring her to look, secure in the knowledge that he had exposed nothing. Bess ignored his false bravado and continued sewing. When finished, she inspected her handiwork and then passed the overalls to Zack. He was examining the results of her labours and was about to express his appreciation, despite her taunts, when a banshee scream assaulted his ears.

Gazing up in shock, which caused him to drop his trousers to the ground, Zack beheld an apparition from the deepest bowels of hell towering above him. It was the Pastor Sneadmore Treadwell, who had been passing along the plank sidewalk on the other side of the bushes.

*

The Pastor had heard their voices. Being a man who never missed a chance to stick his nose where it did not belong, and considering himself the moral guardian of the Earlscourt area, he felt it imperative that he investigate what evil deeds were being committed in the seclusion of the bushes.

He was shocked to see Zack Mercer, his trousers lying on the ground, and a girl with him. Not realizing it was his sister, his suspicious mind conjured visions of sexual impropriety that he was certain would shock the entire community. He had a nose for evil, and he was certain that vile sins were assaulting his olfactory senses.

He shouted, "A tidal wave of boundless devilry is flooding cross the Earlscourt District."

The vocabulary that Treadwell employed in his sermons never deserted him. Besides, he disliked Zack, since he was the younger brother of the precocious Billy Mercer, whom he had once overheard refer to him as Snotty Snotmore.

Without warning, Treadwell seized Zack by the ear and proceeded to march him to Peevy's Jewellery Store to confront his father. Treadwell's oldest son, Ezekiel, trailed behind, the lad's face betraying his unease with the commotion his dad was creating.

Clad only in his shirt and underwear, the humiliated Zack stumbled along beside Mr. Treadwell, who had Zack's ear firmly gripped in his hand. Each misstep caused his ear to stretch, which brought excruciating pain. Everyone along St. Clair Avenue within at least a block heard the commotion and wondered what was happening. Zack's cries filtered through the animated conversation within McCarthy's grocery shop. Billy knew it was his brother. He dropped to the counter a bolt of cloth he had been showing to a customer and then rushed outside.

*

Billy saw that his brother was in the clutches of Mr. Treadwell, who was dragging him along the planks of the sidewalk by his ear. In a hurry to deliver Zack to his father for a fate well deserved, Treadwell ignored the fact that Billy had appeared.

"Mr. Treadwell. What are you doing to my brother? Let him go," Billy demanded.

"Out of my way," Treadwell screamed belligerently. "Your brother is a child of the devil." As Treadwell tugged harder on Zack's ear to position him in front of himself, the boy's cries of agony displayed the pain he was suffering.

"Let my brother go," Billy asserted once more.

"When I get hold of the devil, I never let go," he trumpeted triumphantly.

"You will this time."

With lightning speed, Billy lifted the lid off the water barrel beside the shop door and, using the scoop attached to the barrel's side, threw water in the furious face of Mr. Treadwell. It caught him by surprise, causing him to ease his grip on Zack's ear. Billy grabbed his brother and swept him away from Treadwell's reach, positioning Zack behind himself.

Mr. Treadwell struck Billy a hard blow. He deftly swerved, so it only grazed his left cheek. Treadwell prepared to strike again, intending to push Billy aside and regain possession of Zack.

Billy seized the lid of the water barrel and, like a gladiator holding his shield in the ancient Coliseum, prepared to do battle. As Mr. Treadwell came in contact with the barrel lid, he tried to shove Billy backward to get at Zack, but Billy held his ground and, with all his might, rammed the makeshift shield forcefully against the fuming Treadwell. Caught by surprise, Treadwell lost his footing and crashed to the ground, his well-pressed trousers and white shirt coming into contact with the dry, dusty earth of the street. His hand brushed against the ground, and when he wiped his brow he smudged the dirt onto his reddened face. Soiled and dirty, not realizing how ridiculous he appeared, he continued to rant at Billy.

Stumbling to his feet, Treadwell attempted to lunge again, but Mr. McCarthy blocked his path.

"I've been assaulted," Treadwell shouted. "Send for Constable Sam. I demand that he arrest Billy Mercer. The lad's a criminal. He struck me," he screamed. His cries of outrage rose loudly in the air, causing a small crowd to gather. Mr. McCarthy calmly stared at Treadwell, who was shaking with rage.

Assured that Billy was unharmed, Mr. McCarthy feigned indignation as he bellowed, "Indeed. Send for Constable Sam. I want this man arrested." He pointed accusingly at Treadwell, stifling the satisfaction he felt at finally having a chance to give the haughty Mr. Treadwell what was long overdue.

Mr. McCarthy continued. "I saw the entire episode through my shop window. Not only did Treadwell assault young Zack, but he also struck my employee. The man is a menace. How am I going to operate a business on this street with this man running about assaulting people?"

Insensitive to anyone's feelings other than his own, Mr. Treadwell was unaware that the people assembled in front of Mr. McCarthy's store were unsympathetic toward his cause. He had at some time or other offended most of them.

"I'll go for the Constable," a tall man in a black cap interjected quickly. "I'll tell him to bring handcuffs and a long rope. If the good Pastor Treadwell refuses to be cuffed, I'll suggest that we hang him." The smirk on his face indicated that he was joshing, but the remark served as the spark that ignited the flames of payback.

Another man chimed in and said, "I saw the entire episode, too. Hanging's too good for that sanctimonious prig. He's a menace to decent folks."

Slowly, Mr. Treadwell recovered his wits. Finally realizing that the crowd was not kindly disposed toward him, he bellowed, "I've been assaulted by a devil and you cast doubts on my good character? Sinful men always stick together."

"Men? We women saw the entire episode, as well," an elderly housewife said. "Ladies?" She looked around at the other women present. "We will all go to court and testify on behalf of the Mercer boys. I want that man there"—and she was pointing to Mr. Treadwell—"arrested and charged with assault." There was a murmur of agreement from the other women there.

"Can't you see?" Mr. Treadwell yelled. "The young lad has no trousers on. That girl over there has them in her hands. Heaven only knows what they were doing in the bushes."

"I tore my pants in the apple tree," Zack stammered, his face crimson with embarrassment. "I had to take them off so that my sister could mend them."

"Did you ask the boy for an explanation before you jumped to conclusions?" Mr. McCarthy demanded. "If the boy says that's what happened, then I believe him. However, regardless of the truth of his claims, we all saw you assault Billy Mercer. He had his trousers on. I hope you find our jail comfortable, Mr. Treadwell. You are likely to be in it until far beyond next Christmas. Perhaps that snotty son of yours, Jeremiah, will smuggle in a carpenter's file inside a Christmas cake."

Fearing that the mood of the crowd might become uglier, Treadwell brushed the dust from his clothes, swiped his hand through his dishevelled, oily hair, and, twirling his moustache between his fingers, slithered from the scene.

Watching him depart, Mr. McCarthy commenced laughing. Within seconds, a chorus of laughter rose in the air, adding greatly to the humiliation of the self-righteous Mr. Treadwell, who felt he had battled a horde of sinners who were beyond redemption.

*

When September graced the river valleys and backyard gardens of the city, the nights again grew cooler. The Mercers knew that with the approach of inclement weather, journeying south to the Queen Street Citadel would become increasingly difficult.

In October, Phil and Emmy decided they would attend services at the small stucco-plastered hall of the Dovercourt Citadel of The Salvation Army on Northumberland Street. From their home on Boon Avenue, they could walk there in less than an hour.

The third Sunday of the month, following the morning service, Emmy told Phil, "I heard that the Dovercourt Corps intends to establish an outpost in the Earlscourt area. They said it would be near St. Clair Avenue and Dufferin Street."

"That would be great for us, as it'd mean there would be a place of worship within easy walking distance."

Two weeks later, Emmy heard more news.

"Following through on their plan," she informed Phil, "the Dovercourt congregation has found a rental place here above the hill where services can be held. The rent will be two dollars per week."

"That's a lot of money, but I guess it's a fair price."

"It's at Little's Hall, at 94 Ascot Avenue, one block north of St. Clair Avenue. The hall is on the second floor. The first floor contains a store, a stable, and a warehouse. They've arranged for the official opening to be in January of the coming year. They've decided to name it the Rosemount Corps."

*

During the Christmas season of 1909, the Mercers—until their new church opened—attended the Dovercourt Corps and enjoyed the yuletide services. On Christmas morning, the gifts under the small tree were homemade and humble, even humbler than in other years.

Emmy explained to the younger children, "The money that we usually use for Christmas gifts provided the twenty-dollar down payment on a building lot on Bird Avenue. You know the street. It's to the west of Dufferin Street, two blocks south of St. Clair."

Billy was listening and chimed in, "The lot is twenty-five feet by one hundred and twenty feet. The total cost is fifty dollars. It's an enormous sum of money, but when the thirty-dollar loan is paid, the lot will be fully ours."

Phil added, "Billy's wages contributed to the down payment. Mary and Ruth helped, too."

On Christmas evening after dinner the children performed their annual Christmas Extravaganza. Emmy thought that their instruments never sounded more tuneful as they played the seasonal carols. Bess was almost eleven, and her playing was beginning to rival Zack's. Among the sisters, she displayed the most promise. Mary, now fifteen, had progressed well on her trombone, and Ruth, who was fourteen, created a decent sound on her tenor horn, although her fingering was awkward at times. However, the two older girls did not possess the enthusiasm for their instruments that Bess did.

The scarcity of gifts did not detract from the yuletide celebration. When the family retired for the night, they were rich with contentment despite the poverty of their circumstances.

*

Chapter Five

January 1910 arrived at last. It was to be an important month in the lives of the Mercer family. On Thursday, January 6, in the darkness of the winter evening, they trudged their way through the drifts of snow to Little's Hall on Ascot Avenue.

Surrounding the hall were empty fields, bare trees, and a few small homes. After they entered through the door next to the store entrance, they ascended the narrow staircase to the second floor and then entered the large space. There was a constant hum of excited chatter from the almost two hundred people who were gathered. The people had commandeered chairs of every description to provide seating. The mercy seat at the front, near the platform, consisted of four second-hand kitchen chairs.

When the service commenced, the newly appointed officer of the Rosemount Corps, Captain Samuel Rush, rose to the lectern and expressed gratitude to God for having found a rental property to hold the services. Everyone fully entered into the exuberant mood, the congregational singing vibrating the old wooden beams high above the auditorium.

The Rosemount Corps had been born!

Following the service, Captain Rush approached George Meaford. "I believe that the Rosemount Corps should have its own band. I'm hoping that you'll be our first bandmaster."

Before George was able to reply, the Captain continued. "I know that organizing a band up here in the Earlscourt District will be a challenge. I also realize that you were the bandmaster of the Queen Street Citadel Band. It's an excellent musical aggregation. Our band will be small, and

I wouldn't blame you if you preferred to trek down the hill to play in the more accomplished Dovercourt Citadel Band. However, I was hoping you'd consider the challenge of starting a band up here in Earlscourt."

"I would welcome the challenge, Captain. The Mercer boys are good players. They'll allow me to make a start."

"They're fine musicians, I'm told."

Captain Rush grinned. He was highly pleased that George accepted. He looked forward to hearing Billy and Zack perform on their cornets.

*

Captain Rush was nearly fifty, but in appearance and thought, he seemed much younger. He was more than six feet in height; his handsome face was unlined, his skin, clear and smooth. He possessed a full head of dark hair untouched by greying. On Sunday mornings, when he stood on the hall's platform, he made an impressive figure.

His mind was agile, and though he had little formal education, he was widely read. As a progressive thinker, he deeply pondered the ideas that he read, incorporating some of them into his sermons. However, he was careful not to stray far from accepted biblical teachings. He preferred to ask thoughtful questions on matters of faith, as opposed to providing simplistic answers. A few members of the congregation appreciated his approach, but others felt that he was perhaps straying too far from Army teachings. However, as he was such an affable man with exceptionable abilities in pastoral care, everyone at the Rosemount Citadel was fond of him.

*

George was one of those who appreciated the Captain's sermons. Having accepted his request to form a band, George set to work immediately. Along with Billy and Zack, he rounded up five other players. Though he was the bandmaster, it was necessary that he play his instrument as part of the group since there were so few members. His bandsmen possessed varying abilities, but they all had previous experience, two of them having played in the Chalk Farm Band, a corps near London in England. To supplement numbers, Captain Rush appointed an elderly man to carry the flag.

The fledging group consisted of three cornets, a euphonium, a trombone, a tenor horn, and a bass. They found a man to beat the old bass drum, which George had borrowed from the Dovercourt Corps.

Early on the morning of Sunday, January 9, 1910, amid falling snow, George and the eight other men departed from Little's Hall to conduct an open-air service. With the flag snapping in the brisk winter wind, they trudged east along Ascot Avenue to Boon Avenue, and then they marched south to St. Clair Avenue to assemble near a pasture on St. Clair near Dufferin. Despite the cold temperatures and the blowing snow, they braved the elements, the music sounding cheerful in the cold winter air.

While standing in the open-air service, Zack told Billy, "I've never felt so frozen in my entire life."

"Me, too. My lips keep sticking to the frozen mouthpiece of my cornet."

"I'll be glad when we return to the hall."

"One or two people stopped to listen, but they didn't stay long. I think they left to attend their own churches. It's too cold to stand around listening to music."

As the outdoor meeting progressed, Zack mentioned to Billy, "The snow's becoming heavier. The wind's blowing it into drifts. It'll soon be over top of the fences."

He shivered as he pulled the collar of his coat higher around his neck.

Finally, George Meaford signalled to his bandsmen that it was time to return to Little's Hall, as he saw that the intensity of the storm was increasing.

After they were inside the building, Billy told Bandmaster Meaford, "It was really cold this morning. I'm glad to be back in the warm."

George Meaford grinned. "It was indeed freezing. But when I marched out of the hall this morning, I felt as proud as if I had been in the International Staff Band parading along Queen Victoria Street in London. However, I doubt that any staff bandsman has ever encountered the winter conditions that we faced."

Billy withheld his grin and said nothing, as he was afraid his lips might crack.

For the evening service, people carried coal-oil lamps to the hall. The Mercers brought two of their best. The small wood stove inside was the only source of heat to ward away the chill of the winter's night. Billy and Zack noticed that their mother and sisters were not sitting near the stove.

Billy whispered to Zack, "I think they're singing extra loud to keep their minds off the cold."

"I hope Ruth and Mary aren't upset because they're not playing in the band. I think Bess is sulking."

"She'll get over it. She always does."

*

During the remainder of January, cold winds swept across the empty fields and orchards above the Davenport hill. They slammed against the walls of the humble homes of the Earlscourt area and whistled under their battered eaves. The gnarled branches of the old apple trees in Wilford's orchard were black silhouettes against the pewter skies.

However, there was one place within the orchard that was far from gloomy—Wilford's Pond. Fed by a small underground spring, the pond was the delight of young children for swimming in summer and skating in winter, when its glassy surface sparkled on a frigid sunny day. During after-school hours and in the early evenings following supper, as well as on Saturday afternoons whenever children had completed their daily chores, they gathered at the pond to skate. Knitted scarves fluttered merrily in the air as the skaters whizzed across the surface of the ice, the barking of excited dogs mingling with the high-pitched voices of the children.

On the south side of the pond during the winter months, the plank sidewalk on the north side of St. Clair was visible through the bare trees. Adults who walked along the planking gazed at the children gleefully skating and remembered when they had been young and had the time to engage in the carefree sport. Most people felt happy for them, but there was a noticeable exception—Mr. Sneadmore Treadwell. He was of the opinion that the "heathen brats," as he referred to them, should stay home to read their Bibles, contemplate their sins, and beg for forgiveness for their multitudinous transgressions.

He often told his neighbours, "There's no way I'll allow any of my brood to be wasting their time skating on that accursed pond."

*

One particularly brisk Saturday afternoon, shortly before the supper hour, Treadwell noticed that his son Ezekiel had not yet returned home.

"Where's that lazy, good-for-nothing son of yours?" he growled to his wife. He never referred to Ezekiel by name, as he considered him his wife's son, not his.

"Working below the Davenport Road hill. It's a long trek to get up over that hill," she replied timidly.

The sun was leaning heavily toward the west, and within the hour it would drop below the horizon and the temperature would plummet. Mrs. Treadwell had been patiently urging her husband all day to go to the butcher shop to purchase a pound of stewing beef. He had ignored her requests, informing her that he'd go when he felt like it.

However, the hour was now late. Because he wanted a little meat in the stew, and as Ezekiel was not yet home, he reluctantly sent Jeremiah. Mr. Treadwell regretted having to send him out in the cold to run an errand that his older brother should have done. As he watched Jeremiah depart, Treadwell told his wife, "That lout of a boy of yours will pay for his tardiness."

When Jeremiah returned home with the parcel of meat wrapped in brown paper, the sky was black. Without removing his scarf and wool coat, the boy rushed over to his father, his breath exploding in short bursts.

"Why are you out of breath?" Mr. Treadwell demanded.

"I ran all the way home."

"Why?"

"Because I saw Ezekiel at Wilford's Pond."

"Why was he there? He has no skates."

"He was laughing and joking with Billy Mercer. I'm certain that they're friends," he added smugly. He knew that mentioning Billy would ignite flames of anger in his father.

"Damn that accursed boy," Mr. Treadwell cussed. Then he raised his eyes heavenward as if asking forgiveness for his foul language and muttered, "He would try the patience of Job. The boy's behaviour has caused me to utter a sinful word."

Jeremiah grinned with satisfaction. He had ingratiated himself with his father, as well as succeeded in causing problems for his brother, for whom he felt no brotherly love.

Twenty minutes later, Ezekiel entered the house. After closing the door, he was aware that everyone in the family was staring at him. He knew by the smirk on Jeremiah's face that he was in trouble.

"You've been conniving against me with that Mercer boy," Mr. Treadwell spat in a voice seething with anger.

Ezekiel instantly realized that his father knew where he had been.

"Why were you at that accursed pond?"

"I was passing by it on my way home from work and lingered for only a moment to talk with a few of the skaters."

"Yes, and Billy Mercer was among them."

"He was there, I admit. But I was talking to the others, as well. Billy was just one person in the group."

"You'll rue the day ye turned against me."

Mr. Treadwell's fist struck Ezekiel in the mouth, splitting his lip and drawing blood. The boy staggered backward. He had seen his father enraged before, but never to this extent. His father struck two more blows before Ezekiel fell to the floor.

Refusing to give his father the satisfaction, Ezekiel held back his tears. Through misted eyes, he struggled to swallow his sobs and remained on the floor, knowing that if he stood to his feet, he would receive another blow.

Treadwell thundered, "Come the spring of the year, I want ye out of this house."

"But where can he go?" Mrs. Treadwell interjected meekly, instantly fearing that her husband's wrath might descend on her head.

"He can go to hell, as that is where he will end up anyway." Turning to the trembling Ezekiel, he added, "When spring arrives, I want ye gone from my life. I'd turn ye out of here tonight, but I'll do my Christian duty and allow ye to remain under my roof until spring."

Mr. Treadwell turned his back on his first-born child and sat down at the kitchen table. Pounding his fist on the rough planks of its surface, he shouted, "Fetch me my dinner."

From that moment forward, Ezekiel never knew a moment's peace.

*

By the end of March, winter-weary citizens of Earlscourt felt that the gods of springtime had truly abandoned them. However, eventually the mild breezes of April graced the land. The frozen puddles in the fields and the ice on Wilford's Pond gradually softened. However, in addition to the people's optimism brought about by the spring thaw, the milder weather delivered roadways and streets of slush as well. Muddy Earlscourt appeared in all its ignominious glory.

St. Clair Avenue during the muddy spring season of 1909. *City of Toronto Archives, Fonds 1244, Item 0031*

St. Clair Avenue and the surrounding streets became seas of mud. On Sunday mornings, the narthexes of the large churches and humble vestibules of the smaller places of worship contained rows of boots caked with heavy clumps of mud. The Salvation Army Hall was no exception. When the Mercers arrived at their place of worship, they deposited their boots in the hallway near the stairs that led to the second-floor auditorium in Little's Hall. They did this to prevent the floors of the meeting place from becoming as muddy as the streets surrounding the building.

A mud-filled street in the Earlscourt District. *City of Toronto Archives, Fonds 1244, Item 00216*

*

One morning at the end of the first week of May, a stranger visited McCarthy's store. As it was early in the day, few local customers had appeared, and it seemed odd that anyone would trek up over the hill at such an inconvenient hour. Mr. McCarthy sensed that the man had a tale to tell. He was leaning on the counter when he heard the shocking news from below the hill.

"My good man," he began, "it's all over the city. Our gracious sovereign King Edward VII has passed away. The city has come to a standstill. The Eaton's store has drawn the curtains over their shop windows, and not one home has the parlour blinds open. When I departed from the city, people were already flocking to the churches, where they're holding impromptu memorial services. The bells of the St. James, St. Michael's, and the Methodist Cathedral are peeling at this hour. Except for the bells, silence has descended over the city. The carriages, carts, and motorcars are motionless. As I proceeded northward, I could hear the church bells as far north as Bloor Street."

Recovering from his shock, Thomas McCarthy told Billy, "Scribble appropriate words on a large piece of cardboard, post it in the shop window, and draw the curtain shut behind the sign. There'll be no business today. Within the hour, housewives and workers will've carried the news throughout the Earlscourt District. It won't be long before the area is as mute as the city below."

Mr. McCarthy was correct. In observance of the passing of the monarch, people maintained a mood of respect during the week ahead. Although stores were open, people cancelled any impending parties and social gatherings. Women went quietly about their daily tasks attired in black, the men placing black armbands on their jackets or shirts.

*

The week following the death of the king, Phil Mercer entered the kitchen of his home on Boon Avenue and sat down heavily on a kitchen chair. He was exhausted after his long walk from a lawyer's office down in the city. In his hand, he held the deed to the building lot on which he and Emmy had placed a down payment the previous December. He had paid the final installment, and the property was theirs.

"Emmy, we're now landowners," he declared.

"Yes," she replied with pride in her voice. "Now the real work begins."

"George Meaford was with me today when I made the final payment. He made his final payment, too. We discussed our building plans as we journeyed homeward. We have agreed to build our house first, as we have five children. Working together, it will be easier to do the heavy lifting. Billy will help us. He's seventeen now and a man. I'm certain that Zack will want to help as well."

"Have you drawn up any plans for the house?"

"To call it a house may be a stretch of the imagination. I'm afraid that most people would call it a shack. We've already placed an order for the cedar posts for the frame. We will purchase the other materials we need as we can afford them. George Meaford's building lot is not that much farther west along Bird Avenue, and it is on the same side of the street as ours. We're hoping that both homes will be habitable before the winter."

*

During the successive weeks of spring, the days lengthened, and each evening, toolboxes in hand, Phil, Billy, and George departed from their homes on Boon Avenue and walked the several blocks to Bird Avenue. Two of the bandsmen from the corps volunteered to assist.

Phil told Emmy, “I need to build a home that we can occupy as soon as possible. It’ll have no basement. That must wait for another year.”

By the end of the first week of June, they had finished building the floor of the dwelling and commenced erecting the walls. Next, they placed the support studs for the walls, the studs spaced sixteen inches apart. The large wood beams supporting the flat roof were rough timbers, solid but inexpensive. Then they nailed planks to the exterior walls and covered them with tarpaper to insulate the interior of the rooms against the winter chill. Under the heads of the nails on the tarpaper, they placed thin tin disks, about the size of a twenty-five-cent coin. The disks were to prevent the wind from tearing away the tarpaper. These disks were in regular patterns, positioned on the walls horizontally, then vertically, and finally sideways.

Humble dwellings like the one Phil was building were becoming common throughout the Earlscourt District. They were an interesting sight—all black, with their shiny tin disks reflecting the light on a sunny day. The next project was to build a similar structure for the Meafords.

One evening Phil told Emmy, “The house has progressed well. It’s almost ready for moving in. I’m aware that those with funds will derogatorily call our place a tarpaper shack, which, in fact, it is. However, I don’t care. It might be humble, but at least we own it and we’ll no longer pay rent. Besides, it contains more living space than the place here on Boon Avenue. And it will be less drafty. There’ll be no cracks between the floorboards or the planks on the walls.”

Emmy smiled as she placed her hand in Phil’s. “We’ll have a fine new home. I’m proud of the way you’ve worked. We’ll be very happy under its roof.”

*

The Mercer family’s new home was on the north side of Bird Avenue, three housing lots west of Dufferin Street. Bird Avenue was the second block south of St. Clair, west off Dufferin. In future years, the street would be renamed Rosemount Avenue.

The entrance to the home was on the right-hand side, and inside the door was a narrow hallway, with a parlour located on the left side of the hallway. The parlour was about ten feet square.

They moved in during the late summer of 1910. Phil, Emmy, and the boys slept in the parlour on the ground floor, using the room as a bedroom. They intended to remain sleeping in the room until the second floor was built, which would contain the proper bedrooms where they could erect the beds.

Behind the parlour was the space they intended to use as a dining room. The girls slept in this area. On the left-hand side of the house, behind the parlour, was a small room approximately eight feet square, which they used as a kitchen. It contained a sink, a built-in drainboard, several cupboards, and a small stove for cooking, which was the only source of heat until they could afford a small stove for the parlour. In the kitchen, there was also a rough baking table. Attached to the rear of the house was a lean-to porch.

There was still no basement, but as soon as they had completed the first floor of the Meaford house, they would commence constructing the second storey of the Mercer house. Fortunately, Grandmother Mercer provided a few extra dollars for building materials.

The second floor eventually took shape. It contained three bedrooms, one for Phil and Emmy, one for the boys, and one for the girls. The girls would sleep in one room until the men could build the third level, which would really be the attic. It would contain two more bedrooms, allowing each of the girls to have her own room. Though it would be humble in appearance, they thought that, once completed, it would be an exceptionally fine home.

The Mercers no longer paid rent, but during the days ahead, finances remained tight. In reality, they were pioneers, building a new life in a frontier community. There remained no electricity in the area, no running water, and no sewage pipes. Building codes and bylaws were nonexistent. It was a place where individuality reigned.

Emmy devised many ways to save money, but the one the children were to remember most in the years ahead was the way Emmy saved on sugar, which was expensive. Phil had a sweet tooth. If left to his own devices, he invariably added more of the sweetener to his tea than Emmy thought was necessary. As a result, she developed the habit of sweetening his tea before she gave it to him. He realized the reason for her action and said nothing, though he gave a small grin each time she handed him the cup and saucer.

*

One evening, though the hour was late, Phil and Emmy sat sipping their tea and heard a light tapping at their door. Phil and Emmy gazed at each other with a mixture of curiosity and concern. It was after ten o'clock, and they knew that the streets of the neighbourhood were empty. Phil opened the door cautiously and peered into the darkness. Seeing that the visitor was hidden by the shadows, his concern grew. Then the person slowly stepped forward, a shaft of light from the door allowing Phil to see that it was Ezekiel Treadwell.

"My goodness, lad," Phil sputtered, "why on earth are you prowling about at this late hour? You should be home in your bed."

"Please, sir! May I speak with Billy?" he pleaded, his words muffled, spoken with considerable difficulty.

The boy's face was partially hidden, but Phil caught a glimpse of the blood running from the corner of his mouth. His left eye was swollen and partly closed. He was shivering in the night air as he had no jacket, only a cotton shirt covering his arms. He appeared so vulnerable and lost. Phil, stunned into silence and immobility, did not notice Emmy nudge past him. She reached out to the wounded teenager and placed her arms around him.

Unlike Phil, who had been busy with his job and the construction of their house, Emmy was aware that Billy and Ezekiel had become friends. Emmy had always liked Ezekiel and had often wondered how a creature as odious as Mr. Treadwell had sired such a fine son.

A few months ago, a neighbour had answered her question. She told Emmy, "Treadwell considers Ezekiel a bastard, a result of a premarital affair on the part of his wife."

Then Phil became aware that Billy was standing behind him. Without speaking, Billy eased past his dad and approached Ezekiel, who motioned for him to step aside where they could speak in private. Emmy released her hold on Ezekiel as he and Billy walked a few paces from the house.

Billy immediately reached out to Ezekiel. He placed his hand tenderly on his shoulder, his eyes telling Ezekiel that no matter what had happened, he was there for him.

Slowly, fighting back tears, Ezekiel explained to Billy in a subdued voice, "Earlier this evening, after my father returned home from work, I heard him tell my mother that he'd suffered ridicule from his boss at the lumberyard because he was a bit slow in filling a customer's order. When he saw me come into the kitchen, his anger exploded. He struck me with a piece of firewood and, despite my mother's pleas, threw me out of the house. I landed on the ground in front of the doorway. He shouted at me that he was fulfilling a promise he had made to God many months ago, and then he slammed the door shut. I've been wandering the streets ever since. Finally, I decided to come to you. I've nowhere else to turn. Can you help me?"

Phil observed the two lads as they continued to converse. He whispered to Emmy, "I wonder what has happened to the Treadwell boy. Why's he at our door at such an ungodly hour? I'm certain that his father has played a role in this."

Emmy nodded in agreement.

As Billy and Ezekiel came back toward the doorway, Emmy motioned for them to get inside. Phil closed the door after them. Emmy placed a pot of thick vegetable soup on the stove to heat, and Phil poked a piece of wood in among the flames. Emmy took a washcloth and began gently wiping the blood from Ezekiel's face. She was certain that his family had abandoned him. Why else would he be at their doorstep at such an hour, with a split lip and a swollen eye?

An hour later, Emmy laid several blankets on the floor in the bedroom where Billy and Zack slept. Her heart ached for the Treadwell boy as she watched him gingerly creep under the quilts, his body sore from the beating he had received.

*

Later, the house was quiet. Phil, Emmy, and Billy were the only ones who had not gone to bed. Billy had told his parents what had happened to Ezekiel, and then he, too, went upstairs. As Emmy passed Phil his final cup of tea of the day, she gazed at the frown on her husband's normally placid face.

Phil's deep concern was evident in his voice. "That boy has experienced more violence and hate in his young life than many mature men see in a lifetime."

"Yes, he has endured much."

"His father has turned him out without a coat on his back."

"Treadwell has always been cruel and treacherous."

"I can't help but feel that this is partly my fault."

"How on earth can you reason in such a way?"

"When Treadwell seized Zack and dragged him painfully along the street, I should've insisted on his being prosecuted by the constable. Zack is underage, and the attack was a direct assault. He also struck Billy."

"Well," Emmy replied. "If that is your thinking, then I'm to blame, too. I was the one who convinced you to turn the other cheek, be civil with the man, and pray that he would change."

"The time to turn the other cheek is past. There comes a time when a man must stand his ground and put right that which is wrong."

"But Ezekiel is not our son. You're on weak ground if you interfere. The boy can stay here with us. He's older than sixteen. He need not return home. We can avoid a nasty confrontation and still protect him. He and Billy are close friends. Billy and Zack will gladly share their room. When we build the third floor onto the house, two of the girls can share, and Ezekiel can have the other room. It'll allow him a little space to himself."

"Yes, that's good. But Ezekiel needs to get his clothes and a few belongings. This means I must confront his father. Besides, if Treadwell gets away with this, it's only a matter of time before he strikes another of our children. The matter must be settled once and for all."

"I understand your thinking. But I'm uneasy with the thought of your facing such a violent man."

Reaching out his hand and placing it gently on Emmy's, Phil stated calmly, "Leave it with me. I'll find a solution."

*

The next day, after Phil had completed the day's work at Peevy's Jewellery Shop, he trudged along the dirt road toward the Treadwell home. Beside him was George Meaford. Emmy had confided in Vangie Meaford about the incident of the previous night. George had insisted on accompanying Phil.

"This is something I must handle on my own," Phil insisted.

"Agreed, but I think I should be with you. Treadwell is a thoroughly nasty individual, and though I will remain silent, my presence might help calm the situation."

Reluctantly, Phil consented.

When they arrived at the Treadwell home, the sun was inching toward the horizon, the shadows of the trees lengthening across the roadway. Though the day was spent, Treadwell remained at work in his front garden. Well, that is, his two children were working and he was leaning on the gatepost critiquing their labours. As he saw Phil and George approach his house, he glanced up. When he noticed them entering through his garden gate, his eyes narrowed and his lantern jaw jutted forward. He was certain that an unpleasant altercation was pending. Smiling in anticipation, he twisted his moustache between his fingers.

"Evenin', Mr. Treadwell," Phil began. "I see you're busy in your garden."

"What do the likes of ye want?" he snarled.

George feared the next few minutes. Treadwell was dangerous; his height and weight created a grave threat.

Without any further polite talk, Phil informed him, "I've come for Ezekiel's belongings."

"Have ye, now? What business is it of yours to interfere with my family affairs? Get out of my garden before I throw ye out."

Phil stepped forward, his jaw set in grim determination. Slowly, with a controlled voice that contained a cold edge George had never heard before, Phil said, "It would give me great pleasure, Treadwell, if you would raise your fist and strike me, so that I can ram those ugly teeth of yours so far down your throat that you'll choke. I'd then have the constable on you for striking me first. I have a witness here that will testify I struck you in self-defense. Either strike me or give me Ezekiel's belongings."

George's expression betrayed his fear for his friend.

Phil continued. "There's another matter that'll go against you,

Treadwell. You assaulted my two sons. When we go to court, it will be easy to find witnesses. There's no shortage of people who saw you assault them."

"I'm a leader in this community. No one would give evidence against me."

"From what I hear about the incident in front of Mr. McCarthy's shop, everyone was against you. You're only a community leader in your own mind."

Phil stepped closer to Treadwell. "Strike me or give me Ezekiel's things."

There was no hesitation. Hoping to catch Phil by surprise, an enraged Treadwell struck out with his fist. Phil swerved to avoid the blow. It whizzed past him. When Treadwell delivered another punch, Phil blocked him with his left fist and gave him a punishing uppercut with his right. It landed squarely on Treadwell's jaw.

When Treadwell attacked again, Phil's retaliatory blow hit Treadwell squarely on the nose. The sickening crunching sound caused George Meaford to wince, surprised at the damage Phil was inflicting.

Treadwell momentarily backed off. Phil stood his ground, ready to deliver another blow if one were necessary.

It was!

Treadwell charged, his head lowered like an enraged bull's. Phil calmly stepped aside, allowing Treadwell to connect his skull forcibly with the hardwood gatepost.

Though dazed, Treadwell staggered to regain his balance and then lunged again at Phil, who hammered another forceful blow with his right fist. It connected with Treadwell's cheek, and Treadwell went down heavily. He was now woozy, gasping for breath, and unable to get up.

As George and Phil stood gazing at the wounded Treadwell, Mrs. Treadwell came out of the house and thrust a neatly tied-up bundle into Phil's arms. She whispered, "These are Ezekiel's things. Tell him I love him." Then she turned and crept back inside the house, knowing that she would receive punishment for showing her concern for their son.

As George and Phil walked away, they did not notice Jeremiah gazing at his father, who was lying prostrate on the ground. Slowly, a sneer crept across his young face. He muttered under his breath, "I despise weakness.

My father's pitiful. He's the one who taught me to be strong. And look at him. He's fallen to the ground in defeat."

*

George now looked at his friend Phil through new eyes. "Where did you learn to fight like that?" he asked.

"I grew up in a village where as a lad I quickly learned to defend myself. I tried to forgive Mr. Treadwell for what he did to my boys. I failed. However, I must admit that I enjoyed thrashing him. May the Lord forgive me."

"I think the Lord understands," George responded. "God did not tell David to turn the other cheek to Goliath. You acted on principle. Treadwell received what he deserved, although it was a bit rougher than I had thought it would be."

"Well, I knew that it was something I had to do on my own. I did not want you involved. As bandmaster at the corps, what would people say if they knew you had been brawling?"

George chuckled. "Well, I am not certain that it will do your reputation much good, either." He rested his arm on Phil's shoulder, and the two men continued down the road toward home.

They knew they had likely committed a sin, but their satisfaction outweighed their guilt.

*

Although George continued to labour daily at his carpentry on the building sites and perform endless tasks around the house, he spent one night each week training the musicians of the Rosemount Band. After much intense practicing, the band began to improve.

Each Sunday morning, with flag unfurled and the beat of the borrowed drum setting the pace, they marched south to St. Clair where many people strolled, as it was the main thoroughfare of the district. Their music attracted much attention.

*

At the beginning of August, the Rosemount congregation purchased property on the south side of St. Clair Avenue, a short distance west of Dufferin Street. The corps had chosen a very auspicious location for their new hall. It was in the heart of little Earlscourt, which centred on St. Clair Avenue between Dufferin Street and Boon Avenue. At Boon and St. Clair, Maltby's Drugstore sat prominently on the northwest corner. Tamblyn's Drugstore, painted brightly in green and white, was one block further east, on the northwest corner of St. Clair and Dufferin, and across from this, on the southeast corner, was the Dominion Bank, the first bank to open its doors for business in the Earlscourt area.

At the same intersection, on the southwest, was the Royal George Theatre (previously the Picture Palace Theatre). Fifield's Butcher Shop, another of the district's shops, was a favourite of the residents, as were Peevy's Jewellery Shop and Mr. McCarthy's grocery store. These businesses made up the entirety of Earlscourt's commercial district.

*

A master carpenter by trade, George Meaford organized the plans and supervised the purchase of materials to erect the first permanent hall of the Rosemount Corps. Until the building on St. Clair was completed, services were held in a large canvas tent erected on the site. This saved on rent. By the time summer had faded and autumn approached, the materials were on hand to commence the new building.

On Monday, September 26, 1910, the congregation gathered for the turning of the first sod to begin the construction. Members of the congregation gathered in the autumn air to watch the ceremony.

Billy said to Zack, "I feel really proud to take part in the service today."

"Me, too."

"It's an important moment for the Earlscourt District, as well as in our own lives."

Zack shook his head in agreement.

Then Billy said, "Look over there. It's Zeke." (Both the boys now referred to Ezekiel as Zeke.)

Zack replied, "I see him. He's among a group of men watching the ceremony from across the road, in front of Tamblyn's Drugstore.

"I wonder what Zeke's thinking," Billy said. "His father professes to be a religious man, but he shows no Christianity in either his thoughts or his actions. I hope his father's example has not poisoned Zeke's attitude concerning matters of faith."

*

On October 30, 1910, Phil and Zeke were in the kitchen of the Mercer home. On the table in front of Phil was a large bowl of ripe grapes. Preoccupied with thought, Phil somehow made the grapes disappear.

When Emmy came into the room, she asked, "Where did all the grapes go?"

Phil innocently replied, "What grapes?"

He had been so distracted that he did not really remember eating them.

Zeke was highly amused when Emmy scolded Phil. Anyone observing the teenager could see that he considered Phil his personal hero. Zeke had thought that no one could rescue him from his abusive home, but Phil had accomplished the task. Zeke's love for Billy had also deepened. He had told Zack, "If only my brother, Jeremiah, could be more like your brother, Billy."

Zack had told him, "There's only one Billy in the entire world."

After Zeke departed the kitchen, Phil told Emmy, "Billy and Zack consider Zeke a brother."

Emmy nodded her head in approval. "I must admit that I look upon him as another son. I don't understand how any father could reject such a fine lad."

"I never told you the full story of the day I confronted the cantankerous Mr. Treadwell."

"I know. Perhaps it's just as well that I don't hear all the details. However, I know that on that day you settled the matter."

"True. I'm pleased that Zeke now lives with us."

"Yes, and I'm happy that Mr. Treadwell has not darkened our doorway."

"Zeke is a hard worker. Each day he walks down the Davenport hill to work. His pay is not much, but he never complains, and he readily pays a share of his wages as room and board. I must admit, the bit of money helps us."

"I heard Billy say that he hopes that if Mr. McCarthy's business increases, he might employ Zeke."

"That would be great," Phil replied. "He'd no longer have to trek down over the hill."

"Each morning, when Zeke departs for work, I hand him his lunch in a small cloth bag. Every Saturday, I wash the bag to keep it clean for him."

"You've grown to love the boy, haven't you?"

Emmy smiled. "He always shows such gratitude for the small lunch I pack him. I can't help but love him."

"I hope we're giving him the parental love that his father denied him."

"I hope so, too. Each morning, when I see him depart the house, Zeke brushes his thick brown hair back from his forehead and smiles shyly. He has such big, dark eyes. My heart goes out to him. At five-foot-ten, and as slender as a sapling, he cuts an attractive figure. He's every bit as handsome as Billy and Zack."

"Do you think we should lock up our daughters?" Phil teased.

"If you do, you had best lock up me as well."

They both grinned, enjoying the intimate moment and pleased that Zeke was now a part of their family.

*

Mr. Thomas McCarthy's business had indeed increased over the previous months. With Billy's help, and with the influence of Mrs. McMillan, the widower McCarthy's shop was now an admirable place of business. The women of Earlscourt highly approved of the change and spread the word to those who would not normally have patronized the store.

Billy was unaware that for several months Mr. McCarthy had been journeying down the hill each Saturday evening to Mrs. McMillan's. He was aware, however, that the grocery man quit work early each Saturday, but Billy thought that he departed because it was the end of the week and he was tired, which is why he trusted Billy to close the shop and tally the cash.

Mr. McCarthy's wooing of the widow McMillan had progressed

slowly. After visiting her shop on several occasions, he became aware that several men—widowers and the never married—eyed the attractive woman appreciatively. However, he had an advantage. He owned his own business and, thanks to the frugal habits of his deceased wife, possessed a modest sum in his bank account. His advantages in the marital game emboldened him, causing him to be more decisive than he might otherwise have been. However, he had the good sense never to overplay his hand. His confident manner eventually impressed Mrs. McMillan.

Early in the courtship, which had begun with regular Saturday visits to her store, he dropped into the conversation, "I own a fine grocery and dry-goods business in the Earlscourt District."

She had replied with a chuckle, "That's as impressive as my owning a shop in Timbuktu."

Thomas was crushed, even though he was aware that many people in the downtown area considered the Earlscourt District as remote as deepest Africa.

Despite her lack of interest in his store, late one Saturday afternoon Mr. McCarthy was highly pleased when Mrs. McMillan asked him, "Would you like to escort me to a concert this evening at St. John Anglican Church at Portland and Stuart streets?"

"I know where the church is, and I'd be very honoured to escort you."

She smiled. "Many of the military officers and enlisted men from Fort York will be attending. They're quite handsome in their impressive dress uniforms."

Mr. McCarthy frowned. He considered the military men to be rivals for the attention of the handsome widow.

On the evening of the concert, Thomas noted that Frank and Sarah Mercer sat in the row ahead of them, and across the aisle were Dorothea Mercer and her friend Mr. Gerald Hutchinson, the butcher. He was aware that Elizabeth McMillan knew Gerald, as he was a fellow merchant.

Following the concert, people lingered to socialize, renew acquaintances, and chat with neighbours. Many of those attending knew Elizabeth and spoke to her. Among them were several widowers. Mr. McCarthy eyed them suspiciously.

Shortly before it was time to depart into the chill of the autumn night, Dorothea Mercer and Gerald Hutchinson approached Elizabeth and

Thomas. Dorothea and Elizabeth knew each other quite well and conversed easily, both avoiding any reference to the eligible men accompanying them. Outside the church, the men walked beside the two women as they continued their conversation.

The strong wind slicing from the northwest caused them to tug their coat collars higher around their necks. In the old cemetery to the south of the church, the blackened limbs of the mature trees, now nearly devoid of foliage, crackled in the frosty air. In the moonless sky, a few stars sparkled but provided no illumination on the roadway that led to Portland Street.

Finally, the foursome turned north toward Queen Street. Before the couples each went their own way, Elizabeth extended an invitation to Dorothea to visit her for tea on the following Sunday afternoon.

*

Elizabeth lived in an impressive bay-and-gable house on Bellevue Avenue in the Kensington Market area. She and her husband had purchased the home shortly after they were married. Its soaring gable reached high into the air, and its attractive bay windows overlooked Bellevue Square Park on the east side of the street. After her husband died—since there was no mortgage and because she had the proceeds from the grocery business—she lived comfortably.

After Dorothea entered her friend's home, she seated herself and ran her gloved hand appreciatively over the rich fabric of the Greek-style sofa. The conversation remained polite and friendly, up until Elizabeth poured the second cup of tea. Dropping an extra bit of sugar into the cup for her friend, she smiled. The conversation now became more intimate.

The home of Elizabeth McMillan on Bellevue Avenue.

"I suppose you've heard the gossip making the rounds since Mr. Hutchinson, several months ago, started coming into my store every Saturday afternoon."

"I know that a few tongues have been wagging, but anyone who's your friend wishes you well. I've heard nothing but praise for Mr. Hutchinson. He's a fine man, and his business is prospering."

"I don't doubt that he's a fine man."

"And handsome as well."

Both women smiled, and a bit of conspiratorial giggling ensued. Dorothea sensed that Mr. Hutchinson's character and good looks were not the problem.

"Are you having doubts about committing your life to another man?" Dorothea asked.

Elizabeth nodded her head affirmatively and replied, "I had a marriage filled with much love. I feel that another relationship would be disloyal to my late husband's memory."

"I know how you feel. I am a little older than you are, and my husband passed away many years ago, but I still have doubts about marrying Gerald. He's asked me, you know."

"That's wonderful." She paused and gazed at her friend before she said, "I always thought that if you love a man, the decision to marry him should be easy."

"Such decisions are never easy. A person must consider the feelings of others," Dorothea replied.

"Who would object?"

"My son Frank. I've never told you before, but Frank and I were estranged for many years. Back in the Old Country, a year after his father passed away, I allowed a gentleman who attended St. George's Parish in Dorchester to court me. Tongues wagged. Frank interpreted my acceptance of the man's attentions as evidence that I hadn't loved his father. Nothing could have been further from the truth. Because I'd been in a marriage blessed with love and happiness, I was open to another relationship. Those who've had unsuccessful marriages are the ones who're more inclined to dissuade further offers of marriage."

"Perhaps it was because you waited only a year," Elizabeth said gently, no hint of censure in her voice.

"Perhaps," Dorothea admitted. "But I've a feeling that even if I'd waited for a decade, the results would've been the same. Frank could never picture me on the arm of another man. He doesn't realize that on cold winter nights, the memory of a good marriage isn't sufficient. Life is meant for the living. I need the warmth and security of a man's love."

*

The frankness of her friend's words surprised Elizabeth. However, upon reflection, she admitted that they aptly described her own situation. Thomas McCarthy was handsome, considerate, and, though a bit obstinate, a thoroughly decent man. Though she was not certain if she loved him, she knew that her feelings toward him were far more than merely friendly. Thomas cut a dashing figure when he walked along Queen Street, and she now realized that she was fortunate to have the attentions of such a man.

*

In the early decades of the nineteenth century, Canadians celebrated

Thanksgiving Day in November. In later years, the government decreed that the holiday would be on the second Monday in October.

George Meaford, Phil Mercer, and Captain Rush, along with a few Rosemount bandsmen, took advantage of the holiday in November and laboured building the new hall. They continued during the evenings ahead, as well as on Saturdays, all throughout the remainder of November and the first three weeks of December. George and Phil often worked beyond the midnight hour to gain extra time, and during those times they employed coal-oil (kerosene) lanterns to provide them with lighting.

Emmy could see the construction of the hall from a rear window of the Mercer home, as there were no houses to obstruct the view between her house and St. Clair Avenue. On one particular Saturday night, at the dot of midnight, she watched Phil descend the ladder from the roof with a lantern in his hand. It was not acceptable to work on a Sunday. As she observed him, she knew he was tired as he trudged homeward in the darkness across the open fields. At the door, Emmy greeted him lovingly.

Shortly after Phil came into the house, Emmy passed him a cup of tea that she had sweetened. They chatted quietly, sharing news of the day,

"The days ahead will be extremely busy, I'm afraid," Phil told Emmy.

"True, but the new hall's almost complete."

"It has been quite an experience. I've laboured on the construction of the new building late into many an evening, with Billy and Zeke at my side. I didn't allow Zack up onto the roof, but he helped pass up materials and tools."

"Whenever Billy isn't at McCarthy's store or working with you, he practises on his cornet."

"I often hear him. Zack is becoming increasingly proficient, too. Sometimes, when I listen, I hear them playing duets."

"George often tells me that he's fortunate to have such talented players under his baton."

"He loves the boys as if they were his own sons."

Finally, Phil and Emmy retired for the night. They wanted to be as rested as possible for the activities of the following day.

*

In the third week of December, the men had completed the new Rosemount Hall. The post office registered the building address as 1183–5 St. Clair Avenue. The structure was rectangular, with a roof that slanted steeply to prevent the winter snow from piling too heavily on top of it. Its white unadorned façade, with two windows on either side of the door, faced St. Clair Avenue. Inside the door was a small vestibule where people were able to deposit their muddy boots. The interior door of the vestibule led to the auditorium, which seated about 250 people. To the rear of the auditorium were a small Sunday school room and a band room.

On the evening of Tuesday, December 22, 1910, the new hall was to be officially opened. The weak sun dropped early in the pale December sky, the residual warmth from the daylight hours having dissipated into the clear, cold air of the night. People gathered outside the small-frame building, the biting frost no deterrent to their attendance.

*

When Phil and Emmy arrived at the site, they joined the small group. Emmy told Phil, "Despite my heavy overcoat, I'm shivering."

"We'll be warmer if we move closer to the electric lamp and the small heater over there. They're powered by the small generator."

"The shadows of the people standing around the heater look eerie against the white walls of the Army Hall, and behind them the black shapes of the pine trees resemble the evil forest that Hansel and Gretel entered to find the gingerbread house of the witch."

"I think you're letting your imagination run wild. You sound like Bess."

"Perhaps, but despite the excitement that everyone feels this evening because we are finally opening our new hall, in reality we're all trying to ignore that it's still a bone-chilling night. And despite what you say, I find the darkness a little frightening."

Teasing, Phil said, "The wind is blowing through the trees and whistling along St. Clair as if it were blasting through a wide canyon. I think it's an evil wizard's breath. I'd best hold you tight so you won't be blown away."

Emmy grinned as Phil placed his arm around her. She always felt safer when she was within his embrace. She also now felt warmer. As Phil had hoped, the silly bantering was taking her mind off the cold.

Gazing around, Phil pretended to grin evilly and imitated a monster's voice as he said, "The wicked wizard is on the prowl tonight. The street's empty. We're easy prey. The only sign of life is our small group clustered around the hall. I wonder who the monster will grab? The other people in the neighbourhood are inside their homes, their doors shut against the creatures of the night and the biting cold."

"Oh, shush, you silly goat."

Then Phil corrected himself. "They're as safe and as warm as is possible in drafty, flimsy tarpaper shacks. It's a bad night to endure the whims of the mid-December weather in homes that are like those in the children's story about the little pig who built his house out of straw."

Emmy again told him to shush and stop being silly.

Becoming more serious, he said, "We'll ignore the wind and the cold. For us, it's a 'night of nights.' I'm sure it's the same for George Meaford and Billy. They played a prominent part in the construction of the building."

"I think you contributed the most."

"Not really," Phil replied modestly. "It was a team effort."

"I have a feeling that the official dedication will be a moment none of us will ever forget. For months, you've all worked hard and endured the whine of the saw and bang of the hammer as you constructed the new building."

"That's rather poetic. Well, anyway, the important thing is that it's now ready."

"It's almost seven forty-five at night. Everyone's gathering around the door to witness the key-turning ceremony. I think we should join them."

Following an appropriate speech and a short prayer, Captain Rush solemnly turned the key in the lock and swung wide the doors. People scrambled to secure a seat, some sitting in the aisles on folded chairs that the captain had borrowed from the Anglican church. A few minutes later, they commenced the first service in the new hall.

*

Prior to the sermon, Bandmaster Meaford introduced Billy and announced,

"Bandsman Mercer will perform a cornet solo, with theme and variations based on the familiar hymn of Washington Gladden, 'O Master, Let Me Walk with Thee.' The arrangement is the bandsman's own composition."

Even the invited guests were amazed at the quality of Billy's playing. The arrangement was relatively simple but interesting. The bandmaster of the Dovercourt Band was present, sitting with one of his bandsmen. He knew of Billy's abilities but had not heard him play during the past year. His expression betrayed his amazement.

After the solo ended, the bandmaster was overheard telling his companion, "I think the lad might be a better player than anyone in our band."

His companion nodded his head in agreement.

"His interpretation was sensitive, displaying an intuitive understanding of the message of the words. The music seemed to soar, filling the hall. I think that the warmth of the message in the words of the hymn banished all thought of the bitter cold beyond the walls of the building."

The companion gazed at the bandmaster. "Those are indeed high words of praise."

"True. But I think they're deserved."

When the inaugural meeting ended, although the hour was late, the Dovercourt bandmaster and his companion joined with the others as tea and biscuits were served. They lingered to chat and offer warm congratulations to those who had worked on building the new hall.

When they departed into the frigid cold of the night, it was close to eleven o'clock. It was long after the midnight hour when those living below the hill safely arrived home.

*

It was to be the second yuletide for the Mercer family in the Earlscourt District, and their first in their home on Bird Avenue. Phil and the girls cut a small tree from a copse of spruce to the west of their house. They decorated it with homemade ornaments of paper, wood, and a few small, empty tin cans wrapped in tissue paper. They created garlands by looping together strands of coloured paper from discarded magazines. Bess, who was now twelve years old, and Ruth, fifteen, baked the cookies in the shapes of trees, balls, and stars. Zack helped secure the treats to the branches of the trees. A few of the cookies ended up decorating Zack's stomach instead of the evergreen limbs.

Bess chastised him. "You're always eating something. Don't eat the tree," she said as she bit into a cookie as well.

Before retiring on Christmas Eve, Emmy placed the modest presents around the base of the carefully trimmed tree, which was situated in the corner of the parlour. She had wrapped the gifts in sheets of newspaper to conceal their contents. Her own gift, Phil had placed in an old pillowcase.

A winter morning in the Earlscourt District during the early decades of the twentieth century. *City of Toronto Archives, Fonds 1244, Item 7274*

On Christmas morning, as daylight fully spread across the land above the hill, the Mercer family awoke to a landscape freshly dusted with snow. Bess exclaimed, as she peered out through an open spot on the frosted window, "The trees are covered with icing. They look like sugar cakes."

"Who's thinking of food now?" Zack quipped.

"Keep quiet."

Following a special breakfast of one egg each, a slice of smoked ham, and real cream instead of the usual milk on their cereal, they set out into the frosty air to attend the Christmas morning service. They approached the building from the south, through the laneway at the rear of the hall. They walked past the two outdoor toilets behind the building and entered the band room though the rear door. Later, when their parents and sisters arrived, they walked around to the front entrance.

Inside, the auditorium was warm and cozy. Near the piano, the potbellied stove, which had been fired up at an early hour, generated almost as much warmth as the smiles and enthusiastic conversations of those who had gathered. It was a wondrous Christmas service, the first in the new hall.

*

On Thursday evening, December 31, Captain Rush led the watch-night service to usher in the year 1911. At the stroke of midnight, they all raised a fervent prayer for blessings during the coming year. The women of the congregation served tea after the meeting, and eventually everyone trudged homeward along the dark wintry streets.

Fresh snow had fallen earlier in the evening, but the sky had cleared shortly before midnight, the moon drifting lazily across the great arc of the firmament, its rays reflecting off the fresh blanket of white shrouding the landscape. The wind's breath was reduced to a whisper.

Bess held her mother's hand tightly and edged closer to her as they proceeded homeward. The hulking outline of the trees cast deep shadows, and despite the fullness of the moon, the landscape seemed ominously dark and forlorn. Then, out of the shadows, with a suddenness that caught Bess by surprise, an owl swooped silently to the earth from an old maple tree on her left. The bird's ever-vigilant eyes had spotted a mouse scampering along the thin crust of snow while searching for seeds. The ensuing drama was quick and silent. Bess watched in horror as the owl grasped the little creature in its deadly claws, its plaintive squeaking audible in the still night air. Within seconds, the owl was once again hidden in the shadows amid the treetops, and the world was silent once more.

Bess shivered and held her mitt to her mouth to prevent a quiet cry from escaping. Though a tomboy and brave in many ways, she had always feared the dark. She edged closer to her mother.

Emmy sensed that something was wrong and inquired, "What's the matter, Bess?"

"I don't like the darkness. There are strange things in the shadows."

Emmy replied, "Perhaps. But don't be afraid of the shadows, my darling child. Always remember that God is in the shadows. You can't see him, but he's there, watching over you."

Bess had never thought about such an idea before. God was in the shadows? She recalled that she and Zack had seen birds of prey hunting at night when they lived on Draper Street. However, she and her brother had felt safe. She also remembered that below the hill, houses bordered the few fields that remained in the district, their light illuminating the darkness. However, the Earlscourt area was a world of blackness. Fields resembled extensive graveyards, and in some places they seemed to stretch forever. Her friends on Draper Street had told her that at night the land above the hill was haunted.

However, she now reasoned, if God were in the shadows, then she was safe.

*

The life of a Salvationist bandsman in the year 1911 was one of considerable dedication, especially in the Earlscourt area. They had open-air gatherings in chilling temperatures on streets that were often deep with mud or frozen hard to create an uneven surface, which made marching difficult. People sometimes ridiculed the bandsmen who conducted these meetings, although gradually people were attracted to their services.

Billy was a part of this life, following in the footsteps of George Meaford, his mentor and bandmaster. Billy's ambition was to someday be as proficient a player as he was. He did not realize that he already surpassed him.

He still had not knelt at the mercy seat, but he lived his life in accordance with the teachings of the New Testament. When he played his cornet, he believed that each note was a word proclaiming its message, as he understood it. He was now eighteen, having grown taller during the past year. His shoulders were more muscular. Though his faith had also matured, his thoughts about the mercy seat remained unchanged.

Because he regularly read *The War Cry,* the official newspaper of The Salvation Army, he knew of the recent excursions of the Toronto Staff Band and dreamt of applying to play in the group. However, they only accepted the finest players from among the bands of the city, and he doubted that they would accept him.

*

On Tuesday, January 31, Billy was unable to contain his excitement. The Toronto Staff Band was to come north over the Davenport Road hill to perform in a musical festival at Rosemount Hall.

On the evening of their visit, a snowstorm howled across the city. The steep slope of the hill was almost impassable. It took several hours for the staff bandsmen to arrive in the barren country land above. It was the band's first visit to the young corps, and its members' determination outweighed the possibility of disappointing the congregation. Shortly before it was time for the festival to begin, the bandsmen stomped into the vestibule of the hall, knocking the snow from their boots.

Men working on Dufferin Street on the Davenport Road hill north of Davenport Road in the summer of 1912. Climbing this hill in winter, prior to the construction of the road, was a formidable task. Notice that the roadway was cut deep into the hill to reduce its height. *City of Toronto Archives, Fonds 1231, Item 1218*

George Meaford had invited the staff band to visit because he felt that his own band required some musical inspiration. The proceeds from the festival were to aid the Rosemount Band. It was ten o'clock when the congregation bade farewell to the staff bandsmen, several of whom did not reach their homes until the early hours of morning.

The music excited Billy, and as such, he had difficulty falling asleep. When slumber finally arrived, his arms were cradling his cornet.

*

During the dismal month of February, Billy and Zack engaged in a prank that in hindsight proved to be a rather foolish one. It all began one afternoon after Bess had arrived home from school. She told her brothers, "This afternoon, I saw Jeremiah Treadwell entering the men's outdoor privy behind the Rosemount Hall."

"So what! The church doesn't lock it. They leave it open for anyone who's walking along St. Clair Avenue," Billy said.

"Two nights ago, I overheard Father and Bandmaster Meaford talking. They said that someone's damaging the outhouse. Mr. Meaford said that if the damage doesn't stop, they'll have to lock the outhouse door. It'll only remain open when the church is open. They said they'd have no other choice."

"Do you think it's Jeremiah?"

"I'm pretty sure."

"Are you positive?" Billy asked.

"No, but I really think he's the one."

The following week, Bess considered her suspicions confirmed.

She told Billy, "Twice this week, I saw Jeremiah enter the backhouse. Both times after he visited it, they found that someone had damaged it."

"I know that you dislike Jeremiah. Is this influencing your opinion?"

"No," she blurted out defensively.

"I've heard that he teases you and calls you 'ugly baby.' He also throws hard-packed snowballs at you."

"I know, and I ignore him, 'cause that makes him mad. It really hurts when the snowballs hit me on the face, but I refuse to cry. To spite him, I just stick out my tongue."

"So you admit that you dislike him, but you're certain that you're not seeking a bit of revenge by accusing him?"

"I know what I saw this week," she replied angrily. "The facts are the facts."

"Why don't we do something about it?" Zack suggested. "I don't like Jeremiah either. It'd be fun to do something to stop him from damaging the outhouse. Instead of telling Father what Bess has discovered, let's solve the problem on our own."

It was Zack who came up with the plan.

Bess told them, "I'll only keep my mouth shut about the plan if you let me join in."

Reluctantly, Billy and Zack agreed.

It was Zack who insisted, "Zeke should be with us, as well."

They readily approved.

Zack told them, "The outhouse roof is hinged so someone can lift it to clean it every spring and fall. There's a sturdy padlock that locks the hinge. However, I know where they keep the key to the lock."

"What do you have in mind?" Billy asked.

"A friend of mine has a pet skunk. He captured it when it was a baby. His father removed the stink glands. The skunk is now big, and though it has sharp claws, it's tame. I think I can talk him into letting us borrow it."

They all smirked as Zack told him the remainder of the details of the plan he had devised.

*

Two days later, late on a Saturday afternoon, secure behind a snowbank created by the wind's piling the drifts against a clump of bushes, the foursome observed Jeremiah entering the outhouse. Creeping silently forward, Billy stood on a wooden crate and, without a sound, unlocked the padlock securing the roof.

Billy whispered to Zack, "Pass up the burlap sack with the skunk inside it."

Zack complied. Stealthily, Billy lifted the roof and placed the open end of the sack against the edge of the top of the outhouse.

"Dump the skunk in," Zack said under his breath.

"Shush."

Billy dumped the skunk inside. The animal had been quiet up to this point, but when Billy unceremoniously released it into the open space, it became enraged.

Jeremiah, his trousers around his ankles, was too busy creating damage with his penknife to the walls of the outhouse to notice Billy lifting the roof. When the animal landed on his head and fell to his lap, he was horrified when he realized it was a skunk. He screamed wildly. Not knowing it was a de-scented animal, he feared that the skunk's foul odour would contaminate him for life.

Leaping from his seat in the outhouse, Jeremiah crashed through the door, which slammed against the outhouse wall with a resounding thud. All the while, Jeremiah was screaming as if his life were in peril. Much to his relief, the animal scampered away. It was then that Jeremiah realized that his pants were down and dragging across the ground, his rear end exposed as on the day when his mother had given him birth.

Bess and Zack started to giggle. Jeremiah turned and saw them. Enraged, he lunged at them, his fists clenched, while trying to pull up his trousers. He stumbled. Gazing up at Billy, he saw that Billy's fist was raised in warning. He remembered the evening Billy's father had thumped his father. Jeremiah thought that if Billy's fists were as threatening as those of his father, then he had best not try to fight him. Besides, his brother, Ezekiel, was there and would likely fight alongside Billy.

Jeremiah hastily retreated, trying to button his underwear and pull up his trousers as he departed, his motions resembling someone's stumbling forward in a sack race. People passing on Dufferin Street saw his predicament, since Jeremiah still had not succeeded in fully pulling up his trousers. Snickers and outright laughter arose in the chilly air. Thoroughly humiliated, Jeremiah slinked homeward, his pants finally elevated to where they belonged.

*

If Jeremiah had been wise, he would have forgotten the humiliation the Mercer boys had inflicted on him. However, forgiveness was not one of his characteristics. Feeling that Zack was the more vulnerable of the Mercer brothers, he plotted his revenge.

It did not take long before he discovered that the skunk they had dumped on him was a pet. A little further investigation led him to discover where its owner lived and the fact that the boy kept the animal in a small shed at the rear of his home. Each night, the boy allowed the skunk to roam the fields near the house to dig for grubs and insects.

Late one afternoon, Jeremiah walked to the home of the boy who owned the pet skunk. It was more than a mile to the west of his own house, an area he rarely frequented. When he arrived in the neighbourhood, the streets were empty. He crept into the shed where the pet was housed. As the animal was tame, Jeremiah found it easy to ensnare its neck in a loop of wire and strangle it.

He muttered, "I'll hang the damn skunk's body from the rafter above the door so Zack's friend will discover it when he enters the shed to let it out to feed."

Jeremiah grinned gleefully as he departed.

The following day, he executed the second part of his plan: to inflict pain on Zack. He knew that Zack often skated on the pond in Wilford's orchard. When Zack was returning home, he would grab him.

Though the days of February were lengthening, it was nearly dark by the time Jeremiah saw Zack and Bess strolling along St. Clair Avenue. Zack had removed his skate blades from his boots and had tied the blades together. They now dangled over his shoulder. His blue wool cap was perched on a jaunty angle, and a tuff of his blond hair protruded from under the cap, falling over his forehead.

Jeremiah watched as Zack and Bess reached the corner of St. Clair and Dufferin streets and entered the laneway between the Army hall and the Royal George Theatre, which led to the fields to the north of their home. He knew that the narrow laneway was deep in shadows, as the buildings blocked any remaining daylight from the ever-darkening sky. Jeremiah was certain that his targets were unaware of his presence. He heard them chatting as they entered the laneway.

Moments later, Jeremiah leaped at them from the shadows. He pushed Bess aside and delivered several violent punches to the side of Zack's head. He cried out as he fell to the ground. Jeremiah now kicked his helpless adversary in the ribs with his thick boot.

Zack whimpered in pain, his breath deserting him.

Then, before Jeremiah was able to crash another boot into Zack, he fell forward, sprawling across Zack. Bess had pushed from behind. Unable to fight Jeremiah, who was older and taller than she was, she had had struck him from the rear. She hoped her intervention might provide Zack with a chance to escape.

However, Zack was too stunned to crawl away. Bess raced to the entrance of the laneway. Gazing up and down the street, she saw that no one was in sight.

Jeremiah stood to his feet and kicked his boot, which landed heavily against the prostrate Zack.

Before Bess was able to reenter the alley to assist Zack, someone at the other end of the laneway came out from the shadows and moved swiftly toward the two boys. The figure grabbed Jeremiah by the collar and thrust him forcefully to the ground.

The hunter had now become the prey.

Then, from the shadows, a voice shouted to Bess, "Quick! Check Zack to see if he's all right." Bess recognized Billy's voice.

Turning toward Jeremiah, Billy said, "Get on home, you coward. If you must fight, at least pick on someone your own size."

Jeremiah staggered to his feet. "You're my size. I'll pound the hell out of you."

Anger clouded Jeremiah's brain, his adrenaline causing blood to pound in his ears. Fists raised, he snarled, "You snot-nosed Mercers are all alike. I'll teach you a lesson you'll never forget."

Before he was able to deliver the opening blow, another shadow crept into the laneway and a menacing voice spit, "Stand aside, boy. This Mercer lad is dumb meat for my fists. Keep out of my way as I hammer him to a pulp."

It was Jeremiah's father, the notorious Pastor Treadwell.

*

A shiver ran up Billy's back as he retreated from the infuriated Mr. Treadwell, who was several inches taller than he was and many pounds heavier. Despite being a self-proclaimed religious man, Treadwell also had a reputation as a brawler. His superior size told Billy that it would be prudent to grab Zack and run. He would live to fight another day. However, Mr. Treadwell had blocked the entrance of the laneway ahead of him, and Jeremiah had manoeuvred himself behind him to prevent him retreating.

A fight was unavoidable.

Billy heard Zack whimper as he cradled his ribs to ease the aching.

Zack's outcry of pain infuriated Billy. Though primed to explode, and what with his adrenaline pumping, he controlled his emotions. Breathing in deeply, he allowed calm to flow over him.

Fists raised, he stood his ground, watching his adversary carefully.

Billy was no longer the young lad whom Mr. Treadwell had punched in the face in front of McCarthy's store. The soft flesh of youth had hardened into muscle. He was a natural fighter, instinctively sensing how to manoeuvre, how to punch hard, and when to dance out of reach. As with his other attributes, this skill came from somewhere inside him. He was born to fight. It was not an acquired skill.

Hesitating, Billy allowed himself more time to assess his adversary. Then he stepped back a few paces, hoping to sucker Treadwell into making the first strike. As Billy intended, Treadwell interpreted Billy's hesitation as fear.

The enraged Treadwell lunged forward, striking hard with his right. Billy weaved deftly out of reach, allowing Treadwell's fist to plunge into space. The momentum of Treadwell's failed punch made him lunge forward. He stumbled.

His adversary caught off balance, Billy hammered a forceful blow to the Pastor's gut. Treadwell grunted heavily as the air rushed from his lungs. Though winded, he quickly struck out again at Billy, who deftly stepped aside and once more struck Treadwell hard in the stomach.

The Pastor screamed in frustration. "Stand still like a man and take your punishment, you child of Satan."

Billy sensed that Treadwell's anger was now beyond control. He was right. Treadwell wheeled around and threw his full weight at him. Billy stepped back to avoid contact.

Then, leading with his left, Billy battered his fist into Treadwell's face. The skin on Treadwell's right cheek split open; blood ran down his face. Without waiting, Billy smacked another blow, striking Treadwell above his right eye. Winded and half-blinded from the oozing blood, the Pastor stopped in his tracks and stared at Billy.

Billy watched Treadwell, attempting to determine his next move.

Moments passed.

Billy continued observing Treadwell. He waited and remained alert. Would the man retreat? If Treadwell came at him again, he wondered if he could knock him out. The man was much heavier than he was, even though he was slow and clumsy.

Jeremiah now decided to assist his father. He rushed forward to strike Billy from behind.

Zack clambered to his feet. Despite the pain shooting through his ribs, he moved swiftly toward Jeremiah, who was too enraged to notice him.

Zack's fist collided with Jeremiah's nose.

Jeremiah collapsed to the ground. Treadwell took advantage of the distraction and struck out at Billy.

The blow never connected. Again, Billy feigned to his left and delivered another pulverizing thrust with his right, connecting directly with Treadwell's bloodied face.

There was pause as the two Treadwells evaluated their situation.

Moments later, they retreated down the laneway, Jeremiah shouting curses as he fled.

*

Billy placed his arms around Zack, who winced from his brother's embrace. The side of Zack's face was trickling blood and beginning to swell. Billy gingerly touched his cheekbone.

"Thank goodness it's not broken. It appears worse than it is."

"It really hurts."

"I know it does," Billy said gently, "but you did well. You saved the day by felling Jeremiah."

Bess, who was watching her two brothers, chirped in, "What about me?"

She felt better when Billy said, "You were also great, Bess. By pushing Jeremiah to the ground after his first attack, you delayed him. It gave me time to grab him by the scruff."

Zack added, "Thanks, Bess. I owe you."

They departed from the laneway a happy triumvirate.

"Will we have to tell Father and Mother what happened?" Zack inquired.

"Are you kidding?" Billy responded. "If we don't, what will we say when they see your face?"

"Tell them I fell off a coal wagon."

"I don't think that would work." Billy could not help but smile. "The wagons have long gone for the day. We have no choice other than to tell them. Earlscourt is a small place; news circulates quickly."

"I doubt that the Treadwells will say anything. They won't want anyone to know that they were beaten."

"True, but they may say that we attacked them."

"I guess you're right. We'll have to tell Father and Mother," Zack responded, resignation audible in his voice.

"I don't think Father and Mother will be proud of us for fighting."

"Maybe not, but they can at least be proud we won," Zack responded, grinning despite his pain.

*

On arriving home, Billy explained what had happened, providing as few details as possible. Their father wanted to put on his coat, visit the constable, and request that he press charges against Mr. Treadwell, as Zack was underage. Billy now informed his father of the prank they had played on Jeremiah with the skunk.

After much discussion, Phil told the boys, "Time to go to bed. In the future, try harder to stay out of fights. I'll decide in the morning what to do."

*

After the boys had gone to bed, Emmy and Phil sat alone at the kitchen table, the silence in the room magnified by the contrasting noise of teaspoons rattling against teacups as Emmy stirred in the sugar. Passing Phil his tea, she gently rested her hand on his arm while gazing sympathetically into his face. His having finally confided in her the details of his fight with Mr. Treadwell, she knew what he was thinking.

"They're following in my footsteps," he lamented. "How can I ever face them if they learn about my own encounter with Treadwell?"

"If our sons follow in your footsteps, I'll be very proud of them. Besides, they likely have stopped the vandalism of the Army's outhouse."

Phil gave a small smile, but he remained unconvinced. "Even that old rascal Reverend Wilmot preached that it was our duty to turn the other cheek rather than fight."

"That old rascal Reverend Wilmot never turned his cheek unless it was to position his mouth to suction food. Sometimes when he visited us, the only reason I fed him a slice of pie was that I feared he might gnaw the legs off our kitchen chairs."

Phil smiled half-heartedly as he nodded his head and said, "I know. Wilmot was not a very good example of a man of God. However, I thought that Billy's fighting days were behind him."

"A man's fighting days never end when the cause is justified and there is no other way. Being a Christian does not make a man or woman perfect. It's the striving to be better."

"If that is the case, Wilmot must be the most 'striving' man in the world."

Emmy grinned and said no more.

*

In the morning, as dawn crept through the east windows of the house on Bird Avenue, the Mercers sat around the kitchen table. Phil told his sons, "I've decided to say nothing more about the events of last evening. Your prank with the skunk may have been at the root of the incident, but Mr. Treadwell didn't forgive as a man of God should've done. Under the circumstances, I think we'd best leave things as they are."

Emmy added supportively, "Mr. Treadwell will receive his reckoning someday."

"Yes," Phil added, "and he might be surprised how dramatic it'll be."

"The Lord works in mysterious ways," Emmy said.

Her words ended the conversation.

After the boys departed the kitchen, Phil told Emmy, "I don't understand how on earth Billy managed to whip the Pastor Treadwell. He's a mature man and an experienced fighter. Billy's not."

"Or is he?" Emmy asked.

"Sometimes I wonder if there are there any limits to what Billy can accomplish if he sets his mind to it. You've always said that Billy will make us proud. But now I'm beginning to realize that Billy is different from every lad I've ever met or heard about."

"In some respects, we'll never truly understand our own son."

"I think you may be right."

*

The festering wound of defeat cut deeply into Mr. Treadwell's pride. To make matters worse, he was aware that his son's lack of respect for him had deepened. He knew that his wife, Polly, invariably gazed at him with fear in her eyes. However, Jeremiah was his favourite. It was important that the lad respect him, even though he believed that respect without fear was of little consequence.

Treadwell feared his God and believed that this fear kept him righteous and prevented the world from defeating him. He had bullied and pushed his harsh beliefs on others all his life, and he had never felt the sting of defeat until he met the accursed Mercer family. He remembered the passage in the Bible where the prophet Elijah challenged the priests of Baal that their god bring down the fires of heaven. When they failed, it was proof that Elijah's God was greater than their god.

Could the God of the Mercers be greater than Treadwell's God was? The Mercers seemed stronger than he was. Treadwell did not attend any church other than his own. During the summer months, he preached in a clearing in Wilfred's apple orchard, and during the winter months the apple grower allowed him to use his barn. Though Treadwell had no clerical training, his imposing size and booming voice permitted him to preach mightily. There were many who attended his makeshift services, some out of conviction and others out of mere curiosity. He taught a Christian religion dominated by the fear of fire and brimstone, as he believed the Bible instructed. He had always preached, "Give me that old-time religion."

Was there more to the practice of religion than obeying God out of fear? he now thought. The matter required deep consideration. Something was wrong in his life. His aching bones from the beating he had received at the hands of a teenage boy made him feel like a defeated priest of Baal.

Billy Mercer had stormed Treadwell's Mount Carmel. The Pastor felt as if his God had deserted him.

*

Despite its being the beginning of April, George Meaford feared that the Canadian spring had forever deserted the land. However, as the days passed, hints of the approaching season gradually emerged. The barren, blackened trees finally sported tiny green buds. However, as the temperatures began to rise, some lamented that the sun-filled skies also produced the inevitable seas of mud.

Looking west along St. Clair Avenue from near Avenue Road in 1908. Life above the Davenport Road hill remained primitive compared to life in the city below. *City of Toronto Archives, Fonds 1244, Item 0019*

By April 1911, George noticed that the Rosemount Band had greatly improved. He was delighted. Another occurrence added to his enjoyment. His application for membership in the Toronto Staff Band had been successful.

His responsibilities increased in the days ahead. Along with attending the rehearsals of the staff band, he also worked long hours as a carpenter, since the need for housing in the Earlscourt District was increasing each month. Practising on his trombone, preparing for band practices, performing household chores, and doing other activities at the corps allowed him very little free time. As well, he tutored Zack and Billy. It was often approaching the midnight hour when he extinguished the kerosene lamp and climbed into bed beside Vangie. She always supported him in his work and did her best to assist him, but she became increasingly concerned about the long hours he laboured and his lack of free time.

Another event was soon to place further demands on George. The first week of May, he received an invitation for the Rosemount Band to perform at its first citywide musical festival. He felt the responsibility keenly since he wanted the band to perform well. He held several extra practices and drilled the men thoroughly.

The Army was holding the concert in Massey Hall, with many bands and Army dignitaries in attendance. To perform in Massey Hall was an honour that George did not take lightly.

*

George discussed the pending event with Vangie one evening, shortly before they retired for the night. On several occasions, he had played in the great hall on Shuter Street, a short distance east of Yonge Street, with the Queen Street Band. He knew the history of the hall, even though it was a relatively new building.

He told Vangie, "Massey Hall was the first hall ever built in Canada expressly for concerts."

"It's an impressive building. Its red-brick façade, with the classical figures inside the Greek triangle pediment, dominates the street."

"That it does. It was designed by C. R. Badgeley, a Canadian architect who lives in Cleveland. Hart Massey donated the money for its construction to honour the memory of his son. The great hall cost one hundred and fifty thousand dollars."

"I wasn't aware of that."

"It opened in June of 1894 with a gala performance of Handel's 'Messiah.'"

"I'm not old enough to remember that far back," she teased.

"Neither am I," he countered. "I read about it."

George continued telling Vangie about the hall. "The year after its inauguration, the Toronto Mendelssohn Choir chose it as its home, and in 1906 the Toronto Symphony Orchestra did likewise. Paderewski performed on its stage in that year, and two years later, the great Caruso sang to capacity crowds in the hall. Its reputation has grown quickly. Experts now say that the only concert hall in North America to equal its acoustics is New York's Carnegie Hall."

Toronto's Massey Hall in 1912. *Photo from book published by the City of Toronto in 1912*

George added, "I'm keenly aware that our band is stepping onto a stage upon which some of the world's greatest musicians have performed."

"You also know, of course, that more experienced Army bands of the city will be present and listening carefully when the Rosemount Band plays."

"I'm only too aware. It increases the pressure on us. To make matters worse, on the afternoon of the concert several of my bandsmen will be absent, as they are travelling."

"The band will be fine," Vangie said reassuringly.

*

On the Saturday evening of the festival, Billy entered the hall and climbed the stairs to the stage level. Arriving at the entrance to the stage, he hesitated. Breathing deeply, he took his first step forward, his stomach fluttering with a million swirling butterflies.

Having entered from stage left on the east side of the hall, he kept his head down and eyes lowered to avoid tripping over the chairs positioned on the wooden floor to accommodate the numerous participating bands. He proceeded toward the area reserved for the Rosemount Band, on the far side of the stage, near the west wall.

Billy gripped his cornet tightly as he advanced.

Many of the other bandsmen's chairs were already occupied, a few of the older players gazing at Billy's youthful countenance, some sensing that it was his first appearance at a major festival.

One of the men smiled and said, "Is this your first time in the great hall?" Encouragingly, he added, "I remember my first time. I survived. I'm still here today."

Billy smiled, the man chucked, and Billy continued toward the other side of the stage.

It seemed a lifetime before Billy reached the chair assigned to him. The Colour-Sergeant who carried the flag on open-airs was also the band librarian. As Billy arrived beside his designated chair, the man said, "Lad, I've put your solo cornet music on your chair."

Billy thanked him as he sat down.

He then picked up the tune book, opened it to the page of the hymn, and positioned the book on his music stand. Then he looked up. For the first time, his eyes scanned the audience.

His heart dropped to his boots.

Interior of Massey Hall in 1912, with its high-vaulted ceiling and Moorish arches. *Photo from book published by the City of Toronto in 1912*

A few moments later, Zack arrived. Billy whispered to him, "I've played before crowds before, but never like this."

"Father told me that the hall seats thirty-five hundred people."

Gulping silently, Billy scanned the vast auditorium. He said to Zack, his voice now a little louder, "The ground-floor seats are already full, and in the two balconies there're very few empty seats. I think that the whole city is here for the concert."

"The crowds don't bother me. I've been on the stage here twice before, when my class was in the Toronto schools' May Festival Concert. In the mass choir, we sang British folksongs."

When it was time for the concert to begin, Billy and Zack watched as the bandmasters of the various bands entered the hall to loud applause. Billy felt greatly encouraged when George Meaford had taken his seat.

Then the audience grew silent as Commissioner David Hees, who was the afternoon's chairman, stepped to the podium to offer a few introductory remarks. He concluded by saying, "We warmly welcome the Rosemount Band to this concert, since it's their first appearance at an Army festival."

Then he added, "It's also good to note that five other bands are on the platform—the Riverdale Band, Queen Street Citadel Band, Territorial Youth Band, and Parliament Street Corps Band. The featured group is the Toronto Temple Band."

Billy whispered to Zack, "The Toronto Temple Band's one of the largest and best bands in the city. I don't know what they'll think of us."

*

The concert commenced with the massed bands playing a festival march. Two of the bands performed before it was time for the Rosemount Band to offer their selection. Billy focused on the music. For him, the audience and the great hall no longer existed. He eyed George Meaford's baton as it raised for the opening note.

Within seconds, Billy was lost in the music.

Balancing his sound with the other instruments and forming each note carefully, he manipulated the valves of his cornet as if the music were the only thing that existed in his universe. He poured his heart and soul into it, moving confidently through the difficult passages, never relaxing his concentration when performing the less intricate sections. His tone was full and smooth, especially in the difficult section where he soloed. George had purposely chosen the composition to feature his accomplished young player.

Billy did not disappoint. The rich sound of his instrument poured over the audience, his rendition aided by the warm acoustics for which the hall was becoming famous.

Even before the band's final note ceased, the audience responded with loud applause. Billy gazed at Bandmaster Meaford who gave him a slight smile as he placed the baton at rest on the music stand.

*

Exiting Massey Hall onto Shuter Street, Billy ignored the clip-clop of the horses and the drone of the carriage wheels, which mingled with the noisy streetcars and automobiles. He overheard a few of the comments. Several people mentioned the Rosemount Band and were enthusiastic about its performance.

Billy blushed when he heard a man say, "The band's young solo cornet player was excellent. He performed his solo in the score exceptionally well. He seems too young to play in such a mature manner."

Mingling among the throngs is where Billy and Zack found their parents. Phil placed his arms around his sons and smiled encouragingly. "You did well, boys. The band sounded great," he said.

Zack beamed and Billy smiled, but in truth, they did not know what to think. Billy knew he had done his best, and from what he heard, Zack had performed admirably. As they walked eastward along Shuter Street, Billy placed his arm around Zack's shoulder, his embrace reassuring to his younger brother.

*

The following week, Emmy scanned the pages of *The War Cry* for a report on the concert. The words that jumped out at her were these:

> The Rosemount Band performed admirably. In this *War Cry* reporter's opinion, the young solo cornet player in the band bears watching.

*

In the final week of May in 1911, the Toronto Staff Band travelled to Owen Sound. The band appeared splendid in their scarlet festival tunics. The braid on their uniforms was wider than the one on their regular uniform, and because it was white in colour, it contrasted attractively with the red tunic.

As Vangie Meaford admired the costume, she told her husband, "You look dashing in it."

George replied, "Just think how much more dashing a young man of Billy's stature would appear in it. I look forward to the day he dons the scarlet tunic."

"You look fine, George. But I admit that Billy's trim figure would create quite a sight."

"Are you implying that I'm no longer trim?"

"You have put on a few pounds lately."

"It's because of your excellent cooking."

Though pleased with his compliment, she did not thank him. Instead, she said, "I was thinking the other day. The man within Billy has fully emerged."

"Yes. Though yet a teenager, he's more of a man than many of those who're considerably older, especially in his music and his thinking."

"I know how much you love him."

"He's like a son to me."

"Billy will be nineteen on his birthday."

"Yes," George replied. "He had the ability to be a valuable member of the staff band. I'm wondering how I can draw the staff bandmaster's attention to him. I'm determined that within the year, Billy will don the scarlet uniform."

*

The delicate white blossoms in Wilford's apple orchard burst forth in all their glory to announce the arrival of June. It was now possible to climb the Davenport Road hill without confronting snowstorms or, as earlier in the spring, mudslides. The second week of the month, the Dovercourt Band and Songsters arrived early on a Sunday morning at the Rosemount Corps. The men were grateful for the dry conditions underfoot when they departed eastward from the hall. The Rosemount Band joined them. They had recently acquired several new bandsmen and, with no absentees, now had nineteen players.

The chosen location for the open-air service was on St. Clair Avenue near Wilford's orchard. As the bandsmen stood in a circle for the opening hymn, white petals from the apple blossoms floated lazily downward, scenting the air and scattering amid the tall grasses sprouting among the trees.

Jeremiah's father, the self-appointed pastor, was conducting an outdoor service of his own. When the bands' music floated across the open space amid the apple trees, Jeremiah watched and looked around at those who were attending his father's service of "hell and damnation." Despite his father's obvious disapproval of the music, he thought the sound of the music pleasant. It was a new experience for him. Never before had he really listened to the Army band.

However, as the music continued, his father became more enraged.

Blood rushed to his face, and Jeremiah knew that he was controlling his anger with great difficulty. He also knew that his father was unable to desert his flock to tramp through the orchard to wring the neck of the accursed Bandmaster Meaford.

Frustrated, the Pastor shouted, “Beware of false prophets. They can beguile and enchant as they lead a man onto the paths of unrighteousness.”

As Mr. Treadwell continued to vent his anger, he ignored Jeremiah. He was sitting on an upended wooden crate to prevent soiling his Sunday clothes, having positioned himself on the periphery of the group beneath the shade of a mature tree. It was easy for him to sneak away.

Arriving near to where the band was playing, Jeremiah slid behind several men standing on the plank sidewalk listening to the music. He scanned the faces of the bandsmen. They did not see him, as they were reading the music as they performed. Continuing to observe, Jeremiah saw that Billy was playing without glancing at the tune book, as he evidently knew the hymn by heart. Then Jeremiah became aware that Billy had noticed him. Their eyes met. Coals of enmity burned in Jeremiah’s heart.

As the second verse of the hymn ended, Billy lowered his cornet. Captain Rush preached to those who had gathered. Billy gazed directly at Jeremiah and gave him a friendly smile. Jeremiah froze. It was the last thing he had expected. A sneer or a glance of hostility he knew how to handle. Then he wondered if perhaps Billy was mocking him. However, the smile contained no subtext of malice or mockery. It struck Jeremiah dumb. He turned away. When he looked at Billy a second time, he smiled again.

Next, Billy played the music for the third verse. For this verse, the other solo cornets remained silent while the remainder of the bandsmen accompanied him. Never before had Jeremiah heard Billy play. The sweetness of the sound struck something inside him.

He was unaware that it was to be a pivotal moment in his life.

That spring morning, amid the blossoms of Wilford’s apple orchard, Billy’s cornet planted a seed in Jeremiah’s heart that would grow into something that his father would never recognize.

The trumpet had sounded.

*

Meanwhile, across the sea in London, England, plans for an important event were in the final stages. Also, throughout the far-flung countries of the British Empire, people were greatly anticipating Thursday, June 22, 1911—the coronation of Their Majesties King George V and Queen Mary.

George informed Vangie on the day prior to the event, "The city of Toronto has planned a people's coronation service for two-thirty in High Park. Officials have requested that Commissioner David Hees conduct it, along with other city clergy and members of various Army and church congregations. Massed bands are to be in attendance, as is the Toronto Staff Band. They've invited everyone in Toronto to participate in the service of thanksgiving."

"It sounds as if it'll be an impressive event."

"We're wearing our scarlet festival uniform. Billy and Zack have asked if they can accompany me."

"Of course, you agreed."

"Of course."

Vangie nodded in approval.

*

The next day, when the triumvirate arrived at High Park, they walked southward, finally reaching the hill that overlooked Grenadier Pond, to which people sometimes referred as Grenadier Lake. George listened as Billy chatted with Zack.

Billy said, "The hill surrounding the water on the east side makes a great viewing area. People are already placing blankets on the grass to reserve places to sit."

"I don't see anyone I recognize."

"Look down there, at the bottom of the hill, on the flat area near the water's edge. They've erected a platform and have chairs for the massed bands."

George interrupted them. "I'm going down to the area they've reserved for the staff band. I'll see you later."

Billy and Zack said goodbye and joined the crowds gathering to sit on the slopes of the hill. Finding a place with a great view near the top of the hill, they surveyed the scene.

Zack said, "Wow! Look at all the people who're arriving."

"It's going to be a hot, sunny day. The oak trees behind us will shade us from the sun's heat. The three sides of the grassy slope make a natural amphitheatre. It can hold thousands of people. And it looks out over Grenadier Pond."

"Look at the platform where the Commissioner will stand. They've decorated it with coloured red, white, and blue bunting."

"Do you see the huge banner with the words 'God Bless Our King and Queen'?"

"Of course."

*

Finally, it was time for the service to commence. The Army bandsmen and dignitaries had all gathered. Sunlight glinted through the trees, reflecting from the polished silver of the musicians' instruments and highlighting the scarlet hues of the staff bandsmen's tunics. About five thousand people were present, seated around the slopes and on the hilltop above.

Following the Commissioner's introductory words of welcome, the first hour of the service was devoted to musical selections by the various bands. Then, all of the musical forces united in sounding forth a stirring rendition of Britain's national anthem, which brought everyone in the vast assembly to their feet.

Next, the bands accompanied the throngs as the forest glade echoed triumphantly with the words of the hymn "All Hail the Power of Jesus' Name."

Billy told Zack, "I wish they'd asked the Rosemount Band to participate in the coronation service."

"It would've been great to be down there beside the staff band."

"I agree."

After the people had finished singing the hymn, Zack whispered to Billy, "I have to go to the outhouse to pee."

"Do you know where it is?"

"Sure, it's just behind the brow of the hill."

"Look around and memorize the location where I'm sitting so you can find me again. And don't be too long."

"I'll be as long as it takes," he said with a grin as he sauntered off, weaving his way among the spectators seated on the hillside. Billy was not aware that someone else had observed Zack's departure and decided to follow him.

*

Commissioner Hees now delivered a celebratory sermon. After about fifteen minutes, Billy wondered why Zack had not returned. After another five minutes, he became worried. He decided to investigate.

Before departing, he said to a man who earlier had talked to Zack and him, "Would you please watch for my brother, Zack? If he returns while I'm away, tell him to wait here for me."

Having covered his bases, Billy climbed the hill in search of his brother.

When he was over the crest of the hill, he could see the outhouse in the distance. He saw that a group of boys was merrily tipping one of them, allowing it to collapse almost to the ground before uprighting it and tipping it once more.

Unbeknownst to Billy, it was Jeremiah Treadwell who had seen Zack leave the hillside and, suspecting where he was going, had followed him. A boy inside an outhouse provided unlimited possibilities for pranks. As Billy approached, he could see that the boys were intent on rolling the outhouse down the hill. If it rolled all the way down, it would crash into Grenadier Pond.

Then Billy saw Jeremiah. He wondered if he were a part of the group.

When Billy drew closer, he heard Zack's screams. Billy quickly interrupted the group's laughter by shouting, "Stop! My brother's inside!"

The boys dropped the outhouse to the ground and stared at him.

"Who the hell are you?" a muscular kid about Billy's size snarled. An ugly three-inch scar marred his left cheek, and his nose was crooked, as if it had been broken once, perhaps twice.

Billy quickly scanned the group. Except for Jeremiah, he recognized no one. He sensed that Jeremiah was unfamiliar with the others, too.

"Let my brother out. There's no harm done," Billy said, trying to placate the ugly lad.

"There'll be harm done when I smash in your face," Scarface replied menacingly.

The boy raised his fists. His companions immediately backed away to allow the two space to fight. The boy advanced confidently toward Billy.

Jeremiah continued watching.

The bully threw the first punch. However, as the boy struck with his right fist, his left side was exposed. Billy dodged him and hammered a smashing punch with his left. It was of sufficient force to knock the boy down, but he seemed unfazed. However, being an experienced street fighter, he momentarily backed off.

The boy assumed that Billy fought from the left, and so he grinned confidently. He knew that Billy would expose his right side when he struck again. The boy attempted another crushing blow, this time from the right.

A second time Billy dodged, and then he jabbed the other boy forcefully with his right. The strike almost knocked him senseless, but he remained on his feet. Billy aimed his next blow toward the centre of his opponent's face. The boy was too slow to block it. He went down hard and did not get up, too dazed to stand and retaliate.

The other boys in the gang watched in awe as they saw their leader humbled. In the ensuing silence, the strains of the Army band music were audible from below the hill. The boys did not move as they observed Billy to see if he would attack one of them.

However, when Billy heard his brother cry out from inside the outhouse, he walked over and set it upright. Inside, Zack was awaiting his rescue. Billy unlatched the door, and Zack stepped out into the sunlight. He saw that Scarface was on the ground and guessed what had happened.

Billy and Zack calmly walked away.

As the brothers sat down again on the grassy slope, a senior officer was stepping onto the platform. The people stood reverently to their feet and bowed their heads as he read the Coronation Prayer. Then the massed bands played the "Coronation March."

The people's coronation service in Toronto's High Park was over, and the crowds slowly dispersed.

*

When Jeremiah departed from High Park, many thoughts tumbled in his mind. His hatred for Billy and Zack had mellowed since he had heard Billy perform on his cornet that Sunday morning beside Wilford's orchard. Though he hated to admit it, he harboured a begrudging admiration for Billy. Jeremiah's father had taught him to respect strength, and Billy possessed it in abundance.

What was it that Billy possessed? Nobody his age should have such abilities. He could play an instrument as well as he could fight.

Jeremiah's father had taught him that only the strong and righteous win in battle. Billy was certainly strong, but he was also gentle, and he only fought when there was no other way. Was it possible that Billy's smile and music could win more battles than his father's fists and bullying sermons?

*

By September 1911, the Rosemount Band consisted of twenty-three bandsmen. Each Sunday morning as they gathered for open-air services, it was obvious to them that the autumn season was progressing. By the end of October, the hand of the new season fully gripped the landscape. With the diminished sunshine, the sky billowed with masses of silver-grey clouds that extended from horizon to horizon.

During the blustery month of November, there was a service in the hall that Zack was to remember for a long time. It featured "The Salvation Army cowboy," a Salvationist who was attired in a Texan outfit with all the trimmings. The cowboy also attended the open-air gatherings and drew large crowds. Following these gatherings, many people went to morning service in the hall.

For the afternoon musical service, the Army rented the Royal George Theatre because they expected overflow crowds. It was available since the city allowed no movies on Sundays. The Royal George's large auditorium was ideal for special occasions. Hoping no one would notice them among the crowd, Jeremiah Treadwell and his sister, Annabelle, snuck into the theatre. However, Zack saw them.

He knew that Annabelle was sixteen, a year younger than her brother Jeremiah. Zack was certain that their father did not know they were here. However, he was unaware that Annabelle's motive for attending was to watch Billy. She had observed him many times walking along St. Clair Avenue and had seen him in McCarthy's store. She considered him the most attractive boy she had ever seen.

*

As Billy sat in his chair in the cornet section, which now included four other players, he gazed across the theatre. He noticed Jeremiah and saw that his sister was with him. He told Zack, "Jeremiah's in the hall. We're not exactly friends, but since the day in High Park, we nod to each other if we meet."

"I see him. He's with his sister, Annabelle."

"I've seen her at McCarthy's store. She's pretty. I enjoy talking to her."

"I think she's a hellcat," Zack responded.

Continuing to scan the crowd, who filled almost every seat, Billy noticed someone else he recognized. It was Jenny. With her was her mother, Mrs. McMillan. Billy's heart beat faster, and without his realizing it, his face flushed. However, Zack noticed.

Sitting beside Mrs. McMillan was Billy's boss, Mr. McCarthy.

Billy said to Zack, "Mr. McCarthy and Mrs. McMillan are close friends."

"I hear that they're *very* close," Zack said as he grinned.

Billy ignored the remark.

Then Zack said, "I think that Mr. McCarthy and Mrs. McMillan are much, much more than friends."

"What makes you say that?"

"I overheard Mother say that Grandmother Mercer told her that Mr. McCarthy has asked Mrs. McMillan to marry him, and that she's considering it seriously."

"What else did you overhear?"

"Grandmother Mercer says that some of the bachelors in the Queen Street neighbourhood would ask their cow to marry them if it had a rich dowry." Zack continued grinning.

"Well, Mr. McCarthy has a successful business, so he has no reason to marry Mrs. McMillan for her money."

"Grandmother Mercer told Mother that Mrs. McMillan's visit to the

Earlscourt this afternoon is a scouting expedition. I'm not sure what that means."

Billy explained, "I think it means that she's trying to decide how she feels about Mr. McCarthy. Everyone says he's handsome, and I can personally testify to his kindness. However, she may be trying to decide if she loves him. Love is essential in a marriage. If the love is strong, other difficulties can be managed."

"How do you know all these mushy things?"

"I just know."

Zack started to giggle. He said, "I think it's because you want to marry Jenny."

Billy blushed, which sent Zack into a fit of laughter.

"Keep quiet," Billy told him. "It's time for the band to play."

Billy's gaze turned toward Bandmaster Meaford as he stepped to the dais to conduct the music for the opening congregational song. Zack was now intent on his music, and Billy was grateful that he did not ask any more questions.

*

The afternoon went well. The cowboy thrilled everyone with his stories of the Mexican Highlands where he had been born. At one point, he even swung a lasso wildly in the air, shouting vociferously as if galloping across the high grasslands of Mexico and chasing a herd of cattle.

At the end of the final hymn, Billy quickly tucked his cornet in its case, folded up his music, left the stage, and went into the audience. Weaving his way among the people, he finally connected with Jenny in the theatre's lobby. When she gazed directly at him, he blushed. Instead of talking to her, he shyly turned to Mrs. McMillan and told her how glad he was to see her.

"Billy! It's such a pleasure to see you, too," she responded warmly. "Do you remember my daughter, Jenny?"

"Of course," he replied, as his eyes met hers.

Then Billy shyly dropped his gaze.

Jenny did not.

"Nice to see you again, Billy," she said. Then she coyly added, "I was hoping I'd see you. I've not seen you since you left my mother's store to move up here to the Earlscourt District. I understand you now work for Mr. McCarthy. He often tells me about you when he visits my mother. You've grown since I last saw you."

Because Jenny had begun the conversation and made it obvious she was interested in him, Billy mounted the courage to speak.

"You've grown, too. I've often wondered how you were doing. I bet you have many boys admiring you."

Billy instantly regretted having uttered the last remark, fearing it was obvious that he was asking if she had a boyfriend.

Jenny laughed softly. Leaning closer to him and glancing directly into his eyes, she said in a quiet, conspiratorial tone, "I always hoped you'd be an admirer, Billy."

If the roots of the hair were capable of burning, Billy's would have been a raging fire. Without thinking, he gazed back at her, smiled, and said, "I will if you want me." Then, feeling he had been too forward, he instantly regretted his words. Fortunately, he continued to hold his gaze and this was his salvation. It was all the encouragement Jenny needed.

"I hope we see each other again, Billy," she told him encouragingly. "Perhaps on one of the Saturday evenings when Mr. McCarthy journeys down the hill to visit my mother, you'll accompany him."

Billy never knew where he received the courage to utter the words, "I would enjoy that."

Jenny smiled enchantingly, obviously pleased at his response. Billy felt as if he were floating on air. Pleasing Jenny was now the most important thing in his life. The auditorium and the crowds disappeared from view. He only had eyes for her.

*

Billy was unaware that Annabelle Treadwell had witnessed the exchange of words from a distance, his and Jenny's body language telling her what had occurred. He also did not know that jealousy had seized her heart and that she now despised him. From that moment onward, she would plot his downfall, certain that Jeremiah would assist her.

*

In mid-December, Bess helped her mother prepare for the yuletide season by assisting her with preparations for the all-important days ahead when visitors would be calling and family and guests would share the cookies and cakes. Although Bess was now thirteen, her older sisters were better suited to assist their mother with the cleaning chores, allowing her to have a little more free time. As soon as her homework was complete, Bess grabbed her skate blades and bolted out the door to race over to the pond in Wilford's orchard.

Bess skimmed across the surface of the ice at unbelievable speeds, laughing and carefree as she enjoyed the delights of a Canadian winter. Friends she knew from school and others from the church skated beside and around her, a few of the boys close in age trying to grab her hat to catch her attention. She was maturing attractively, and the boys had certainly noticed. Some admired her smile and pert little nose, while others were attracted to her flashing blue eyes. Whatever the reason for it, Bess was enjoying the attention. It was a new experience for her, and new experiences are always a delight for any thirteen-year-old.

As she skated, she was aware that four teenagers had gathered at the east side of the pond, and she noticed that they were discussing something serious with Annabelle Treadwell. Bess paid little attention to them.

Bess was unable to hear them, but one of the teenagers was questioning Annabelle, who knew the teens from the services her father conducted in the barn. They were loutish lads, unkempt and coarse in their habits.

"You want us to beat up Billy Mercer?" the shortest of the foursome said.

"Yes. Are you afraid of him?" she taunted.

"Why do you want him thrashed?" another asked.

"He's a heathen, and as my father says, 'The hand of the righteous should smite the wicked.' He needs a good beating." Annabelle, similar to her father, knew how to twist words to suit her own purposes, as well as how to mimic her father's preacher's vocabulary.

"I hear he's an awesome fighter," the short boy said.

"So you *are* afraid of him."

The boy now remained silent.

The tallest boy inquired, "Isn't he the one who works at McCarthy's and is a sissy player in that heathen circus band?"

"That's him," Annabelle replied. "My brother Jeremiah will help you. I see him at the other end of the rink. He's just arrived. Billy will be here in a few minutes, too. He always escorts his sister home."

Then Annabelle told them her plan to entrap Billy, enabling them to "smite the evil sinner," as she had phrased it.

*

Five minutes later, as the last light of day drained from the sky, Annabelle noticed that Bess had sat to rest for a few moments on a snowbank at the edge of the pond. A cute boy was trying to impress her, but Bess seemed indifferent. Then, as Annabelle had instructed, one of her cohorts pushed the boy aside while the three others boys grabbed Bess from behind, pinning her arms so she was unable to escape.

Annabelle growled to the four lads, "Hold her until her brother arrives. I see him coming along St. Clair now. Twist her arm and make her scream. When he comes to her rescue, pounce on him."

The final hint of daylight had now disappeared. In the shadows, Annabelle watched as Billy walked along St. Clair Avenue and approached the pond. When he was not too distant, the boys, as planned, twisted Bess's arm forcefully, but she refused to scream. However, Billy saw what was happening and came rushing to her aid.

It was then that Annabelle saw it was not Billy.

It was Ezekiel, her older brother.

Annabelle noticed that Ezekiel remained calm as he faced the tormentors. She thought it was likely Billy who had taught her brother to size up his opponents. *It will make no difference,* she thought. She had selected those who were more mature, almost men. Three of them were in their late teens, and the fourth was nearly twenty. Ezekiel was nineteen, but it was four against one. Annabelle smile as she realized that the wheels she had set in motion were now set to roll over her brother. She was not concerned, as she considered him a traitor to her family. She sneered at him as she said, "Father says that you're a child of the devil, and I believe it."

Then, turning to her other brother, she yelled, "Jeremiah, punch the snivelling traitor in his ugly face."

*

Ezekiel ignored his sister as he stood his ground. However, he noticed that Jeremiah had edged toward him.

Ezekiel tensed and tightened his fist.

Then, to his surprise, he heard his brother snarl to Annabelle's cohorts, "If you want to whup my brother, you'll have to go through me."

Ezekiel grinned as Annabelle's mouth opened wide in surprise. Jeremiah now stood beside him.

However, it remained two against four.

Then, from out of the shadows, Billy appeared and stood beside Jeremiah and Ezekiel.

Now it was three against four.

Annabelle had listened to far too many of her father's sermons.

She screamed, "The Lord is with ye. Who can smite ye if he is on your side?"

There was a pause before the lads obeyed Annabelle's order. However, their opponents were prepared.

A slight nod of Billy's head notified Ezekiel of what he was to do. Jeremiah sensed what was about to happen, as he had witnessed Billy in action before. The oldest of Annabelle's thugs was standing behind the other three boys, who were protecting him even though he was the heaviest and the tallest of them all. Ezekiel was certain the tall boy was a coward who possessed no ability to lead.

Then in a flash, the action began.

*

Billy lunged forward, crashing through the three protectors. Into the opening that Billy created—before the three defending boys had a chance to recover—the Treadwell brothers rushed. The big lad never knew what hit him. The minute he fell to the ground, the flying fists of Jeremiah and Ezekiel struck the other three. It was only seconds before they fled,

Annabelle behind them. It was clear that she had no desire to face the wrath of her two brothers.

Billy and Ezekiel stared at Jeremiah, who grinned sheepishly.

"Thanks for helping us," Billy said.

"No problem."

"You have quite a right hook," Billy said.

"Thanks." Then Jeremiah added, "Can I ask for a favour?"

Billy gazed at him suspiciously. "What is it you want?"

"Will you teach me to fight?"

The request surprised Billy. He paused and peered intently into Jeremiah's face as he decided his response.

"I don't think that would be a wise thing for me to do."

"Why not?"

Ezekiel now interrupted. "As our father might say, you only fortify the arms of the righteous. Heaven knows what you would do if you had Billy's skills."

"I'll make a deal with you, Jeremiah," Billy said. "If you learn to play a brass instrument, I'll teach you to fight. You may find that the sound of a single trumpet wins more battles than all the warriors of a mighty army."

"I know the story of the battle of Jericho," he replied. "I don't want to bring down any walls. I simply want to know how to fight better."

"Fine! Then learn an instrument first."

"I'll think about it."

Billy walked away into darkness of the evening, his arm around Bess.

*

As Jeremiah watched Bess, Billy, and Ezekiel walk away, he was lost in thought. He knew that an inner strength possessed Ezekiel and Billy. He longed to possess their strength. He despised weakness, yet he was now consorting with two boys to whom his father referred as "the princes of darkness."

His father's sermons echoed in his head and he was confused. However, he knew that he wanted to learn to fight, not make music.

*

As the final days of 1911 plodded forward, Christmas music, yuletide festivals, and sacred carols rose to the rafters of the Rosemount Hall, drowning out the cries of the wind echoing along St. Clair Avenue.

As the season intensified, open-air services again became more difficult. Billy and Zack applied kerosene oil to the valves of their cornets to prevent them from freezing. It was not always successful, and the valves often became stuck, causing missed notes in a few of the songs and extra notes in others. On a few occasions, their lips became glued to the mouthpieces of their instruments.

At least Bandmaster Meaford's baton was immune to the harshness of the weather. It never froze. But on the occasions when he played his trombone to assist the small group, he, too, suffered the ill effects of the freezing conditions. Despite these barriers, people heard the sounds of the carols throughout the Earlscourt District. Billy performed cornet solos, and increasingly, Zack played a few as well. Many people throughout the neighbourhood recognized the Mercer brothers by sight. Sometimes they saw Jeremiah in the background listening to the band, although he never approached Billy.

With the conclusion of the nativity season, the watch-night service heralded in the New Year. Everyone shouted joyously, "Happy New Year."

Chapter Six

During January 1912, the weather continued to create hardships in the district above the hill. However, time continued its unalterable course, and slowly, the months of winter dissolved into spring.

On the morning of April 15, Mr. McCarthy was a few minutes late unlocking the door of his shop. It was a Monday. The previous evening he had been late returning to his home on Earlscourt Avenue as he had been down in the city attending church with Mrs. McMillan. Billy was already waiting for him at the door, and beside him stood Zeke Treadwell, his new employee. Business had improved during the previous year since Mrs. McMillan had assisted McCarthy in employing several promotional techniques that had increased profits. The cleanliness of the grocery and dry goods store and its improved organization had also helped. Because of the increased business, Billy had suggested that Mr. McCarthy hire Zeke. Billy's recommendation was sufficient reference as far as the shop owner was concerned. Zeke was grateful for the opportunity, as it meant that he no longer had to journey down the hill to earn his wages.

After the three of them entered the shop, the bell above the door fell silent. A few minutes later, a breathless woman pushed the door open so forcefully that she almost knocked the bell from its fastenings.

Without any greeting, she gasped, "Have you heard the latest news?"

Gazing at the three males, she knew by their puzzled looks that they were not aware of the recent events. Sticking her tongue to the side of her mouth in satisfaction at being the first to deliver the news, she stared at them.

"My goodness, woman," Mr. McCarthy exclaimed. "Say what you have to say before we all die with curiosity."

"Early this morning, the son of my neighbour, Mrs. Martha Simpson, arrived from down in the city."

"Get on with it. What did she tell you?"

"The *Titanic* struck an iceberg in the North Atlantic."

Silence fell across the shop.

Stories of the *Titanic*'s maiden voyage had been in the newspapers for weeks. Through the miracle of the wireless aboard the ship, reporters had chronicled her progress across the Atlantic. The great ocean liner was unsinkable. How could this have happened?

Over the next hour, people arrived at the shop and, in quiet, sombre tones, talked about the disaster. Shortly after 10:00 a.m., a man entered the store carrying a newspaper he had brought during his early morning journey down to the city. For the first time, the Earlscourt area saw the news of the sinking in print and learned details of the disaster.

PAGE ABOUT DR. BEATTIE NESBITT

THE TORONTO DAIL

CANADIAN LINER TOWING STEAMSHIP TITANIC TO H

WORLD'S LARGEST STEAMSHIP CRASHED INTO ICEBERG AND AT LAST REPORT WAS SINKING

LINERS PARISIAN, VIRGINIAN, CARPATHIA, OLYMPIC, AND BALTIC TAKE PART IN THE RESCUE

SUMMARY OF THE DISASTER

FACTS ABOUT S.S. TITANIC, VICTIM OF OCEAN DISASTER

SOME VIEWS OF

CANADIAN LINER'S TOWING

Front page of the *Toronto Daily Star* on Monday, April 15, 1912. *Photo from digital files of the Toronto Reference Library*

*

The Salvation Army planned memorial services to honour those who had perished and to comfort those who had lost loved ones. Billy and Zack attended the events. Although Billy felt the sorrow of the tragedy deeply, the sinking of the great ship haunted Zack.

On the Sunday afternoon of May 4, 1912, Billy and Zack were with the Rosemount Corps at The Salvation Army memorial service in Massey Hall for the victims of the *Titanic*. They listened to the tributes and watched as the relatives of those who had perished on the ship wept openly. The experience left an indelible mark on Zack.

The stories of the *Titanic* haunted Zack's slumber for many weeks. Just when he thought they had disappeared, the nightmares returned. In the dreams, he had escaped the cabin in panic, but the swirling waters trapped him in the ship's corridor. Vainly, he struggled to find Billy. At times the water rushed over his head and he was unable to breathe. Then the death waters retreated to his chin as the nightmare continued. The screams of those around him drowned out his own panicked cries for help. Where was Billy? He had always been there. Where was he when he dropped into the nightmare waters of his dreams?

Then Zack awoke. Billy was there, his arms cradling him, his hand wiping the sweat from his brow. There was no need for Billy to inquire about the dream.

"Don't worry, Zack. It's all right," Billy said as he reassured his brother. "Nothing will ever separate you from me."

*

The spring days of June rolled forward in rapid succession, and eventually another summer solstice faded into history. Within what seemed like an instant, the languid days of July fell across the open fields, leafy orchards, and dusty streets of the Earlscourt District. In the first week of the month, Emmy decided to apply to send Zack and Bess to summer camp to escape the sultry days of heat that were wrapping around the tarpaper shacks of the district. Conditions were not as severe as below the hill in the crowded city streets, but she was convinced that it would be better if they attended summer camp.

In 1912, The Salvation Army operated its summer camp at Clarkson, on the shores of Lake Ontario to the west of the city. The cooling breezes and the refreshing waters of the lake provided relief from the sweltering conditions of the inner city. A large section of land adjoining the lakeshore site provided a spacious playground for the campers. Clarkson was well beyond the city. A fortunate few maintained summer homes at Mimico and Long Branch. Torontonians considered these areas "cottage country."

In the poorer districts of the city lived hundreds of children whose only playgrounds were the streets, which reflected the poverty of their families. Harsh economic circumstances forced their parents to dwell in these congested quarters, and though some often longed for the sight of a green countryside, with its pleasant and healthful offerings, they accepted their conditions as they discovered the truth of the motto, "What can't be cured must be endured."

Slum housing on Terauley Street (now Bay Street) in 1908. The west façade of today's Old City Hall can be seen in the background on the right. *City of Toronto Archives, Fonds 1244, Item 3101*

*

On Sunday, July 14, Zack and Bess departed Toronto's Sunnyside Station for the camp at Clarkson. When the train arrived at its destination, Bess and Zack gazed around warily as they climbed down from the train and onto the platform. In their hands, each clutched a small canvas portmanteau bag containing the necessities for their two-week holiday.

An adult volunteer from the camp informed them, "We only transport the smaller children from the train station to the campsite. Because you're older, you're expected to walk."

While they trudged along the road to the camp, the sun beat down on them. When they arrived at the site, the volunteer informed them, "Last year, some of the campers slept in an old barn that we'd divided with partitions into dormitories. The only other wooden building we had was the cookhouse, so the overflow from the barn slept in tents, rows and rows of them."

Zack's concern showed on his face. He whispered to Bess, "I hope neither of us is in a room with hordes of other children."

Bess nodded in agreement.

The volunteer ignored their worried expressions and proudly continued, "This year we've a new building. It has replaced most of the tents. It opened two weeks ago. It has long rows of bunk beds. We can accommodate about seventy-five children in it."

Then the volunteer asked them their names and checked a list. "Let's see. Oh, you're not in the new building. Both of you have been assigned to tents. You'll each share your tent with three other children."

Zack whispered to Bess, "I'd rather bunk in with three others than be in the building with a large group, all in a single room."

The volunteer added, "Our camp has no running water like you have in the city. We have a well and a hand pump. You'll bathe in the lake. And, of course, we've no electricity. A row of outhouses meets our sanitary needs."

As Zack departed for the tent that he was to share with three other lads, he quipped to Bess, "Everything sounds just like home."

Bess smiled at Zack and then left him as she was shown to her tent. Zack followed an older boy to the tent he was to occupy. He had never been away from home before and missed Billy. However, he was determined not to allow Bess to know his fears.

*

In the boys' dining room, Zack's first meal at the camp was baked beans and two thick slices of bread that the cook had baked the previous day, as they did not allow baking on the Sabbath. Following the evening meal, Zack assembled with the other children near the water's edge for an open-air church service. A group of twelve Army bandsmen from Port Credit had arrived to provide music to accompany the singing. Zack watched the musicians intently, wishing that they had allowed him to bring his cornet. Despite his disappointment at not participating, he enjoyed the lively singing and spirited choruses. When he became bored with the sermon, he amused himself by gazing out over the expansive blue waters of the lake.

At the end of the service, the Captain in charge inquired, "Does any boy or girl wish to sing a solo, recite a Bible verse, or quote the words of a favourite hymn? Any child who participates will receive an extra slice of raisin bread at bedtime."

Several lads succumbed to the obvious but well-intended bribery and raised their hands. After a stumbling rendition of the first three verses of "Jesus Loves Me," a small boy recited a passage from St. John's Gospel, and a girl who had taken elocution lessons from her mother "executed" a poem.

Zack raised his hand hesitantly. The officer gazed down at him. "Captain," he inquired, "may I borrow one of the band players' cornets?"

"Well, now, sonny," the Captain said, condescendingly gazing at Zack, "can you play a solo for us?"

"I can try," Zack responded.

Taking the cornet gingerly from one of the bandsman, Zack opened the spit valve to allow any moisture to drip out of the instrument. Then he removed his own mouthpiece from his pocket and inserted it into the cornet. He never went anywhere without his mouthpiece. Producing a few trial notes on the cornet, he adjusted his embouchure. Standing up straight to increase his height, he was ready to begin.

The Captain smiled benevolently to encourage him.

*

Zack commenced his solo. It was only a few seconds before the Captain realized that he had severely underestimated Zack. The notes were clear and confidently produced. The older bandsmen listened with amazement.

Zack had chosen to play a variation that centred upon the hymn "O Boundless Salvation." It was not really a composition but rather an improvisation that Billy had devised as a practice exercise. Billy had eventually expanded it, and it had slowly evolved it into a set format. Zack and Billy often employed it when they practised together, although they had never performed it in public. Zack knew every note by heart.

He began by playing the melody of "O Boundless Salvation" as it had originally been written. Then he proceeded through an intricate series of variations during which the music changed keys twice. At times, the effect was rather strange, but Zack's confidence never wavered. Then he played the original melody of the hymn once more, but this time the music was soft in volume, each note melodious and sure. Then the music abruptly changed again. Zack introduced more intricate variations on the original tune and fingered rapidly, as the passage was extremely complex and demanding. As he neared the conclusion, he played a simplified version of the part Billy usually performed—a trumpeting fanfare culminating in a high note that rang to the treetops.

The children whistled and screamed with delight; the adults applauded enthusiastically. Some of the playing had been a bit rough and a few of the passages had been rather weird, but it was a remarkable performance for a boy Zack's age.

At the end of the service, the Captain walked beside Zack as the two strolled toward the bunk house.

"Where did you learn to play like that?" he inquired.

"My brother taught me."

"Where did you find the music that you played?"

"Nowhere. My brother made it up in his head. We use it as an exercise drill when we practise."

"You mean that no one has ever written it down?"

"That's right, sir!"

"My! My!" the Captain said as he meditatively stroked his chin. He now knew why some of the passages sounded as if they lacked something. The boy had been performing one part of a duet.

"Does your brother also know the music by heart?"

"Yes, sir."

When they reached the bunk house, the Captain led Zack and the other children who had participated into the kitchen.

"Here, lad!" the Captain said as he passed Zack the promised slice of raisin bread. "You earned this. What's your name, boy?"

"Zack."

"What's your last name?"

"Mercer."

The Captain paused as he gazed at him. Recognition dawned in his eyes. "Are you the younger brother of Billy Mercer?"

"Yes, sir."

"Well, bless my old Army cap. I heard your brother play once in an open-air service in the Earlscourt District."

"That's where my family lives, sir."

"God has given you a great talent, boy. Be certain you always use it for his glory."

"Yes, sir!" Zack replied meekly.

In the days ahead, Zack fell into the routines of camp life. Some activities he enjoyed, some he tolerated without complaint, and others bored him stiff. The thing he disliked most was the constant routine. It was as if the camp counselors believed that a boy was incapable of amusing himself.

He was grateful when camp ended and he and Bess returned to the city, where his family awaited them with open arms.

*

At the beginning of August, the Rosemount Band visited Brampton, their first trip beyond city limits. Most of the bandsmen had worked a full day on Saturday, so it was quite a rush for them to leave by train for Brampton at the early evening hour. Billy and Zack, along with the other bandsmen, boarded the train at the West Toronto Station located on Keele Street, a short distance north of Dundas Street.

Zack told Billy, "This is great! It's the longest trip we've had since leaving Comstock."

Then Zack nodded with his head to indicate where Billy was to look. "See over there? That's the Captain who was in charge of the summer camp where Bess and I were, at Clarkson."

Billy gazed at the man. "I think he's the guest preacher for the weekend."

At about 6:00 p.m., shortly after their arrival in Brampton, Billy, Zack, and the other bandsmen had tea, which consisted of soup and sandwiches. Despite their arriving late in the day, they had a busy schedule ahead of them.

Over the course of the weekend, they performed at many services and open-air meetings. Following the final event of the weekend, even though the hour was late, they performed an extra musical program. After the band presented a stirring march, a hymn tune arrangement, and a devotional selection, the guest captain stood to the podium and gazed across the crowd. The crowd's applause indicated that were thoroughly enjoying the band's visit and did not wish to see the weekend's activities end.

"I know how much everyone has appreciated the efforts of the band," the Captain said. "I feel honoured to have travelled with the band this weekend and to have participated in the activities. However, I know a secret about two of the bandsmen that I believe even the bandmaster does not know."

There was a dramatic pause before the Captain continued. "I am going to ask two of the young bandsmen of the Rosemount Band to indulge us and play a duet that one of them composed. One of them performed the music at this year's summer camp at Clarkson."

The Captain now introduced Billy and Zack to the audience. He thought that the duet would be an amusing and highly entertaining ending to the weekend. He was certain the crowd would appreciate the novelty.

Zack turned and looked at Billy, shrugging his shoulders to signify that he was as surprised as Billy was. The Captain continued to exhort Billy and Zack to step to the front of the platform. They finally agreed, although Billy's reluctance was evident, since he had not intended anyone other than his family to hear the music. The music had sprung from within him. It was not a polished composition. He feared that some people would consider it disrespectful of the grand old hymn "O Boundless Salvation," as it contained several rollicking variations on the original melody.

Standing on the dais, Billy was tired after the day's many activities. He gripped his cornet tightly in his hand, feeling the perspiration building on his brow. Gazing out over the congregation and sensing the anticipation of those who had gathered, he stuck his index finger in the collar of his uniform and tried to loosen it.

Billy gazed down at Zack. He realized that his brother was calm and confident, full of energy, beaming at him as if he had not a care in the world.

He whispered, "Let's show them what we can do!"

Zack felt ready to take on the world, musically or otherwise. He raised his cornet to his lips, gazed at Billy, and waited to begin.

Giving in to the inevitable, Billy blew air through the mouthpiece of his cornet and then moved the valves up and down a few times to prepare for playing. Next, he adjusted his embouchure on the mouthpiece. The numbing tiredness from the exhausting weekend's activities slowly drained from his body and was replaced by adrenaline. He allowed the rush to crest and subside, and then, as calmness returned, he concentrated on the music.

Raising the cornet to the playing position, he gave a slight nod to Zack to coordinate their entries. With another nod, they began. The instant the first notes sounded forth, the music seized Billy and flowed effortlessly from his instrument.

The music that followed took the Captain by surprise. He should have expected it, as he had already heard Zack's performance the previous summer and he was aware of Billy's reputation. Within moments, he realized that this was no novelty item. With Billy's supplying the missing parts of the piece that Zack had performed, the music acquired harmony and depth. Zack's playing was also much improved with Billy at his side.

The boys moved through the melodic opening with such grace that it mesmerized the audience, and the duet accomplished the intricate variations with artful professionalism. The variations included an assortment of rhythms, some alien and others vaguely familiar. A few caused the audience to tap their feet, while other people swayed in their seats. However, other than the soft tapping of feet, the audience was hushed, intent on every note. As the performance drew to a conclusion, there was another section of scintillating variations which drew the piece to an ending that included a trumpeting rendition of "O Boundless Salvation," in which Zack played the melody while Billy's instrument danced around it, adding harmonized countermelodies and brilliant staccato effects. Both players built slowly in volume to the final high-pitched notes that brought the music joyously to a fulfilling climax.

The audience stood to their feet, clapped their hands, and joyously sang the words to the grand old hymn.

> O boundless salvation! Deep ocean of love,
> O fullness of mercy, Christ brought from above,

The whole world redeeming, so rich and so free,
Now flowing for all men, come, roll over me.

No words could ever express how successfully the weekend ended. Billy and Zack had performed beyond the expectations of Bandmaster Meaford, even.

*

As the band travelled on the train back to Toronto, many thoughts tumbled through Bandmaster Meaford's mind. Billy had impressed him since the first day he had set eyes on him in the corridor of the *Southwark,* which had transported them to Canada. However, on this occasion, it forcefully dawned on him that Billy was far more talented than even he had ever dreamed. The lad was not only capable of performing on his instrument superbly, but he was also able to compose.

In his mind, he replayed some of the passages he had heard in the duet. Instinctively, he commenced thinking of a band score to accompany the two instruments. Finding some advertising flyers in the coach, he grabbed a pencil and, using the blank sides of the flyers, quickly drew groupings of five lines with treble clef signs in front of them. In rapid succession, he penned a few bars of the music he had heard, adding more as he remembered them. Finally, in frustration, he walked down the train car to where Billy was sitting.

"Lad!" he blurted out. "Can you write down the music that you two played tonight?"

"Sure," Billy said, taken by surprise. "But why? I already know it."

"The music needs to be placed in written form. Get started! I'll assist you."

Billy took the pencil. At rapid speed, he placed the notes of the cornet parts onto the staffs. By the time the train reached Toronto, a lot of the solo parts of the composition were on paper. As George Meaford observed Billy write, he could almost envision the score for the brass instruments that would form the accompaniment. He was unaware that Billy could easily write that, too.

That evening on the train, they began the score for what they would eventually name "O Boundless Salvation—Symphonic Variations for Cornets and Brass." George suggested the title. He felt that to title it as a mere cornet duet would simply not do justice to the complicated composition.

*

On Tuesday, August 20, 1912, General William Booth was promoted to glory. Salvationists employed the term *promoted to glory* to denote the promotion of a member of their congregation into the glories of heaven.

The death of the General extinguished the great fire of Salvationism that had been present at the founding of the organization. The world of the Army mourned the loss of the man who had led them for so many years, exhorting his followers to give assistance to the poor. The General had believed that if people were to find God, then the Army must first feed them. The mighty and the humble of the land paid tribute. Even King George V stood beside the coffin and offered homage to the grand old man who had advanced the cause of social justice for the less fortunate of Canada.

In Toronto, on Thursday, August 23, in the early evening, the city held a memorial service in front of the City Hall on Queen Street (now the Old City Hall). Later, they held another service in Massey Hall to honour the memory of the Founder. Members of all denominations thronged into the spacious hall, the size of the crowd indicating the respect people held for the late General.

*

Rosemount bandsmen were a part of the massed band assembled for the memorial service for the General. Billy and Zack were among them, even though Zack was only thirteen years of age. It was at Bandmaster Meaford's insistence that Zack play in the Rosemount Senior Band, despite his age.

Following the service, Billy and Zack sat beside George Meaford on the streetcar as they journeyed homeward, listening to the noise of the wheels on the tracks.

The memorial service had struck a chord deep in Billy's heart. He turned to Mr. Meaford and said, "The first Army hymn I had ever heard was 'O Boundless Salvation.' I heard a band play it in Comstock. The next time I heard it, you performed it in your cabin on the ship that brought us to Canada."

George replied, "I know the hymn is special to you."

Billy's next statement caught George by surprise. "I've been thinking about the manner in which they said the General died."

"You're young to be thinking about such ideas."

"Perhaps, but the service in Massey Hall has caused me to wonder—can a person face death calmly, knowing that life is ending?"

"I'm not certain I know the answer to that question."

"It makes me think about those who drowned after the *Titanic* sank. The disaster gave Zack nightmares for weeks. He awoke screaming in the night, telling me his fear of being trapped in the ship's narrow corridor, the waters of death swirling around him, creeping higher and higher."

The conversation began to worry George. Billy's dramatic choice of words showed that he had given the matter too much thought.

Billy added, "I wonder what thoughts ran through the minds of those aboard the *Titanic* as they faced death."

George felt that Billy was pondering issues that, at his age, he should not be thinking. He replied, "You're too young to brood over questions that have stumped humanity since time immemorial." Even before George spoke, he knew his words were redundant. Billy had always pondered the mysteries of life.

Changing the subject, George's voice broke Billy's reverie. "I want to begin rehearsing 'O Boundless Salvation' at band practice on Thursday evening. I think we've worked on the score sufficiently. I'd like to present your composition to the congregation on Harvest Festival weekend. That gives us two months to rehearse and eliminate any problems with the harmonic structures."

"I think that would be great," Billy responded, his voice indicating that his gloomy thoughts were dissipating. "However, you've done so much work on it that I think it should be called your composition."

"Nonsense! You handed me the solo parts, already finished, and together we polished the accompaniment. If the Music Editorial Department in London, England, ever publishes the piece, it'll have your name on it."

"Publish it?"

"Well, we will see how it is received by audiences before we submit it. But, yes, I think it's of a quality they would definitely consider."

Billy's gloom flew out the window of the swaying streetcar as he thought about the music. But in the recesses of his mind, ideas lingered about what a man thinks when he faces death.

*

In mid-September, an event occurred that provided Billy with an opportunity to visit Queen Street, where he might call on Jenny McMillan. For several months, each Saturday afternoon, Mr. McCarthy had journeyed down over the hill in his cart pulled by his old horse, Dancie, to the streetcar stop at Dovercourt Road and Van Horne. There, he left the horse and cart stabled with a man in the district and climbed aboard a streetcar to travel to Queen Street.

He and Mrs. McMillan looked forward to their Saturday evening rendezvous, especially now that their feelings for each other had deepened. Billy frequently hinted that he would like to go down to Queen Street, but Mr. McCarthy had scrupulously avoided any indication that he was aware of Billy's wishes. As fond as he was of the lad, he did not view him as part of an evening's visitation with the love of his life.

By mid-September, Mr. McCarthy was transporting more and more produce from the local harvest of the Earlscourt area to Mrs. McMillan's shop on Queen Street. She sold some of it wholesale to other stores and merchandised the remainder in her own shop. On days when it was necessary to transport produce southward, Mr. McCarthy left Billy and Zeke to tend his store and loaded his cart with the bushels of fruits and vegetables to trek down over the hill. Exhaustion caused the horse to clip-clop ever slower as it reached the downtown area. Mr. McCarthy accomplished these visits during business hours on weekdays. His Saturday trips were for pleasure only.

However, an unexpected delivery of apples arrived on the afternoon of Saturday, September 14, at 1:00 p.m. A Sunday delivery was out of the question, and since some of the apples were nearly overripe, the situation demanded that Mr. McCarthy transport them to Mrs. McMillan's shop immediately so they would be ready for sale early on Monday morning. This entailed taking his cart and horse all the way to Queen Street instead of riding the streetcar for the main part of the trip, as was his usual custom on Saturdays.

He asked Billy, "Will you ride with me, to assist me in unloading the heavy bushels?"

Billy was delighted.

A half hour later, as Dancie ambled along St. Clair Avenue toward Dufferin Street, Zeke Treadwell stood in the doorway of the store and waved to Billy. He would inform Billy's parents that he had gone down to the city for the evening.

*

Arriving at Mrs. McMillan's shop, Billy, while unloading the cart, glanced up and saw Jenny peering through one of the small panes of the shop's large windows. The smile on her face made his heart race. He felt the blood rushing to his cheeks. After returning her smile, he dropped his head to hide the glow of his blushing face. He was certain that it was illuminating the entire street even though it remained daylight.

After unloading the apples, it was 4:00 p.m., and as his assistance was no longer required, Billy asked Jenny to walk with him. She suggested that they stroll westward along the north side of Queen Street.

*

The afternoon sun felt warm on their arms, dispelling the chill from the breezes blowing from the west, indicating that the days of autumn were fast approaching. In the late-day light, Billy noticed that Jenny's brunette hair contained a hint of red, making it to appear auburn as the long strands cascaded enchantingly over her shoulders. As she brushed away the hair that the wind had blown over her forehead, he thought how beautiful her hands appeared, delicate and perfectly formed. Her fingers were long and graceful. He longed to hold them in his. The thought caused him to blush. Sensing his inner embarrassment, Jenny smiled at him encouragingly.

As they continued strolling along the street, they peered into the shop windows at the varied array of goods. Residing in the threadbare Earlscourt area, Billy thought that the shops of Queen Street appeared crammed with exotic items. The pair greeted and smiled at those whom they recognized from either Mrs. McMillan's shop or the Army congregation. Jenny laughed quietly at Billy's attempts to inject humour into the conversation. He was clearly entranced to be with her, thinking he was in the company of the most beautiful girl in the world, giving no thought to his own appearance. However, others noticed and remarked on what a handsome couple they were.

*

When Billy and Jenny passed the Snipe sisters, two elderly spinster women, the younger of the two, Freda Snipe, who was over eighty, said breathlessly, "Good gracious, Martha! Look at that young couple. He's like a Viking warrior, and she's like the long-haired maiden-mistress of a southern plantation."

"It sounds as if you received in the mail this week another ten-cent nasty," her older sister huffed accusingly. The term *nasty* was the common adjective given to describe romance novels that cost a dime to purchase.

Ignoring the remark, Freda continued breathlessly. "I can picture it now. When the blond warrior takes the fair maiden in his arms, she'll swoon with the rapture of being held in his manly embrace. As her brave warrior kisses her passionately on her full, moist lips …"

Her voice trailed into silence. In her excitement, Freda was unable to catch her breath. To push oxygen into her lungs, she breathed deeply, causing her corset to tighten, which further restricted her breath. Martha noticed her sister's distress.

"Calm down, Sister," Martha snapped. "If your breath becomes any more irregular, you'll swoon right here on the sidewalk, and there will be no warrior's manly arms to lift *you* up."

Billy and Jenny had not heard the sisters' conversation and continued their journey along Queen Street. They had entered a world of their own, insulated from everything around them.

*

Though the Snipe sisters had not caught the attention of Billy and Jenny, there was another on the street who had been observing them closely. It was the thief who had attempted to lift the billfolds of Billy and his father when they had been on Queen Street years ago. The man had noticed the expensive clothes the sisters wore, and because of their ages, he was certain that grabbing their purses would be easy. He had noticed Billy and Jenny but had not recognized Billy as being one of his earlier victims. However, he knew that the handsome lad with the pretty young woman appeared athletic and strong, so he waited until the couple had strolled farther along the avenue before he made his move.

Stealthily approaching the Snipe sister from behind, he pushed Freda to the ground while deftly grabbing her purse. Martha was so shocked that for several seconds she was unable to react. When she finally screamed, Billy turned around, instantly knew what had happened, and rushed toward the two sisters. Martha was already assisting Freda to her feet, and though the woman seemed all right, with no broken bones, it was obvious that she was going into shock. Jenny appeared within a few seconds, immediately comforting Freda while trying to calm Martha. Realizing that the elderly sisters were physically unharmed, and reassured that Jenny was there, Billy chased after the callous thief.

Because the criminal ran while favouring his left leg, limping slightly, Billy soon overtook him. However, at the moment when Billy reached him, the thief sensed his presence and swiftly turned to deliver a quick punch that struck Billy on the chin. Caught by surprise, Billy was knocked to the ground by the force of the blow. Dazed and unable to immediately get to his feet, Billy watched helplessly as the man disappeared into an alley.

As Billy sat on the sidewalk nursing his chin, Jenny appeared and helped him to stand. A police constable had appeared and was tending to the needs of the Snipe sisters. He insisted that Freda Snipe receive an examination at the Toronto General Hospital. He suggested that Billy do likewise, but Billy refused. He decided that continuing his stroll with Jenny was the best medicine he could possibly receive.

*

The bubble in which Billy and Jenny had floated minutes ago had burst. However, they decided that they would make the best of the situation and continue their walk. Jenny clung to Billy's arm to comfort him. Billy imagined that they were strolling like a married couple. The thought cheered him as the pain in his jaw receded. Though Billy had been unable to capture the thief, he had bravely chased after him.

Jenny told Billy, "You're my hero."

Lost for words, he remained silent.

For Jenny, fantasy and dreams were a part of young love.

Despite the ugly incident, the two slowly recaptured the magic that had existed prior to the robbery. For them, their world of love was unique and exclusive, and they felt that no one had ever journeyed along this path before.

A short distance ahead, Jenny saw the new library on the south side of Queen Street, near Lisgar Street. She told Billy, "It will soon be time to turn back and retrace our steps to my mother's shop."

"Yes, it's almost five-thirty, and within a half hour the stores along the avenue will shut their doors for the day."

"After my mother closes her store, she and Mr. McCarthy are retiring to our house for tea. They would be expecting us to join them shortly after the hour of six."

"I think we might be late returning."

"True. I'm enjoying myself too much to walk faster. I've waited several months to be alone with you, and I don't want our time together to end."

Billy blushed at her honest admission and was at a loss for words.

Jenny continued. "Let's cross the street and enter the library. It will close at six, but that'll give us a few moments to be alone together among the shelves with their rows of books."

Impressive door of the library on Queen Street West near Lisgar Street, as seen today.

Billy was puzzled as they pushed open the door of the new library, passed through the small, high-ceilinged vestibule, and entered the room that housed the many rows of books. He was too entranced to question why they were there.

Jenny told him, "At this late hour, most library patrons have departed, and the section at the rear of the building, where they shelve the reference books, will be empty."

Slowly, Jenny led Billy into one of the aisles where the bookshelves almost touched the ceiling.

"We're alone at last," she said, looking directly into Billy's blue eyes. She ran her fingers through his thick blond hair, her fingertips drifting down over his face, caressing it where he had been struck by the robber. "I see that a bruise is forming. It must be painful?"

"Not really. It's fine." He smiled.

Then, before he knew what was happening, Jenny stretched upward on her toes to compensate for their difference in height and tenderly kissed his jaw. Then her lips reached up toward his. It was a magical moment.

After their lips parted, she confessed, "That was my first time kissing a boy."

"It was my first real kiss, too."

Awkward at first, they now embraced each other, their bodies touching, the thrill of their first kiss and romantic embrace delighting them. Then it was over. Jenny dropped her arms and withdrew, allowing space to creep between them as she slipped her hand into his. Their first kiss was something that neither of them would ever forget.

That evening, Billy thought that the library on Queen Street was his "Elysian paradise, where the thrill of romance captivated his heart." Of course, he never told anyone of his flowery allusion, not even Zack. When he revisited the library the following week and gazed at the lines of bookshelves, he altered the poetic wording somewhat and referred to his first kiss as "love among the stacks."

*

On an afternoon during the first week of October, Emmy received a five-page letter from Grandmother Mercer in the mail. Emmy and Phil each read it several times before they discussed its contents.

"My goodness!" Emmy said. "Your mother says that she intends to marry Gerald Hutchinson."

"My mother is a headstrong woman. If she says she's going to wed him, then she will."

"What did you think about her explanation of your brother's reaction?"

"Well, it explains a few things that I've wondered about over the years. I never knew the reasons for Frank's estrangement from Mother. She says that he thought that she had allowed a gentleman caller to court her a mere year after Father died. He thought that she exhibited undue haste."

"Did you agree with Frank's thinking at the time?"

"Well, not really. A person is not meant to be alone in life, and besides, my mother was a handsome woman in those years."

"She remains a handsome woman."

"Yes, I am aware of that. Now let me finish." Emmy smiled as Phil continued. "I think if my mother had waited for fifteen years, Frank's reaction would have been the same. Father's death devastated him. He couldn't understand Mother's ever wanting another man."

"She says that Frank has given his blessing to the marriage."

"Yes! I think that after he immigrated to Canada, he learned what it was like to be lonely. I believe that is the reason he reconsidered his position. Sarah is the most important person in his life, but blood relatives are important to him, too. I think this truth dawned on him during the many years he remained separated from us here in Toronto, while the rest of us remained in the Old Country."

"It's a good thing that Frank approved. According to your mother, it made it easier to sort out other difficulties before she accepted the proposal of Mr. Hutchinson."

"Yes, my mother mentioned those things in the letter as well."

"Do you think she was correct to insist that the marriage be held in St. John the Evangelist Anglican Church?"

"I don't object, and I'm certain that Frank approved, but it was likely difficult for Gerald. He's an Army bandsman, and as my mother has been attending the Army services regularly for quite some time, he likely expected that they would marry in the Queen Street Citadel."

"The compromise they made has been agreeable to them both, or so your mother says."

"Yes! The marriage will be in the church, and the wedding banquet will be in the Army hall."

"What do you think about the one condition that Mr. Hutchinson imposed?"

"You mean that Billy be allowed to play a cornet solo at the wedding?" Phil smiled, knowing that it was not much of a demand. How could a grandmother not wish her talented grandson to play at her nuptials?

*

As October 1912 progressed, it dropped its inevitable seasonal transformations across the avenues, fields, and laneways of the Earlscourt District. Summer's hazy days were now a distant memory, and the nights were increasingly infused with cooler temperatures. During the early morning hours, the garden gate of the Mercer house banged loudly in the stillness of the chilly air as Phil departed for work at Peevy's Jewellery Shop. He hunched his shoulders against the wind, pulling his wool scarf tighter around his neck

Sunday, October 21, was the Harvest Festival Service at the Rosemount Corps. The hall was decorated with the fruits and grains of the season. Phil, Emmy, and the girls attended the festive morning service.

In the afternoon, Phil attended the musical program. When he and Emmy entered the hall shortly before the three o'clock starting time, he told Emmy, "The auditorium's even more crowded than for the morning service. I think the news had spread that the band is presenting Billy's music. The Rosemount Band has been at it for many weeks."

"Yes, and the word has spread."

As the service was about to begin, Billy and Zack took their seats among the other bandsmen. Phil felt proud as he watched them enter. He told Emmy, "I see that five young bandsmen from the Dovercourt Band are sitting in the front row, their uniforms clearly identifying them. I'm certain that they've come to hear Billy."

The musical program commenced. Later, at the appropriate moment in the afternoon's proceedings, Bandmaster Meaford stepped to the lectern and explained about the music that the band was about to perform, "O Boundless Salvation—Symphonic Variations for Cornets and Brass."

He concluded his introduction by saying, "Now that everyone appreciates the origins of this music, and the youthful age of the soloists, I am certain that I needn't say that this is an historic occasion for our congregation. Billy Mercer not only composed the music, but also wrote the band score that accompanies it."

George did not mention that he had assisted Billy, as he felt that his role had been minor. The music had sprung from the heart of Billy, and he felt that the credit belonged solely to him.

George's words of introduction completed, Phil watched with great anticipation as he stepped onto the bandmaster's podium, gazed around at the bandsmen, and smiled encouragingly. Before raising the baton, he turned and glanced at the two soloists.

Phil knew that George could not see their faces, as they were facing the audience. However, he was certain that George could sense their tension by observing the way they were standing, especially the stiff angle of their shoulders. Phil was aware that George knew the boys well, as if they were his own sons.

Phil prayed silently for their success as George raised the baton.

*

The band commenced with a full-score harmonic rendition of the Founders' Song. Then the intricate solo parts entered, their rich sound engulfing the hall. The boys easily moved through the difficult score, which contained intricate rhythms demanding rapid fingering. They played the mournful passage in the minor key with haunting brilliance. Billy had added it to the piece shortly before the band accompaniment had been completed.

Near the conclusion, which featured a joyously harmonic version of the hymn tune, the solo instruments floated a full octave higher than the accompaniment, like angel voices above an earthly throng. Billy's brilliant trumpeting effects, while Zack replayed the melody, brought the piece to an exhilarating climax.

The applause was thundering. The five Dovercourt bandsmen were the first on their feet. They could not believe that fourteen-year-old Zack and twenty-year-old Billy were capable of playing so skilfully. Similarly, many found it amazing that such a young musician had written the band accompaniment.

Phil was grateful that his sons' playing had pleased those who had gathered. As he turned and scanned the many smiling faces, he noticed that in the back row, slouched low in his seat, was Jeremiah Treadwell. He wondered if Billy had seen him. Phil thought that the expression on Jeremiah's face gave no indication as to whether or not he had enjoyed the music.

*

Throughout the days ahead, Phil learned that Billy's performance was the talk of the Earlscourt District. The Dovercourt bandsmen had carried word of the new music to the Army congregations below the hill. The following Sunday, the Rosemount Corps was packed to capacity to hear Billy's composition. Extra chairs were found and placed in the aisles.

*

By the beginning of November, farm produce had been harvested, the remaining field stubble now dry, blanched white from the killing frosts and biting winds. In the farmlands surrounding the city, fields were bare of crops, the grain's having been gathered into the barns. The trees in Wilford's orchard contained only a few shrivelled apples, lonely reminders of autumn's earlier bounty. Citizens daily anticipated the first snow of the season to swirl and drift upon the ever-increasing chilling winds.

The Mercer family welcomed the Christmas season of 1912 as joyously as ever. It represented a bright and hallowed time in an otherwise dark and dismal month. In the evenings, the family gathered around in the kitchen, close to the warmth of the wood stove. Decorations appeared as if by magic, but the humble gifts that Phil and Emily had purchased remained well hidden, ready for Christmas morn.

The music heard on the streets or in the shops was live, as recordings from a sound system had not yet appeared on the scene. During the week prior to Christmas, yuletide bells rang out across St. Clair Avenue and people gathered in the churches in anticipation of the season.

*

Despite the overwhelming appeal of Christmas, the event that dominated the Mercer family's yuletide season was the marriage of Grandmother Mercer at the Church of St. John the Evangelist. It was where she had attended her first services in Canada.

Several weeks prior to the wedding, Grandmother Mercer requested permission from the priest of St. John the Evangelist to allow her grandson to perform a cornet solo during the service. After meeting Billy, the elderly clergyman readily agreed. The choice of music was to be Billy's.

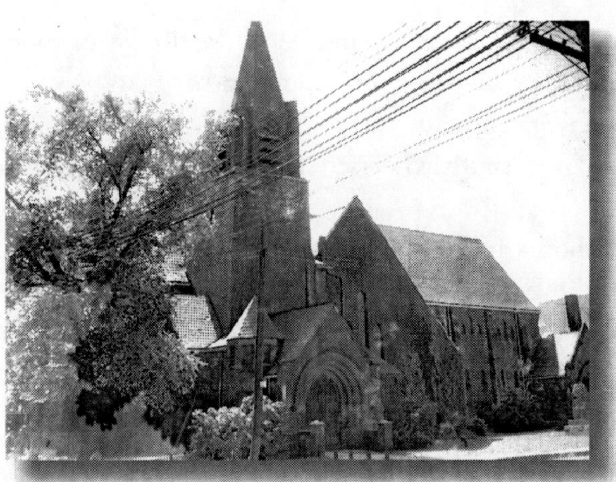

The church of St. John the Evangelist at Stuart and Portland streets (built 1893, demolished 1963). *City of Toronto Archives, Series 380, Item 111*

*

The week before the wedding, Billy and Jenny had strolled along Queen Street. Jenny told Billy, "I'm pleased that your parents are allowing you to journey down to Queen Street more often."

"They're agreeable as long as I travel with Mr. McCarthy and return before the hour of eleven."

"I understand that, at first, Mr. McCarthy was hesitant to allow you to travel with him."

"I think that he was reluctant to accept the responsibility should he return later than the designated time."

"I can understand. It's easy to be delayed. The trip after the streetcar drops you off is lengthy, and climbing the hill at Davenport to the Earlscourt District at that time of the night is difficult."

"That's for sure. Every night, old Dancie plods up the steep incline as if it's the last climb she'll ever make. However, Mr. McCarthy now allows me to accompany him whenever I wish."

"Perhaps he doesn't wish to stand in the way of our love."

They both grinned, and Billy gripped Jenny's hand tight.

While they ambled along Queen Street, the shops were closed for the day, but they peered into the windows at the display of goods, smiling at each other as they saw their reflections in the glass. A chilly west wind had been blowing throughout the day, and after sunset the temperature plummeted. They snuggled closer as they walked, oblivious to the frigid night air.

In the shop window of a music store, Billy noticed a poster that declared, "'I Love You Truly'—the first song to sell almost a million copies of sheet music."

"It's a parlour song," Billy explained. "It's by Carrie Jacobs-Bond, published this very year. It's been popularized by the famous singer Elsie Baker. I really like the title of the song."

"If you'd like, tomorrow I can purchase a copy of the music for you."

"That'd be great. I'll give you the money the next time we meet."

"I'll mail the music to your home."

"After a few embellishments of my own, I'll have a solo that might be appropriate for my grandmother's wedding. You'll be at the service. When I perform the song, the words will be for you, as well as to honour my grandmother."

"Oh, Billy, you're so romantic."

*

On the wedding day, Saturday, December 14, Grandmother Mercer requested that the ends of the church pews be adorned with simple white ribbons, draped along both sides of the centre aisle. As it was nearing winter, the decorators added green sprigs of holly atop the ribbons in lieu of fresh flowers. The simplicity of the display complemented the simple architecture of the old brick church, built in 1893 to replace a previous frame building.

The sun slipped from behind a cloud bank as the wedding ceremony commenced. Its golden rays bathed the narrow streets surrounding the church, splashing across the tombstones in the old garrison burial grounds. Sunlight pierced the church's narrow Gothic windows, dispelling the gloom of the interior and casting ribbons of shadow and light across the nave. Radiant beams flooded across the sacred altar and lectern—a fortuitous omen, many thought.

At the appropriate time in the wedding service, Grandmother Mercer listened as Billy stood beside the altar and played "I Love You Truly." She knew the words and silently sang them as the fullness of the harmony flowing from Billy's cornet sounded forth. She knew that she would never love him more than at this very moment, her precious grandchild.

> I love you truly, dear.
> Life with its sorrows, life with its tears
> Fades into dreams when I feel you near,
> For I love you truly, truly, dear.

A tear trickled down Grandmother Mercer's cheek as she listened. Many thoughts flowed through her mind—sweet memories of past loves, hardships of bygone years, and present-day happiness. The death of her first husband had devastated her, and she had believed that joy had fled her life forever. However, the years had flown by, and she was now marrying a man whom she loved dearly. As well, she was reconciled with Frank and had five beautiful grandchildren. Gazing at Gerald in his new navy serge band uniform, she smiled. He adoringly returned her smile. She wondered if he knew that her wedding dress was from one of the most fashionable shops in the city, and then she felt guilty about being vain.

She admitted to herself, *I suppose I am a little "man crazy." At least I'm crazy about my Gerald.*

Following the wedding reception, Grandmother departed with Gerald from Union Station on the evening train to Niagara-on-the-Lake. The family gathered to see them off.

*

After the train pulled out of the station, Billy said to Zack, "There goes Mr. and Mrs. Hutchinson. I can't quite believe that our grandmother is a newlywed."

"I don't care what her new name is. To me, she'll always be Grandmother Mercer. I will never call her by any other name," Zack replied.

Sometimes the young as well as the elderly refuse to relinquish tradition.

*

Dorothea and Gerald arrived at Niagara-on-the-Lake in the darkness of the near-winter evening. Arm in arm, they walked from the small peak-roofed train station located on King Street, crossed the roadway, and went into the Prince of Wales Hotel at the corner of King and Picton streets. They remained for two days in the quiet town where the Niagara River flowed into Lake Ontario. Even though it was their honeymoon, their time together was brief, as Gerald was unable to be absent more than a few days from his butcher shop.

On Sunday, walking amid the snowdrifts on the town's Queen Street, the happy couple peered into the small-paned windows of the closed shops. They strolled along Front Street and later walked beside the frigid waters of the Niagara River, viewing the quaint homes on the Canadian side and the stone walls of historic Fort Niagara on the American side. Despite the freezing winds blowing from the lake, Dorothea Hutchinson was warmed by an inner glow that only love creates.

*

Two weeks later, in Toronto, Christmas descended upon the Mercer household on Bird Avenue, with all the glorious magic that the blessed event entailed. The excitement was multiplied by the presence of children in the home, who, although no longer of an age to believe in Santa Claus, remained entranced by the yuletide traditions. It was difficult to decide who was more enthralled, Emmy and Phil or their children. The spirit of the season prevailed, gift-givers as blessed as those who had received.

Chapter Seven

In no time, the new year of 1913 crept across the city. At the midnight hour, the bells of the churches once more rang out across the rooftops of the tarpaper shacks and frame homes of the Earlscourt District.

In January, at the first Sunday afternoon musical of the year, Billy noticed that Bandmaster Greenway of the Toronto Staff Band was sitting in the centre section of the hall, about a third of the way back from the platform. Two officers were with him; Billy knew they were cornet players in the staff band. Billy was performing no solo during the program, but one of the pieces of music that Bandmaster George Meaford had selected for the afternoon contained a cornet solo, which Billy had been assigned to play.

When they commenced the selection in which Billy was featured, Bandmaster Meaford gave him a small wink. The other bandsmen noticed, suspecting that their star member was in fact auditioning for a place in the staff band. They all thought that Billy should have been in the staff band the previous year, and they were anxious that he perform well.

When the program ended, George Meaford descended into the audience to greet Bandmaster Greenway. Within moments, George turned and, beckoning with his hand, indicated for Billy to join them.

"Son," Bandmaster Greenway said to Billy, "following discussions with several interested parties, I am prepared to offer you a position in the Toronto Staff Band. Some have voiced the opinion that you are too young. However, Bandmaster Meaford has assured me that you possess the spiritual and musical maturity to cope with the arduous demands of the staff band."

Billy's heart thumped in his chest as he gazed at the staff bandmaster. A few moments passed, and then he looked into the eyes of George Meaford, who was unable to resist a wink and a small smile.

"Well! What do you have to say for yourself, lad?" Bandmaster Greenway inquired.

There was a hint of impatience in his voice, as he was not accustomed to a man's taking his time to consider such an offer. Besides, he had never before granted membership in the band to a player who was barely twenty years old.

Billy was thrilled. He had dreamt of playing in the staff band but had doubted that the honour would ever come his way. However, he was troubled and uncertain how to reply.

"Well, lad? The cat got your tongue?"

It was then that George Meaford nudged Billy in the hollow of his back.

"Give him your answer, Billy."

Hesitantly, Billy finally said, "I'm deeply honoured, sir, but I need time to consider the matter."

Bandmaster Greenway was shocked. He had taken considerable risk offering Billy the position. There were those who would criticize him for accepting a player who was so young.

"Well, let us know what you decide," Greenway said, irritation evident in his voice. Then, in a bit of a huff, he walked away.

Later, Billy walked beside George Meaford as they plodded homeward across the snowy field that led to Bird Avenue.

"What's the problem, Billy?" George inquired gently. He realized that Billy was tormented by the decision ahead of him.

"What if Bandmaster Greenway asks me if I've ever been to the mercy seat?"

"Then you tell him the truth."

"Won't this disqualify me from being a staff bandsman?"

"Perhaps it will, but not necessarily. Billy, answer me honestly. If I asked you if you were 'saved,' what would you reply?"

Billy gave a slight smile. "I remember when I used to say, 'Saved from what? A runaway horse?'" The smile disappeared and there was silence as Billy seriously considered the question.

"I haven't been to the mercy seat, but I live my life according to Christian teachings."

"You are saved, Billy. You metaphorically went to the mercy seat when you made the decision to dedicate your life to God, expressing your beliefs through your music and the life you live. This is what the kneeling at the mercy seat means. It's not the mercy seat that's important; rather, it's how you live your life. Being a Christian does not mean performing rituals and obeying the rules of a church. Men, not God, create church structures. Being a Christian means living a life in harmony with the teachings of Christ. If anyone asks you if you've have been to the mercy seat, I personally believe that you can look them in the eye and reply yes. Though you have never knelt physically, your life reflects the ideas that the mercy seat represents."

Billy nodded his head, as Mr. Meaford's words made sense to him. However, he harboured doubts.

*

Later, in the darkness of the bedroom, he talked over the matter with Zack, who listened and asked Billy several thought-provoking questions.

Finally, Zack made a suggestion.

"Billy, if we knelt at the side of our beds and prayed that we live our lives in harmony with God, wouldn't that be the same as if we went to the mercy seat?"

Billy paused before he answered. "If the ideas represented by the mercy seat are more important than the act of kneeling, then you're right."

In the cold damp air of the bedroom, they both knelt beside Zack's bed, their heads resting on the homemade quilt their mother had lovingly stitched, and prayed that God would guide them to live a life that reflected the humble teachings of Christ. Without knowing it, their prayers harkened back to the earliest days of the Christian faith when there were no churches or ritualistic ceremonies. Believers were simply trying to follow the teachings of their Master, whom the Romans had crucified.

Before they climbed back into bed, Billy placed his arm around Zack and gave him a brotherly hug. He was grateful that his younger brother had helped him make his decision. He also remembered that he had read, "And a child shall lead them." Zack was hardly a child, but Billy felt that the old expression remained apt.

The following morning, he sent his acceptance of Bandmaster Greenway's proposal on the back of a postcard. He wrote, "It would be an honour to serve as a member of the Toronto Staff Band," and signed his name. It arrived in at The Salvation Army Headquarters on Albert Street the same day, in the afternoon post; the mail-boy had placed it on the bandmaster's desk.

*

When Bandmaster Wilford Greenway read the card Billy had sent, he smiled. He admitted that at first he had felt offended that Billy had not immediately accepted his offer. However, from what he had heard of Billy Mercer, he knew him to be a highly moral and intelligent lad. *Whatever reason he had for pondering the offer at some length, it must be a good one,* he thought.

Having Billy in the band, he felt, was to be "interesting." He had never before had a musician of Billy's expertise under his baton.

*

The week after Billy was accepted into the staff band, Captain Rush asked him to step into his office for a moment. He congratulated him on his commission as a staff bandsman and presented him with a book from his private collection. He thought that Billy might enjoy reading it. The title of the book was *Is Anyone beyond God's Love?*

"Thanks for the book, Captain." He gazed at the book's title and added, "I've often asked myself that question."

Unable to resist, the Captain inquired, "What have you concluded?"

"I think that no one is beyond the love of God."

"Then you think that God loves unrepentant sinners?" The Captain wanted to hear Billy's opinion on the subject.

"If no one is beyond the love of God, then I guess he does!"

"Isn't that a contradiction?"

"Perhaps. But shouldn't a father love all his children, not just those who obey him? That's the lesson in the parable of the Prodigal Son."

"If God's love includes sinners, then do you think that unrepentant sinners are in heaven?"

"If Jesus could forgive a thief who was dying on the cross, then why cannot God forgive a sinner after the cross has claimed his life? Isn't his love unconditional?"

"But remember that the thief on the cross repented."

"True, but if no one is beyond God's love, then he will not deny his love to an unrepentant thief. I don't think that God gives love to one but withholds it from another. His love is available to all."

"Then you think that those who do not repent won't burn in the fires of hell?"

"God loves everyone. I don't presume to know how God will judge unrepentant sinners, but I am sure that he loves them, regardless of their sins. If he does, then isn't it possible that he will take them into heaven?"

"So they will not burn in hell?" the Captain repeated.

"I think that defining hell as a place of fire and brimstone is metaphorical. Hell is anywhere where there is no God of love. That's worse than fire and brimstone. Don't you think that after we pass over beyond the cross, there's only God and his love?"

"An interesting question," the Captain replied. He hesitated and gazed thoughtfully at Billy before he continued.

Then, the Captain asked, "Are you suggesting that hell is here on earth, in any place where God is not present?"

"I think that the newspaper reports during the past week suggest this."

"I know what you mean."

Billy now asked, "Captain, do you think that those who don't believe in Jesus are denied entry into heaven? Because if this were true, then it would imply that some people are beyond God's love."

"Well, the book of John, chapter fourteen, verse six, says, 'I am the way, the truth, and the life: no one cometh unto the father, but by me.'"

"Yes, I know that verse. However, if we take it literally, then we see that God's chosen people, the Jews, are unable to come to God the father."

"What do you think?" the Captain asked.

"It's possible that Jesus did not mean those words to be taken literally. After all, if a person cometh unto the father through the teachings of Jesus, then he or she is still doing so 'by him.'"

"That idea has implications."

"Yes, it does. It implies that all those whose lives reflect the teachings of Jesus are able to reach God and receive his love. When we lived on Draper Street in downtown Toronto, we had a neighbour, Mrs. Greenberg. She's a Jew, yet she lives her life in harmony with the teachings of Jesus. Is she denied being able to 'cometh unto the father,' as the verse says? If this were true, then she would be beyond God's love."

"That's an interesting point of view."

"Yes, and I will be interested in reading the book you gave me to see what the author has written."

Captain Rush and Billy chatted for several more minutes, and then Billy departed for home. The Captain thought about their conversation. Billy's ideas certainly showed insight, but they were not within the scope of the present-day teachings of *any* Christian church. However, his ideas were true to the spirit of St. Paul's letter to the Galatians: "For ye are all children of God by faith in Christ Jesus. … There is neither Jew nor Greek, there is neither bond nor free, there is neither male nor female: for ye are all one in Christ Jesus."

However, the verse in Galatians contains a contradiction. It states that "we are all one" and then stipulates that the "oneness" is attainable only through Christ. If that were literally true, then Jews, God's chosen, as well as Muslims and Buddhists, could not "cometh unto the father." The Captain understood what Billy was saying. If a person interpreted the Bible too literally, then contradictions appeared. The Captain wondered if Christ considered the spirit of the law to be more important than the letter of the law. He had heard George Meaford express similar sentiments.

Then another idea crossed his mind. He wondered if Billy had missed his true calling. The young bandsman would make an ideal Army officer! This brought a smile to his face, as he knew that it was unlikely they would accept him as a candidate if they knew his biblical interpretations. However, he was confident that in the future, such thinkers as Billy would enter the Army's Training College, and one day one of them might become the General.

*

The Toronto Staff Band visited Lisgar Street Corps in February. It was Billy's first time performing with the band. The following week, *The War Cry* reporter wrote that the cornets in the band performed particularly well, especially the youngest addition to the section, a newly appointed member from the Rosemount Corps.

Salvationists throughout Toronto and the surrounding area were quite familiar with the staff band, as the bandsmen were engaged constantly to perform at Army and civic functions. During these occasions, Billy attracted much attention. There were rumours that he might soon be allowed to perform a solo. His handsome appearance and polite, friendly manner added to the interest people paid to the talented young man. Whenever possible, Jenny attended the programs, and afterward the couple strolled along the quiet streets of Toronto. Nothing deterred them from sharing their young love.

During the weeks ahead, Zeke Treadwell asked Billy to give him trombone lessons. Although Billy played the cornet, he knew the slide positions on the trombone. Zeke quickly became a decent player. In March 1913, Billy was highly pleased when Captain Rush commissioned him as a member of the Rosemount Citadel Band. He knew the story of Zeke's life and was aware of the abuse he had endured within his family home. Zeke might have become a truant from school in his early years and engaged in criminal activities, yet he was now an Army bandsman, dedicating his life to spreading the gospel through the ministry of sacred music.

*

Not everyone was pleased. Pastor Sneadmore Treadwell brooded over the loss of his son to the ranks of the Army. He had never cared for the boy, but when Ezekiel joined the Army band, he felt that it was a smack across the face and an abnegation of the way he preached the Christian faith. He was convinced that the boy would burn in hell for his sins. He had often quoted to his flock at his Sunday morning gatherings the words of Paul to the Galatians 6:7: "God is not mocked: for whatsoever a man soweth, that shall he also reap."

It never dawned on him that this might also apply to him.

*

Although not of sufficient age to be in a staff band, Zack also had a demanding life. At fourteen years of age, he still attended school. He was now in his second year at Oakwood High School, located at the corner of Oakwood and St. Clair avenues. The eighteen-room building had opened two years previously with an enrolment of seven hundred students. The following year, it would be renamed Oakwood Collegiate Institute.

In this decade, most boys had quit school by Zack's age, but Emmy had insisted that he continue. Emmy and Phil expected him to apply himself well to his schoolwork, especially because he needed to achieve sixty percent in each subject once his final examinations were graded.

Another stressful situation facing Zack was the threat of bullies in the schoolyard or on the streets while he walked to and from school. The older children soon learned that although Zack was short in stature and unmuscular, he was capable of defending himself. The bullies were usually able to win in fight against him, but Zack got in his "licks." They soon learned to leave him alone. He had absorbed more than just music from his older brother.

Oakwood High School, which opened in September 1911. In this year, there was not yet a St. Clair streetcar. *City of Toronto Archives, Fonds 1257, Series 1057, Item 0240*

Some children worried about their friends accepting them. This was no problem for Zack. The other students liked him, as he was mischievous and possessed a good sense of humour. The girls were attracted, considering him "cute." Some of the other children longed for the latest clothes and possibly a winter sled. Zack never thought about such things. He had his cornet. Whenever he had finished his schoolwork, he practised on it. The one thing that bothered him was that recently he was unable to spend much time with Billy since he was in the staff band. Any free time that came his way, his brother spent with Jenny.

However, one problem presented itself that Zack found difficult to solve. To his great surprise, Jeremiah Treadwell, whom Zack despised, had quietly approached him. He requested that Zack teach him to play the cornet.

Zack refused.

However, as he thought about the request, he remembered that Billy had told him that he should reach out to everyone who needed his help, even those he disliked. Two days later, he informed Jeremiah that he would teach him. The boy asked Zack not to tell anyone, as he feared his father's wrath if he were to discover that they were even communicating, never mind cooperating on music lessons.

Jeremiah was not as thick in the head as Zack had thought, and the lessons progressed well. Within a few months, Jeremiah belted out the hymn tunes with confidence, each note correct and well placed, even if lacking in finesse. However, eventually his style smoothened and it became a delight to hear him play. Zack wondered what Jeremiah would do with his newfound skill.

*

The weeks of March slowly disappeared, each day bringing new challenges as well as rewards and disappointments. The chill of winter gradually softened into the milder breezes of spring. On Easter Sunday of this year, 1913, at an afternoon service in the Massey Hall, the staff band presented a cornet octet. Billy performed in the ensemble. The staff band selection in this program was "My Guide."

Bandmaster Greenway knew that Billy was the finest instrumentalist in the band. However, he remained unsure what people would say if he allowed a bandsman as young as Billy to be a soloist.

*

Household tasks changed with the season, and what with the increasing sunlight during the month of May, Emmy planted seeds in the kitchen window boxes in preparation for the coming season. Phil turned over soil in the backyard garden to ready it for planting on the twenty-fourth, weather permitting. Emmy scrubbed the floors and railings of the veranda so the family could sit outside on balmy evenings soon to come. When she had thoroughly scrubbed the porch, Phil applied a fresh coat of paint, working after supper in the lengthening light of the evening.

Spring-cleaning became Emmy's main occupation as the month progressed. She swept cobwebs away with her cloth-covered corn broom. She turned over the mattresses and placed the floor rugs on the garden clothesline for beating with her long-handled wire beater. She accomplished all these chores manually. There was now electricity in the Earlscourt area, but the Mercers could not afford to connect it to their house.

The Twenty-Fourth of May holiday was on a Friday, and the city shops and factories closed in honour of the former monarch's birthday. Early in the morning, Emmy and her family journeyed to the Toronto Islands, which was the domain of those unable to afford cottages in Muskoka.

When the city had presented its final homage to the late Queen Victoria and the last crackling fireworks displays had died in the night sky of May Twenty-Fourth, Torontonians felt that the long-awaited season of summer had officially arrived.

Emmy observed as Phil browsed the seed catalogue in Mr. McCarthy's store. He had already inspected the back garden to determine which annuals had survived the winter.

Emmy told Phil, "The hollyhocks have reseeded and are already seven or eight inches high."

"Yes, I noticed. These days, when neighbours lean over the garden fences to discuss their gardens, they never fail to mention the height of their rhubarb or the progress of their strawberries."

"The spring of the year is advancing. Tonight, despite the cool temperatures, I hope we can sit out on the veranda."

When evening arrived, it was indeed chilly, even though it was of the last week of May. However, as Emmy intended, they sat chatting and listening to Zack and Zeke practising their instruments in their upstairs bedroom.

"Even though the days remain cool," Phil told Emmy, "the open-sided trolleys are in service on Sherbourne, Yonge, and Bay streets."

"Aye, I remember the trip we made on one of them the first year we were in Canada. It was quite an adventure. As we grow older, memories of simple outings in bygone days become more precious. Small wonder that we tend to exaggerate them."

"Aye, reminiscing makes liars of us all," Phil replied as he laughed quietly. "However, we are creating new memories, too. I enjoyed my trip downtown last week. I saw many fascinating sights."

"I know what you mean. Sometimes when I go downtown, I wish we still lived below the hill. In the springtime, we did not wade through pools of mud. We could join the picnickers who flocked to the ferries, where the sparkling surface of the water glistens like mercury in the noonday sun."

"My, aren't we waxing poetic," Emmy teased.

"Well, after enduring the long months of winter, it was glorious to be out on the lake."

"I understand. I suppose the end of a winter can turn any Canadian into a poet."

Changing the subject, Emmy inquired, "Have you heard any news from your mother and Gerald over the past week?"

"Nothing since I received the postcard in Monday's morning mail that they were considering buying a new house—a larger one. Do you think they're planning on starting a family?"

"Don't be so cheeky," Emmy replied, grinning as she gently rebuked him. "I know your mother likes to keep up with the trends, but at her age having a child is not a trend she can follow."

Continuing his teasing, Phil added, "Well, I heard that they were looking for a house near a school. They might be planning a family."

Emmy ignored the remark, even though she smiled. "As a matter of fact, I think your mother has her eye on a house on Draper Street."

"Well, it's close to Brant Street School."

"True, but we will soon have a new school near us, as well. They're building a two-classroom school on Regal Road, on the brow of the hill.

However, because a school will be close by us, don't get any ideas about another child in our family."

Phil grinned. "Stranger things have happened. Another Zack or Bess in our home would be great."

Emmy said nothing, but the thought stayed with her. She was now thirty-two years old. It was possible that she could have another child, but Zack's birth had been difficult. She wondered if this was why he was not as strong as her other children. If she became pregnant again, would the birthing be dangerous?

*

As the weeks rolled onward, the heat of the summer poured forth. Many people sought to escape it in the emerald river valleys of the city or beneath the shade of their backyard trees. A scoop of ice cream became the favourite treat. Vanilla, chocolate, and strawberry were the only flavours available—at the grand price of five cents a scoop.

In the city's parks, arguments sometimes arose over the picnic tables, which were now in great demand. Bandstands and gazebos throughout the city offered musical concerts where off-key vocalists warbled as if they were among the finest singers on the great stage at Massey Hall. People applauded politely, sometimes because they were relieved that the renditions had ended.

On the Toronto Islands, young men rented canoes, embarking on idyllic voyages with their sweethearts. The lagoons between the islands possessed an alluring atmosphere, which in the eyes of Torontonians was more romantic than the canals of Venice or the banks of the River Seine in Paris. Summer was a magic time in Toronto of old, especially when it included a journey to the Islands.

Unfortunately, the Mercer family was rarely able to enjoy the Toronto waterfront, the city's parks, or the Toronto Islands. Free time was scarce, and the trip down over the hill required more time than was available to them.

*

In July, the Toronto Staff Band visited Hamilton, Ontario, for the weekend, and the new staff band colours (flag) were unveiled on this occasion. By visiting other cities such as Hamilton, Billy attracted much attention. More and more, Bandmaster Greenway appreciated the abilities of his youngest bandsman.

He knew he had a star on his hands.

*

In mid-August, Billy travelled with the Rosemount Band to Orangeville to the northwest of Toronto. The weather was steaming hot and Billy was uncomfortable in his wool tunic as the band departed by train. Zack was pleased that he was travelling with his brother. He never tired of gazing out the train window at the passing landscape.

Because the band was performing for an audience that had not previously heard them play, Bandmaster Meaford requested that Billy and Zack play their duet.

The audience enthusiastically received the music. George decided that at the first opportunity he would show the manuscript to Bandmaster Greenway. He wondered if the bandmaster had already heard about the composition, as it was common knowledge throughout the city among many Salvationists.

*

On August 23, the Canadian National Exhibition (CNE) opened on the shores of Lake Ontario. It created a grand flourish as it returned to the Toronto scene for its thirty-fourth year. The CNE was a fascinating world where pavilions displayed the latest technology and the most up-to-date consumer products. The buildings had been constructed to mirror the styles popular during the 1893 World's Fair in Chicago. The CNE Horticultural Building was a prime example.

Billy was granted time off from work and attended the exhibition, accompanied by Jenny and Zack. They were among the excited crowds pouring through the gates of the CNE on opening day. Zack stared in wonder at the myriad of food kiosks. He exclaimed, "I bet they have thousands of gallons of lemonade and millions of tons of food."

When he saw the samples at the Pure Food Building, he declared, "I was right. Look at all the stuff. Old Wilmot would be in heaven if he ever saw all this food."

Billy grinned and then did his best to ignore Zack as he continued to eye the special treats and yearningly watched the other boys his age go on the amusement rides. Finally, Billy told his brother, "We've no money for the rides. I'm saving our coins for something special."

They entered the new Government Arts, Crafts, and Hobbies Building that had opened the previous year. They also enjoyed visiting the Music Building, which was constructed in 1907, the year after Billy and Zack had arrived in Canada. Groups performed recitals and chamber music in the structure, but on occasion modern popular music was featured. Billy, Zack, and Jenny were highly entertained by a local singer who performed "Brighten the Corner Where You Are," "Peg o' My Heart," "Danny Boy," "It's Great to Get Up in the Morning," and "There's a Long, Long Trail." However, they were even more entranced listening to a recording of Al Jolson singing "The Spaniard That Blighted My Life."

Jenny whispered in Billy's ear, "It is not a dark-haired Spaniard that has blighted my life but a blond-haired Englishman."

"Are you certain that you don't mean 'delighted,' not 'blighted'? And besides, I am a Canadian."

They both laughed. Zack was certain that their comments were "mushy" and so he ignored them.

In the late afternoon, they strolled over to the Grandstand Building, now seven years old. Billy quietly produced the necessary coins for three tickets for the auto polo game. In this year, the fascination with automobiles, the latest mode of travel, had never been greater.

Auto polo at the 1913 Canadian National Exhibition. *City of Toronto Archives, Fonds 1244, Item 0211*

As they entered the stadium, Zack asked Billy, "What's auto polo?"

"To play it, mechanics strip cars down to their chassis and, on the skeletal frames, mount two seats over the gas tanks."

"How many people does it take to play?"

"In each auto there's two passengers—a driver and a man with a mallet."

"What does the guy with the mallet do?"

"Like in polo, he swings the mallet as he tries to hit the ball into the opposing team's goal. The driver has to manoeuvre the auto through vicious turns and twists as he follows the ball. Sometimes he crashes into other autos, and there's always the danger that the auto will roll over."

"It sounds great," Zack exclaimed.

Jenny grimaced as she listened to the conversation and then said, "It sounds pretty rough."

It was indeed rough, but Zack loved it. At the end of the match, while exiting the grandstand, Zack oozed, "That was super. Didn't you think so, Jenny?"

Jenny offered a weak grin and said nothing.

For their supper, Jenny had brought a picnic meal, which they devoured while sitting on the grass near the Horticultural Building. After they visited a few more pavilions, the day was ebbing to a close. The increasing darkness of evening threw ever-lengthening shadows across the grounds, the tops of the buildings reflecting the glow of the sun as it dipped toward the west.

At 10:30 p.m., after the grandstand performance ended, fireworks illuminated the darkened sky. The sparkling images were visible for miles around. Sometimes residents of the Earlscourt area sat on the brow of the hill to observe the display.

After the last of the illuminations and crackling bursts had died away, the skies fell once more into silent darkness. The happy threesome slowly wandered toward the gates to exit the grounds, another eventful day having ended.

The midnight hour chimed before Billy and Zack arrived home.

*

The following Monday, August 25, was another day Billy would never forget. He was standing beside Mr. McCarthy in front of the store when the first St. Clair streetcar rumbled along the wide avenue, separated from the traffic on its own right of way.

"Thank goodness," Mr. McCarthy exclaimed, "the construction in front of the store has ended. The Toronto Civic Railway Company has finally completed the new line."

Billy replied, "I can't wait to travel on it to Avenue Road. For the first time, I'll be able to go downtown by public transportation."

"Yes. At Avenue Road, we can connect with the streetcars operated by the Toronto Railway Company. Their streetcars go down the hill to Bloor Street and then turn east to Yonge Street and south to the downtown area."

"We'll no longer be living in the middle of the wilderness," Billy said. "The isolation of the Davenport Road hill has ended. It also means that Salvationists living downtown can attend special services and musical programs at the Rosemount Corps without having to climb the steep incline."

Laying the streetcar tracks on St. Clair Avenue in 1913, west of Dufferin Street. *City of Toronto Archives, Fonds 1231, Item 1787*

A St. Clair streetcar in the winter of 1914 on St. Clair Avenue near Wychwood Avenue. *City of Toronto Archives, Fonds 1231, Item 0245*

St. Clair Avenue looking west from near Christie Street in 1914. Oakwood High School is visible in the top left corner of the picture. The streetcar tracks are visible in the foreground.
City of Toronto Archives, Fonds 1244, Item 5006

*

In September, the CNE shut its gates. As the days passed, markers of the approaching season became increasingly evident across the forested city. Autumn signalled the beginning of special activities in the Rosemount Corps. In October 1913, the Toronto Staff Band again visited the corps above the hill for the weekend, for the first time arriving by streetcar.

At the end of their visit, George Meaford gave Bandmaster Greenway a hand-penned copy of the score for "O Boundless Salvation—Symphonic Variations for Cornets and Brass."

In November, Gerald Hutchinson became a member of the Toronto Staff Band. However, for the weekly services he decided to take advantage of the new streetcar line along St. Clair Avenue and transfer from the Queen Street Corps to the Rosemount Corps. He knew that his friend George desperately needed a bass player.

Bandmaster Meaford was very pleased with Gerald's decision, as he was well aware that Gerald was a superb instrumentalist. There were now three members of the Rosemount Band in the staff band.

Meanwhile, Elizabeth McMillan worried about her fiancé travelling such a long distance for band practices and Sunday services, but Jenny was delighted, since she journeyed with him each Sunday to the services above the hill.

*

In the middle of December, following a weeknight staff band practice, Bandmaster Greenway decided that the staff band should visit the home of Commissioner David Hees to render a few hymns and seasonal carols to the Canadian leader of The Salvation Army. He had been ill. That he had allowed the band to visit was a sign that the Commissioner was gaining strength and recovering. The Salvationists of Toronto held him in high regard and eagerly sought any news concerning his health.

In the days ahead, amid the numerous yuletide activities, Bandmaster Greenway continued to labour long over his decision whether or not to allow the band to perform Billy's composition. He knew it was a remarkable piece of music, but he considered some of the rhythms provocative and perhaps too "worldly" for Army audiences. However, unable to deny its overall beauty and artisanship, he finally asked that the band librarian distribute the music one evening at band practice. The rehearsing began.

The enhanced abilities of the staff bandsmen made the music transcend to a level of harmonic excellence that the Rosemount Band had never attained. The more the bandmaster heard the music, the more he appreciated it. However, it crossed his mind that other than bandsman Billy Mercer, not many instrumentalists would ever be able to perform the intricate music.

On Sunday, December 21, the staff band conducted services in a theatre in the east end of the city, at the corner of Queen Street and Lee Avenue. In the afternoon musical program, the staff band publicly performed Billy's composition for the first time. Greenway paired Billy with another highly skilled member of the band who performed Zack's part.

When the band completed the final notes of the music, spontaneous applause erupted from the audience. The reaction to the music removed any reservation that Bandmaster Greenway harboured about the piece. He vowed that, when possible, he would arrange for Billy's younger brother to perform the music with the staff band. It was sure to draw crowds to the concerts, and besides, he wanted to hear Zack play.

*

In the few days prior to Christmas, George Meaford and Billy, as well as Gerald Hutchinson, had few minutes to spare. Not only did they go "serenading," as Salvationists referred to carolling on the streets, with the Rosemount Band, but they went serenading with the staff band as well.

On Thursday, December 25, after the morning service, at which half of the Rosemount Band played (while the others were serenading), the Army held a program for needy children in the area. Later in the day, it was finally time for the Mercers to celebrate the yuletide event at home. Snow surrounded the house and drifted over the lanes and walkways. The scene resembled the front of a Christmas card.

Within what seemed to be a wink of an eye, the old year slipped away and a new one appeared. At the stroke of midnight on December 31, at the watch-night service in the hall, the Mercers shook hands with others at the service and wished them a happy New Year. The year 1914 dawned, bringing with it all the promises of a new beginning.

Fortunately, a benevolent future hid from view the tragic events that would unfold in the months ahead.

Chapter Eight

During January 1914, details appeared in the press regarding the International Congress Conference of The Salvation Army in London, England, from June 11 to June 27. It was to be a gala occasion, with more than fifty countries represented. There were rumours that the Toronto Staff Band would represent Canada at the Congress. The final decision was in Commissioner David Hees' hands, and he had not yet declared his intentions.

David Hees was very popular among Salvationists. Because of his many responsibilities as head of The Salvation Army in Canada, and because he often led the organization's charitable efforts, he often met with important businessmen as well as civic and provincial officials. Those he met quickly respected his organizational skills and appreciated his considerable intellect, but they also came to realize that he was a man of great compassion, one who also had a delightful sense of humour.

One afternoon he was standing near the reception desk of the prestigious Queen's Hotel, one of the finest in the city. The builders had originally created the four-storey building in 1843 by altering a row of terrace houses. The Queen's boasted marble fireplaces, rooms with piped-in water, and the finest hand-carved furnishings in the city. It had been the first hotel in Toronto to install a central hot-air furnace. Within its precincts, Sir John A. Macdonald had held meetings that had led to the formation of the Canadian nation. The city eventually demolished the hotel and constructed the Royal York Hotel on the site.

Queen's Hotel on the north side of Front Street in 1908, today the site of the Royal York Hotel. The Queen's Hotel closed in 1927. *City of Toronto Archives, Fonds 1244, Item 0333*

On this occasion, Commissioner Hees was at the Queen's. He was to be the guest speaker at a monthly businessmen's luncheon held in the hotel's grand ballroom. An imperious woman wearing three stands of pearls and a satin dress noticed the Commissioner's uniform and the letters *SA* on the collar. She assumed it signified that he was a staff assistant at the hotel.

"My good man, take my luggage and the portmanteau to my suite," she demanded haughtily.

"Certainly," Hees responded. "Immediately!"

The woman proceeded to the stairway. She regally lifted the hem of her floor-length gown, and with ramrod straight posture, her chin held high, she gracefully mounted each step as if she were ascending a staircase in Buckingham Palace. Commissioner Hees dutifully trailed behind her, his back bent as he lugged her two suitcases up the sixteen steps to the second storey of the hotel. He was later to tell his friends, "I prayed to the Lord that the good woman did not reside on the fourth floor."

When they arrived at the door of the woman's suite, a bellboy arrived to unlock the massive mahogany door. The boy realized that the Commissioner was not a member of the hotel staff, and he stared. Then, recognition dawned on the lad. In the lobby, he had seen the Commissioner's picture on a sandwich board advertising the businessmen's luncheon.

"Sir," the boy exclaimed, "aren't you the guy who's the head of that there Salvation Army?"

The grand woman gazed at David Hees, and suddenly she, too, realized who he was. Surreptitiously, she placed the five-cent tip she had intended to give him into the side pocket of her gown. The bellboy retrieved the luggage from the Commissioner, who smiled, gave the woman a small salute with his right hand, and retraced his steps back down to the first floor.

Commissioner Hees apologized for his late arrival at the meeting, telling the gathered assembly, "I was delayed, as God sent me on a mission of mercy to aid one of the unfortunate of the land who was in need of a little assistance."

The incident would have never received any attention, but the bellboy was unable to resist having his moment of glory when, later that morning, he travelled up the staircase with a reporter. The story appeared under the title, "Commissioner Hees Commissioned to Haul Luggage." The article endeared Hees to the citizens of the city.

David Hees had trained as an officer in London, England, and served many years in small congregations throughout Britain. As the years passed, the Army promoted him. When he sailed to Canada to become the head of the Canadian Territory, he was only fifty years of age, relatively young to be appointed to a position of such responsibility. His hair had greatly thinned, but the fringe that surrounded his head remained dark brown. He often told people that he had not gone bald, but had simply become so tall that he had grown right up through his hair. Since David Hees was only five-foot-four, the remark always created a few smiles, even though it was corny. Despite his lack of stature, he was an imposing man, as he was athletically proportioned. His goatee and handsome features added to his appeal. He also had the booming voice of an orator. Salvationists adored their leader and eagerly attended any service where he preached.

*

In Canada, great excitement was generated by the advance news of the International Congress Conference (ICC). Details were appearing weekly in *The War Cry.* The Salvation Army maintained a Travel Department in Toronto at 20 Albert Street, and already people were booking passage on the various ships that crossed the Atlantic. Amid the bustle and excitement over the anticipated events, life in the various congregations continued.

*

On January 4, the Rosemount Corps held another Theatre Campaign, the special services occurring on four successive Sundays. As usual, they rented the theatre next door. Great crowds attended. The staff band conducted the afternoon and evening meetings.

On the first Sunday, more than six hundred people attended the event. The second Sunday, eight of the staff bandsmen travelled to Woodstock to perform as an octet, while the remainder attended the Rosemount Corps to continue the campaign. Billy was not among the group that journeyed to Woodstock.

When it was time for the afternoon service to begin, Bandmaster Greenway felt ill. He handed the baton to Billy. "Son, I want you to conduct the staff band."

"Me?" Billy responded.

"Yes, you. The deputy-bandmaster is in Woodstock. I have every confidence in you. The reputation of the band is now in your hands."

Billy's conducting style proved an instant hit, especially since the congregation had never seen anyone as young as Billy conduct such a prestigious band.

On the third Sunday, crowds filled the theatre beyond capacity, with chairs placed in the aisles and across the back of the theatre. Some people stood in the theatre lobby, and although they were unable to see the band, they could hear the music.

On the final Sunday, many people were turned away from the doors of the theatre because there was no space for them. Following the service, the band provided a short musical concert. By now, the audience was unable to contain its enthusiasm for watching Billy conduct. When the concert ended, as the applause died away, an elderly man shouted, "Praise the Lord—and let's see Billy lead the band."

Several others shouted, "Amen."

A woman in the back row called out, "Fire the volley. Let the boy conduct."

Prepared for this moment, Bandmaster Greenway grinned, nodded to the bandsmen, and motioned for Billy to step to the dais.

He told him, "While the bandsmen are placing the music for the march on their stands, take a look at the score."

Billy obeyed and examined the score as he pulled on his tunic collar, which had suddenly become too tight. He had considered his previous conducting of the staff band a fluke and never dreamt of a second chance. It thrilled him, but he was also fearful. With a degree of trepidation, he picked up the baton. He gazed around at the bandsmen. Every eye was on him. Billy again tugged on his uniform collar, which was becoming damp. He looked again at the bandsmen.

Then his instincts took over.

Closing the score, he raised the baton and conducted the march from memory. He knew the scoring for every instrument and could instantly recall each sectional entry. Establishing the rhythms expertly, he altered the interpretation of the music in the melodic parts of the march. The bandsmen instantly followed him, creating a different effect than what the composer had intended. It was scintillating. The audience swayed in their seats and tapped their feet to the distinctive beat of the music.

When it ended, the audience thundered their appreciation. Billy briefly acknowledged the applause and quickly returned to his seat. Amid the clapping, he heard an elderly man shout from the congregation, "Let's have Billy and Zack play 'O Boundless Salvation.'"

A loud chorus of "Hallelujah" and "Praise the Lord" followed.

Bandmaster Greenway was again ready. Knowing that Billy was a prodigy, he ceased caring about what others would say. He would not hide the lad's talents under a bushel. He also knew that this was an excellent opportunity to have the brothers perform the composition. If it were a success, then the band could present it to audiences downtown. Zack looked younger than he actually was, and his youth would be a great drawing card.

Motioning for Billy to approach the dais again, he inquired, "Where's your brother?"

"My brother, Zack?"

"Why, do you have more than one?"

"No, but …" Billy stammered.

"Get him up here on the platform. We'll give him a cornet. Let's hear the Founders' Song as it has never been played before."

While the band librarian handed out manuscript copies of the music to the bandsmen, Billy looked toward where Zack was sitting in the audience and motioned for him to come to the platform. A member of the congregation shouted hallelujah as Zack walked down the theatre aisle to join his brother.

Upon reaching the platform, Billy handed Zack one of the bandsmen's cornets, and Zack extracted his own mouthpiece from his pocket. They fiddled with the valves of their instruments to ensure they were lubricated and were moving smoothly. Billy nodded to Bandmaster Greenway to signal that they were ready to begin. They required no music.

They progressed smoothly through the composition, creating an elegance that lifted the music to a level they had never before attained. The intricate sections they breezed through without splitting a note. Their timing and entries were flawless. When the trumpeted version of the old hymn concluded, the audience again stood to its feet. Bandmaster Greenway knew exactly what he intended to do with both the players and the music.

The following Thursday at the staff band practice, he announced that Commissioner Hees had decided that the Toronto Staff Band would represent Canada at the International Congress in London. He also informed them that they must find a way for Zack Mercer to accompany the band as a guest performer.

Bandmaster Greenway was British and was aware of the degree of excellence in The Salvation Army bands in his homeland. He also knew that not one band within the British Territory had any players of higher caliber than Billy and Zack Mercer, especially considering their ages. They would attract great attention at the Toronto Staff Band's concerts.

*

When the bitter months of January and February finally disappeared, windy March blew across the city. When it ended, no one mourned its demise. The fifth day of April was Phil and Emmy's twenty-third wedding anniversary. It was a mild and sun-filled day, and since it was Sunday and their anniversary, Emmy purchased a roast of lamb. She served it in the parlour rather than in the kitchen.

After the meal ended, Mary and Ruth retired upstairs to their bedrooms to read. The boys had by now departed for the open-air service. Up in her bedroom on the second floor, Bess was practising on her cornet.

Phil smiled as he listened. He told Emmy, "I don't think that Bess will ever play as well as Billy, but I must admit that she's becoming quite good."

"Don't ever underestimate her."

"I don't, but I think she wants to be in the staff band."

Emmy smiled. "Who knows? She just might do that. Someday, the Army will have to accept women into the staff band. But at the very least, she should be allowed to play in the Rosemount Band, alongside her brothers."

"Perhaps one day she will."

"But when?"

"By the way, has Zeke told you about his plans?"

"Yes, he has."

"What do you think?"

"I think it's a good thing that he has reconciled with Jeremiah."

"Has he told you that he and his brother intend to share a small flat above a shop on Dufferin Street?"

"Yes, and I think that's good, too. He should be with his brother, although I'll greatly miss him."

Changing the subject, Emmy said, "I still cannot believe that Billy will be attending the International Congress Conference. It worries me that he will be so far from home."

"That's why I need to talk to you. In the postcard from Frank last week, he told me that he wanted me to meet him on Saturday to discuss an important matter. I assumed that it was something to do with Mother."

"You didn't tell me that you met with your brother," Emmy replied, a puzzled look on her face.

"I thought it best not to mention it, as I thought it was likely trivial and not worth your worry. After the meeting, I needed time to think over his proposal."

"Proposal?"

"Yes. He knows that Bandmaster Greenway has expressed the desire that Zack travel with the staff band to London. Of course, the staff band will pay for Billy's passage, but there's no budget to pay Zack's fare. We cannot afford it, so I had assumed that the matter was closed."

Alarmed, Emmy said, "Isn't it?"

"No, it's not. Frank and Mother have talked it over. They wish to pay Zack's passage to enable him to travel with Billy. They know how Zack hates to be separated from his brother."

"Zack is only fifteen. People will think that we are reckless to allow a boy Zack's age to travel overseas. To make matters worse, because of his size, people think he is younger than he really is. Billy is now twenty-one, and I think that even he's too young."

"Mother and Frank are aware of Zack's age, obviously, so they want me to accompany him. I will be able to keep an eye on Billy, too. Mother and Frank will not only pay the passage for Zack and me, but they will also provide a few dollars for you and the girls to live on while I'm away. I spoke to Mr. Peevy, and he is willing to grant me a two-month leave of absence."

"It sounds as if matters have already been arranged."

"Not at all. Mother and Frank told me that they would not go ahead with the plans unless we both approve. The decision is in our hands."

"I want the boys to have a chance to travel back to England. From everything I've heard, the Congress will be a magnificent affair. I realize that the offer from Frank and your mother is generous, and I appreciate their thoughtfulness. But Zack is so young. He's not as strong as the other children."

"I realize this, my love. I'm also greatly concerned about leaving you and the girls alone for eight weeks. It's a long time for us to be parted. However, I admit that if Zack attends, I would feel better accompanying him. I also know that both of us must be comfortable with the decision."

"We don't have much time to decide."

"True. I must conclude the arrangements soon."

"I'll sleep on it."

In the darkness of the bedroom, Emmy "slept on it" without ever falling asleep. When she heard the clip-clop of the milkman's horse and then the rattle of the milk bottles, she rose from the bed. She was busily preparing Phil's breakfast when he entered the kitchen. Glancing up at him, she noticed the bags under his eyes. He had slept poorly as well.

After supper that evening, Emmy and Phil again sat at the kitchen table once the children had gone to bed. They resumed their conversation from the previous evening.

"Phil, this has been one of the most difficult decisions of my life," Emmy began.

"More difficult than deciding to marry me?"

"Deciding to marry you was easy," she replied as she smiled weakly. "When I married you, I knew we were to be together. This decision means that we must be apart."

"Then you've decided?"

"Yes! Even though we'll be separated for two months, I cannot find it in my heart to deny Zack the chance of a lifetime. He and Billy have worked hard at their music, and we should allow them an opportunity to share their love of music together."

"Then I will make the arrangements, as I feel the same. I must also inform my mother. She says that if Zack and I go to England, she'll go as well to accompany Gerald, who will be playing with the staff band. I will book a cabin with four bunks in the second-class section. Billy, Zack, and I will bunk in together. The band will choose another bandsman to occupy the fourth bunk, as this will save us money."

"There is some other news that you should hear," Emmy said. "Mrs. McMillan and Mr. McCarthy intend to marry the day before you sail, and they will go to England on the same ship as you and the boys."

"You mean they'll be honeymooning with the band?" he replied with a grin.

"Not exactly, but in a way I suppose they will. It's the second marriage for both of them, and they don't want a fuss. It will be a small wedding."

"What about Jenny? She's twenty-two and an adult. Does her mother intend to leave her on her own in Toronto?"

"No! I understand that Jenny will travel with them, in a cabin she'll share with another young lady."

"My goodness, this will indeed be a voyage that people will talk about for many years." Phil added, "Billy will be ecstatic when he learns that Jenny will be aboard."

"I think you should be the one to tell him. It also may be a good time to have a quiet discussion with him about the 'birds and the bees.' Moonlight reflecting from the water affects young men strangely."

"Young women, too, I believe. However, I think Billy already knows about the birds and the bees. I must admit, although the thought of the birds and the bees and the moon dancing on the waves makes me wish that you were sharing my cabin."

Emmy glanced at Phil, who grinned naughtily. Then a wide smile broke out across his handsome face. He crooned a few lines of "I Love You Truly." Emmy told him to hush, but she was unable to refrain from smiling.

Phil rose from his chair and swept her up in his arms. Holding her tightly against himself, he kissed her tenderly. She was still in his arms as they slipped quietly up the stairs to their bedroom.

Emmy purred, "At least we have our own cabin for the night here in our home."

Phil replied, "There may be no moonlight over the waves tonight, but there's plenty of wind billowing my sail."

The following Saturday, Phil travelled downtown and discussed the pending journey with his mother. Later in the day, he arranged the fares to England. On Monday morning, Bandmaster Greenway was thrilled to learn that Zack would be accompanying the staff band on their journey to the ICC. Elizabeth McMillan was pleased that she and Gerald would honeymoon in the British Isles.

When Jenny heard the news, visions of romance and adventure swept through her mind. Sailing aboard a ship to England with Billy was a fantasy beyond her wildest dreams.

*

One evening in April, Phil and Emmy sat at the kitchen table. Phil was reading the newspaper while Emmy placed the supper dishes up into the cupboard after drying them with the new tea towel that Grandmother Mercer had sent them. On it were pictures of City Hall. Similar to the children, Emmy and Phil found it difficult to refer to her as Mrs. Hutchinson.

Phil placed the newspaper on the table and then heard a gentle knock at the door. The hour was not late, but it was after dark. It was unusual for someone to be outside at such an hour. If it were a close friend, then he or she would have knocked and opened the door. Who could it be?

Phil opened the door a crack and peered out into the gloom of night. A shaft of light from the interior of the house fell across the face of Mr. Sneadmore Treadwell. Phil's body tensed and his fist tightened as he gazed at the man. He feared he had come about Zeke. Then Phil noticed that Mr. Treadwell's shoulders were stooped, his hands were thrust deeply in his pockets, and there was anguish in his eyes.

"Mr. Mercer," Treadwell began, "would ye please step outside and grant me a few minutes of your time? I wish to talk."

Phil considered Mr. Treadwell a dangerous man, but on this occasion he sensed no hostility, so he stepped out and closed the door quietly behind him.

"It's about my boy Jeremiah. He's changed. He no longer fights for his rights as I've taught him. He does not attend my preaching services. Yesterday, I discovered that your boy Zack has been giving Jeremiah cornet lessons. Last night, I confronted Jeremiah, and he told me that not only has he learned to play the cornet, but also he wants to start attending The Salvation Army. I threatened to throw him out of the house, but he told me that he plans to leave anyway. He's now eighteen, and he and Ezekiel intend to rent a flat together. I believe they've already found a place. Mr. McCarthy has even agreed to give Jeremiah a job at his store."

"It sounds as if your sons have given this matter considerable thought."

"You don't understand. Jeremiah is my favourite. I always knew that other son of mine would turn against me, and that daughter of mine is a child of hell. I never know what she's thinking. On the other hand, I thought that Jeremiah would continue in my footsteps and preach the word of the Lord."

"He may still do that."

"He'll not preach the *real* word of the Lord. Anyone can preach that mushy religion you follow. It takes a man to preach the fire-and-brimstone faith of our fathers. Fear of hell keeps a man on the straight and narrow. Give me that old-time religion."

"Have you ever considered that a love of God is more powerful than a fear of God?"

Mr. Treadwell paused for a moment, but he dodged Phil's question. Finally he said, "I love Jeremiah and don't want to lose him. Can ye help me?"

"Have you told Jeremiah that you love him? Love may be part of a mushy religion, but you may find it stronger than all the fires of hell."

Ignoring Phil's question, he responded, "Can you stop Zack from giving my boy music lessons?"

"Wouldn't that be like locking the barn door after the horses have fled?"

Mr. Treadwell gazed at Phil. His shoulders drooped as he gave a quiet sigh. Turning away slowly, he slipped silently into the night.

*

Early morning on Good Friday in April 1914, the staff band, along with many corps bands, assembled at the armouries on University Avenue. This was the assembly point for The Salvation Army's annual parade. They marched to Massey Hall where they held the sacred Good Friday service.

Phil and Zack walked along the parade route, keeping pace with the band. Zack longed to apply to become a member of the staff band. He found it difficult to wait for the years to pass so that he would be of age. Phil smiled when Zack exclaimed in exasperation, "Time goes too slowly."

On May 16, people filled the Rosemount Hall. Among the three hundred people crowding the space, Phil noticed Mr. Treadwell sitting with his wife and son Jeremiah. Phil wondered what had transpired.

Contrary to Zack's opinion, time continued to roll forward rapidly. Canadian delegates who were crossing on the ship the *Royal Edward* arrived in Toronto from western Canada on the following Sunday afternoon, departing the same evening for Montreal. Within a few days, the first party attending the ICC would be gazing upon the waves of the mighty Atlantic, on their way to the "great event."

Toronto Armouries on University Avenue north of Queen Street West (the site today contains courthouses). *City of Toronto Archives, Fonds 1568, Item 0220*

*

The month of May brought forth the perennial blossoms on the trees in Wilford's orchard. Under the warm sunshine, the Earlscourt District burst into the fullness of spring. Fragrant white and purple lilacs scented the laneways and back gardens. Nature was reaching upward to touch the face of God.

As spring progressed, and with the completion of the St. Clair streetcar line, the Mercers were able to travel on public transit to visit Kew Beach on Lake Ontario. One weekday, Emmy took Zack and Bess to High Park. They walked there from Lansdowne Avenue and Bloor Street, as that was where the Bloor streetcar line terminated. Summer outings were few for the Mercer children, but they created treasured memories.

Emmy kept in touch with her family living downtown by sending postcards. From Monday to Saturday, the postman delivered mail every morning and every afternoon. If she mailed a card before 10:00 a.m., it arrived at its destination by 3:00 p.m. the same day.

Since Emmy and Phil lived in the west end of Toronto, they rarely visited the east end. Yonge Street was the great divide, a place where east embraced west. Once or twice a year, Emmy journeyed downtown to Eaton's or Simpson's. For these occasions, she donned her Sunday best" She highly approved of the large "restroom" on the third floor of the Eaton's Queen Street Store. It provided armchairs where she could sit and rest from the labours of shopping. Eaton's had been the first store in Toronto to provide women's washrooms, allowing female customers to shop longer. Emmy appreciated this convenience and was a loyal customer.

*

As the time for the International Congress neared, excitement increased. All eyes were on London. Contingents of representatives from distant lands were arriving daily in the city. People living in other parts of the British Isles were already journeying toward London. There were to be five contingents of Canadian delegates: more than 400 people. Of this number, 170 would be in the group that would depart from Toronto. Available space for overseas bookings, especially in third class, was quickly disappearing.

Billy and Zack often shared their thoughts after they were in bed. In the darkness of the room, they talked about their forthcoming journey.

"When we arrive in England," Zack inquired, "what sights do you want to see?"

"I've read all about London. I want to see Westminster Abbey, the Guild Hall, Buckingham Palace, and Big Ben."

"You know where I want to go?"

"Where?"

"I want go to Comstock to see our old house on South Street."

"It's strange that you mention Comstock. I want to see Mrs. Rowntree again. I'll never forget the day she rescued me with her broom."

Zack giggled. "I bet if she sees you, she'll pee her pants," he said, his laughter increasing.

"Do you remember how I used to play pranks on her?" Billy asked, ignoring his brother's mirth. "She was the last person I ever thought would show up to see us off at the train station."

"I thought she was a strange old woman."

"Perhaps she was. But now I feel guilty about the many times I teased her."

"Crabtree, Crabtree's a mean old bag, drop her in the river in a burlap bag," Zack chorused and then chuckled quietly.

In the quietness that followed, a clumsy May beetle hit against the window glass with a dull thud. When the noisy insect flew away, silence returned. Zack's voice broke the tranquility when he asked, "Do you think the Reverend Stinky Wilmot will be glad to see us?"

Billy was unable to resist smiling. "I think I should ask him if he still has the cow-dung Christmas wreath that I hung on his door."

"Naw! He doesn't have it. I bet he ate it."

Billy now broke out laughing. An annoyed voice from his parents' room requested that they settle down.

Zack waited a few moments before he said, "I bet that Stinky Wilmot has never kissed a woman, because if his lips ever came near a woman, she'd be afraid that he was going to eat her."

More laughter ensued. They shoved the edge of the quilt in their mouths to stifle the noise so they would not disturb their parents. When they were in control again, Zack said, "Billy. Do you kiss Jenny?"

"Every chance I get. Why do you want to know?"

"I always thought that kissing a girl was mushy, sissy stuff. But lately I've been thinking about it."

"What caused this change?"

"There's this girl at school. Her name is Peggy, and she's real cute. Should I walk home from school with her?"

"Sure, you said you thought she was cute. But find out her last name before you kiss her. If it's Peggy Wilmot, then she may be trying to eat you."

They again broke into laughter and, despite the thumping on the wall, were unable to stop. Finally, silence descended. Zack gazed at the outline of Billy's body under the quilt. *I bet no one in the whole wide world has a brother like Billy,* he thought. *I wish I were more like him.*

Billy was silent. He was thinking of Jenny.

*

In the days ahead, Phil and Emmy observed the anticipation intensifying in their two sons. At times, they were too excited to sleep, talking quietly late into the night, sharing hopes and dreams. The age difference between them did not exist. They were soul mates sharing a mission.

Whenever possible, they practised on their instruments. Billy made several changes to the solo parts of the manuscript for "O Boundless Salvation," being certain that the cornets would not harmonically clash with the band accompaniment, as there was insufficient time to alter it. The changes enhanced the music, making it more difficult to play and more interesting for listeners.

*

In Toronto, the final practice for the staff band was on Thursday, May 21. Commissioner David Hees attended the session and afterward shared tea with the bandsmen in the band room at the Territorial Headquarters.

At the end of the serving of tea, Commissioner Hees stood to his feet to speak. He remarked that the band had had a highly successful winter season, the best in its history. Then he added his personal thoughts: "I have sailed the Atlantic three times during the month of May and never had a decent crossing. I suppose this voyage will be no different. On my first trip, I spent more time leaning over the deck railing than I did in the dining room. At one point, I thought that I would arrive in Canada without my stomach."

This remark brought an amused reaction from the men. As Commissioner Hees continued, he reminisced about the Congress of 1904, in which he had participated. He told the assembled group, "In that year, it seemed as if all Londoners ceased their daily activities to gaze upon the Army. I am not certain how the city managed to receive their bread and milk deliveries." Then he winked at the bandsmen and added, "Perhaps the deliveries of gin and ale were also disrupted."

Speaking in a more serious voice, he continued. "I know that the staff band will be touring Scotland and Ireland after the Congress ends. I express my deep regrets that I will be unable to accompany the staff band on the tour. However, I look forward to sharing time with you all in London."

*

Three days after the final band practice, May 24 was the final Sunday before the band departed. They held a pre-farewell service for the staff band at the Temple Corps on Albert Street. The staff bandsmen wore full Congress regalia (scarlet tunics with thick white braiding on the shoulders).

The Toronto Temple Corps (now demolished) on the northeast corner of Albert and James streets, headquarters of The Salvation Army in Canada. *City of Toronto Archives, Fonds 1244, Item 1998*

The next event planned for the staff band was a final farewell program on Wednesday evening, May 27. Following this service, the bandsmen were to depart by train for Quebec City to board the *Empress of Ireland.*

*

Finally, the day of departure, May 27, 1914, dawned. It was frantic inside the Mercer household.

Phil told Emmy, "I've completed most of the household chores that need to be done before I leave."

"I'm grateful for all your help."

"I know only too well the daily problems you'll confront during the weeks while I'm overseas."

"It has been a rush to complete everything. Mary and Ruth are helping me to place the final items into the suitcases that you'll be carrying with you on the streetcar."

Ten minutes later, the morning mail arrived. Phil shouted to Emmy, who was upstairs in one of the bedrooms, "I received a postcard in the morning mail. Bandmaster Greenway has requested that all bandsmen arrive at the Toronto Temple by one o'clock."

"That's earlier than I'd planned."

"Yes, it is."

"It's not so bad for delegates who live in the downtown area. They've already walked over to Union Station with their hand luggage and had it checked in. Today, they can proceed on foot to the Temple Corps."

"I know," Phil said. "Because we're in remote Earlscourt, we must carry our hand luggage with us to the temple, and later have it delivered to the station."

"Well, we have no choice. If you and the boys must depart early, I'll hasten the last of the packing."

Phil gazed longingly at Emmy as he told her, "I'm looking forward to the departure with mixed emotions."

"I am, too. I'm grateful that my men—and I include Zack as one of my men—are journeying to Britain. However, I'll be apart from the three of you for eight weeks."

"It bothers me, too. You'll never know how much," Phil replied.

They gazed tenderly at each other and then embraced. Finally, Emmy said, "Enough. We must finish our chores."

*

Emmy watched Phil don his blue serge suit, knowing the departure hour had arrived. She smiled bravely as Phil hugged and kissed the girls. Bess was the first to have tears in her eyes.

Phil placed his arms around her and tenderly kissed her cheek.

"You're a young woman now. Look after your mother," he whispered tenderly.

"I want so much to be with Zack!" she replied, careful that Zack did not hear her.

"Oh, darling! I wish you could."

"I know! I know! If wishes were horses, then beggars would ride," she said, trying not to show her disappointment.

"My princess, when I return home, we shall ride a streetcar for a whole day."

"Is that a promise?"

"I give you my word on it. Bess, you will be the first one I hug when I return."

Phil was aware that Bess was not completely mollified. He noticed when she attempted surreptitiously to wipe her eyes with the sleeve of her dress.

Then a flood of emotional goodbyes ensued. Love had always dominated the family, and never before had they been apart, other than on band trips or for the week when Zack and Bess had been at the summer camp in Clarkson. Other than the final goodbyes at the streetcar stop on St. Clair Avenue, this was the last private parting for the family as a group.

Ruth and Mary elected not to attend the concert, as the hour would be late when it was over and they must rise early the next day for work. Bess reluctantly agreed to stay with her sisters. As her daughters were not attending, Emmy decided that after the concert she would walk to the train station to see Phil and the boys depart.

After Phil offered a prayer for the protection of his family, he and the boys walked the two blocks to the streetcar stop. They soon reached St. Clair Avenue. In the near distance just west of Boon Avenue, they could see an eastbound streetcar approaching. It was time for a quick and final goodbye. As the streetcar arrived at the stop, Phil and his sons moved their suitcases to the small platform in the centre boulevard. When the streetcar doors opened, tearful eyes from the sidewalk watched the Mercer men climb aboard.

Billy and Zack raced down the aisle of the streetcar, struggling with their instrument cases and suitcases. They located seats on the south side of the streetcar, placed their luggage in empty spots, and quickly slid along the wooden bench seats. Then they shoved up the windows and, along with their father, poked their heads through the openings to obtain one last glimpse of their family. Billy tucked his band cap under his arm and leaned out as far as possible. Zack copied him and almost tumbled out the window. A breeze ruffled Phil's hair; he attempted to rearrange it as he waved to his wife and daughters with his other hand.

Then the streetcar began its eastward journey, leaving behind the lonely figures on the sidewalk. Inside Phil's suit-jacket pocket was a postcard he intended to mail to Emmy from Quebec.

*

As the streetcar continued eastward toward Oakwood Avenue, Emmy walked south on Dufferin Street, the parting scene vivid in her mind. She smiled to herself as she thought about Phil, his hair dishevelled from the wind, appearing so youthful and boyish. She knew that it was typical of him to struggle to straighten his hair rather than ignore the sudden untidiness. Gazing at Mary and Ruth, and then at Bess, Emmy noticed that Bess was nearly as tall as she was, maturing into a beautiful young woman. She reflected on this for a moment, realizing that all her children were now young adults. It seemed as if it had happened without her realizing it.

Motioning for the girls to continue homeward, Emmy reflected upon her situation. She was now without a husband in the home, and so she thought about the tasks ahead. Bess sensed her mood. As they walked along in silence, she slipped her hand into her mother's. Emmy gazed at her daughter and smiled.

She told Bess, "When I get home, I must prepare to journey downtown for the evening's farewell concert."

*

Phil and the boys journeyed along St. Clair Avenue, and at Avenue Road they transferred to the Avenue Road streetcar, which soon rumbled down the steep incline of the hill toward Bloor Street. From there, the tram turned eastward to Yonge and then proceeded southward to the downtown area. The warm temperatures had enticed Toronto's citizens to venture forth into the spring sunshine, making the downtown a hive of activity.

Alighting from the streetcar at Shuter and Yonge streets, Phil, Billy, and Zack walked south a half block to Albert Street and turned right, since the Toronto Temple Corps was located slightly to the west of Yonge, at Albert and James streets. Its imposing, ornate façade dominated the north side of Albert, although it appeared insignificant compared to Eaton's store across the road on the south side of the street and to the nearby towering 1899 City Hall.

After climbing the steps of the Temple Corps, they walked into the foyer. From the moment they entered the building, an atmosphere of anticipation and excitement surrounded them. Officers, bandsmen, and family members rushed about offering farewells and last-minute instructions as well as best wishes. Luggage, suitcases, and boxes were everywhere, many of the suitcases reinforced with leather straps, the rest secured with rope. Because corrugated cardboard cartons were not yet in use, people had sewn some parcels into cloth bags to protect their contents during the journey.

In the early afternoon, the staff bandsmen had assembled at the east side of the Toronto City Hall (now the Old City Hall) to have an official band photograph taken. Bandmaster Greenway had thought that it would be a good idea to have a picture of the band in their Mountie-style fedoras, on the front of which were small crests consisting of a white maple leaf on a red background. The bandsmen posed proudly, wearing their tunics with the white braids on the shoulders.

Meanwhile, departing passengers continued to pile luggage into the vestibule of the Temple Corps, while carters attempted to arrange for its delivery to the train station. Phil and Zack's luggage was among the mountains of suitcases. The staff bandsmen were unable to carry their own belongings, as they were to march in formation to the train station after the evening festival in a triumphant parade of witness. As a result, Headquarters had arranged for a horse-drawn wagon to take their luggage and instrument cases to the Union Station in late afternoon. It was imperative that the lobby area be cleared to accommodate the huge crowds that would soon pour into the temple for the great Farewell Festival. The logistics of the entire operation required immense planning.

The Mercers had taken their midday meal at home, but a substantial supper was essential because they would not have another opportunity to eat before the following morning, when the attendants on the train would offer them a breakfast. Few of the bandsmen could afford to eat in restaurants, so they arranged to serve a supper in the basement level of the Temple Corps where there was a fully equipped kitchen.

Upstairs in the temple, people were busy with the final preparations for the evening's Farewell Festival, placing the chairs and music stands in position on the platform. The auditorium of the Temple Corps was enormous, the extra-wide platform capable of holding at least four full-size bands.

*

Elizabeth McMillan and Thomas McCarthy, who were now Mrs. and Mr. Thomas McCarthy, had shipped their luggage to Union Station earlier in the day, as had Grandmother Mercer and Gerald. Jenny's suitcase and steamer trunk were among the bags.

*

As the appointed time for the festival approached, the audience buzzed with anticipation. Well over a thousand people were in attendance. On this evening of evenings, when the all-important moment finally arrived, the audience hushed when the doors on either side of the platform opened and a flag party entered. The standard-bearers marched proudly across the platform, the audience standing to its feet, loud applause breaking forth in great waves across the expanse of the auditorium.

After the flag party had entered, the Toronto Staff and the Toronto Temple Bands came in from opposite sides of the platform. As Billy marched onto the stage, he tugged nervously at the collar of his uniform, not quite believing that he was taking the first steps of a journey that would lead him to London.

For a split second, Billy glanced back at the doorway leading to the platform, as he knew that Zack was watching the procession while awaiting his turn to walk onto the platform later in the evening. Zack was poking his head from the right-hand side of the doorway, craning his neck to see into the platform area. In that brief moment of time, Billy caught sight of his brother's impish grin. Billy quickly turned away and looked ahead to avoid bumping into the bandsman ahead of him. Then he heard an explosion of applause from a small group in the balcony.

In the congregation, soldiers from the individual corps tended to sit together in groups, so the clapping was louder when one of their bandsman entered. The applause Billy had heard was from the Rosemount group sitting in the balcony; it had erupted when George Meaford, Gerald Hutchinson, and he had entered the platform area. He felt slightly embarrassed by the attention he and the Rosemount bandsmen were receiving, but he was grateful for their support.

When all the bandsmen were in position, Bandmaster Greenway and the bandmaster of the Temple Corps entered from opposite sides of the platform to assume leadership of their respective bands. Finally, the platform party entered, led by Commissioner David Hees. Now that everyone had arrived, the platform was transformed into a panorama rich in Army symbolism and pageantry. From the moment Bandmaster Greenway raised the baton for the bands to play the opening notes of the first song, the emotions of the crowd electrically charged the air.

*

The evening unveiled prayerful hopes, inspirational singing, a few too many grand speeches, and certainly great instrumental music. The rhythms of the combined bands soared to the lofty ceiling, filling the auditorium. In recognition of the staff band's pending journey, the Temple Band performed a composition titled "Songs of England." Each band played separate items as well as massed numbers, the combined renditions drawing a great response.

When it was time for Billy and Zack to perform "O Boundless Salvation," the audience burst into wild applause as the duet stepped onto the dais. It was difficult to imagine a single person in the crowd who had not heard about this piece of music. It had been the talk of the town for weeks, especially after the announcement that young Zack was to accompany the staff band to England. The crowd's anticipation was intense; the applause increased.

Then, it was as if a great hand silenced the throngs.

Billy gazed at Zack, an unspoken communication passing between them. Then Billy nodded to Bandmaster Greenway to indicate that they were ready to begin. The boys raised their cornets to their lips and adjusted their embouchures. The bandmaster lifted his baton. The course of events was now unalterable. Fate would unfold in its inimitably impartial and unpredictable manner. The outcome now rested on the shoulders of the two young men standing before an audience wrapped in anticipation.

From the opening notes until the climactic end of the music, every sound was true and clear. Zack's part was not as difficult Billy's, but he never split a single note. The melody of the old hymn soared gloriously. The intricate sections involving triple-tonguing clipped along flawlessly. The staff band's accompaniment was the finest it had ever given, and the combination of two highly skilled soloists and a superbly trained band produced a performance that was beyond the expectations of even the most optimistic.

When they had finished playing, the applause was thunderous. As it died away, Commissioner Hees stepped to the podium. He was lost for words. Slowly recovering, he said in a voice choked with emotion, "Is the mother of these two lads present here tonight? If she is, would she please stand?"

There was silence as everyone glanced around to see if anyone had stood. Then they heard the loud clapping of hands in the balcony as Emmy hesitantly rose to her feet. The audience below realized what was happening, and though they were unable to see Emmy, they broke out into energetic applause that filled the auditorium. Before the Commissioner could say another word, Emmy quickly sat down.

"Comrades!" the Commissioner began, "Tonight, we all give thanks for the life of Emily Mercer, whose sons thrilled us this evening."

More applause!

Gazing up into the balcony, the Commissioner added, "My dear comrade, do you have any more sons at home to give to the musical ministry of the Army?"

Emmy nodded her head, not because she had another son, but because she had a daughter, Bess, who, if given a chance, might someday perform every bit as well as her brothers.

Following a few more words of praise for Billy and Zack, the Commissioner read aloud a message of best wishes sent by the New York Staff Band. Loud and warm applause greeted the announcement. The festival closed with the hymn "God Be with You till We Meet Again." As the audience stood and sang, Commissioner Hees leaned over the podium and shook hands with a group of young men seated in the front row.

He said to them, "It's time for you lads to rush home for tea and biscuits."

The boys grinned. Their names were unknown to the Commissioner, but he considered no one a stranger, especially the young. He was a man who was well known for such spontaneous acts of cordiality and fellowship.

At the festival's conclusion, jubilation engulfed the crowds as they surged out of the doors of the temple and poured onto Albert Street. Within a short space of time, the staff and temple bands assumed an orderly formation in the centre of the street. Behind them, another four or five corps bands assembled. With flags unfurled and to the beat of the bass drum, the musicians marched east to Yonge and then south on Yonge toward Front Street. It was well after the hour of ten, but the few people remaining on the street applauded. Many Salvationists, including Emmy, marched behind the bands, their hearts lifted and inspired by the stirring sound of the music.

*

When the throngs arrived at Front Street, the marchers turned west toward Union Station, which in that decade was between York and Simcoe streets. This venerable station, built in 1884, has since been demolished. The city replaced it with a newer structure, which is also on Front Street, but to the east of the original. The old station possessed an impressively ornate stone façade and a large square tower. At the rear of the station, on The Esplanade, were several pointed towers near to where the train tracks were located. South of the tracks was the shoreline of Lake Ontario. Because of landfill, the city eventually pushed the lakefront farther to the south, reducing the size of the harbour.

The parade came to an orderly halt in front of Union Station. The *Toronto Daily Star* reported this:

> There was an animated scene and the station was crowded with the many friends of the travellers. Many of the bands from other sections of the province were there, and the leave-taking was a most impressive one.

The music ceased and silence fell over the street. To the beat of the drums, row after row, the bandsmen left the formation and entered the tall doors that gave access to the Great Hall in the interior of the train station. It had a high domed ceiling and amenities typical of most stations in major Canadian cities—huge bench seats without armrests, a souvenir stand, ticket cages with barred windows, a newspaper and tobacco shop, and a row of shoeshine chairs. Other passengers gazed with interest at the bands and their followers as they filled the hall to near capacity.

The delegates proceeded toward the swinging doors at the south end of the departure hall. The station permitted only ticketed passengers beyond this point, but some purchased a ticket for twenty-five cents, allowing them to travel to the Sunnyside Station. They never intended to use the fare, but it gave them access to the platform level, and thus they were able to be with their loved ones until the final moment when the train departed. Emmy was one of these people, grasping Phil's arm tightly as they walked slowly toward the doors.

Rear view of the departure area and tracks of the old 1884 Union Station. *City of Toronto Archives, Fonds 1244, Item 5021*

On the other side of the doors, the staff band and the delegates walked along the crowded, covered passageway that crossed over Station Street below, where the streetcar circled the station. The elevated passageway gave access to the long flights of descending stairs that led to the platforms, where the hissing of steam escaping from the trains was audible.

Descending the staircase to the track level, the Salvationists proceeded to the seven coaches reserved for the Army to transport them to Montreal and eventually onward to Quebec. By this time, quite a large crowd had assembled at the platform level. Before they entrained, the staff band played another hymn, the music blessing the hearts of those who listened. Finally, the music ceased, and delegates exchanged their last hugs, tearfully gave final words of farewell, and commenced climbing onboard.

*

Phil and Emmy walked along the platform. Behind them were Grandmother Mercer and Gerald, as well as Thomas and Elizabeth McCarthy and Jenny. When Phil reached the narrow stairs that permitted access to the interior of the coach, he stood aside to allow the others to climb aboard. Billy and Zack were already in the coach, having accompanied several younger bandsmen.

Departure area of the 1884 Union Station. *City of Toronto Archives, Fonds 1244, Item 5040*

Placing his small carry-on suitcase on the ground, Phil took Emmy in his arms. She clung to him. He held her close. The commotion of the passengers surrounding them, the hissing steam from the engine at the front of the train, and the porters shouting for people to climb aboard made it difficult to talk. The noise was akin to a cacophonic opus beyond the abilities of future composers of discordant symphonies.

"Emmy," Phil said, his voice husky with emotion, "I can hardly bear being separated from you. It's like denying breath to my body."

"You're my life," she replied, a sob choking her words.

Trying to regain his composure, Phil looked deeply into her eyes as he continued. "You're my strength, Emmy. It was you who pushed me to immigrate to Canada. Everything I have, I owe to you. Ever since the day when I was a lad and saw you with the other children, I've never loved anyone else."

"Hush!" In truth, however, she relished hearing his words.

"The children are what they are because of the guidance you gave them. I see your influence in Billy and Zack every day. The girls reflect you, too—beautiful and smart."

"They're *our* children, Phil."

"I've told you many times how much I love you, but I also want you to know how grateful I am for all you've given me these many years. You're the reason today I carry great happiness in my heart."

Emmy's hand brushed the hair that had fallen over his forehead, her fingers lingering on his cheek.

"No matter how great the distance between us," Phil said, "we'll always be together. You'll always feel my presence beside you, even when you're unable to reach out and touch my hand. I'll be away in the Old Country for two months, but I'll be beside you in my heart."

"I'll love you forever, Phil."

"Be brave, my darling, until we're together again."

The coach gave a sudden shudder, metal grinding on metal, indicating the forward thrust of the mighty steam engine. Their parting kiss, tender but brief, ended. Breaking from Emmy's embrace, Phil picked up his suitcase and climbed up the stairs and into the coach. As the train slowly moved forward, Phil peered at his beloved Emmy from the opening between the coaches.

Emmy gazed up into Phil's face, and for a fleeting moment she saw the boy within the man. His smile contained the innocent bravery of a child who was watching parents depart, fearful that they might not return.

Such instances in life are rare, when an adult's smile or unguarded moment reveals the child within. Emmy knew that she was experiencing such a moment. The boy within Phil had surfaced. Capturing the tenderness of the moment, she lovingly placed it in her heart.

Then the final glimpse of the love of her life vanished amid the hissing steam and the foreboding darkness of the night. The noise of the engine's rhythmic chugging lessened when the train escaped from beneath the canopied dome above the departure area.

Phil entered the coach to locate the seat assigned to him. He removed his pocket watch from his vest and glanced at it. Due to the delays, the train had not departed until almost 12:30 a.m., an hour later than the scheduled time.

*

The train lumbered eastward, passing the level crossings at Bay, York, Yonge, and Jarvis streets. Passengers gazed from the coach windows at the dark shapes of factories and industrial buildings. As the train gathered momentum, it rumbled among quiet residential avenues flanked by small cottage-like dwellings, passing row houses, semidetached homes, and several impressive mansions. A few lights from kitchen windows penetrated the inky darkness of the early morning, as at this late hour most residents of Toronto were snugly tucked into their beds.

Inhabitants near the railway tracks often found the hollow, deep-throated whistle of the train to be a familiar-sounding source of comfort. The coaches continued their journey, racing over street crossings and over steel bridges. The click-clack of the wheels became increasingly hypnotic, producing a steady rhythm that was persistently audible in the coaches' interiors. Eventually, the deep shadows of the countryside enveloped the train, with only an occasional feeble light in a farmhouse window piercing the dense blackness.

For about ten minutes, Billy and Jenny stood outside on the space between the coaches. They peered into the darkened landscape as it raced past. The noise from the wheels was intense, but they managed to chat intimately, Billy's arm around Jenny's shoulder to keep her warm against the chill of the wind created by the speeding locomotive. Finally, as the hour was late, they returned to their seats inside.

Billy found it difficult to settle into the coach seat. Near the front of the car, a small group had gathered, and though at times their voices were louder than they intended, eventually Billy managed to fall asleep. Zack had been asleep for the past twenty minutes. Phil remained awake, thinking of Emmy. When the coach was quiet, though his seat was uncomfortable, Phil eventually fell into a fitful slumber.

The Mercers went to the dining car for breakfast. Jenny was already seated at a table with her mother and stepfather. Zack had difficulty eating the scrambled eggs, even though they were his favourite, as he was unable to take his eyes from the landscape racing past the windows.

Later, near the midday hour, they arrived in Montreal's Windsor Station. It was not necessary to change trains, so after a brief delay they were eastbound again as the coaches sped along the north shore of the St. Lawrence. In the afternoon, at about 3:30 p.m., the train arrived near Quebec City and stopped at the Canadian Passenger Railway (CPR) pier at Wolf's Cove. Moored at the wharf of this historic landing site was their transatlantic steamer, the *Empress of Ireland.*

*

Captain Henry George Kendry of the *Empress* was on the bridge, anxiously awaiting the appearance of the large party of Salvationists. At age thirty-five, he was relatively young, but he was a highly seasoned marine officer. However, it was his first voyage as captain of the *Empress.*

He informed his first mate, "Throughout the day, about a thousand passengers have boarded, but I'm becoming increasingly concerned that the large group of Salvationists hasn't yet appeared."

"Yes, it's puzzling that they're not here," the mate replied.

"I am unable to give the order to sail without them."

"Perhaps their train departed late from Toronto."

"Possibly, but the hour is growing late."

"Look, Captain, over there, I can see the members of the band coming along the wharf."

"I see them. Their uniforms are certainly colourful."

"I overheard a Salvationist who is already aboard say that their bandmaster chose the Mountie-style hats for the trip. He wants people in London to recognize instantly that the band is Canadian."

"It's a good choice," the Captain replied. "The Mountie uniform, of which the Stetson is an important part, is a world-famous symbol of Canada."

"I notice that there are many passengers leaning on the deck rails, looking down at the bandsmen in their colourful outfits. Some are undoubtedly wondering about the identity of the group."

"True. But many know that it's a Salvation Army band, and they have chosen passage on this sailing of the *Empress* because they know there'll be inspirational music aboard."

"Aye, Captain. I think you're right."

*

Down on the wharf, Zack gazed up at the ocean liner and dropped his jaw in amazement. His only ship of comparison was the *Southwark,* which had brought them to Canada. The Royal Mail Steamer the *Empress of Ireland* was a sight people never forgot. Trudging along the pier with his suitcase, Zack chatted with Billy.

"Is this a super-ship?" Zack inquired of Billy.

"I suppose that's one way to refer to it."

"Well, it looks like a super-ship to me."

"They launched it in Glasgow in 1906. It has twin propellers just below the waterline. You can't see them from here."

"It's long and cigar-shaped."

"Actually, it's an elongated torpedo shape. It can travel at speeds of up to twenty knots an hour."

"How fast is that on land?"

"About twenty-three miles an hour."

"That's as fast as a motorcar." He paused and gazed across at Billy as he asked, "How do you know all this stuff?"

"There was a sheet of information about the *Empress* on the bulletin board in the staff band room back in Toronto. I read it."

"Anything else that you read?" Zack inquired.

"There was a list of remarkable statistics about the *Empress*. It requires almost a week to load the twenty-six hundred tons of coal to create the heat for the boilers. Almost the same amount of time is needed to replenish the food and other supplies onboard."

"I guess I don't have to worry about starving," Zack quipped.

"Just be grateful that we don't have to lug the food onboard. These suitcases are heavy enough."

***RMS Empress of Ireland* sailing at full speed. Owned by the Canadian Pacific Railway, it was built in Govan, Scotland, and launched on January 27, 1906.** *Photo courtesy of the George Scott Railton Heritage Centre*

Gazing intently at the ship and barely noticing where he was going, Billy continued talking about the vessel. "Look, the hull of the *Empress* is huge."

They both gazed at the coal-black hull with its narrow band of scarlet red at the waterline. The decks were white, gleaming as the sun reflected off of them. The two towering funnels were copper-coloured with solid black bands at the top stretching high into the air.

Finally, Zack told his brother, "I think the *Empress* really deserves her regal name. She looks like an empress of the seas."

*

The steamer represented one of the finest achievements of the Edwardian Age. The *Empress* was one of the few ships that provided direct train service, complete with sleeping cars, from Toronto to shipside in Quebec. Travellers thought so highly of the quality of the ship that the June 25 sailing was reasonably well booked for so early in the season. The ship inspired confidence and awe in those who beheld her, and Billy and Zack were no exception. Similar to the other bandsmen, as well as to Commissioner Hees, the Mercers possessed a second-class ticket.

Loading the passengers' luggage was a formidable task, since for this particular voyage more than three thousand pieces were involved. From the CPR shed, baggage handlers took the steamer trunks and piles of luggage and carted them down the gangways on two-wheeled dollies. The workers resembled a long line of constantly moving ants.

When the Mercers arrived at the end of the gangway, an officer from the ship greeted them. Phil indicated to an attendant which bags he and his sons did not require during the voyage, and the attendant attached labels to them that stated, "Unwanted." Workers lifted them onto a dolly to deliver them to the storage hold. The Mercers' smaller suitcases, containing personal items and clothing needed for the days ahead, were labelled with "Wanted" tags. The hall stewards carried these directly to the cabin.

The arrival of passengers created a flurry of activity onboard, as over a thousand people had booked passage. It was not yet the high season, but the third-class section, formerly referred to as steerage, was fully booked. Second-class was about half-occupied. Only the first-class section had plenty of space; it was two-thirds empty. Very few Salvationists could afford a single cabin. The majority were sharing berths in the second- or third-class section, which were assigned according to gender.

*

Sean Brownslea, who was crossing the ocean on the *Empress* in the first-class section, was travelling alone. A professional thief by trade, he stood on an upper deck observing the passengers as they boarded. He took no notice of The Salvation Army bandsmen in their colourful scarlet tunics. He was interested in those who were more prosperous, aware that people sailing overseas invariably carried cash to pay expenses during their journey. He smiled to himself as he thought about the thick money belts they often wore. It was not difficult to spot a wealthy businessman and discreetly follow him to his cabin. If he were unable to pick the gentleman's pocket or money belt, then he was sure he possessed the skill to open locks on the cabin doors and relieve his chosen victims of their funds. He never stole jewellery, as it was too easily identified if he were to be caught with it in his possession. Cash, on the other hand, was anonymous.

Brownslea was an Irishman. Born in Belfast, his parents abandoned him when he was ten years of age. Falling under the tutelage of a pair of elderly thieves, he had proven to be an apt student in the art of burglary and picking pockets. When Sean was thirty-five years old, both his teachers had passed away, leaving him alone. Prospects in his native city were limited, as few had any money to spend, and those who did have money lived in areas of the city it was difficult for him to frequent. He tried his hand on stage in a few run-down theatres, but his talents had been insufficient to earn him any decent money. However, he gained an extensive knowledge of stage makeup, which was to become useful in the years ahead. One day he relieved a woman of a heavy purse, and with the illicit funds he decided to invest in his future. Purchasing a second-class ticket aboard an ocean liner, he immigrated to Canada.

In Toronto, disguising himself as a humble labourer, he picked pockets in the downtown area of the city and burgled houses in Rosedale. For more than two decades, he earned enough to feed and clothe himself, enjoy a few luxuries, and, on some occasions, live in style. However, he struck it big when he turned his hand to bank robbing. He studied a prospective bank for weeks before he struck. Much to his surprise, he discovered he possessed a natural talent for bank robbing—as he did for other criminal enterprises. Each time he committed a robbery, he disguised his appearance, employing the skills he had acquired in the theatre. It was not long before he had amassed considerable savings, which he stored in safety deposit boxes in the same banks he had robbed. No one ever recognized him. It was his own private joke that he deposited in the banks the money that he had taken from them in the first place.

He was now returning to the British Isles in style. He purchased a first-class ticket, and so his cabin was spacious and luxurious. When the ship's security men found out that a passenger had been robbed, they would scour the third-class section, never suspecting that a prosperous gentleman in first class was the thief.

Sean Brownslea felt smug and quite secure.

*

A seemingly innocent incident occurred shortly after Billy and Zack boarded with their father. It had escaped their notice. The ship's cat, Bonita, a yellowish brown tabby of dubious descent, jumped ship at Quebec even though she had a litter of kittens on the *Empress.* The cat was the pet of a Mexican dishwasher who worked in the kitchen. He attempted to lure the fickle feline back onboard, but all his efforts failed.

The cat's owner later jokingly told his fellow workers, "For all I know, Bonita is involved with a cute Quebecois tomcat that lives in an alley off Rue du Porche in Lower Town."

Ah! Sí! The romance of travel!

*

Billy glanced around the ship. He knew that Jenny and her family had already boarded, but they were nowhere in sight. Gazing at the teak planking on the deck, he noticed that it was reflecting the late-day sun like a polished mirror. The railings were similarly manicured, their shine displaying evidence of the great care lavished on this CPR vessel. On the various deck levels, it was nearly impossible to find a smudge or dirt mark. In these surroundings, the white gloves of the ship's officers were most appropriate.

Onboard the *Empress of Ireland*'s decks. *Photo courtesy of the George Scott Railton Heritage Centre*

Billy noticed that some of the passengers who strolled on the uppermost deck (the boat deck) were well dressed, their attire clearly obtained from the prestigious shops of Toronto, Detroit, Montreal, or London. Billy heard a woman whisper, "I hear that Mr. Hyrum P. Graham from Toronto is sailing on this trip. He has so much money that it grows out of his ears."

The other woman replied, "I've oft heard that the rich are deaf."

Her companion chuckled and replied, "How true."

Billy had never heard of the man.

On the promenade deck below, the less opulent onboard walked about as if they, too, were a part of the more affluent scene. Mothers, trying imposing a sense of order and dignity, scolded any child who dared to run or shout. For most onboard, this was their only opportunity to roam all the decks of the ship, since after it sailed, the various classes of passengers were strictly separated from each other by small gates that formed barriers between the areas of the deck allotted to each class of passenger. Decks, dining rooms, parlours, and social rooms were similarly labelled according to class.

As Billy and Zack walked along the deck, their father told them, "On our previous Atlantic voyage aboard the *Southwark* eight years ago, the passenger list was considerably different."

"It was an emigrant ship," Billy reminded his father.

"True, but at least on that trip your mother was with us. The voyage to Canada was a nightmare for her."

Billy changed the subject, as he knew that his father was greatly missing Emmy. "I see that our cabin's on the main deck, third deck down, on the port side and toward the bow. It has two sets of bunk beds."

"You and I will take the berths nearest the bow," Phil suggested.

Zack interjected, "Can I have the top bunk on the opposite side?"

"That's fine," Phil said. "Mr. Meaford will sleep in the berth below you."

"I'm pleased that Mr. Meaford's bunking with us," Billy told his father.

"Yes, he's good company."

Phil now informed his sons, "The Captain has scheduled the sailing time for shortly after four o'clock this afternoon. Between now and departure time, we had best unpack our belongings."

Down in the cabin, Phil and his sons chatted while they stowed their personal items. They were in a buoyant mood, with much good-natured joshing and friendly banter. Though their cabin was far from commodious and the furnishings were relatively sparse, nothing could dampen their spirits.

Billy told Zack, “Look out the porthole. We’re on the side of the ship that faces the dock.”

Zack gazed out and exclaimed excitedly, “I can see the cliffs of Quebec.”

His father explained, “Atop the cliffs are the Plains of Abraham, the site of the legendary battle of September 1759. More than a mile east are the towering walls of the ‘Citadel of Canada’—the Quebec Fortress.’”

Billy told his dad, “I know the story of the battle. However, I think that we’re creating our own important event—a trip to England on the *Empress*.”

After unpacking their personal items, they walked out into the passageway and strolled toward the stern. Locating the stairs, they ascended to the deck above to find the second-class dining room. The three of them, especially Zack, considered the posting of the menu an important event. Although the doors remained closed, the stewards were preparing for afternoon tea.

Zack exclaimed, “Listen. Inside I can hear the clinking of the knives and forks and the rattle of the china plates.”

“I think I can hear your stomach rumbling,” Billy teased.

Zack grinned impishly and rubbed his belly.

“You sound like the Reverend Wilmot,” Billy added.

“I don’t eat chair legs and tabletops,” he replied.

“Then look at the menu and be content.”

They eagerly surveyed the menu.

Zack began to recite, “For breakfast tomorrow morning they’ll be serving hot oatmeal with fresh cream, a choice of fried meat or vegetable stew, toast with marmalade, and hot tea. For dinner they’ll serve soup, roasted mutton accompanied by several root vegetables, and pudding for dessert. Tea consists of cold roast meats, cheeses, cold hash, pickles, buns, and bread with butter.”

“Your recitations of the menus are almost as long as Reverend Wilmot’s sermons,” Billy told Zack.

Refusing to be deterred, Zack continued. "Supper is served at seven p.m. It only offers broth, cabin biscuits, tea buns, cheeses, and tea."

"What do you think of the menus?" his father asked.

"I think the choice of food's quite good."

Phil nodded. "I'm pleased that they've included the meals in the fare. It'll extend the six dollars I'm carrying in cash. I hope to have a little remaining after the voyage to supplement the bank draft of one hundred dollars that I have for expenses in England. It's in Canadian currency, which I must exchange for pounds sterling. I hope I have enough money to purchase gifts for Emmy and the girls."

"We'll have enough money," Billy assured his father. "Zack can always recite menus in the ship's lounge to earn extra funds."

*

As the stewards roamed the ship's passageways and decks, Zack heard their voices proclaiming loudly, "All ashore who's going ashore." He imitated their voices, cupping his hands to form a megaphone, until his father ordered him to desist.

As the final preparations for cast-off were in progress, Billy joined other bandsmen who were going below to a small storage room where the band instruments were located. It had been arranged that the band would perform as the ship set sail. While the staff band was assembling on the promenade deck, they heard the sounds of the crew removing the gangways. It was a cloudless day, the blue sky stretching endlessly behind the steep, rock-faced cliffs of old Quebec.

The deckhands lifted the thick mooring lines from the bollards, dropped them into the water, and pulled them aboard. Slowly, the gap between the ship and the wharf widened. The grand majesty of the waves, the *Empress,* was now free from her bonds to land and floating in her natural element. At approximately 4:20 p.m., the tugs manoeuvred the *Empress* into midstream, the twin propellers at the stern slowly coming to life. The twenty-foot blades, four on each propeller, began to rotate, the first of many thousands of revolutions which would not cease until they secured the mooring lines in Liverpool.

When the ship cast off, the Mexican dishwasher noticed that his pet cat, Bonita, was among the well-wishers at dockside. “Look,” he told a mate, “she’s offering a final farewell, waving her tail to say ‘adios’ to her kittens that are onboard the ship. For her, the call of romance is more important than her family.”

A blast from the whistle of the *Empress* split the air.

The mate said, “Captain Kendry has given the order from the ship’s bridge to set sail. We’d best man our stations.”

“Listen, I think I hear music on the promenade deck.”

“It must be that Salvation Army band.”

As they listened, the sound drifted on the quiet afternoon air. At first, the notes were soft, but soon the volume of the music increased.

“Blimey,” the crewman said, “They’re singing ‘O Canada.’ It’s not the national anthem. They should be singin’ ‘God Save the King.’ And now they’re singing ‘Auld Lang Syne.’ I doubt there’ll be a dry eye on any of the decks.”

“Maybe that’s why my cat left. She hates to get her paws wet.”

*

After the band finished playing ‘Auld Lang Syne,’ a man stepped forward and spoke to Bandmaster Greenway, leaning in so that only the bandmaster could hear. The man was elegantly attired, obviously a passenger from first class. His suit, expensive hat, and polished shoes indicated that he was likely a prosperous businessman.

“Bandmaster!” he began in a soften-spoken but authoritative voice. “I am Hyrum P. Graham from Toronto. One of my employees attends The Salvation Army and informs me that the band possesses a young musical prodigy of considerable note. I am a lover of brass band music. I would consider it a great honour if you allowed me to write a cheque for a hundred dollars, drawn on my London bank, so that the lad may perform a solo.”

The request took Bandmaster Greenway by surprise. A hundred dollars was a significant sum of money. The band could use a little extra cash during their tour of Scotland, and this was a golden opportunity.

“What would you have him play?”

“Well, I have been informed that the older boy has written a duet, and though I would enjoy hearing it, I realize that that it would not be appropriate for this occasion. I understand that the lad has a few other compositions based on well-known hymn tunes. Does he possibly have one for my favourite hymn, 'Abide with Me'?"

"I'll certainly inquire."

Bandmaster Greenway motioned for Billy to step to the podium. He introduced him to Mr. Graham, they shook hands, and he told him of the man's request, mentioning that Graham had offered to donate a hundred dollars to the band fund.

Billy nodded his head, consenting to the request. He had no such composition but felt that he could improvise something.

He inquired of Bandmaster Greenway, "Is it possible for Bandmaster Meaford to conduct the staff band while I play? He is accustomed to accompanying me when I create variations on a hymn tune when I play with the Rosemount Band."

Bandmaster Greenway was puzzled, as he had never heard Billy perform such music. He handed the baton to George.

George informed the band of the hymn's number in the Band Journal and explained to them that Billy would perform the hymn as a cornet solo, while the remaining musicians would softly play the full score to accompany him. He explained that they were to watch the baton closely, as he would indicate when they were to stop playing and when to resume. Then he looked at Billy, who indicated that they would play all five verses of the hymn. George held up his fingers to indicate Billy's instructions.

Bandmaster Greenway then announced the name of the hymn to the throng gathered on deck and explained that Bandmaster Meaford of the Rosemount Corps would conduct the band as Bandsman Mercer performed a cornet solo.

*

The light from the setting sun reflected on Billy's youthful face and highlighted his blond hair, which was already bleached fair from the spring sunshine. Because of his broad shoulders and narrow waist, he wore the scarlet uniform splendidly. The crowd was captivated even before he raised his cornet to his lips.

Billy commenced playing Henry F. Lyte's hymn "Abide with Me," and the staff band softly accompanied him. The scintillating notes of the cornet floated above the gathered throng, drifting across the spacious deck. People leaning on the rails who had not intended to listen to the band turned toward the source of the rich, heavenly sound. Slowly, they edged toward the music's point of emanation. Many in the crowd knew the lyrics of the first verse.

> Abide with me; fast falls the eventide;
> The darkness deepens; Lord, with me abide!
> When other helpers fail, and comforts flee,
> Help of the helpless, O abide with me.

As the second verse began, George Meaford watched for a signal from Billy, stopping the band at the end of the phrase where Billy wished to improvise. Then, when Billy indicated that his improvised part was ending, George's baton instinctively brought in the band once more, and the music continued seamlessly until the next improvisation. Billy knew the score of the music from memory, as he did for every other hymn he had ever played from the Army tune book.

In the third verse, Billy played alongside the band, the notes of his cornet distinct and clear above the band's accompaniment as he deftly switched into an embellished blend of the solo cornet, tenor horn, and euphonium parts. Bandmaster Greenway stared in disbelief as he listened to the intricacy of the music, marvelling how Billy was able to switch effortlessly between the various parts. Silently, he was grateful that he was not conducting.

In the fourth verse, Billy continued his improvisations. When he soloed, he created countermelodies with rhythms that complemented and contrasted with the original music. Then, when the band inserted itself into the composition, he played alongside it in perfect pitch. It opened an entirely new dimension into the old hymn, but at no time was the original beauty of the melody lost. He enhanced it, creating a symphonic rendition that captivated those who listened. It was as if the skills he had learned when composing "O Boundless Salvation" had been transferred to this old hymn.

The audience had thought that up to this point the music had been glorious, but they were soon to learn that the final verse was to be the most emotional of all. The cornet began unaccompanied as Billy switched into the minor key, creating a haunting version of the hymn. Then, as the band again entered, Billy returned to the melody as written by the composer, but at an octave above the band's. As the final notes drew near, because of the cornet's high pitch, the music ended on a note of triumph—"In life, in death … abide with me."

Then there was silence.

No one on deck moved or spoke. Many knew the words of the fifth verse of the song:

> Hold thou thy cross before my closing eyes;
> Shine through the gloom, and point me to the skies;
> Heaven's morning breaks, and earth's vain shadows flee;
> In life, in death, O Lord, abide with me!

Mr. Hiram P. Graham knew that Billy had transformed a simple hymn tune into a complicated musical composition, creating an experience he would never forget. The businessman was also aware by his tone and his technique that Billy was indeed an accomplished musician. He noticed that as Billy returned to his chair among the bandsmen, many of those who had gathered wiped tears from their eyes.

A woman standing near Mr. Graham said, "When I hear the angels play for me in heaven, the sound will not be any sweeter."

The woman beside her chimed in, "That boy could play his way right into heaven."

*

As George Meaford handed the baton back to Bandmaster Greenway, he had never felt prouder of Billy. He knew that if Billy were not in the staff band, then he would be the featured soloist on the trip. But he harboured no envy. He loved Billy, immensely enjoyed listening to him play, and did not wish it to be any other way. He also admitted that Billy was the better musician—a Mozart of the cornet.

When Billy had performed "Abide with Me," George thought that his tone had never been fuller and sweeter—nor had the improvisations ever been more amazing. The ease with which he manoeuvred the cornet's valves had never been smoother. His ability to switch parts and keys with ease had been superb. George knew that Billy was determined that when he performed in London, the voice of his cornet would echo the depths of his faith.

Aware of Billy's convictions, George knew that he wanted each note to encompass the compassion and love that he believed his faith taught. He saw little relevance in the rituals, church edicts, and great sacred buildings. George had discussed these issues with Billy many times and felt that Billy was correct. Maybe the problem with Christianity was that its message was too simple and unselfish to be widely accepted. Humankind had chosen to embellish it with the trappings of wealth and power.

Walking to his chair among the bandsmen's, George saw that the others were preparing to play another hymn. The words of this hymn would also haunt the memories of the *Empress* passengers in the days ahead. People were to hear its timeless message down through the decades. It expressed the thoughts and prayers of those who waved goodbye from the shore, as well as the passengers who lined the decks of the *Empress* on this gloriously sun-filled afternoon of Thursday, May 28, 1914. Many of the passengers had been singing along with the band, the words to the music echoing hauntingly across the decks.

> God be with you till we meet again;
> By his counsels guide, uphold you;
> With his sheep securely fold you;
> God be with you till we meet again.

The music ended, the words dying in the stillness of the springtime air. Now the rippling of the waves from the water below the deck rails filled the vacuum as the ship eased into the river's current.

*

As the men had ceased playing, the soft mood of late afternoon descended. The rays of the sun glistened on the bandsmen's silver instruments as they packed them away to place them in the allotted storage place in the interior of the ship.

Mr. Graham now approached Bandmaster Greenway to shake his hand.

"My secretary will give you my cheque for the agreed sum. I truly believe that that is the best value for the money that I've ever paid for a musical rendition."

"The band is very grateful for your generous donation."

Mr. Graham smiled. "Where can I get my hands on a copy of the composition that the young lad played?"

"I think you had better ask George Meaford, who conducted the band while Bandsman Mercer played. He can tell you more about it than I can."

Bandmaster Greenway caught George's eye and motioned him to join them. After he introduced the two men, he told him of Mr. Graham's request.

"I'm afraid there is no copy of the composition," George explained. "Billy composed the music as he performed it."

"But that's not possible. It was letter-perfect. It requires many hours to create such a composition—and many more hours to learn to play it," Mr. Graham replied.

"I couldn't agree more. It's amazing. I can't explain it. But there's something else that's even more amazing. Young Billy could play that exact music a year from now and it would be exactly the same, not a note different. He can also write it down from memory, and when it appears on the pages, it is a completed composition that requires no corrections."

Mr. Graham's expression displayed his surprise. He looked at Bandmaster Greenway as if to ask if this were true. The bandmaster did not know what to say. After a few more questions, Mr. Graham asked to be excused and walked over to talk to Billy.

As the important businessman chatted with Billy, Jenny watched them. After five or six minutes, she saw Mr. Graham place a small card in Billy's hand. When the man walked away, other well-wishers surrounded Billy. Finally, Billy saw Jenny. He quickly folded up his music stand and packed away the Band Journal as she approached him.

"Your playing was never better than today," she told him.

Billy hung his head shyly and simply replied, "I did my best."

"I saw Mr. Graham give you his card."

"Yes, he said that when I get back in Toronto, I am to visit him at his office on Bay Street. He's a patron of the Toronto Symphony Orchestra, and he wants me to meet its conductor."

"That's wonderful, Billy."

"I suppose, but for me, playing in the staff band is more important."

Billy did not tell Jenny that Mr. Graham had also told him that he intended to hear him play in London. He said that if he performed as well as he expected, he wished to arrange for him to play for King George V. Billy had thought this a dream too unreal to be true and had already dismissed the idea from his mind.

*

The propellers of the *Empress* began their forward thrust to continue the journey downriver. The amber rays of late-afternoon sun reflected from the rocky shoreline, distilling the romantic scenery into an unforgettable moment.

Billy and Jenny were now strolling along the deck. He had his arm around her. They chatted quietly, anticipating the thrilling days ahead. As they continued their stroll, Zack joined them. Even though Billy wished to be alone with Jenny, he smiled at Zack. He was aware that the excitement of the *Empress*'s setting sail was a moment his brother did not want to experience without him.

Surrounding the happy threesome, passengers bubbled with excitement. The *Empress* was afloat with patriotic fervor, British and Canadian pride being indistinguishable from one another to those onboard. Most of the passengers were similar to Billy, making a journey to see their homeland again. They loved their adopted land but retained great pride in their British roots. Even those who were born in Canada identified with the ideals of the British Empire.

It was now time for Billy to descend to the cabin and change out of his band uniform. When he returned to the deck, he and Jenny resumed strolling about, enjoying the final minutes of the day's warmth. The river had widened abruptly after the vessel sailed beyond Quebec. The Île d'Orléans loomed port side of the bow.

*

Though the ship had set sail, the crew had not yet positioned the barriers to segregate the three designated classes. Second- and third-class passengers continued roaming the various decks, peering into the lounges and dining room reserved for those who had paid higher fares. It was their last chance to view them before the barriers were put in place.

Sean Brownslea decided to take advantage of the situation. In fact, he had already determined which passenger he would rob. In the privacy of his cabin, he prepared for his caper and talked merrily to himself, asking himself questions and answering them, as well. He had acquired this habit many years earlier when he had lived alone and had no one with whom to chat.

"Well, Sean, me old chappie, today Mr. Hiram P. Graham is to be relieved of a little of his money. You ask me, 'Why him?' He's a natural mark—wealthy, thinking he knows it all, and brimming with self-importance."

As Sean selected a cheap suit from his steamer trunk, he said, "This will do nicely. Then I'll glue on a fake moustache and grab a pair of eyeglasses that have plain glass lenses."

Gazing at himself in the mirror, he told himself, "You're not quite a third-class passenger yet. You need to darken your face with makeup."

Standing back from the mirror to inspect his handiwork, he muttered, "Now, that's more like it. You can mingle among the crowds on deck and nobody will ever suspect that you're in first class."

Not content with his self-praise, he continued, "No one would ever suspect that you're older than fifty. You look much younger. When you tip your hat and nod to the women on deck, giving them a naughty grin, they'll smile back and nod their heads in return. You're a winning lad, Sean Brownslea."

Closing the lid of his trunk, he stepped out into the corridor. A few minutes later, he was strolling along the deck.

It was not long before he spotted Mr. Graham, who was leaning on the rail observing the scenery. He muttered to himself, "Sean Brownslea, me lad, this is your chance."

He ambled over to where Mr. Graham was standing and stood beside him. After a few moments, he pretended to lose his balance on the slightly swaying deck. Nudging gently against his victim, he required mere seconds to deftly remove Mr. Graham's billfold.

Quickly apologizing, Sean tipped his bowler hat deferentially and pretended to continue his stroll. He said under his breath, "Not too fast, Sean, me boy. Easy does it. Don't attract any attention. People are busy observing the scenery. No one saw you lift the old sod's billfold."

In a casual manner, Sean Brownslea departed the scene.

He continued talking to himself, although his lips did not move. He had learned this trick from a ventriloquist he had met in his theatre days. Talking to himself in this manner, quite certain that no one could hear him, steadied his nerves.

He told himself, "For every pocket you've picked and for every bank job, you've always planned excellent escapes. Today when you reach the cabin, Sean, me boy, dump the glasses and moustache, wash off the makeup, and change into an expensive suit. It'll make you look more like your real self—a man of first class. They'll never recognize you if they see you again. Besides, if they search the ship for a thief, they'll never look in first class."

Busily occupied talking to himself, Sean did not notice that one person had witnessed him at work.

*

Billy and Jenny, accompanied by Zack, had arrived on deck a few moments before Sean had lifted Mr. Graham's billfold. The young couple were too engrossed in each other to notice what had happened, but Zack had observed it. There was something about the way the man pocketed the billfold that he recognized. He was still grappling with the memory when he saw Sean strolling away. From the distinctive way he walked, Zack knew instantly who he was and what he had done.

"That man just stole your billfold," he shouted at Mr. Graham.

"Young man, I am certain that you are mistaken. I have my ..." Feeling for his billfold, Mr. Graham realized it was missing. Zack pointed to Sean, who was hastening his retreat.

The moment Zack shouted, Billy sprang into action. He raced forward and stood in front of the thief, firmly blocking his retreat and allowing sufficient time for two men to seize him.

"I know that man," Zack asserted heatedly. "He tried to take my brother's and father's billfolds a long time ago in downtown Toronto."

Sean gazed sneeringly at Zack and replied angrily, "The lad is either mentally deficient or a liar. I've never set eyes on him before."

"It's him," Zack asserted. "Make him take off his glasses. And I bet the moustache is not real."

One of the men restraining Sean looked at him closely. "I think the lad's right. The moustache is a fake."

When the glasses and moustache were forcibly removed, Billy stepped forward. "My brother's right. That is the man who tried to grab our billfolds in Toronto. He's a thief." Billy could never forget his face, as he was also the man who had attacked the Snipe sisters, and he recalled the blow he had received on the chin.

It was then that Phil Mercer arrived on the scene. He identified himself and confirmed that what the boys had said was true. He, too, recognized Sean as the man who had tried to rob them so many years ago.

However, Sean refused to accept defeat.

"These boys are liars." Then, pointing to Phil, he declared, "The father of the boys has trained his sons to be thieves. They work as a gang."

Mr. Graham smiled at the irony of Sean's accusation.

He said, "My good man, are you aware that these two lads play in The Salvation Army band that is aboard the *Empress*?"

Sean's mouth dropped open. He had never taken any notice of the boys before, and as they were not wearing uniforms, he had not realized their connection with the Army band. Being busy searching for victims, he had never paid any attention to the band members.

One of men holding Sean now reached inside Sean's jacket and pulled out the billfold he had stolen. As Sean Brownslea was escorted to the brig, Mr. Graham praised Zack for his quick thinking and thanked Phil and Billy for their assistance.

Jenny and Billy strolled off, and Zack joined his father.

*

After the excitement of the attempted robbery died down, passengers returned to viewing the scenery. From the stern, the steel girders of the Pont de Québec (Quebec Bridge) were visible. It was under construction. When completed, it would span the width of the St. Lawrence.

Gazing at the Beauport Shore to the north behind the Île d'Orléans, Phil drew Zack's attention to the mist rising from Montmorency Falls. In the breathless afternoon, vapour rose straight into the air. The waterfall was more than a hundred feet higher than Niagara's. To sail past the south shore of the Île d'Orléans, the *Empress* veered starboard and into the south channel.

The sun was leaning toward the west, silhouetting the Laurentian Mountains on the north horizon as Phil and Zack approached the stern of the ship, where many passengers had assembled to observe the magnificent panorama. The sun reflected from Phil's handsome face, breezes blowing through his dishevelled hair. He struggled to rearrange it with one hand as he placed his other on Zack's shoulder. Zack gazed at his father and grinned. It was a touching scene, father and son sharing a personal moment as they watched the glorious landscape drifting past the ship.

Phil noticed that his mother and Gerald Hutchinson were among the crowd to his left, arm in arm and enjoying the view. He wondered where Mr. and Mrs. McCarthy were. Then Phil smiled sheepishly, remembering that they were on their honeymoon.

As the ship progressed downriver, at the stern, from both port and starboard, the hills of pine and spruce on either side of the river etched dark lines alongside the mighty river. Visible in the soft light hugging the water's edge were the long, narrow farms with their family houses of ancient stone. Their steeply sloped metal roofs painted brightly in colours of red, yellow, or green, along with the gabled windows, reflected their French heritage. No two houses were identical, but well-tended gardens surrounded every one of them. It was a scene reminiscent of the old colony of New France, as eternal and endearing as any portrait of rural Canada.

With the waning of the day, the sun continued its skyward progression as the temperature slowly dropped. Phil and Zack drifted inside to explore the ship further. Twenty minutes later, Phil decided that they should return to the cabin, as he had one small task to perform before the supper hour.

When they stepped into the cabin, they saw that Billy was there. He was stretched out on his bunk, hands clasped behind his head, staring dreamily at the ceiling. Mr. Meaford was nowhere in sight.

Phil retrieved the picture postcard that he had purchased a few weeks earlier in downtown Toronto. He had already addressed the card, "Mrs. P. Mercer, 6 Bird Ave., Toronto." He wrote a message on the blank side and asked Zack to go to the lounge upstairs and insert it in the mail pouch. It would go ashore prior to the ship's departure from Quebec. The postcard carried a one-penny green stamp with the profile of King George V in the upper right-hand corner. When the post office received it, they stamped the card with the date and time: "Quebec, 8:00 p.m., May 28, 1914." Phil's message was as follows:

> My dearest Emmy,
>
> Just a line to say we have settled into our cabin. Billy and Zack are fine. We have an outside cabin with a porthole in it. Everything is spotlessly clean. We sailed at four o'clock. Love and kisses to Mary, Ruth, and Bess. Keep a good heart. Miss you dearly. I send you all my love.
>
> Phil

*

At 5:00 p.m., passengers gathered in the third-class dining room for the first and only meal of the day. It was a light meal consisting of smoked herring, cold meat, pickles, and tea. At 7:00 p.m., the passengers in first- and second-class cabins were to be served. The number of meals served and the menus reflected the class structure of the vessel.

As a special gesture, the staff band assembled and played well-known hymns for the third-class passengers as they dined. The people were grateful and applauded enthusiastically when the band concluded.

At 7:00 p.m., the staff band assembled outside the second-class dining room on the upper deck. Inside, there were rectangular alcoves on both sides of the room, wherein tables were located to create intimate dining areas. In the open space of the salon, there were also neatly arranged tables covered with white cloths of starched linen. For this trip, the crew had combined tables and reserved them for the exclusive use of The Salvation Army officers and the Toronto Staff Band.

Relish dishes with celery and olives in them were positioned in the centre of the tables. The passengers already seated ceased conversing as the band, dressed in scarlet tunics, marched into the dining room. Some wondered about the handsome teenager who marched with the adult bandsmen. Bandmaster Greenway had decreed that Zack had earned the right to be included among the men at the table.

In a formal manner, standing behind their chairs, the bandsmen waited for the signal to sing the grace. Then, with heads bowed, they sang the well-known blessing to the tune of "Old Hundred." The dining room remained quiet as the men sang in harmonized parts.

> Be present at our table, Lord,
> Be here and everywhere adored;
> These mercies bless and grant that we
> May feast in paradise with Thee.
> Amen!

There were muffled sounds as the bandsmen pulled out their chairs and sat down. The seating arrangement reflected the friendships within the group, as friends sought the companionship of friends. In some cases, men who played similar instruments sat side by side, their long hours rehearsing together as a section drawing them into bonds of fellowship. Sometimes those who were close in age chose to sit together. Because they had selected cabin mates in a similar manner, the seating arrangement was at times a mirror image of their accommodations.

*

Billy sat with Zack and George Meaford. As the other passengers in the room continued dining, the bandsmen ceased to be the centre of attention. The stewards brought food to the tables, and the noise of conversation increased. Billy glanced at the far end of the room where Jenny was dining with her mother and stepfather. She caught him looking and gave him a discreet wave with her hand. Billy's father was also at their table. Since he was not a staff bandsman, he was unable to sit with his sons.

Infectious laughter surrounded the table, animated voices drifting across the room. By the time the soup arrived, Billy felt that the good times of the long-anticipated trip had actually begun.

Zack whispered to Billy, "If Reverend Wilmot were here this evening, all the food would now be gone, as well as the tablecloths."

"I think the tables' legs might have disappeared, too."

"Do you think old Wilmot might be a cannibal?"

"Why?"

"If he is, then a few waiters might disappear, too," Zack smirked.

"Judging by the way you're slurping your soup, you and Wilmot may have something in common."

Zack grinned and slurped louder than before. Billy rolled his eyed and added, "I should have kept quiet. I forgot that you're the slurping champion of our family."

Billy again glanced the length of the room at Jenny and forgot about Zack. The other bandsmen encouraged Zack by making humorous comments about his noisy eating habits. Zack continued slurping, enjoying the teasing of the bandsmen. Their attitude demonstrated that they had fully accepted Zack as a member of the band.

Billy's thoughts about Jenny were interrupted when Zack asked, "Do you think Reverend Wilmot ever has indigestion after he eats a chair leg?"

"Perhaps!"

"I bet he belches sawdust."

"Hush! Eat your tapioca pudding."

When they finished their dessert, the meal was over. The bandsmen bowed their heads to offer gratitude to God for the food. Salvationists referred to this as returning thanks—"Praise God, from whom all blessings flow." Within minutes of making this meaningful gesture, the men began leaving the table. It was now about 8:30 p.m.

*

Billy went immediately to Jenny's table to escort her from the dining room. The couple ascended the stairs to the deck and, once outside, glimpsed the last rays of the setting sun. At the final moment it hovered on the horizon, splashing its last crimson rays across the darkening sky. Then it slipped beneath the water, creating the soft amber glow of twilight. Sailing toward the northeast, the *Empress* continued its path downriver.

Billy told Jenny, "I only had a few hours of sleep last night on the train, but being with you has made me feel I never need to rest."

Jenny smiled and gripped his hand a little more firmly.

They strolled about the public areas of the ship, chatted with friends, and exchanged words with other passengers. Some of those on deck noticed the handsome young couple and smiled, realizing that Billy was the young man who had performed as the ship set sail.

As they gazed out across the darkening waters, a mood of inner reflection enveloped them. The setting sun reminded them that the long day had truly drawn to a close. Billy hugged Jenny closely. Meanwhile, the ship's deck grew ever quieter.

The first-class lounge of the *Empress of Ireland*. *Photo courtesy of the George Scott Railton Heritage Centre*

Finally, the deck was deserted, the only sounds being the ever-constant lapping of waves against the ship's bow. There was no one present to observe the young couple huddled at the stern on the leeward side of the lifeboats, protected from the wind. The moon was rising, its pale light falling across the smooth planking on the deck and reflecting off the brass trim on the wooden rails. In the shadows, Jenny gazed into Billy's face, his features soft in the diffused light.

"Billy, I love you so very much."

"I love you, too. I loved you from the first moment I saw you in your mother's store."

"My stepfather says that 'love at first sight' is romantic nonsense. He says that love is something that grows slowly and matures with age."

"I think he is talking about the mushrooms that grow in the boxes in the back of his store."

Jenny laughed quietly as she reached up and tenderly stroked Billy's face.

"Billy, from the first day I saw you, I wanted to be your girl. You'll never know how much courage it took for me to devise the plan to get you into the library on Queen Street. I visited it dozens of times to determine the best hour to lure you in among the tall shelves of books."

"You 'lured' me, did you?" he replied with a quiet chuckle.

"Yes. Just like the legendary Lorelei."

"You've never sung to me."

"I would have if the library hadn't imposed strict rules about silence."

"The kiss we shared was silent."

"Yes, and truly wondrous. If I had been the Lorelei and you a handsome sailor, I could not have kissed you with any more love."

Billy nibbled gently on her earlobe and began softly humming the haunting melody of the old folksong "The Lorelei." In an attempt to cheer Jenny, he sang a few lines of the song, transforming the tragic ballad into a tender melody of love.

O tell me what it meaneth,
this sad and tearful eye,
The memory that retaineth
a tale of years gone by.

A touch of melancholy crept into Jenny's heart, and a tear trickled down her cheek as she realized that in England, Billy would be travelling with the staff band and they would be apart.

"Don't be sad, Jenny. We're together right now," Billy pleaded softly as he wiped away a tear from her cheek.

"Billy, I want to be beside you forever."

"We will be! I promise. Our love will never die. Nothing shall ever keep us apart."

Billy held her close and they kissed, the passion of their love transcending to new heights of intimacy. Their love was indeed eternal.

The hour was late, the breezes on deck becoming chillier as the young lovers returned inside the ship. Billy gave no more thought to Jenny's having mentioned the German legend of the Lorelei. The Lorelei was an enormous outcropping of rock that towered 120 metres above the Rhine River. Situated on the narrowest part of the river between Switzerland and the North Sea, in bygone centuries it was treacherous to navigate. Because so many shipwrecks occurred on this section of river, a legend arose about a maiden who sat atop the rock and sang enchantingly, luring sailors to their deaths in the river's depths. For Billy and Jenny alike, the ominous portent of the song remained hidden.

The mighty *Empress* ploughed through the darkened waters of the historic St. Lawrence River, which the mariners of old had referred to as the gateway to Canada. Jenny was the gateway to Billy's happiness.

Billy and Jenny kissed tenderly and said goodnight outside Jenny's cabin door. Their arms reached out toward each other as Billy began to step away. Finally, only their fingers touched. As Billy's hand dropped and he turned to walk down the corridor, the ship was quiet. Passengers and crew were preparing for the night.

*

It was shortly after 10:00 p.m. when Phil passed the stewards whose job it was to circulate through the hallways and decks and close the portholes in the public areas. They locked them with a special key, and the portholes remain locked until the crew members performed the task of opening them in the morning. The stewards were also gently rapping on the cabin doors to remind passengers to shut their portholes. It was a customary routine performed prior to the ship's entering the open waters of the Gulf of St. Lawrence.

When Phil had departed the cabin, Zack was reading a book and George Meaford was asleep. Billy was gazing out into the darkness through the porthole, a faraway look on his face. Phil wanted a few minutes alone before retiring for the night, so he had decided to ascend to the deck, which at this hour, he thought, would likely be deserted.

He stood near the bow, the breezes buffeting his suit jacket and ruffling his hair. His mood was quiet but happy, even though he was exhausted. The previous evening he had not slept much on the train.

Thoughts of Emmy, Mary, Ruth, and Bess comforted him. Leaning on the rail, he glanced skyward at the star-filled firmament that was graced by the hint of a new moon—a sign that, for centuries, mariners had welcomed as an omen of a safe voyage. The river was exceedingly smooth, barely a ripple disturbing the surface. It was so calm, he mused, that even Emmy might not be seasick on a voyage such as this.

With this thought, Phil yawned and descended below deck.

*

By midnight, the *Empress* was sailing parallel to the south shore, the tide running swiftly. The temperature on deck was barely above freezing. Officers on the bridge noticed that beyond the distant hills, fog was building ominously. Where the warmer air from land swept over the frigid waters of the river, fog was a constant danger. Ice had disappeared from the river a mere week or so before, and the water remained extremely cold. Forest fires along the river's banks added to the misty scene.

The *Empress* was a ship sailing silently into the darkness of the night, unheeded by its surroundings. Below deck, the rhythmic vibrations of the engines' twin propellers were the only sound audible as the ship slashed smoothly through the water, the ripples spreading gently from either side of the bow. On the velvety black surface of the river, reflections of the ship's lights sparkled like silver coins tossed randomly on a tranquil sea. It was a moment of peace and calm. To paraphrase William Wordsworth,

> Ne'er saw I, never felt, a calm so deep!
> The river glideth at its own sweet will;
> Dear God! The very "world" seems asleep;
> And all that mighty heart is lying still.

*

The helmsman on the bridge told Captain Kendry, "It's almost zero–zero hour. Mist is increasingly rolling across the river from the southwest. It's obscuring our masthead lights."

"Give three short blasts on the ship's whistle to warn any approaching vessels."

"Aye, aye, Captain."

"I am becoming alarmed. The fog is intensifying. Reduce the *Empress*'s speed to eight knots."

"Aye, aye, Captain."

"I'll remain on the bridge. Fog is the worst of the dangers that can develop on this stretch of river."

"At oh-one-fifty hours, the mail cutter *Lady Evelyn* will meet our ship. The small vessel is from the river port of Rimouski."

Kendry replied, "I've been to Rimouski several times. It has about two thousand inhabitants. It's a hundred and eighty miles northeast of Quebec City. The *Lady Evelyn* will unload the last of the mail destined for Canada, and we'll place it aboard with the outgoing mail to Great Britain."

As the Captain fell into silence, fog continued to settle snugly around the *Empress,* obscuring the waters of the river.

A mile or so offshore, at 1:20 a.m., Captain Kendry remained on the bridge. He told the helmsman, "Slow the *Empress*'s speed to five knots; the pilot tender *Eureka* is coming alongside."

After the river pilot departed the ship, the helmsman reported, "We're about a mile north of Father Point."

"Father Point," Kendry replied, "is an important post on the river. It has a government wharf, a wireless station, a lighthouse, and an office of the Great Northwest Telegraph Company."

"The houses of the river pilots are there, too."

"Yes, I know. After we clear Father Point, set our course to the northeast. At this point, the river's about thirty miles in width. The sea remains calm, with no wind. However, the thick mist overhead entirely hides the sliver of a new moon."

"'Tis an eerie night to be on the river, Captain."

*

Had any passengers chosen to be on deck at the soulful hour, they would have gazed into an eerie, mist-wrapped world. Dense grey vapour had settled heavily across the decks. A dank atmosphere enveloped the ship, the type that chills a body to the bone by sucking the warmth out of it. The thick air muffled any deck sounds. Tiny water droplets smothered the rails and lifeboat covers. The masthead lights and the huge funnels had disappeared into the fog. Through the half-drawn curtains over cabin portholes on the promenade deck, shafts of light glowed from inside, spread outward, and evaporated into the thick nothingness of the fog. The *Empress* was an island unto itself, and the living world was far beyond its decks.

At approximately 2:00 a.m., the *Empress* was more than four miles from shore. At this distance out into the river, the fog was beginning to clear. Several minutes later, through a wide gap in the mist, a horrifying sight confronted Captain Kendry.

"My good God," he shouted. "There's a small vessel steaming toward us on our starboard side."

"I see it, Captain. It's at a right angle to our hull. Its masthead lights are approaching us at a speed of at least ten knots."

For the Captain, it was the ultimate horror.

There was a sudden jolt. The *Empress* shuddered slightly as the other ship struck her.

Immediately, Captain Kendry barked, "Launch a lifeboat to inspect the damage."

As crew members scrambled to obey, the ship began listing slightly starboard.

Several minutes later, a crew member reported to the Captain, "From over the rail, I got a report from one of the men in the lifeboat."

"Quick, man, what did he say?"

"The other ship's bow has penetrated our hull midway between the bow and the stern. It's opened a wide gash. Water's pouring in."

Minutes later, another crewman rushed to the bridge. He had been in the lifeboat and inspected the damage firsthand. "The ship that rammed us has a steel-reinforced bow. I saw the name on it; it's the *Storstad*."

"I know the vessel, Captain. It's a coal ship of Norwegian registry."

"Never mind the accursed name of the ship. What's our damage?"

"The depth of the hole's at least fourteen feet. I'd say that the gash is about twenty-five by fourteen feet. Part of it's below the waterline. Water is pouring in."

The helmsman added, "We're already listing to starboard."

"May God help us all," the Captain said, shock evident on his face. "The *Empress* may be mortally wounded."

*

At the moment of collision, below deck in the cabin the Mercers shared with George Meaford, everyone was sleeping soundly. They had retired for the night with little knowledge of the layout of the ship, the positions of the stairs, or specific safety details. Even the locations of the lifeboat stations were not clear in their minds. The collision sliced so smoothly into the ship that hardly anyone noticed the impact. It was more like a dull thud than an explosive blow, as if the ship had nudged against a mud bank or hit a sandbar.

Although many passengers did not even roll over in their bunks, those who had cabins located near the point of impact on the starboard side were at once aware of the true situation. The collision killed many on impact. Later, blood was found on the bow and anchor of the *Storstad.* Other people were violently thrown from their berths, many rolling about on the flooded floor. However, except from these passengers, there was little panic. Most people were unaware that anything of significance had occurred, while others, awakened by the bump, rolled over and went back to sleep, deciding that the ship could not possibly be in trouble. They had no idea that water was entering the ship at a rate of sixty thousand gallons per second.

However, in the wireless room, the situation was already obvious. The Marconi wireless operator of the *Empress* tapped out a message to the marine station at Father Point. The operator knew it was unlikely that experienced personnel would be on duty ashore at this early morning hour, so he took his time, slowly and deliberately sending a clear, strong signal.

"SOS."

The return message was, "Okay! Here we are." It was followed by, "Okay, sending *Eureka* and *Lady Evelyn* to your assistance."

The telegraph tower of the marine station was located four miles southwest of Rimouski. From there, messages were transmitted by wire to Quebec City. Meanwhile, the final events of the disaster were swiftly unfolding.

Within minutes of the withdrawal of the *Storstad* from the hull, the *Empress* listed nine degrees toward starboard, and as the ship continued to tilt, more and more of the gash fell below the waterline, which hastened the flow of water into the battered hull.

Realizing that the ship was unable to stay afloat for long, Captain Kendry made an instant decision. He shouted, "Signal the engine room—full steam ahead." He said to the helmsman, "I pray that we can beach the *Empress* on the shore. It's a little more than four miles away."

The response was, "Captain, the engine room says it's already flooded, and it's impossible to provide any power at all."

The fate of the *Empress* and many of her passengers was sealed.

The crew of the *Storstad* remained unaware of the enormous injury that their small ship had inflicted on the larger vessel. At this point in time, they were more concerned about their own fate. In the darkness, they did not realize that the large vessel was rolling to starboard and taking on water at a prodigious rate. It did not occur to them that the *Empress* was about to sink, nor did they know that the third-class section was already mostly submerged.

*

In the cabin where the Mercers and George Meaford slept, the ship's list was increasingly evident. Zack awoke. Rubbing his eyes and gazing about, he was the first in the cabin to become aware that something was terribly amiss. His cry of alarm awakened the other three, but by this time vital minutes had already elapsed.

Billy was instantly awake. He instinctively reached for the cork-filled life jackets in a cupboard above the bunks. Leaping out of the bunk, he reached for his trousers on the chair. He pulled them up while stumbling forward, reaching for the bolt on the cabin door. The deadly reality of the danger swept over him, and he wondered if someone had awakened Jenny. He knew it was to be a struggle for any of them to survive.

Grabbing Zack by the arm, Billy propelled him toward the cabin door, while his father shook George Meaford awake, as he remained yet in deep slumber. The noise and commotion slowly aroused George, but he behaved drowsily as Phil helped him to his feet. When Billy opened the cabin door, he was horrified at the sight of the water swirling through the passageway. He knew that they were three levels below the top deck, and to reach it meant navigating through the rushing water which, minute by minute, was slithering higher up the corridor walls.

Billy now pushed Zack through the cabin door. A quick look backward assured him that his father was following. As Phil departed the cabin, he glanced over his shoulder and saw that George Meaford was stumbling in his wake.

Glancing up and down the passageway, Billy realized that pandemonium reigned. He knew that it was a race against time. The corridor was flooding fast. Before passing Zack into the care of his father, he hugged him.

"Go with Father," Billy said in a calm but firm voice. "I'll see you up on deck. Never fear, we'll be all right."

After assuring Zack that he was safe, Billy gazed at George Meaford, his mentor and friend. He looked directly into his eyes. They had shared many experiences and ideas through the years, and for Billy to leave Mr. Meaford behind was almost as painful as leaving Zack and his father. However, time was of the essence. He must find Jenny.

George winked at Billy, and an understanding passed between them.

"Go ahead, son. Find Jenny." He nodded to send Billy on his way.

Billy turned and sloshed through the water toward Jenny's cabin. Zack saw his brother struggling down the corridor and gripping his father's arm tighter. All his life, Billy had been at his side during times of trouble. Fear seized Zack's heart, but he refused to allow it to deter him from reaching the upper deck.

*

Phil and Zack continued along the passageway toward the stairs. Then the lights faded and the corridor became as black as ebony. Engulfed in darkness, Zack clung to his father for dear life.

As Phil entwined an arm around Zack, he told him, "Hold on to me tight. If we lose each other, it'll be nearly impossible to find one another again."

"I'll try, but people keep bumping into me and things are hitting against me."

Then, several panicked passengers crashed directly into them. Phil lost his grip on Zack. The force of the water was sweeping Zack away.

Phil reacted quickly.

"Quick, reach out and grab my hand."

Luckily, Zack succeeded in finding it, despite the near-complete darkness. Within moments, Phil had pulled him back into his arms.

As the floor tilted at a terrifying angle, Phil grabbed hold of the carpet, which broke away in his hands, sending him and Zack tumbling into the swirling water, gasping for breath as they resurfaced. The angle of the ship was so severe that the right-hand wall was swiftly becoming the floor under their feet. Zack lost his footing on the smooth wall surface and fell, pulling his father down with him. They scrambled about helplessly. For every two steps forward, one was taken backward. They were unable to see what was happening, which was making their escape almost impossible. Sometimes, someone lit a match and the small light glowed for a brief span of time. Then darkness prevailed again.

As the minutes passed, more and more debris floated in the hallway. Phil did his best to protect Zack from the floating objects continually crashing into them. As Phil struggled to find the stairs, he and Zack collided with walls and metal stanchions, often bumping into individuals who had stumbled and fallen.

Since the angle of the staircase had altered so severely, they found that they must crawl up each step hand over hand. As the ship listed even more, the staircase angled more acutely; now it was almost on its side. To add to the confusion, the set of stairs led to a landing where the steps divided to the left and right. This added to their difficulty.

*

Meanwhile, Billy had miraculously reached Jenny's cabin. Within seconds he had his arms around her. "Thank God you found me," she told Billy.

"Where are your mother and Mr. Hutchinson?"

"I don't know."

"We must hope for the best and concentrate on getting to the top deck."

Overcoming the force of the water surging into the cabin, Billy pulled Jenny out the door. They stumbled along the corridor amid the crush of other people who were also desperately pushing their loved ones to safety. Husbands assisted their wives. As parents valiantly fought to protect their small children, the terrified cries of the toddlers added to everyone's sense of desperation.

Billy and Jenny clung to each other as they struggled along the hallway. The ship's tilt was swiftly increasing, adding to their terror. If only there was more time. At this point, more than five hundred passengers were below deck and were facing the possibility of being entombed within the hull of the ship, their mortal remains to rest for eternity in the dark, slumberous waters of the Gulf of St. Lawrence.

Billy heard a young woman's voice cry out, without the slightest trace of hysterics, "We're trapped down here. May God have mercy on us all."

The calmness of the woman's statement sent shivers up Jenny's spine. Billy felt her body tense up, and he held her even more tightly as he pushed along the corridor to the stairwell, praying that Zack and his father had already reached it. By now, the water was up to their chests, but because numerous people and debris were floating in the water, they couldn't swim their way out.

"I can't swim. There's no space," Jenny cried.

"Don't give up. We're almost at the bottom of the staircase."

"More and more people are crushing against us."

"I know. But we must keep moving."

"The ship is tipping more on its side."

Then a small beam of light penetrated the darkness of the stairwell.

Billy's voice betrayed his excitement. "Look up there, high above. I see a glimmer of light. Someone outside on the open deck is holding a lantern."

"I see it."

"Its small beam will help guide us upward. Come on, we'll make it."

Painfully slowly, they climbed ever upward until they were near the top deck. When Billy looked down, in the dim light he saw that the last corridor they had climbed out of was now completely submerged. He said nothing to Jenny.

In the next instant, Billy looked up and caught a glimpse of Zack and his father. Extra adrenaline pumped through his veins.

They clawed their way up the final set of stairs.

Billy told Jenny, "I've rarely lost a fight, and I don't intend to lose this one."

*

Those who had succeeded in reaching the outside areas were confronting a vision of unbelievable horror. There were sufficient lifeboats, but it took five minutes to launch each one. People watched in dismay when the crew released several lifeboats on the port side. They crashed over the deck, crushing people and sweeping others over the side. The crew and passengers now realized that it was impossible to deploy any of the remaining lifeboats. The two lifeboats that the crew had managed to place in the water on the starboard side were in danger of capsizing, and to make matters worse, the men were having difficulty loading passengers into them.

With each second, the ship listed further to starboard. People on deck endeavoured to reach the side of the ship that remained above water and cling to the rail there. The numbers increased as more people escaped from the lower decks. The vessel continued to roll, some passengers climbing over the railing and walking out onto the smooth steel plates of the hull. Many were unable to hold on; they lost their footing and slowly slipped into the frigid water. Even those with surer footing soon realized that within minutes the ship was going down and they would be forced into the sea.

Those who could pulled a few people through the portholes, but it was extremely rough going because the openings were small. The ship's doctor, Evans, escaped in this manner. Some of those who were stranded on the hull jumped. Those who were in the water without life jackets clung to any debris capable of keeping them afloat.

Within minutes, the ship gave an enormous shudder, which passed from bow to stern along the steel-sheathed plates, as the leviathan of waves commenced plunging downward. There was an explosion as water encompassed the ship's boilers, a murderous cloud of hot vapour scalding many people as the compressed steam blasted to the surface. Next, there was the gushing sound of air being pushed out of the submerging hull. More masses of white bubbles seethed and foamed furiously to the surface, contrasting ominously with the raven-black sea. A geyser fountained furiously upward as if a giant seltzer bottle had exploded.

The final few seconds of the great ship's life were terrifying. The hull floated almost horizontal to the surface, momentarily suspended on the waves. It hovered for a few seconds and then commenced sinking from sight. It was as if a destructive monster from the river bottom had reached upward and pulled the ship into its depths. Beneath, the water was a hundred and fifty feet deep. The vacuum-like pull created by the ship's descent sucked people who were in the water near the hull into the vortex of the funnelling sea, which boiled and foamed in a great cauldron of people, debris, and bodies. Many went down and were never seen again. Others pulled themselves free and surfaced three or four times before they were finally free of the violent suction. Frantic people who were unable to swim dragged some people under. In the pitch darkness, terror was supreme.

Within minutes, the only reminders of the massive ship were the floating pieces of wreckage and the people bobbing about helplessly in the pitch-black waters. Their faces contorted with shock, their eyes wide with uncontrollable fear, they floated in the oily water, which stung their submerged cuts and bleeding wounds. They collided painfully with the sides of the few lifeboats, half-submerged boxes, splintered oars, and other broken objects.

By now, the fog had mostly disappeared and the lights of the *Storstad* were visible to those struggling in the water. Its crew finally realized what had occurred. They were able to hear the great swelling tide of the voices of men, women, and children in the water, pleading for someone to save them. Then, as the emergency flares from one of the lifeboats of the *Empress* illuminated the night sky, the enormity of the disaster became even more apparent. The *Storstad* hastily launched its lifeboats and began to pull people aboard, while the *Empress*'s few lifeboats continued rescuing as many as possible.

When the lifeboats' crews tried to pull people from the water, at the last moment they lost their grip. Too exhausted to continue struggling, they fell beneath the waves, never to surface again. Others, when immersed in the depths, kicked and clawed upward to fight against the burning pain in their lungs brought on by air deprivation. Their feet became leaden from the drag of the water that pulled them downward. The coldness of the icy waves sapped the warmth and strength from their bodies. People bobbed about, their faces as pale and lifeless as the dead. Within a short span of time, many more slipped below into dark oblivion.

Grandmother Mercer was in one of the lifeboats. Dazed and in darkness, she gazed across the water at the catastrophic scene. She murmured aloud, addressing no one in particular, "Where is Gerald? I saw him jump from the ship into the water, but he's nowhere in sight. Where are Billy, Zack, and Phil? Where is Jenny?"

An elderly man placed his arm around Grandmother Mercer to comfort her. He was aware that she was going into shock. He took a blanket a sailor had handed him and placed it around her.

"Madam, your relatives are likely in another lifeboat."

*

In Rimouski, officials had summoned two rescue vessels, but they needed time to prepare them to set sail, as they had to recall the crews and bank the fires in the ships' boilers. Meanwhile, lives continued to be lost to the depths of the river. From Quebec, news of the tragedy soon spread to the press throughout Canada and the United States, and within the hour newspaper reporters were booking train space to travel to Rimouski.

*

After a night of terror, it was now dawn on Friday, May 29. Near Rimouski, the sun broke across the surface of the St. Lawrence River, the warmth lifting the spirits of those who had toiled throughout the cold hours of the night to "rescue the perishing and care for the dying." As the light of day increased, the search for bodies intensified, and the grim task of harvesting the dead continued. In Canada and in other countries around the globe, people awakened to discover the news of the *Empress.*

Meanwhile, in Toronto, the sun emerged above the horizon about an hour later than at Rimouski, splitting asunder the darkness, slivers of light creeping into an indigo sky. One newspaper, *The Telegram,* had forecasted that Friday was to be a day of fair weather with light winds from the southwest and pleasant temperatures. As the sun climbed higher, it washed over the walls of the downtown buildings, casting grey shadows into the narrow alleys. Its morning rays draped across backyard fences and then splashed across neighbourhood gardens. As people emerged from their beds to begin another day, there was no hint of the storm clouds that were soon to enshroud the city.

However, details of the disaster were already trickling into the newsrooms. Apart from word-of-mouth, newspapers were the only source of information. Each of the four Toronto daily papers had a staff of telegraph operators with machines connected by wires to news sources around the world.

The editor of one of the newspapers had been summoned to his office by his assistant, who had sent for his demanding boss shortly before daybreak.

When the boss arrived, his uptight assistant told him, "The information on the wires is continuing to trickle in as we speak."

"Trickling? Isn't it arriving up to speed?"

"Of course, of course," he replied testily, "at a rate of thirty to forty words a minute on the Morse code machine."

"Have the operators written out the messages and delivered them to the typists?"

"Yes, and they're being edited and retyped right now."

"Good. Get them to the Linotype casting machines as fast as possible."

"Whom do you want to write the lead article?"

"Jim Corrigan, and tell him to get it ready for the 'extra' edition as fast as possible. We want it in print within the hour."

"Yes, sir. How many pages should we prepare?"

"Between four and eight—whatever it takes. We want to create for our readers the true extent of the disaster. When the extras are ready, insert them inside the regular daily editions."

"Right." The assistant's expression indicated that his editor needn't have given him this obvious directive.

The editor continued, "And by the way, have they placed the large sheets of paper telling of the tragedy in the row of billboard stands in front of the building?"

"Certainly." By now the assistant was becoming exasperated.

Ignoring him, the editor barked, "I want each sheet to give a different summary of the latest news. Have Miss Smith print them out in her usual thick black lettering. She's excellent at it. Tell Sam to open the wooden frames covered with chicken wire."

"It's already done."

"Excellent! Be certain that Miss Smith updates the messages hourly. It will keep Sam busy inserting them in the billboards."

"Yes, Boss. I was told that crowds are already gathering in front of the billboards. Many of the people working in downtown offices and stores will receive the news ahead of the printed editions, like always."

"Good. But for more details, they'll purchase a newspaper. Tell the print room to prepare five hundred extra copies of today's edition."

"Right, Boss." The assistant departed the editor's office shaking his head. "I could run this accursed newspaper myself," he muttered.

*

Since the events remained unknown to many in the early hours of Friday morning, those awaking from their slumber followed their usual routine of retrieving the bottles of milk from the verandas, lighting the stoves, and preparing the first meal of the day. There was the rattle of dishes in kitchens throughout homes all across the city. Despite the bustle of activity, the scene reflected a mood of calm and tranquility. However, before the day ended, May 29 would come to be known as Black Friday.

When the first details of the disaster reached Toronto, the editor of *The Globe* phoned a staff captain who worked at The Salvation Army Headquarters, and he in turn notified other officers who worked there.

In downtown Toronto, the first editions of an "Extra" were rolling off the presses. Boys waited near the newspaper offices to receive an armful of papers to sell on the streets. There was great competition among the lads to be the first to arrive at the busiest corners. Sometimes a smaller boy was pushed from his spot and forced to retreat to a less desirable location.

Newspapers were two cents a copy, and as they were the main source of information, residents of the city eagerly sought them. Within minutes of the boys' hitting the streets, people heard their cries: "Read all about it. Ship sinks, with great loss of life."

The extent of the disaster became clear when people read that only six passengers had wired a telegram to notify their relatives that they had survived. The *Toronto Daily Star* proclaimed across the top of its first page:

> **ONLY 337 SURVIVORS OF 1,422 SOULS**
> ***EMPRESS* CARRIED 121 FROM**
> **TORONTO— SIX WIRED BACK**

On the front page was a picture of the staff band, but it was not the photograph taken two days earlier, as that one remained unavailable. The first editions of *The Telegram* and *The Globe* carried details of the disaster, but no headlines referred to the event.

It was not long before carriers and vendors rushed newspapers to the far corners of the city, and within the hour the Earlscourt area was overwhelmed with the news. Folks went from door to door to spread the details, neighbours speaking in hushed tones as they chatted over backyard fences. Some enterprising boys peddled the papers up and down the streets. Since this was an "Extra" edition, they knew that people would eagerly purchase the papers.

People gathered near the doors of The Salvation Army Territorial Headquarters on Albert Street where bulletins were posted to inform the public of the events. A crowd of onlookers, family members, and reporters from the press stood in silence. The quiet was awesome. At one point, a reporter stated that most aboard the *Empress* were safe, but people later learned that, in the confusion, the reporter had exaggerated.

As the morning hours progressed, the Army posted a list of the survivors, and the terrible truth slowly became evident. Eyes anxiously scanned the bulletins, but only a few persons gained a sense of relief. They were the fortunate few who saw the names of their loved ones appear in print as having survived.

*

Inside the Mercer house, Emmy was preparing breakfast. After cooking the oatmeal, she spooned it into bowls for the girls and sat down to enjoy a cup of tea. She smiled as she remembered how she had always placed the sugar in Phil's cup to presweeten it. Other than the muted sounds outside on the street, inside the kitchen she could only hear the ticking of the clock and the clink of the teacup as she placed it on the saucer.

She had suffered a few lonely hours during the night because Phil and the boys were absent, but she consoled herself with the thought that in eight weeks they would return. Other than the absence of Phil in the bed beside her, the thing she missed the most was the muffled laughter in the bedroom shared by Zack and Billy, when they carried on mischievously instead of going to sleep. She admitted that she also missed the sounds of their cornets.

From the kitchen at the rear of the house, Emmy heard a knock on the front door and proceeded down the hallway to see who was there. A neighbour woman who lived on a street nearby stood on the veranda. She silently passed a newspaper to Emmy, whose eyes widened in horror as she saw the headline in bold letters. The words made her feel as if she had been cut in half. She clung to the doorframe to steady herself. The headline read as follows:

***Empress of Ireland* Sunk—All Lost.**

Throughout the day, Emmy continued to hear more details as they poured into the newsrooms and the newspapers disseminated them across the city.

*

At Rimouski, in Quebec, people throughout the day brought ashore the dead and placed them in the coal sheds, the coal having been shovelled aside to allow space on the floor to accommodate the bodies. Surviving crew members were requested to identify their shipmates. It was a gruesome task. The storage areas were cold, damp, and dimly lit, the long rows of corpses creating a scene that was beyond a person's worst nightmare.

An Army officer who was walking toward the sheds told another officer,

"I fear that in many instances, identification will be almost impossible. I understand that the bodies are badly bruised due to the ordeal they suffered during the final minutes aboard the ship, or when floating debris crashed against them in the water."

"I'm afraid you're right," the other officer replied. "Many were crushed when the funnels and masts toppled into the water. Most of those who perished did not have time to properly dress. They're in their nightclothes, pyjamas, or housecoats. Some are without any clothing at all. Wallets, purses, and identity papers are mostly missing, meaning that rings and personal jewellery may be the sole items that will allow us to make an identification. A sailor told me that on one body, a wristwatch stopped ticking at precisely two-eighteen in the morning."

"The hour of the tragedy," the other replied solemnly.

"People took almost no baggage from the ship. Some of the men were wearing trousers, but on many, they found nothing but a few coins in their pockets. I hear that inside there's a woman holding a young child in her arms. They perished together."

Both men paused, the extent of the tragedy gripping their hearts.

"In order that each body can be respectfully contained, the residents of Rimouski are bringing us every available casket. They're working throughout the day to build makeshift coffins from boxes and crates."

"Inside the coal shed, the bodies are in long rows on the floor. We have the terrible ordeal of trying to identify as many as possible."

"Thank the Lord that so many are anxious to help with the needs of the survivors."

"Yes. The inhabitants of Rimouski are donating much-needed clothing and food."

"And the CPR has dispatched to Quebec a special train with eight coaches to carry the survivors back to Toronto."

"The survivors I've talked to seemed unaware of their surroundings. They cared little about their ragged appearance. They hardly spoke a word."

"Indeed. They're in deep shock."

"I understand that the railway attendants will convert one of the sleeping cars on the train into a mobile hospital."

"Yes, the survivors will arrive tonight at Levis at eight o'clock, on the south shore. They will be met by a chartered ferry that will carry them across the river to Quebec. I'm told that they'll arrive on the other side about eight-forty p.m. They have arranged to accommodate the first-class passengers in suites in the Château Frontenac Hotel. The second- and third-class survivors are to be housed in smaller rooms in the same hotel. The injured are to be transported to the Jeffery Hale Hospital and later transferred to various institutions, as their injuries dictate."

"Further information is trickling in about the extent of the disaster. Last night, the *Storstad* rescued three hundred and thirty passengers, and when the *Lady Evelyn* finally arrived on the scene, its crew plucked five more survivors from the frigid water."

"This is a nightmare that none of us will ever forget."

*

It was almost a week before it was confirmed that only 217 of the 1,057 passengers on the *Empress of Ireland* had survived. Of the 420 crew, only 248 escaped. Including the 134 children, 840 passengers had perished, along with 172 crew.

It was to be Canada's greatest maritime disaster.

*

In Toronto, throughout the long day, Emmy remained unaware of the fate of Phil and the boys, as well as Grandmother Mercer, Gerald Hutchinson, Mr. and Mrs. McCarthy, and Jenny. She also wondered if George Meaford had survived.

Vangie arrived from her house on Bird Avenue to be with Emmy.

"We suffer the same fate," she told Emmy as she sighed deeply, holding back tears. "Neither of us knows where dear Phil and the boys are, or where George is."

"We've only the comfort of our company and trust in the Lord."

"I pray that they'll arrive home safely."

"Frank remains downtown at The Salvation Army Headquarters seeking information from the constantly changing bulletins. He has promised to take the streetcar up here to Earlscourt as soon as he receives any news."

As the two women tried to comfort each other, rain descended across the city in the early evening hours, appearing as an ever-darkening curtain, pouring horizontal windblown sheets of water across the streets and laneways. Trees and bushes drooped heavily toward the sodden earth as the skies wept with those who mourned. The thoroughfares became as empty as graveyards after the midnight hour. In homes throughout Toronto, people huddled close to the warmth of their stoves to avoid the cool, damp air. Like tears, the raindrops dribbled down the windowpanes.

In the hours ahead, Emmy and Vangie, along with the Mercer girls, sat beside the warmth of the stove and pondered the events of the day. Sleep was impossible.

*

In Quebec, during the late hours of Friday night, workers recovered the ship's log from the water. The first mate had placed it in a watertight tin box and had carried it with him when he abandoned the vessel. When he sank beneath the frigid waters, his hands released the box, which floated to the surface. When rescue workers were searching for bodies, they found it bobbing on the waves.

The next morning, the survivors departed from Quebec City to travel westward to Montreal and onward to Ontario. Meanwhile, throughout the day in the cold, damp coal sheds at Rimouski, Army officers attempted to identify Salvationists. They examined more than two hundred bodies, repeating the gruesome task many times to be certain that they had not overlooked anyone. An officer painted small red crosses on the coffin lids of Salvationists, and the men arranged them in a group so they might be placed together aboard the transport ship.

At 4:30 p.m., the bodies were finally carried to the *Lady Grey,* and the vessel set sail. The Canadian Government steamer was a small, white-hulled, single-funnel vessel. Accompanying her was a British cruiser, the *Essex,* a first-class armoured cruiser of the British fleet that King George V had personally ordered to the scene. The vessels steamed out into the river and passed near the spot where the *Empress* had gone down, the crews pausing from their tasks and gazing out over the water.

An Army officer wrote in his journal, "The sun broke through the clouds at the moment the ships sailed away from the spot, and proceeded toward Quebec City."

*

In Toronto, the morning headline of *The Globe* newspaper read:

> ***EMPRESS* CARRIES ALMOST 1,000**
> **PASSENGERS**
> **TO THE BOTTOM OF THE ST.**
> **LAWRENCE RIVER**

The newspaper published a list of names of the survivors, but no Mercer name was among them, although their names did appear in the late edition of *The Globe,* which stated that they were missing. The same edition also reported that they had recovered 250 bodies, but many remained unidentified.

While reports continued in the papers, a train departed from Toronto's Union Station during the morning hours with the close relatives of some of the survivors aboard. These passengers were to meet those who had departed from Quebec, at the Locust Hill Station, northeast of Toronto, to allow them a few minutes' privacy with their relatives before they returned to the city and confronted the waiting crowds at Union Station.

On the journey from Toronto, the atmosphere in the coaches was subdued, almost prayerful. People spoke to each other in voices barely audible above the clatter of the coach wheels. Though there was certain to be much joy in meeting the relatives who were returning, there was also a terrifying dread of hearing the names of those who were not. Arriving at Locust Hill, the people detrained and assembled near the platform to await the incoming train with the survivors aboard.

Frank Mercer was among the crowd.

*

Finally, the train travelling westward from Quebec City arrived. People in the coaches leaned out of the large windows to catch a glimpse of their loved ones. They waved handkerchiefs and wiped tears of joy from their cheeks when they recognized someone. As people stepped down from the coaches, some hugged and kissed. The restraint that had been so evident earlier now fell away, and within a single moment it seemed as if a million questions exploded.

One man aboard the train from Quebec inquired of a friend from Toronto, "Does my wife know? She's ill at her mother's in Detroit, you know."

The reply was, "Yes. We have wired her. She knows you're safe."

*

Frank Mercer felt immensely relieved when he saw his mother descending from the train. He rushed to her and wrapped her in his arms.

"Did you see any of the others?" he asked as he comforted her.

Tears streaked her exhausted face as she replied, "I never saw any of them. Not Phil, Billy, or Zack after I retired to my cabin for the night. It was Gerald who managed to get me outside onto the deck."

"Mr. Hutchinson is also missing?" Even though he was his stepfather, Frank referred to him by his formal name. His mother nodded and burst into tears.

"My Gerald helped me into the lifeboat but refused to get in beside me, giving the space to a young woman. He donned a life jacket after he helped me into the lifeboat. When he saw them lower it, he jumped from the ship's railing. I lost sight of him. Then I saw him struggling to keep afloat. He was not more than thirty feet from the lifeboat. I noticed that he was no longer wearing a life jacket. He must have given it to someone else. I saw him slip under several times, but someone pulled him to the surface. Finally, he sank below the water and disappeared from sight. The nightmare will haunt me until the day I die."

Frank held his mother close as she convulsed into uncontrollable sobbing. After assisting her to board the train departing for Toronto, he sought out a Salvation Army officer who knew the Mercer family. Approaching the Major, who had his back to him, he touched him on the shoulder. The officer turned around and gazed at Frank's worried countenance. In a soft voice, he inquired, "Did you see my brother, Phil, or my nephews, Billy and Zack?"

There was a short pause before the Major slowly replied, "I never saw any of them."

"Did you see George Meaford?"

Again, he shook his head sadly in a negative response.

Frank turned away to hide the tears that flowed down his cheeks. Then, to his relief, he spied Mr. and Mrs. McCarthy walking toward him on the platform. At least someone he knew had survived. Mr. McCarthy was assisting Jenny, who was in a daze, her eyes blank and lifeless. Frank spoke to them briefly, and they informed him that Jenny had not uttered a word since the disaster. Doctors would provide medical treatment for her when they arrived in Toronto.

The coach that was to carry the survivors and their family members to Union Station was soon ready to depart. Frank boarded and sat beside his mother. Frank's world was crashing around him. Boyhood memories of his brother flashed through his mind. Even when the vast Atlantic had separated them, he had felt close to Phil. He remembered the evenings in the parlour in the house on Draper Street when he had talked about Toronto to his nephews. Billy and Zack were dear to him. Would his world ever again be normal?

*

Eventually, the train departed from the Locust Hill Station to make its journey to Toronto. As the engine gathered speed, Frank noticed that his mother's eyes were glassy and motionless, as if she were in a trance. He turned away from her and stared blankly out the train window at the scene that flew past him. The spring sunshine bathed the landscape in evening's warm light, the fields reflecting green hues of the patchwork fields that contrasted with the brown of the freshly ploughed earth. The feathery treetops of emerald green caught the rays of the setting sun, the shadows lengthening behind the houses, barns, and trees. Dairy cows slowly wandered toward the pasture gates, unmindful of the surrounding events, for to them it was merely the end of another day. Frank gazed at the scene, wondering if the quiet contentment of a normal day was now forever beyond his grasp.

The train rushed onward, the noise of the coaches producing a constant rhythm. Within thirty minutes, the engine slowed its pace, the click-clack of the wheels also slowing as the train arrived in Toronto.

It was 7:45 p.m. when the first group of survivors arrived at Union Station. Joy seized the waiting crowd as the survivors appeared. People cheered. Men threw their hats into the air. The exuberance died quickly as people realized that of the group that appeared, only fifteen persons were actually survivors. Then the crowd saw people unloading a body from a baggage car at the rear of the train. Reality set in.

The gathered crowd on Front Street, in front of the Union Station, blocked the street in either direction. Beyond the horizon, the last rays of the dying sun were departing, dampness penetrating the night air. From somewhere in the crowd, a group commenced singing a well-known hymn. The throngs soon joined in, their voices rising into the evening sky as they sang.

> O God, our help in ages past,
> Our hope for years to come,
> Our shelter from the stormy blast,
> And our eternal home!
>
> Time, like an ever-rolling stream,
> Bears all its sons away;
> They fly forgotten, as a dream
> Dies at the opening day.

After the singing ended, a hush fell across the assembly. It was unbelievable that a street filled with such crowds could be so silent. It was as if at the same moment, the reality of the situation gripped everyone as they all confronted their own mortality. The stillness was deep and hung in the air, louder than any spoken words.

*

Sarah met Frank and Grandmother Mercer at the station. Leaving his mother in her care, Frank then spoke with an officer who had been at Quebec. He ended Frank's last hope of finding his loved ones alive. Since he now possessed the information that he had sought, he rejoined his mother and they stole away from the crowds, departing Union Station. After arriving at the house on Draper Street, Sarah agreed to sit with Frank's mother, since it was now his responsibility to travel to the house on Bird Avenue and relate the details. Many thoughts whirled through his mind as he travelled on the streetcar to the Earlscourt District.

When he opened the door to the small house, Emmy, Vangie, and the three Mercer girls gazed intently at him. There was no need to explain the situation. They saw the look on his face.

Emmy softly asked, "All of them?"

"My George too?" Vangie stammered.

Frank nodded his head in response. Vangie burst into tears as Emmy placed her arms around her. No one could possibly ever explain the depth of sorrow that gripped their hearts. George, Phil, Billy, and Zack were gone forever. Emmy's heart bled as she realized that she would never again wrap her arms around her husband and two beautiful sons. The girls hugged their mother to comfort her while trying to ease the pain in their own hearts.

*

Meanwhile, in the house on Draper Street, Grandmother Mercer remained in shock, having endured the unendurable. Her beloved Gerald was gone. She had also lost a son and two grandchildren. She refused a cup of tea, and Sarah helped her into the bed. The elderly woman rolled over on her side and faced the wall. Her life was over. The indomitable woman of old was no more.

In the Toronto General Hospital on College Street, Jenny was in a ward with seven other people, white cloth screens surrounding her. The doctor had sedated her. The tragedy had crushed another indomitable spirit. In the days ahead, she would remain comatose most of the time, rarely uttering a word.

How she had escaped and what had happened to Billy remained locked inside her.

*

On Sunday, May 31, in Quebec City, the sun rose in a sky of brilliant blue. A few cumulus clouds blossomed in the distance, not daring to intrude on the scene.

News of the impending arrival of the *Lady Grey* and the *Essex* had spread throughout the city in both Upper and Lower Towns. In the morning, while the clarion bells rang out in the towers of the old basilica and other churches in Quebec City, people gathered below the cliffs of Quebec. Despite the early hour, the docks were soon crowded, some climbing on the roofs of the sheds and warehouses to catch a glimpse of the scene.

It was almost 7:00 a.m. when the people at Quebec sighted the outlines of the two ships sailing upriver. Within twenty minutes, the small steamer and British cruiser were approaching the docks, their funnels outlined against the sky. The crowd patiently waited. It was not long before the vessels nudged into port. The sight was a sombre one.

Onboard the ships, the union jacks were at half-mast. In the cool morning air, the flags fluttered in the breeze and then became limp as the wind reverently ceased, as if an unrelenting power had forced stillness upon the scene. On the deck of the *Lady Grey* were rows of wooden coffins, two to three deep in several places. There was no one there to wonder if Phil, Billy, or Zack's bodies were among them.

While the men secured the vessel to Pier 27, people noticed a group of small white coffins—the children who had perished. Until this moment, the crowd had remained hushed, but the pitiful sight of the children's caskets caused the onlookers to gasp in shock. Except for the coffins on which a Salvation Army officer had placed a small red cross, the boxes were impersonal and unmarked as they rested on the deck of the ship in the stark morning light.

On the *Essex,* more than a hundred sailors appeared on deck attired in navy blue jackets and trousers and stood in formation. A small group of them commenced unloading the coffins. The silence of the Marines cast symbolic significance onto this deeply powerful scene. Throughout the history of the Royal Navy, the admiralty had called upon British tars to perform difficult deeds in stressful situations, but this was surely one of the worst. Despite the many hands assisting, it took over an hour to complete the sad task. When the fourteen Marines brought the small white coffins ashore on their shoulders, muffled weeping rose in the still air and remained for several minutes. Finally, the last twenty coffins were placed on the wharf to be taken to a nearby freight shed for storage.

*

At this same hour in Montreal, the Peterborough Temple Band of The Salvation Army was boarding the *Alaunia,* the ship that was to transport them to England to the ICC. Their final concert had been in Montreal the previous evening. It had become a memorial service instead of a farewell musical festival.

Another ship, the *Teutonic,* sailed from Montreal with twenty-seven Salvationists aboard on this Sunday morning of May 31. The morning service, delivered by the purser on the deck of the *Teutonic,* included the hymn "Eternal Father, Strong to Save."

Eternal Father, strong to save,
Whose arm hath bound the restless wave;
Who bidd'st the mighty ocean deep,
Its own appointed limits keep;
Oh, hear us when we cry to Thee,
For those in peril on the sea.

Salvationists who participated in this meaningful gathering thought of those who had been on the *Empress* and knew that they were now among those who had perished on the sea. During the singing of this hymn, and by grim coincidence, the *Storstad* with its crumpled bow passed by as it steamed upriver. This was the vessel that had collided with the *Empress.* Later in the day, when it arrived in Montreal with its load of coal, government officials impounded the ship.

Captain Andersen of the *Storstad* asked, "By whose authority do you seize this ship?"

The reply was, "By the authority of the British Empire."

The *Storstad,* its bow crushed after colliding with the *Empress of Ireland.* *Photo courtesy of the George Scott Railton Heritage Centre*

*

On this same Sunday morning, deep sadness entombed Toronto. Early in the day, three more survivors arrived at Union Station. People found it difficult to cope with the extent of the disaster. They filled the churches, where the congregants sought words of comfort. At the Sherbourne Street Methodist Church, they sang "O God! Our Help in Ages Past" as a prayer for those who mourned. The minister of St. James Cathedral on King Street had chosen as his text, "Ye shall receive power, after that the Holy Ghost is come upon you: and ye shall be witnesses unto me." Though the clergyman had chosen the biblical verse prior to the tragedy, he altered his emphasis to render it more appropriate for the occasion.

*

In the Mercer home, the hearts of Emmy and her girls were heavy. Emmy was in shock, unable to release her tears and experience the relief that crying might have provided her. However, a visit from Zeke Treadwell and his younger brother, Jeremiah, *almost* caused her to break into tears. The Treadwell brothers reminded her of her own boys.

She appreciated their visit and hugged them both. For Emmy, the boys were proof that miracles did indeed happen. Sibling rivalry had turned into brotherly love. She smiled sadly as she threw her arms around Jeremiah. It was something that she thought would never happen. Emmy never noticed the look in Bess's eyes as she watched Zeke.

*

The Salvation Army cabled details of the *Empress* tragedy around the globe to sixty-nine countries and colonies in thirty-four languages. On Sunday, May 31, they estimated that almost three million Salvationists and friends of the Army gathered in the various corps and public buildings throughout the world. A service held in the Royal Albert Hall, London, was led by General Bramwell Booth, son of the Founder of the organization.

The Territorial Headquarters in Toronto issued orders that they *not* fly Army flags at half-mast. The fronts of the corps buildings were to be draped in white, not black, and Headquarters requested that Salvationists not wear black as a symbol of mourning. The faithful aboard the *Empress* had not died in defeat. They had been "promoted to glory."

*

On Monday, June 1, the wells of sadness had not yet drained from the city of Toronto. In the afternoon, another CPR locomotive steamed into Union Station carrying four more survivors and fifteen bodies.

Mr. A. W. Miles, a Toronto funeral director, had accompanied the bodies from Quebec City. Within minutes of unloading the coffins, Mr. Miles and his assistants issued the necessary instructions to transport the bodies that had been assigned to their mortuary. The caskets were placed on two lorries—actually, coal carts—covered in purple and black, each cart pulled by a team of horses draped with long ribbons of funereal crepe.

It was a solemn moment as the cortege left the yards of the train station on The Esplanade. Automobiles were supplied by the City of Toronto to transport the close relatives of the victims. Along the streets, crowds stood silently in reverence of those who had perished. The coffins were delivered to the private mortuary of A. W. Miles at 326 College Street, where the bodies were to remain until the funeral service.

On Tuesday, June 2, early editions of the newspapers announced that there were sixty unknown bodies remaining at Quebec, where the awesome task of examining the dead continued. The Salvation Army posted a list of the bodies that they had identified.

Gerald Hutchinson's name was not on that list. Emmy received no news that might end her family's grief-filled vigil. In an attempt to receive information, Frank Mercer travelled to Quebec. He failed to locate the bodies of his brother and nephews.

On Wednesday, June 3, an officer from Headquarters arrived at the home of Frank and Sarah Mercer on Draper Street. He bore the sad news that Gerald's body had been found. It would arrive in Toronto in time for the mass funeral service.

*

On Thursday, June 4, and Friday, June 5, the Mercers attempted to console each other. Friends visited the home, as did members of the Rosemount Corps. Emmy found the visit of Captain Rush the most comforting, since he truly appeared to understand her grief. Emmy was aware that Vangie was caught in the same web of despair, not knowing the location of George's body. She and Vangie continued to spend much time together, finding comfort in each other's presence.

Now that all hopes had been dashed, Emmy knew that it was necessary to notify the relatives in Comstock about the deaths. She discussed the situation with Frank, and they decided to telegraph a message to Emmy's brother, Bill, asking him to notify other members of the family. Emmy also asked Frank to indicate in the telegram that she would write her brother as soon as she was able.

Emmy realized that Mary and Ruth, despite their intense sorrow, were managing to cope, if only barely. However, Bess's grief fell into a bottomless pit from which she could not ascend. Bess voiced aloud the questions that tumbled within all their minds. "How could God allow this to happen? Where was God when Zack needed help? Zack had served

God faithfully. Why didn't God help him?" Also, "Why did God take our father and Billy?"

Emmy could find no answers to give.

When Emmy heard Bess crying during the night, her heart ached. She knew that at some point she must find the wisdom to answer her youngest daughter's questions. However, she was also aware that her three daughters were without a father and needed her strength more than ever. Her devotion for Phil must now be gently placed aside, not forgotten or lost, but swept into the depths of her precious memories, so that her love for their children may take the fore.

*

On Saturday, June 6, the newly appointed Commissioner of The Salvation Army for Canada arrived by ship in New York from London, and he would journey by train to Toronto. He was to replace the missing Commissioner Hees. As the new Territorial Commander for Canada, he was to represent the General at the forthcoming memorial services in Toronto. In his absence, Headquarters released the following to the press:

> **Services in Toronto for our comrades "Promoted to Glory" from the SS *Empress of Ireland* on May 29, to be held in the Mutual Street Arena at Mutual and Shuter Streets.**

Then they posted the following dates:

> **Lying in State: Saturday, June 6, 10:00 a.m. to 2:00 p.m.**
> **Public Service: Saturday, June 6, 2:30 p.m.**
> **Public Memorial: Sunday, June 7, 3:00 p.m.**

*

Early on the morning of Saturday, June 6, A. W. Miles Funeral Home transported the coffins from their mortuary to the Mutual Street Arena. The building was the city's main sports arena. Outside the doors, a long line of mourners waited patiently to enter and pay their respects. They arranged the open coffins on the floor of the arena, and people slowly walked between the three rows. They estimated that between twelve thousand and fifteen thousand people filed past.

Mutual Street Arena in downtown Toronto. This was the city's main sports arena in 1914. *City of Toronto Archives, Fonds 1257, Series 1057, Item 0964*

An enormous Army flag hung from the north end of the building, and the platform area was edged with smaller Army flags of yellow star and red and blue, as well as the bold colours of the union jack. In front of the platform, in large blue letters on a white background, was the word that delivered an important message for the occasion: *Victory.*

When it was time for the service to begin, the entire building was fully occupied. Officers and soldiers wore white armbands. There was a children's choir attired in robes of white, standing in formation in the shape of a large cross. The traditional colours and symbols of death were absent from the scene.

Behind the platform, tier upon tier, was a massed band of bandsmen from Toronto and the surrounding areas. The Rosemount Band, Billy and Zack's, was a part of this group. At the opposite end of the arena were the bands provided by the Toronto Musicians Protective Society. Among these were the famous 48th Highlanders.

They sang "Abide with Me" as a processional while the platform party entered. The mourners sat at either side of the caskets. On the left-hand side of the platform were the few survivors, and behind them were thirty-seven empty seats, an emotionally fraught symbol of the Army's losses. Emmy and the girls, along with Frank, sat with Grandmother Mercer, whose hand rested on Gerald's coffin.

Funeral service in Mutual Street Arena for victims of the *Empress of Ireland*. *Photo courtesy of the George Scott Railton Heritage Centre*

Finally, the service began. The new Commissioner read the lines of the first song in a voice thick with emotion. He then spoke a few words to those who had gathered.

"I wish to offer the condolences of the General, who has expressed deep sympathy for those who lost loved ones. On my own behalf, I wish to add my condolences."

He paused before he added, "I also wish to pay tribute to Commissioner David Hees. He was a humble man who treated everyone with respect and friendly courtesy. I know that he was loved by all. I'm told that he will be remembered for his keen wit and good sense of humour. He was a great Salvationist."

The Commissioner went to say, "Of the forty-one members of the Toronto Staff Band who were aboard the *Empress*, only twelve survived. These are all that remain of the band."

He slowly read the list.

Next, he read the names of those who had perished. Zack's name was included, alongside that of his brother, as Bandmaster Greenway had insisted that the teenager was an honorary member of the staff band.

When the last verse of the final hymn ended, they offered a prayer, and then the congregation quietly departed from the arena. Dignitaries, bands, officers, and soldiers arranged themselves outside the building on Mutual Street.

In orderly groups, the great funeral procession commenced to march to Mount Pleasant Cemetery, about three miles' distance. More than six thousand people joined in the procession.

*

Hushed crowds lined the streets of Toronto as the procession passed through the city. It was an impressive sight that confronted onlookers as the Salvationists marched north on Yonge. Many said that it was the greatest funeral procession ever to have been seen in the city. An estimated hundred thousand people or more stood along the route. When the cortege reached the Yorkville area, the crowds were six or more deep, people row upon row, standing shoulder-to-shoulder. The sidewalks, house windows, shop doorways, and sometimes even roofs were crammed. As the procession passed, men removed their hats and women bowed their heads. Holding the hand of a mother or father, children stood beside their parents sensing the great sorrow that the scene represented, but unable to fully understand its meaning.

Funeral procession for the victims of the *Empress of Ireland*. *Photo courtesy of the George Scott Railton Heritage Centre*

Funeral procession on Yonge Street, Toronto. *Photo courtesy of the George Scott Railton Heritage Centre*

When the procession finally reached the Yonge Street gates of Mount Pleasant Cemetery, the crowds were immense. Police on either side of the entrance restrained the onlookers so as to allow the cortege to enter. Inside the ornate iron gates, the cortege proceeded along the south road, stopping a short distance to the east. Near the south wall of the cemetery, not far from Yonge, the procession came to a halt, and people assembled around the open graves. The ensuing ceremony was brief but filled with meaning.

Following the service, the crowds departed. Most walked away in silence, though a few remained staring into the open graves, standing like statues, unable to cope with the loss of their loved ones. A few sobs broke the depth of the silence.

*

Frank and Sarah, as well as Vangie, were among those who stood silently. Emmy and the girls supported Grandmother Mercer, who was gazing at Gerald's grave. Emmy understood the pain that sliced into her mother-in-law's heart, as she suffered from death's cruel blade as well.

Funeral service in Mount Pleasant Cemetery. *Photo courtesy of the George Scott Railton Heritage Centre*

Funeral service near the south wall of Mount Pleasant Cemetery. *Photo courtesy of the George Scott Railton Heritage Centre*

Finally, Grandmother Mercer smiled weakly and gathered what remained of her family around herself. Though it seemed impossible, she was already rallying her strength. Emmy had thought that her mother-in-law was defeated, but she was not. Without speaking a word, she encouraged the others, despite her deep-felt sorrow.

Mary and Ruth quietly cried but maintained their composure. As they walked out of the cemetery, Bess looked back at the numerous graves and asked her mother, "Is this where they will put Father, Billy, and Zack when they find them?"

"Yes, my love, but they won't really be there."

*

Following the service in the cemetery, Vangie Meaford joined with the Mercer family to share a light meal. No one had much appetite. Sitting around the kitchen table, their conversation was quiet and at times strained. Finally, after assuring Emmy that she would be okay, Vangie departed for home, walking a short distance along the street.

When she arrived in the house, she placed her hat in the hall cupboard. After positioning it on the shelf, her eyes fell on George's winter uniform coat. She gently caressed it. How many times she had watched him don it on a winter morning to attend an open-air service with the band! She remained unable to dispose of her husband's belongings, as to do so was to lose the last few connections she had to the man she loved. On the floor of the cupboard was his toolbox. She would never again see him lift it to go out the door to work. His work clothes and shirts remained in the bedroom closet. Vangie had also been unable to relinquish them from her world. However, the worst reminders of her loss were George's empty chair beside the kitchen table and his vacant space beside her in the bed.

As twilight was creeping across the landscape, she decided to sit on the veranda. A soft, warm breeze gently blew from the west, bringing with it pleasant air. She recalled the many times she had sat out here with George. Despite her loneliness, thoughts of her precious husband comforted her, helping to ease her melancholy.

Just then, a small brown hare hopped across the lawn in front of her, darted across the roadway, and disappeared into the tall grass of the empty lot across the street. The small creature led her to remember the Easter season that had recently passed. Her mind turned toward a conversation she had shared with George on the previous Easter Sunday morning.

As he sat sipping on his tea, she had noticed an odd look on his face and said to him, "A penny for your thoughts, George."

"Normally, I would say that my thoughts are not worth a penny, but perhaps on this occasion I'm wrong."

"What were you thinking about?"

"I had a strange dream last night. I've been thinking about it ever since."

"Care to share?"

"Well," he began, "I was standing high on a hill overlooking an enormous valley where everything was in deep shadows. Despite the darkness, the valley was not threatening. From within it rose to my face a fresh, caressing breeze fragrant with spring, the season of new beginnings. I was drawn toward the valley, a powerful presence beckoning me while it comforted and guided me. As I stepped into the unknown, I felt that you were there beside me, Vangie. Actually, I think it was your love that I was sensing. When I finally arrived at the far end of the valley, I knew I was in the presence of the divine. I was home."

"That was a strange dream."

George was silent for a few moments.

Then he said, "Vangie, I believe that the dream mirrors my life, not my journey into heaven. All my life, I have travelled through a seemingly endless valley in search of spiritual understanding. Despite my failings, doubts, and shortcomings, I have travelled far toward 'home.' During the years, whenever I succeeded in gaining spiritual insight, it was as if the curtain separating me from the face of the divine was drawn back slightly. With each new insight, the curtain parted a little more, and I drew closer to understanding how God wished me to live my life. Each step along the path was a beginning—a resurrection. I came to view a resurrection not as something to be experienced after I had passed beyond the cross, but as a part of my daily life. This is the Easter message that dwells within me."

"I am not certain that I understand all you have said, but your contemplations have obviously brought you peace."

"True. I believe that losing one's fear of death is less about bravery than it is about faith—a faith that assures you that you are in safe hands, the hands of the divine. I accept the Easter message. Death is not to be feared—it has been conquered. The resurrection is a beginning, not an end. Therefore, I have already experienced my resurrection while still here with you."

Vangie gazed at him but remained silent.

George continued. "Vangie, I'm at peace. When I do pass through that valley, your love will be within me, as it has always been—constant, never-ending, and true. When I'm at home with God, the answers to the questions that have confounded me all my life will finally be revealed."

Vangie had reached out her hand and held his as he spoke again.

"You know, I remember a particular evening, many years ago, when I had finished a tutoring session with Billy in our apartment above the hardware store on Queen Street. Billy confided in me some of his thoughts about spiritual matters and asked questions. Now, after all these years, I realize that—although I was unable to successfully provide answers to the questions he asked—the way he has lived his life has helped me along my spiritual path. He forced me to examine my beliefs. I have been richly blessed by his life. I believe that his example and music have also helped others."

As Vangie sat on the porch on this mild spring evening, she remembered George's words. She was comforted by the thought that, although she did not know where her husband's earthly remains were resting, he was at peace with his Creator. She now realized that George had been trying to tell her that he had experienced the resurrection prior to his death, since a resurrection was a new beginning, not an end.

The words of Horatio Gates Spafford's hymn crept into her heart as she looked out across the spring greenery, the shadows of evening increasingly enveloping the landscape. Her dearest George had been a living testament to Spafford's lyrics,

> When peace like a river attendeth my way,
> When sorrows like sea billows roll,
> Whatever my lot, thou hast taught me to know,
> *It is well, it is well with my soul.*

*

Less than a week later, on Thursday, June 11, the International Congress of The Salvation Army commenced in Britain, and from the far corners of the globe, the flags of many nations paraded through the crowded streets of London.

Emmy lamented that Billy and Zack were not among the marching bandsmen. Londoners and people who had gathered from around the world would never hear the golden tone of Billy's or Zack's cornet. She was unaware they had scheduled a performance of Billy's composition "O Boundless Salvation" in the Royal Albert Hall. This, too, would never happen.

Billy and Zack had wanted to visit Comstock with their father, see the old homestead on South Street, and visit Mrs. Rowntree. A faint smile crossed Emmy's face as she remembered her cantankerous elderly neighbour. Emmy thought of the day the woman had come to the train station to see Billy before he departed for overseas. Despite the way he had tormented her, she had finally realized how much he meant to her.

Emmy thought, *I've always known how much they all meant to me, and right now, I've never loved them more.*

*

Despite the tragedy, the ICC was a great success. King George V and Queen Mary sent their best wishes; leaders of government cabled their congratulations. The ancient city of London had never before witnessed such a vast throng of Christian warriors. However, a cloud of sorrow permeated the celebration, as thoughts of the *Empress* hovered in everyone's mind. There was a great wave of emotion when the twenty-five contingents of the Canadian delegation marched past the reviewing stand, led by the Peterborough Band. Bystanders were unfamiliar with the words of "The Maple Leaf Forever," but they instantly appreciated the stirring melody.

On Saturday, June 13, a celebratory march snaked its way through the grand thoroughfares of London, the parade having begun at Victoria Embankment and terminate in Hyde Park. As a salute to the work of the Army, ten thousand British troops participated. People marched in the parade eight abreast. It took more than an hour for all of them to pass through Oxford Circus.

In Hyde Park were a dozen reviewing stands with loudspeakers, constructed for this occasion. It was estimated that over a million people lined the route and mingled in Hyde Park. Later, in the Strand Hall, General Bramwell Booth conducted the Peterborough Band in a tribute to the late Commissioner David Hees. A Toronto staff bandsman gripped the audience as he spoke to the gathered crowd about his miraculous escape from the *Empress.*

The Canadian delegates marched through the streets of London's West End to visit Canada's new acting High Commissioner, who was at Canada House on Trafalgar Square. The Peterborough Band performed a number of pieces outside the government building, with the hymn "Nearer My God to Thee" played in memoriam of the *Empress of Ireland* disaster.

*

In Rimouski, Quebec, on Friday, June 26, divers recovered five more bodies from the *Empress.* Among them was a man with the initials *D. H.* stitched on his pyjamas. A Salvation Army major who was at the scene made the positive identification. They had found the earthly remains of Commissioner David Hees. They transported his body immediately to the A. W. Miles Funeral Home in Toronto. It arrived the next day at the North Toronto Station on Saturday, June 27, at 8:00 a.m.

*

In London, the sun set on the International Congress the same day the body of Commissioner Hees arrived in Toronto. Despite the sombre mood created by the Canadian disaster, an uplifting sense of faith had prevailed. Inspired, the delegates left London and returned to their congregations throughout the British nation, as well as to the many countries around the world.

In Britain, because of the demise of the majority of the members of the Toronto Staff Band, there was no tour of Scotland. The people of this nation never heard its music. Billy's cornet never echoed through the narrow streets of the cities of the ancient land. The intricate rhythms of "O Boundless Salvation" never graced the concert halls of London, Edinburgh, or Glasgow.

On July 10 the *Empress* was to have set sail from Liverpool, but on this date, the pier at the great port city was empty. The *Empress* had already sailed into the everlasting sagas of the sea.

*

During the final week of June, the Rosemount Corps held a memorial service to honour the Salvationists who had perished on the *Empress*. Among the names they read aloud were Billy's and Zack's, as well as those of George Meaford and Gerald Hutchinson. It was a staggering loss for the congregation of "little" Rosemount, which four years earlier had been an outpost of the Dovercourt Citadel, one of the largest congregations in the city.

An Army major led the meeting. The tragedy had personally touched him, as he had been one of the officers who had assisted in identifying the bodies in the coal sheds at Rimouski. People read letters of condolence from various churches and organizations in the Earlscourt District.

One of the hymns sung during the service had been written by James Milton Black: "When the trumpet of the Lord shall sound, and time shall be no more …"

When the singing ended, Emmy turned to Bess and said, "Yes, the trumpet of the Lord has sounded, but it's Billy's trumpet that we shall hear no more."

At the conclusion of the service, the Major asked everyone, "Please rise as the band plays 'Promoted to Glory' for those who perished on the *Empress of Ireland*.

*

Emmy attended the service. She knew that for her, the terrible effects of the tragedy were far from over. Divers were exploring the wreck, and although they had recovered more bodies, they had not found her loved ones. She felt trapped in an ongoing nightmare that promised no awakening from it.

Emmy and the Mercer girls were not the only ones suffering. Vangie was managing a brave face, but Emmy knew her thoughts, as did Grandmother Mercer. Meanwhile, Jenny remained in the hospital in downtown Toronto.

*

The final days of June passed in rapid succession. The strawberry season ended, the berries now tucked away in preserving jars in cold cellars. Late spring mellowed into the lazy days of the new season as summer spread out its hand. The humid heat of July descended over the streets and homes of the Earlscourt District and across the verdant vacant lots.

Early each morning, Emmy toiled in the backyard garden. She told Bess, "Families in the neighbourhood are taking the streetcars down below the hill to seek relief from the heat alongside the waters of the lake."

"I know," Bess replied. "I don't really care."

"It's just as well. We don't have the carfare, and I don't have the energy for such trips."

"Me neither."

"In the worst of the afternoon heat, we can sit in the shade under the maple tree here in the backyard."

"That's fine with me. I don't feel like going anywhere."

"Since Mary and Ruth are both at work below the hill, you and I are left to keep each other company. I suppose you'll soon seek a job, too."

"I suppose. I don't really care. Now that Billy and Zack are gone, I don't even feel like playing my cornet."

It worried Emmy that Bess was no longer a happy teenager, as she was in earlier times. She was oblivious to the hot temperatures as well as to most other things in her surroundings. The lustre of her eyes seemed to have dulled.

Later, in the waning light of day, Mary and Ruth returned home from work. When supper was over, the four of them sat on the veranda, anxious to feel the cooling effects of any slight breeze that might appear. With the setting of the sun, silence dropped over the street like a soft summer curtain. Although the humid air was now devoid of children's voices, adults walking along the street continued to chat in quiet tones, while others, like the Mercers, sat in the darkness on their large verandas.

Bess said, "If I were older, I'd run away to Africa to hide in the jungles, where no one would ever find me. If I were older, I'd …"

Emmy sighed as she told Bess, "My darling, the young always wish to be older, while older folks fondly cherish the days of our youth and wish to return to the security of the past." She paused before she added, "If I had my wish, I'd return to the wondrous days of the past. The past was safe; the future is uncertain."

Bess gazed at her mother but said nothing.

*

On Friday, July 3, a letter arrived in the afternoon post. Emmy knew by the handwriting that it was from her brother, Bill. It was the second one he had sent following the long letter she had mailed to him in the week after the tragedy. Loneliness gripped her heart as she reflected on the great distance between them. A letter required almost two weeks to arrive from England.

Rather than returning inside the house, she decided to sit in a chair on the veranda. She opened the envelope, her hand trembling slightly.

South Street
Comstock, Dorset
24 June 1914

My dearest Em,

It is often said that time heals all wounds, but for me, the healing has barely begun. No words can ever portray the depth of sorrow that I continue to feel since the day I read the telegram that Frank sent. I wish I were there in Toronto to place my arms around you and the girls. I feel so helpless being so far away. The tragedy increases my guilt, as even when you were residing in Comstock, I rarely saw you and your family. Billy was the only one I became close to, and I failed even him.

I cannot help but feel that if I had not encouraged Billy in his love of music, he would not have been aboard the Empress on that fateful voyage. I realize that such reasoning is senseless, but it has entered my mind nevertheless. I loved him deeply and was in awe of his talent. I have never met anyone, even those much older than he, who possessed so much natural ability. I always felt that he would achieve greatness, and now this opportunity has been denied him.

My love for the other children is also deep, though I admit that I did not have the chance to get to know them as well as I did Billy. I will live with this regret forever.

Whenever I think of Zack, I see his smiling, angelic face, and tears come to my eyes.

I always respected Phil, but after our parting at the train station in Comstock, I fully realized the depth of his compassion and understanding. Before he departed, he told me that Billy was a better person because of my influence. I treasure those words, but I feel that Phil was being overly kind. Billy and Zack reflected the upbringing that you and Phil gave them. The generosity and compassion they showed others were a result of the values you instilled in them.

Now, my dearest sister, I must impart news to you about recent changes in my life. My earnest prayer is that they will offer a bit of cheer. As you are already aware, in the past I lived hand-to-mouth with the few coins I received playing the piano at the alehouse. All that has changed. At the tannery, where I am now employed, they recently promoted me to foreman in the dyeing department. The increase in wages has allowed me to put aside a little money. I will tell you more about this later in the letter.

Last winter, The Salvation Army established an outpost congregation in Comstock. It has only a dozen members at present, but I play the piano for them. They are a wonderful group of people, and I treasure the friendship and emotional support that they provide. They have become a family to me. I know that you have been attending the Army for many years now. I hope that the news of my joining the church will cheer you.

There are few stories about happenings in the town that I wish to share with you. I am certain that you remember Mr. and Mrs. Bailey, who owned the butcher shop, and their son, Freddie. The boy died two weeks past in a tragic accident in a copse of trees in the woods to the south of the town. Freddie was a mischievous lad, and as a teenager, though never in trouble with the constable, he was frequently involved in some prank or other. Despite his mother's pleading, he had not attended St. Mary's for several years. The week after his funeral, Mrs. Bailey went to church to find solace among the faithful. On the morning she attended, Reverend Wilmot delivered a two-hour sermon condemning those in the parish who did not attend church.

He insisted that they were all "doomed to bottomless perdition," and that they would "dwell in adamantine chains and penal fire for eternity." I understand that this is one of the Reverend's favourite ways to describe the fate that awaits sinners. I was not in attendance when he delivered this insensitive sermon, but I heard about it. The Reverend's words paraphrased those of John Milton in his epic poem Paradise Lost. They were repeated to me verbatim by a close friend. Mrs. Bailey was shocked and saddened, as she considered the sermon a direct attack on her Freddie, since the boy had not attended church for several years. The reason he had not attended was that the Reverend had repeatedly verbally attacked Freddie and also ridiculed him.

The following Saturday morning, Mrs. Bailey encountered the Reverend on the High Street, at the farmers' market. Mrs. Bailey has a stall at this market, where she sells her pork pies. The Reverend was attempting to purchase several of them, and he demanded a lower price, as he was a man of the cloth.

Remembering his sermon the previous Sunday, and confronted with his condescending manner, Mrs. Bailey's temper got the better of her and she threw a pork pie in his face, after which the pie fell to the ground. Enraged, he shouted at her, "You, too, are bound for hell."

Mrs. Rowntree was standing near the Reverend as he delivered his tirade. Moments before, she had purchased a new straw broom. She was so incensed at the Reverend's raving that she swatted him with the broom. The force of the blow caused him to fall to the roadway and atop the pork pie, which was crushed beneath his prodigious rear end. While prostrate on the ground, he continued to protest, so Mrs. Rowntree struck him a second time. Fearing another blow, the Reverend made a hasty retreat.

However, the matter did not end there. The news of the incident spread quickly, as many had witnessed the Reverend's encounter with Mrs. Rowntree's broom. The following Sunday, he did not conduct the service at St. Mary's, having requested that a church elder take his place. The next Sunday, the church was more heavily attended than usual, as people knew that he would be returning to the pulpit.

The events on that day, people said, were "mighty to behold." The Reverend was completely contrite. He said that all his life he had prayed for the souls of others, but during the past two weeks, he had prayed for his own. He realized that he had drunk from the sacred waters that the church offered without ever considering the thirst of others. God had reached into his heart. He openly confessed his sins of pride and sought forgiveness. He promised that he would be less judgmental and preach more about forgiveness and love. After the sermon, Mrs. Rowntree declared, "The age of miracles has not passed."

Although Freddie's death was tragic, it seems that much good has resulted. The change in the Reverend's attitude has changed the tone of the services at the church, which in turn is reflected in the way people greet each other on South Street. Indeed, the age of miracles has not passed.

Now I return to the subject of the money that I have saved. Having sufficient funds to purchase passage on a transatlantic steamer to Canada, I have arranged a booking. I sail out of Liverpool for Halifax on 10 July. I have no real emotional ties here in Comstock, and as soon as possible, I wish to be reunited with you and the girls. I presently rent a furnished room in the home of a member of the Army congregation, so I have few possessions. I estimate that I will arrive in Toronto around 20 July. I will send a wire from Halifax to inform you when the train departs for Toronto.

I find it difficult to express the joy in my heart at the thought of seeing you and the girls again. Until we meet.

Your loving brother,

Bill

*

A tear trickled down Emmy's cheek as she placed the letter on her lap and gazed across the roadway at the fullness of the summer greenery. It was a stifling evening.

She told Bess, "Your uncle Bill's presence will be a blessing."

Ignoring her mother's optimism, Bess replied, "The divers are still searching the *Empress,* and they're finding bodies."

"Please, my dear. I don't need to be reminded. We'll find out about your father and brothers when we find out. Try to push it from your mind."

"I can't. Every day they release more information. I read that officials have instructed the divers to probe only the decks and passageways of the sunken ship. It's too dangerous to enter the submerged cabins. Each day, I await the announcement of the names of the bodies that they've recovered."

Fearing that Bess was obsessing too much on the happenings surrounding the dives into the *Empress,* Emmy tried to change the subject.

"We may find the hot days of summer tedious, but they're a respite from the freezing days of winter."

Bess replied, "I don't care about either summer or winter."

Knowing that further pleasantries about the season would fail to distract Bess, Emmy picked up the daily paper. Its news was also depressing. In addition to the reports of the dives into the *Empress,* other events were troubling as well. The newspapers warned that the turmoil in Europe was developing into a political powder keg that was in danger of igniting.

Emmy knew that ominous days lay beyond the horizon.

*

Several days later, another letter arrived in the afternoon post. Emmy was surprised when she opened it and saw the signature at the bottom of the page. It was from Mrs. Rowntree.

It began:

Me dear Mrs. Mercer,

Me hopes you forgives me for writing you. It has taken me several weeks to work up the courage to send this here letter. It has been so long since I put pen to paper that I was not certain I remembers how. But I needs tell you a few things. Since

I hears the news of the tragedy, I have thought about the days when we all lived together in Comstock. I've knocked me old noodle on the wall trying to discover why I was so difficult and harsh with yur young brood.

I've come to believe that each time I saw yur children, I thought of the children I had wanted when I was first married to Harry. Your youngins reminded me of my loss, and in my way, I tried to guide them as if they were mine, by scolding them and telling them to behave or else they were bound for hell. I did the same with me poor dear Harry. I scolded he for coming into the house with mud on his boots and for smoking his stinky tobacco pipe in the back porch. When he passed away, I realized that the love of me life was gone, and I had never told him how much I loved he.

I made the same mistake with Billy. He was the only one on South Street who reached out to me with a smile, and I never gave him a smile in return, until he was departing the town and it was too late. I knows now that all I had to do was to reach out and love him, but I was unable to do it. May God forgive me my sin of not doing what in me heart I knows was the right thing to do.

Whenever I thinks of yur Billy, I remembers the day he put the puff mushroom under the Reverend's cushion. After I comes home from the service, I laughed so hard, I almost split me corsets. Despite the sadness I feels when I think of him, I also remembers the many smiles he gave me. Just this morning, when I saw the fish at the bottom of the well, I thought of him. Heaven is a better place now that he's there. God will give him the love I never gave him.

I can never undo the past. 'Tis gone. Billy and the other of yur brood will always be in me heart. At my age, 'tis only the memories that I have left to treasure. My memories of yur Billy will remain with me always.

I sends you me love, Mrs. Mercer. Try not to hold me sins against me.

Faithfully yours,

Mrs. Rowntree

P.S. I ran into yur brother day before yesterday on the High Street. He told me that he wrote you about me hitting the old Reverend Wilmot with me new broom. I did not tell yur brother that when I swatted the Reverend the second time, I said under me breath that it was for Billy, as he made the lad's life so miserable when he was here in Comstock.

*

Despite being July, the fullness of summer having descended over the north hemisphere, the waters of the North Atlantic remained unpredictable. Due to stormy weather, Bill Thompson did not arrive in Halifax Harbour until July 21, and because of a delay in the trains, it was July 23 before the engine of the train he was aboard thundered into Union Station, clouds of hissing steam in its wake.

Bill's reunion with Emmy was tearful and warm. She was unable to stop hugging him, as if trying to reassure herself that he was actually in Toronto. For Ruth and Mary, Uncle Bill was almost a stranger. They had seen very little of him when they lived in Comstock, and they had not laid eyes on him for many years. However, their mother's tears of joy melted the barriers, and they hugged their uncle.

The reunion cheered Bill greatly. He was with his family once more and so pushed the regrets of former years from his mind. Then he was aware that his youngest niece, Bess, had not hugged him. She stood beside her sisters, smiled, and offered her hand. Bill accepted it and gazed into her intense blue eyes. He saw the sadness in them, but he also saw that they hinted at a maturity beyond her years. With his suitcase in his right hand, he slipped his other arm around Bess as they all departed the platform.

Bill was unaware of the reason that Bess was hesitant to open her heart to him. Every male she had ever loved had died. To accept Uncle Bill into her life might cause him to die, too.

*

By the early years of the century, Germany's population had grown considerably, creating massive industrial might and excellence in technology. Germany viewed England as its commercial, naval, and territorial rival. The world watched. An assassination in an obscure part of the Balkans became the spark that ignited the flames, and in early August the tense rivalry developed into open conflict. England and Germany were at war.

On Tuesday, August 4, 1914, the sleepy citizens of Toronto awoke to learn that their nation, as a part of the British Empire, was embroiled in the conflict. They eventually called it the Great War and The War to End All Wars. It was neither. Over one million Allied troops were to perish, untold thousands drowning in mud in pursuit of the enemy across perilous battlefields. It was certainly not the war to end all wars, but it did set the stage for a further conflict. However, with the new weapons of mass destruction, it was to be the world's first modern war.

None of this was evident on the morning of August 4. Except for a very few, Canadians were not a people who relished the idea of wars and battles. However, because Canada was mainly a rural society, most men were familiar with the use of firearms. They had harnessed their nation's energy to clear land for farming, open the west, and construct railways, and thus people were not reticent to tackle massive projects. They were accustomed to planning, implementing, and accomplishing difficult tasks. The newspapers declared that the war was a cause for justice to triumph, and so it became a conflict imbued with the highest of ideals. To participate was noble.

Within weeks of the declaration of war, men commenced labouring in industries geared toward the war effort. The nation that had triumphed over the wilderness now funnelled its energy into the new task. The tragedy of the *Empress* receded from the conscious minds of most people, as within months the first fatalities of battle overshadowed the losses in the waters of the St. Lawrence.

*

In the days ahead, the Rosemount Corps, like the nation at large, felt the effects of the war, as more and more men of the congregation enlisted. Families prayed earnestly for the safety of their loved ones. Five members had been lost on the *Empress,* which left many wondering how many more lives the battles would claim.

Bill Thompson was now too old to serve the nation. He settled into his new life in the Earlscourt District. During the first service he attended at the Rosemount Corps, he was drafted to play the piano. He accepted, and the same morning he was asked if he were able to play a brass instrument. Informing the corps that he played the trombone, he was immediately inducted into the band, which—because a number of men served overseas—was made up of only a dozen bandsmen.

Similarly, as there was a shortage of labour in the community, Bill had no problems finding employment. Thomas McCarthy hired him immediately, happy to have assistance with his booming business and pleased to have an uncle of Billy's in the store. The memory of Billy established a bond between the two men.

On the afternoon of August 2, Bill was practising the piano in the Rosemount Hall, and as no one was around, he played from memory a few of the rollicking songs the men at the Oak Leaf Ale House had enjoyed. Because The Salvation Army often set sacred words to secular tunes, he decided that he would write lyrics suitable for congregational singing to some of the better melodies.

Then he sensed that someone was standing beside him. Turning his head, he saw that it was Bess. He had not heard her enter the building, and her presence caught him by surprise. She said nothing, only stared at him with her deep blue eyes and sat on the bench beside him. Bill resumed his playing, all the while remembering how Billy had sat beside him in the alehouse those many years ago. Almost without realizing it, he began to explain the basics of the music to Bess. She listened but said nothing. After four or five minutes, he stopped and looked at her.

"Have you ever played the piano?" he inquired.

"No."

"You play the cornet, so you can read music, right?"

"Yes."

Reaching for a book on the top of the piano, he selected a hymn. He played it with both hands and then separated the parts and played them each separately. "Want to try it?" he asked.

Bess shrugged her shoulders indifferently, but she was unable to resist. A tear crept into Bill's eye. Her first attempts were more awkward than Billy's had been, but similar to her brother, she quickly corrected herself and remembered each correction. It was not long before Bill realized that behind those blue eyes was a mind as alert as Billy's had been.

In the evenings ahead, each time Bill slipped away from the house to play the piano in the hall, Bess trailed behind him. The lessons continued, and by the next week she had dropped all pretences. Whenever he departed the home on Bird Avenue, she was beside him, her arm wrapped around his. By the end of the month, she was playing with both hands. Her errors were fewer, and though her style remained awkward, it improved each time she performed.

One evening, after a three-hour session, Bess said, "Uncle Bill, I love playing the piano, and I love playing the cornet, but do you know what I really want to learn?"

"Tell me, my dearest Bess. You surprise me in so many ways each day that I have no idea."

"I want to learn to write music. I practised with Billy and Zack many times. I can remember the entirety of Zack's cornet part in 'O Boundless Salvation.' I can remember most of Billy's, too. Billy and Zack can never return to my life, but perhaps their music can be raised from the depths of the St. Lawrence River. Will you help me?"

Before Bill replied, he admitted to himself that writing music on paper had never been his strong suit. However, he knew he could do it if he tried. They would learn together.

"Yes, my darling Bess, I will assist you as best I can. We'll see what we can accomplish as a team. Is there anyone who might remember the score to accompany the duet?"

"I don't know. But I do know that I can hear it in my head."

"Then we will see how the music unfolds. I've heard so much about Billy's composition. I'd welcome an opportunity to resurrect it."

Bill had been with Billy the first time he had heard the hymn played, outside the alehouse. It was now special to him, as well.

"There's something I want you to promise."

"What's that?"

"Uncle Bill, I want you to promise that you'll never leave me."

"I promise."

*

During the month of August, Emmy remained unaware of the final resting place of Phil and her sons. On Thursday, August 20, as Emmy was in the kitchen peeling the carrots for supper, she heard a soft rap on the front door. Before she had time to go down the hall to answer it, the door opened and in walked Grandmother Mercer. Emmy was immediately alarmed. What had happened to cause her mother-in-law to travel so late in the day from downtown Toronto to the Earlscourt area?

Grandmother Mercer removed her broad-brimmed hat and pulled out a kitchen chair. Bill came from the parlour, greeted Grandmother Mercer, took a chair, and sat down.

"My dears," she began, "we've things to discuss."

"Have you received any news?" Emmy asked.

Grandmother Mercer nodded her head. "Divers have now recovered two hundred and fifty bodies from the wreck. Phil and the boys were found this morning, during the final salvage dive, which ended today when they retrieved the purser's safe. Their bodies had been hidden under a large pile of debris. They said that no more bodies would be recovered from the ship. It has become too dangerous. It means that they will never recover the body of dear Bandmaster Meaford."

Emmy stifled a sob as she said, "It's over."

Bill rose from his chair and placed his arm tenderly around his sister.

"Yes, my dear. We can now bury Phil and the boys. We will no longer be left wondering where they're resting."

"Did you receive any details?"

"Yes! An Army officer at the site spoke to one of the divers and then phoned an officer at the Army Headquarters on Albert Street. He said that they found my dearest Phil, and my precious grandsons, huddled together in a corridor near the top of a staircase."

"They spent their last minutes of their lives together."

"Yes! They perished in each other's embrace."

"There is a degree of comfort in knowing that none of them was alone. I've had nightmares about Zack crying out for Billy, and about Phil struggling valiantly to reach them."

"You can put your mind to rest. They were together. However, I have more details to tell you. Throughout the past few months, I've visited Jenny in the hospital many times. She's sometimes coherent for a moment or two, and then she lapses into a state that is much like a coma. From the few times she's been able to speak, I've slowly gleaned some of the details of her final moments aboard the *Empress*. It's no small wonder that the memories of what she saw have almost driven her to insanity."

"What did she tell you?"

Grandmother Mercer placed her hand over Emmy's to comfort her as she began. "She and Billy reached the top of the stairs and were almost out on the deck when from behind themselves they heard Zack cry out.

They looked back and saw that Phil was trying to free Zack. Something had ensnarled his leg, and he was unable to break free. Billy told Jenny to go out on the deck and grab hold of the railing. Then Billy plunged back inside to help his father free Zack. The water was rising swiftly."

Emmy remained silent, her breath suspended.

Bill's arm tightened around his sister.

Grandmother continued. "Jenny did not cross the deck and grip the railing as Billy had instructed, but she remained rooted to the spot, peering down into the stairwell. She said when it became obvious that they could not free Zack, Billy placed his arms around him, holding him close. Jenny sensed that Billy was telling Zack that he would never leave him. Jenny said that Phil placed his arms around his sons, refusing to leave them as the waters rose. His love for his sons transcended his fear of death."

Sobbing quietly, Emmy realized now that both Billy and Phil could have escaped, but neither of them would leave Zack to die alone in the icy water. If they had left him, then he would have seen them abandoning him as the water closed over his head.

Comforting Zack had been more important than surviving.

Emmy knew that Billy had always reached out to comfort others. He viewed life as a journey whereupon a traveller helped those he met along the way. He embraced each day with curiosity and exuberance, always protective of those he loved, whether it was Zack, the other family members, or Jenny. Even those who were strangers or enemies he had embraced. He had used his fists when a loved one was threatened, but only as a last resort. Through his music, he had reached out to others, sharing his enjoyment of life, each note a testimony to his commitment to his beliefs. When the sacred drew near, without hesitation he embraced it. Phil had done likewise.

Emmy said quietly, "Greater love has no man than this: that he lay down his life for his brother or son."

Grandmother Mercer knew that her daughter-in-law was paraphrasing the words of the Gospel of John, 15:13.

Slowly, Grandmother Mercer continued. "Jenny said that just before the water rose over their heads, Billy looked up at her, smiled, and gave her a small wave of goodbye. Then the water closed over them. She passed out and remembered nothing until after she awakened in a lifeboat. The memory of her final moments aboard the *Empress* will haunt her as long as she lives. She might never find peace."

"My heart and prayers are with her," Emmy said.

"I think that at times she feels grateful that she survived, and then she feels guilty that she did not go back and try to help them."

"She could have done nothing. Billy and Phil were strong. If they could not free Zack, then Jenny's help would have been to no avail."

"We know that, but Jenny is not consoled. She may be trapped within the nightmare until the day she dies."

"We'll all be. But somehow we must find the strength to go forward."

"Yes," Grandmother Mercer declared softly, "but can we explain to Jenny how to do it?"

"Perhaps not. But I must find a way to explain it to Bess. Mary and Ruth are managing to cope. But Bess is more like Billy. She questions everything and will not allow the matter to rest until she has found an answer that she can accept."

"Then you have a problem."

*

Emmy arranged the funeral services for her husband and sons to take place at the A. W. Miles Chapel at 10:00 a.m. on Monday, August 31. Bandsmen from the Rosemount Corps were the pallbearers. They placed Phil in a single plot and buried Billy and Zack together in the same grave, not far from The Salvation Army plot in Mount Pleasant Cemetery. In death, they were together, as they had been all their lives—spiritually and physically.

The Rosemount Band played as those who had gathered sang the hymn "Abide with Me." The plaintive singing carried gently on the breeze, floating across the quiet forested cemetery. It drifted across the lawns, dying among the silent tombstones nearby. Among those at graveside were Mr. and Mrs. Greenberg from Draper Street. Mr. Greenberg appeared frailer than ever, but he wanted to pay his respects to the boy to whom his wife always referred as "my Billy."

As they slowly lowered the caskets into the graves, Captain Rush spoke the final words: "In the sure and certain hope of seeing them again on the resurrection morn."

Then the band played the majestic melody of "O Boundless Salvation" with an upbeat cadence. Everyone present knew the significance of this song for the Mercer family—indeed, for the entire Toronto banding community. In their minds, Billy and Zack had immortalized it. The words of William Booth, the Founder of The Salvation Army, had taken on new meaning and greater depth. They would never again hear its stirring melody without remembering the Mercer boys.

*

Emmy's heart was breaking, but she remained unable to cry. For a mother to lose one child was a tragedy. But to lose two, along with a husband, was beyond her ability to endure. She gazed at her three daughters, knowing that she must be strong for their sakes. She hoped that the great hymn of Salvationism would be their final memory of the scene, not the open graves.

Emmy and the girls, along with Grandmother Mercer, left the cemetery. Bill accompanied them, his arm around Bess. Mary and Ruth walked beside their mother as they trudged toward the cemetery gate on Yonge Street.

"Somehow we'll survive this day, and the sun will rise again tomorrow," Emmy told them.

*

On the following Sunday, September 6, they held a memorial service in the Rosemount Hall on St. Clair Avenue to honour the memory of Phil and his sons, as well as to pay tribute to their former bandmaster, George Meaford.

Zeke Treadwell had enlisted in the military, but as he had not yet been shipped overseas, they selected him to perform a trombone solo at the service. He chose to play, "In the sweet by-and-by, we shall meet on that beautiful shore ..."

As Bess watched Zeke perform, she realized that he was like a brother to her. His presence at the service was comforting, creating fond memories of her own brothers. She remembered the evening when he had appeared at their home, bruised and bloodied, and they had taken him in.

However, as she gazed at his handsome face, she sensed a stirring within her heart that she had never felt before. For the first time, she realized that her affection for Zeke was much deeper than she had realized. Was it possible that she harboured love for him and had not realized it?

She felt confused.

*

Bess was not the only one in the congregation who was experiencing mixed emotions. Among the gathered crowd was a confused Pastor Treadwell. Beside him sat his wife, Polly, and their son Jeremiah. The brotherly love between Zeke and Jeremiah had blossomed. They were now each other's best friend.

Pastor Treadwell knew that in the boys' lives, God's love had broken the power of his "fire and brimstone" teachings. Recently, Jeremiah had expressed a desire to play in the Army band. Pastor Treadwell had reluctantly consented, but only because he had no other choice if he wished to remain a part of his son's life. As well, for the first time, he discovered that he had feelings of affection for Ezekiel, and he could even say his name without feelings of anger and resentment.

This added to his confusion. The Pastor now wondered what the future held for him. Was he capable of embracing God's love, leaving behind a faith based on fear of condemnation? The fires of hell that had burned within his imagination were being extinguished.

Treadwell's thoughts returned to the events at hand as he listened to the tribute to Bandmaster Meaford. The corps officer expressed appreciation and thanks that George Meaford had passed their way in life. He had supervised the construction of the Rosemount Hall, organized the first Rosemount Band in 1910, and served as its first bandmaster. He had been a soldier and a musician who had dedicated his life to the success of the small corps. His contributions to the staff band had been superlative. The officer ended the eulogy with the words, "George Meaford's life was a testament to God's love as expressed through the Christian experience."

*

Captain Sendry was present in the congregation, listening intently as the officer spoke of George Meaford. The Captain recalled his numerous discussions with George and realized that, despite George's many doubts and failures while searching for an understanding of the divine, George had no fear of death. The Easter message dwelt within him. Yet Captain Sendry, who felt secure in his unquestioning faith, had discovered that when he was faced with his own demise a few months earlier, he had been terrified. He discovered this when what had appeared to be a heart attack turned out merely to have been severe indigestion. The incident left an indelible impression on him.

He had always placed his faith in the Bible's stern edicts, as well as in church rituals and regulations. Now he longed to hear the quiet voice of God within him—the voice that George had heard. However, when he had thought that death was inevitable and had reached out for the hand of God, he found that he was too terrified to grasp the divine and allow his faith to sustain him. He feared death. In his greatest moment of need, there was only silence. He was alone. The message of the resurrection did not dwell within him.

Captain Sendry was a deeply troubled man.

*

At the conclusion of the eulogy for Bandmaster Meaford, Captain Rush spoke of Billy. "We will never again hear the composition that Billy composed based on the Founders' Song. All the manuscript copies are now at the bottom of the St. Lawrence River. The only person, other than Billy, who could have written another score was our dear bandmaster, George Meaford, and he has also departed from our midst."

Bess gazed at Uncle Bill, but neither of them said anything. Then she looked up at the Captain as he requested the congregation to stand and sing "O Boundless Salvation." She was standing beside her mother.

*

When the congregation sang the fifth verse of the old hymn, Emmy felt the voice of the divine strengthening within her.

O ocean of mercy, oft longing I've stood
On the brink of Thy wonderful, life giving flood!
Once more I have reached this soul cleansing sea,
I *will not go back* till it rolls over me.

She realized that she never would "go back." The strength to remain faithful had seized her, and she was comforted by the thought that someday, when the trumpet sounded, it would summon her to join Phil and her precious sons. Then, as the congregants and she sang the sixth verse, its message truly entered her heart. It was as if William Booth had composed the first two lines of the verse especially for Phil, Zack, and Billy. But the final two lines of the stanza spoke personally to her.

The tide is now flowing, I'm touching the wave,
I hear the loud call of the mighty to save;
My faith's growing bolder, delivered I'll be;
I plunge 'neath the waters, they roll over me.

As Emmy sang, she remembered the many times she had listened from her kitchen as Billy and Zack played the hymn. The mellow sound of their instruments now resonated in her heart. From somewhere deep inside her, she slowly became aware that she possessed the strength to survive the terrible tragedy. Her faith was growing bolder. She was determined that she would be delivered as she plunged beneath the healing waters of her faith.

How could she explain this to Bess?

Finally, the tears that previously had been denied her now trickled down her cheeks. Bess slipped her arm around her mother. Now sixteen, Bess was a young woman. Her embrace assured Emmy that she would always be at her side. Emmy gazed into her youngest daughter's face. It was as if Billy were looking at her. She had always known that despite Bess's dark complexion, she resembled her older brother in appearance, and even more so in personality. However, she had never seen the resemblance so forcefully as at this moment. Bess's eyes expressed the same intelligence and empathy as Billy's.

As the tears flowed, Emmy gave Bess a reassuring hug.

She recalled that Billy had always reached out to others. It was as if she could feel his presence comforting her from beyond the grave, his voice softly telling her, "Everything is all right, Mama." It had only ever been in intimate moments that he had referred to her as Mama.

She knew that Billy had loved her dearly and also adored his sisters. His love for Jenny had been deep and abiding. However, when the waters of death swirled around him, he gave up his life for his brother. Zack had not been as strong as his other siblings, and Billy had always reached out to comfort and protect him.

Billy gave his life for Zack.

Then, it was as if Phil were wrapping his arms around her, and she could feel Billy and Zack at her side. Phil had kept his promise. They would never be separated. Tears of relief continued to flow down her cheeks. Then she felt another presence embrace her, more overpowering than anything she had previously experienced.

It lifted her up.

She knew it was the hand of God.

*

Emmy did not notice, but as she wept quietly, her arm around Bess, the Pastor Treadwell slipped from his seat beside Jeremiah and knelt at the mercy seat. He, too, finally found peace in the love of God. It flowed over him as a balm from Gilead. The final verse of "O Boundless Salvation" expressed the revelation that Treadwell beheld on this occasion.

> And now, hallelujah! The rest of my days
> Shall gladly be spent in promoting his praise
> Who opened his bosom to pour out this sea
> Of boundless salvation for you and for me.

*

The following week, Bess and Emmy were alone in the kitchen. Emmy placed a meat pie in the oven as Bess poured hot water from the boiling pot on the stove to wash the cooking utensils that she had used. She gazed at Bess. The afternoon light from the west window highlighted her profile as she poured the water into a pan to rinse the dishes.

On this day, Emmy was aware that Bess was quieter than usual. As she turned and faced her mother, Emmy saw the frustration in her daughter's eyes. As was often the case with Billy, her eyes betrayed her inner feelings.

"What's troubling you?" Emmy inquired as she wiped her hands on her apron.

"I've been trying to understand why God allowed the *Empress* to sink."

"What have you decided?"

Emmy considered it best if she remain silent and allow Bess to explain her thoughts.

"Well, I've listened to what people have said about it, particularly at the funerals and memorial services."

"What have you concluded?"

"Several persons said that those who died on the ship have gone to a better place, because they're with God in heaven."

"What do you think?"

"I think that the best place for Father, Zack, and Billy is right here in our home."

Emmy remained silent.

"Another minister said that God does not prevent tragedies, but he never gives us more sorrow than we can bear. If this were true, then there would be no suicides. Sometimes God does give some people more than they can bear. Of course, that's assuming that God gave the person the sorrow in the first place."

"I see that you have given this much thought," Emmy replied, realizing that Bess's last remark resembled Billy's characteristic way of reasoning.

"One minister said that in every tragedy there is a divine plan. We may know what it is and may not understand it, but God knows."

"What do you think?"

"No God of love would sink a ship to fulfill a divine plan. That's too preposterous to even seriously consider."

"These are very difficult ideas you have been considering."

Bess paused and gazed intently at her mother. Then she said in a hesitant voice, "There's more."

"Really?"

"Yes! Is it right to question matters of faith?"

"I have a feeling you have already thought about it." Emmy paused and looked at her daughter, and then she asked, "Can you tell me what you have concluded?"

"Reverend Wilmot in Comstock believed that a good Christian was anyone who believed the same as he did. Captain Sendry, at the Queen Street Corps, believed that a good Christian was someone who faithfully obeyed the rules and rituals of the church as it interpreted them to be. Pastor Treadwell always said that the path to Christianity was found in fearing and obeying God. If you didn't, then you'd burn in the fires of hell."

"And what do you believe?"

"I believe that I should think carefully about matters of faith. That's what Bandmaster Meaford believed. He thought that the path of a Christian's life included behaving as Christ taught. He believed that compassion, forgiveness, and love were the most important. If someone believed something different than Mr. Meaford did, as long as that person's beliefs showed the same love that Jesus showed, he did not condemn the person for those views. He regarded others' ways as another path, even though it was different than his own."

"Yes, I remember Mr. Meaford discussing these ideas with your father."

"Billy thought that way, too."

"Are you accepting something just because Billy considered it to be right?"

"No! I've given it much thought. I reasoned it out. But that's my problem. I can't for the life of me find a reason for why the *Empress* sank. Can you, Mother?"

Emmy was unsure how to answer. She remained silent, gazing at her daughter.

Bess now asked, "Do you think that God was on the *Empress* when it sank?"

"God is everywhere, so I am sure that he was there. I'm certain he was with your father and Billy when the waters swept over them. Perhaps that's how they found the strength to remain beside Zack. And through their love, Zack was comforted."

"If he was with them, why didn't he stop the *Empress* from sinking?"

"My darling, I don't know."

Placing her arm around Bess, Emmy hugged her. After releasing her embrace, she gazed directly into her eyes and said, "Perhaps we should be wary of those who think they have all the answers. Because we cannot truly understand God, or prove his existence by tangible evidence, it does not mean that he does not exist. Being a Christian, or being a part of any faith, involves a constant search for truth. Be thankful for your doubts. Doubts cause you to ask questions, and questions lead to answers. Sometimes it is the person who asks the seemingly impossible question who discovers that an answer can be found. However, it is true that for some questions, you'll never find an answer. Don't be discouraged by this, and never lose faith. One day, in God's time, the answers may come. Then, perhaps, you'll say, 'Why, it's so clear. Why didn't I think of that before?'"

"What do I do until the questions are answered?"

"The important thing is that you keep searching. The search for life's meaning is eternal. When the trumpet sounds and you are called to face your Creator, I know that you, my precious child, will be able to say that you honestly tried to understand the mystery of God and that you lived your life according to what you believed was right."

Bess hugged her mother. They would never understand why Phil, Billy, and Zack lost their lives, but they found comfort in the love and faith they shared.

A lone lifeboat from the *Empress* floats on the empty waters of the St. Lawrence River in the early morning hours after the disaster. *Photo courtesy of the George Scott Railton Heritage Centre*

When our earthly days are o'er and we sail upon eternity's endless sea, hopefully in our wake is love.

Author's Notes

I am indebted to many sources and individuals for the information and ideas contained in this book. Hilda Whealy and Bernard Aldridge were my original inspiration. Even when they were more than ninety years of age, they painted a vivid picture of the difficulties their parents faced in the first decade of the twentieth century as immigrants crossing the treacherous Atlantic. They also related details about the hardships they experienced as children in Toronto's Earlscourt District. In those days, Earlscourt was a pioneer community, remote from the downtown area of the city, the great Davenport Road hill creating a physical barrier that isolated the community from the city below. I have attempted to remain as true as possible to the images they provided about the early days of Earlscourt, which I supplemented with information from various research sources.

The Aldridge home on Bird Avenue, since renamed Rosemount Avenue, served as the inspiration for the Mercer home. Bernie Aldridge and Hilda Whealy provided many of the details about this house, including those of its construction.

However, the most poignant memories of Bernie and Hilda were of the sinking of the great ocean liner the *Empress of Ireland.* I was amazed how vividly they recalled the details, unlike those to whom the tragedy was merely a horrific newspaper headline. They provided firsthand sources of information—an invaluable asset for any author. They also shared their family's personal letters, photos, and documents.

When Ernest (Ernie) Aldridge, who was the father of Hilda and Bernie, drowned aboard the *Empress,* their mother, Mrs. Charlotte Aldridge, struggled to raise her children in an era when government assistance was almost nonexistent. As young children, Bernie and Hilda, along with their younger sister, Dora, suffered through the aftermath of the disaster. The details they related about their parents are entwined with the background information for several of the book's fictional families—George and Vangie Meaford, and Philip and Emmy Mercer. However, apart from these background details, any similarity between the Aldridge family and the fictional characters is coincidental.

The resources and staff of the George Scott Railton Heritage Centre of The Salvation Army were invaluable to me in writing this novel, as were the microfilm copies of *The War Cry* that the Heritage Centre faithfully maintains. The publication was an invaluable source, relating much information about Toronto during the early days of the twentieth century, particularly of The Salvation Army. I am particularly indebted to Karl Larson, who has now retired from the Heritage Centre.

The most difficult task for me in writing this book, and perhaps for the reader as well, is to separate fact from fiction. The story is fictional, as are the characters. However, much of the story is based on real events. The inspiration for the imaginary Rosemount Corps was the Earlscourt Citadel Corps of The Salvation Army. This congregation has since relocated, and it is now known as the Yorkminster Corps. The concerts, festivals, and travels of the Rosemount Band reflect the history of the Earlscourt Band. Most of the titles of Salvation Army music mentioned in this book are accurate. The Earlscourt Band performed them at the concerts mentioned, which are also real. One of the exceptions is Billy's composition, "O Boundless Salvation." The hymn is real, but Billy's composition never existed. What a pity. Perhaps some composer in the future may write such a piece of music. The concerts and services in Massey Hall are based on real events.

The Toronto I Corps located at Queen and Tecumseth streets was the basis for the fictional Queen Street Corps of The Salvation Army. However, in 1906, the Toronto I Corps occupied a small building on Tecumseth Street and did not possess a large band. Thus, other than its location, any similarities between the two congregations are coincidental. The Dovercourt Citadel Band and the Toronto Temple Band were real. Neither remains in existence today.

The Toronto Staff Band never existed. However, the inspiration for it was the Canadian Staff Band of The Salvation Army, which was aboard the *Empress* when it sank. The events in which the Canadian Staff Band participated provided the details for the fictional Toronto Staff Band's concerts and trips. Information about the *Empress* and the meals served onboard is a matter of record. After the demise of most of the members of the Canadian Staff Band in 1914, there was no similar band until one was reinstituted in 1969.

In 1914, the Canadian Staff Band did in fact play the hymn "God Be with You till We Meet Again" on the deck of *Empress.* However, Billy's impromptu playing of "Abide with Me" is fictional. Information is accurate for the funeral service of the *Empress*'s victims, the processional march up Yonge Street, and the interment service at Mount Pleasant Cemetery. The funeral for the Phil, Billy, and Zack is imaginary.

Commissioner Hees is fictional, but I based the character on Commissioner David Rees, who perished on the *Empress.* The conversations and information about Commissioner Hees were invented. The first bandmaster of the Earlscourt Corps was Ernest Aldridge, not the fictional George Meaford. The religious views of George Meaford do not reflect those of Ernest Aldridge. Any similarity is coincidental.

The location of the Rosemount Corps was actually the site of the first permanent building of the Earlscourt Corps, with the Royal George Theatre beside it. The laneway behind the theatre, where Billy fought the Treadwells, actually existed, but the story is fictional. Wilford's orchard, the Treadwells, Mr. McCarthy's store, and Mr. Peevy's Jewellery Shop never existed. The other businesses mentioned as being on St. Clair are historically accurate.

Mrs. McMillan's Grocery Store and Mr. Hutchinson's Butcher Shop on Queen Street never existed. However, the shops mentioned during the Mercer's outing to Centre Island are real, as are the details about the Toronto Islands. The library building where Jenny and Billy first kissed remains today on Queen Street West, but it is no longer a functioning library. The information about the Canadian National Exhibition of 1913 is also accurate, although Billy, Zack, and Jenny's visit to the late-summer fair is, of course, fictional.

The town of Bridport in Dorset, a mile north of the English Channel, was the basis for the story's fictional village of Comstock. My great-grandfather immigrated to North America from Bridport, and in light of my research into my ancestry, I became quite familiar with the town.

It was thus easy for me to change Bridport into Comstock. The ravenous Reverend Wilmot never existed. The Church of St. Mary's Bridport was the inspiration for the fictional church where the Reverend Wilmot preached. Other than the appearance of the church, any similarity between the real and fictional congregation is a coincidence. Similarly, Mrs. Rowntree is imaginary.

Readers will have noted that the narrative contains constant references to the changes of the season. This is intentional. During the time in which the story is set, the seasons dominated people's daily lives more than in the modern era. Lacking air conditioning, central heat, Thermopane windows, heated automobiles (including taxis), and high-quality insulation, the residents of Toronto were far more at the mercy of the elements. In the early twentieth century, they were unable to import fresh fruits and vegetables. Since they lacked food freezers and refrigerators, it was necessary to preserve in jars the bounty of each harvest for the lean winter months ahead. Thus, the Mercer family lived in harmony with the seasons, adjusting their lives and daily habits to suit the weather.

Canadians today sometimes forget how much their lives remain influenced by the changing seasons. Every three or four months, food, drinks, clothing, entertainment, and habits change according to the weather. Because the winters seem interminably long at our latitude, we often forget the beauty and blessings that the changing seasons bestow. I hope that the descriptions in this book will remind Canadians of the intense beauty that each season imparts, and perhaps readers will appreciate anew their splendour.

The spiritual ideas expressed in this book, I have attempted to match with the characters who spoke them. Many of the thoughts concerning faith were derived from the teachings I received as a child. Others are from personal reading and from my own search for spiritual truth. At the end of the book, when Emmy attempts to help Bess cope with the sinking of the *Empress,* the words of the composer Eric Ball influenced me. He spoke about his struggles to cope with the doubts and questions that sometimes haunt people of faith. His words made a profound impression on me.

I am also grateful to the Reverend Doctor G. Malcolm Sinclair and the Reverend Doctor John Mastandrea of the Metropolitan Church for spiritual guidance as expressed in their sermons, although the views expressed in this book are not necessarily theirs. I am also thankful for my Salvation Army heritage and the teachings of my parents. As a child, I was encouraged to explore spiritual matters for myself, as opposed to merely accepting the edicts of others. As well, I wish to express my gratitude to Doctor John Joseph Mastandrea, Ellen Willows, and David Moore for reading this book's manuscript and offering suggestions. David Moore also assisted in proofreading the book. His assistance was much appreciated.

Some may feel that the Christian faith of George Meaford, as well as that of Billy, is too liberal for the decade in which these imaginary characters lived. This is a valid criticism. However, in any era there are always individuals who think beyond the accepted norms of the day. I created George and Billy to fulfill this sort of role. The reader may accept or reject their expressions of faith, but to deny that they might have existed is perhaps a lack of faith in the people's ability to search for understanding and truth. I feel that to simply accept teachings blindly, without examining them thoughtfully, is not true faith but is, rather, the denial of faith in one of the greatest gifts that God bestowed on humankind—the ability to reason. The acceptance of certain teachings, generation after generation, without question is one reason that bigotry and prejudice survive today within some communities of faith.

The Salvation Army portrayed in this book is not the Army of today. Founded in 1865 and organized as an Army of God, it borrowed military terminology. Many of these terms have since disappeared. Some of the Army's places of worship are now referred to as community churches, rather than citadels and temples. Many people today are not even aware that The Salvation Army is a religious denomination. They view it solely as a social organization. In the 1950s, there were almost thirty congregations within Toronto. Five or six of those remain today.

The hymn "O Boundless Salvation" was for many decades the first hymn in *The Song Book of The Salvation Army.* It has since been placed elsewhere in the book. The hymn seems to have lost much of its appeal to modern congregations. At one time, it was included in the hymnal of the United Church of Canada, but it has since been removed. If anyone wishes to hear the melody and examine the lyrics of the verses of the song, he or she may Google its title. However, in my prejudiced viewpoint, only when a brass band performs it can a person appreciate the full beauty of the melody. I sometimes wonder if William Booth was ever aware of this.

A nonfictional account of the Aldridge family and the tragedy of the *Empress of Ireland* is contained in my book *The Pathway of Duty.* Many of the details therein were placed verbatim into this book. In *The Pathway of Duty,* which was a title chosen by Bernie and Hilda, when the news of the deaths aboard the ship reached the house on Bird Avenue, its inhabitants learned that five members of their household had perished. In the Earlscourt Corps, the waters of the St. Lawrence claimed ten lives from among the congregation, three of whom were Canadian staff bandsmen. In some small way, this story might assist readers to comprehend the depth of the congregation's grief, and in particular that of Mrs. Charlotte Aldridge and her children.

Every year since the sinking of the ship, The Salvation Army has held a memorial service in Mount Pleasant Cemetery on the last Sunday in May to remember those who perished. They gather at the section of the cemetery where the victims are buried. A large stone memorial commemorates the shipwreck. It is an emotional and meaningful ceremony. Each year, on the day of the service, they place small Army flags on the graves, including the resting place of Ernie Aldridge. The flags help those who attend to appreciate the extent of the disaster.

The saga of the *Empress of Ireland* will always remain one of most tragic of maritime disasters and the greatest in Canadian history.

*

Some historians refer to the sinking of the *Empress of Ireland* in the St. Lawrence River as Canada's *Titanic.* The parallels to the *Titanic* are appropriate, as 1,012 people lost their lives on the *Empress* during the early morning hours of May 29, 1914. On the *Titanic,* 807 passengers drowned—the *Empress*'s death toll was 840 passengers. The final death count was higher on the *Titanic,* as more of its crew perished.

The question sometimes asked is, "Why is the sinking of the *Empress* so relatively unknown?" By contrast, almost everyone is familiar with the story of the *Titanic.* There are several reasons for this, but none of them provides a satisfactory explanation. The *Empress* deserves a more prominent place in our history than it has received.

One of the reasons that the *Empress* fell into obscurity was that two months after it sank in the cold dark waters of the St. Lawrence River, Canada entered the First World War. The latter event eclipsed the maritime disaster, pushing all other stories from the pages of the newspapers. When the war ended, four years had passed, and remembering those who had paid the supreme price in Europe became more prevalent.

Some suggest that because the passenger list of the *Empress* did not contain the rich and famous, the public lost interest in the disaster. Whether this is true or not, it is a fact that the majority of those aboard were middle-class citizens or people who earned their livings through manual labour. The first-class cabins of the ship were sparsely occupied.

Perhaps another reason that the *Empress* has not captured the imagination of the world at large is that it plunged to the bottom in a mere fourteen minutes after a Norwegian collier, the *Storstad,* rammed into its starboard side. The event did not readily allow authors or filmmakers much opportunity to create imaginary heroes and romantic scenes, compared to the *Titanic,* which took several hours to sink to its watery grave. There was no time aboard the *Empress,* as illustrated by the fact that the crew managed to lower only four of the ship's forty lifeboats into the water. When the *Storstad* struck the *Empress,* the collision killed or maimed many passengers, while trapping scores of others below deck. Many perished before the ship sank.

I find it strange that some authors consider a tragedy that begins and ends within the space of fourteen minutes as lacking in literary appeal. I believe that the story of the *Empress* is intensely dramatic. The heartrending catastrophe deserves a more prominent place in our historical memory. Perhaps this narrative, in some small way, will help redress the lack of attention that the ship's sinking has received.

CPSIA information can be obtained at www.ICGtesting.com
Printed in the USA
LVOW06s0907031213

363585LV00002B/40/P